DANCING WITH SIN

In an America of soft gaslight and horse-drawn cabs, Rose Beaudette is an innocent in many ways. Raised to become a nun, she shocked her family by marrying Luke Beaudette, the handsome assistant prosecutor of Springfield, Massachusetts. But now Luke seems a stranger, a cold, aloof man who doesn't share the desires that burn so deeply in her soul.

Then Rose meets a fashionable Boston beauty who introduces her to a thrilling new world of excitement and adventure. It is also a place where betrayal—and murder—will test her courage and devotion. Suddenly Rose needs Luke to fight for her, to possess her completely with the only thing that can save them both—a love stronger than scandal, lies, and an enemy determined to destroy them both. . . .

Dancing With Sin

Jane Goodger

A TOPAZ BOOK

TOPAZ
Published by the Penguin Group
Penguin Putnam Inc., 375 Hudson Street,
New York, New York 10014, U.S.A.
Penguin Books Ltd, 27 Wrights Lane,
London W8 5TZ, England
Penguin Books Australia Ltd, Ringwood,
Victoria, Australia
Penguin Books Canada Ltd, 10 Alcorn Avenue,
Toronto, Ontario, Canada M4V 3B2
Penguin Books (N.Z.) Ltd, 182–190 Wairau Road,
Auckland 10, New Zealand

Penguin Books Ltd, Registered Offices:
Harmondsworth, Middlesex, England

First published by Topaz, an imprint of Dutton NAL,
a member of Penguin Putnam Inc.

First Printing, July, 1998
10 9 8 7 6 5 4 3 2 1

To Louise Blackwood,
whose bedtime stories always included
a little girl heroine named Jane.
Thanks, Mom.

Special thanks to:

Karen Levin, for her invaluable help
researching this book;

Maggie Humberston, head librarian at the
Connecticut Valley Historical Museum,
for help finding the little details;

Pam Bernstein, who suggested my story
needed some bad guys;

and Hilary Ross, for unwavering support.

Chapter One

1

"Bless me, Father, for I have sinned."

Rose Beaudette bowed her head in the gloomy confessional, her senses filled with the comforting smells of beeswax, incense, and the dusty thick velvet curtain that separated her from the others waiting to confess their sins.

"It has been one week since my last confession," she said in a soft voice that Father Beaulieu instantly recognized. He let out an inaudible sigh, asking God for patience as he settled in to hear Mrs. Beaudette recite sins that weren't really sins at all. Quite simply, the woman had fewer sins on her soul this Saturday than most parish priests.

Rose bit her lip. Surely she could come up with something to say. She was no saint, after all. Ah, yes. She had admired her neighbor's new draperies. Perhaps she had coveted them? No, she decided. She didn't truly care for the draperies for herself. Rose heard Father Beaulieu shift on the other side of the thin wall that separated sinner from priest. She knew it was him for she recognized his smoke-gruff voice, but he was only a shadow behind the small opaque screen.

A sin, a sin. Surely she had committed one sin in an entire week. Oh, why hadn't she better prepared? she thought as the silence grew. Then she remembered and almost brightly recited her transgression, so happy to affirm that she had, indeed, sinned.

"Last Wednesday I continued to eat after I was filled. It was the lamb, Father. I do enjoy it and was rather gluttonous." Rose smiled, pleased with both her sin and her memories of the succulent lamb. She'd eaten so much, she'd stolen away after the meal to loosen her stays.

Father Beaulieu prayed in Latin, something mysterious and awesome, Rose was certain.

"Your penance is one Hail Mary."

"Yes, Father." One Hail Mary. Rose tamped down the sense of disappointment over such a small penance. She should be pleased that her sin had been so small as to require such a light punishment. As she stepped out of the confessional and into the church, Rose headed for the pews, pausing to genuflect before taking a seat, kneeling and reciting her prayer. Thirty seconds later, Rose stood, almost embarrassed when the others awaiting confession looked up at her in surprise that she should be done so quickly. She imagined they were all thinking the same thing: "That one must not have told the father all her sins. No one could have such a light penance."

Rose almost knelt again to pray a bit longer when her brown eyes met the smiling blue ones of a pretty young woman she'd seen for the first time last Saturday. Rose gave the woman a tentative smile then began walking down the aisle, eyes straight ahead, ignoring the curious stares of the others. As she passed the woman, she fell into step beside her, and Rose wasn't sure she was pleased or annoyed. Rose dipped her finger into the holy water and made the sign of the cross; the woman followed suit.

"We're neighbors, you know," the woman said when they reached the outside steps. She held a hand over her eyes to shield the sun, squinting in the brightness. "My name is Collette Taylor. I know what you're thinking," she said with an impish smile. "Taylor is my married name. My maiden name is LaFrenier. I married a Protestant boy." She whispered the last with mock horror, then laughed at her own theatrics.

"I wasn't thinking . . ." But Rose stopped herself. It was *exactly* what she had been thinking, that "Tay-

lor" didn't sound Catholic, that it sounded decidedly
Protestant. For years she had heard her mother repeat
nearly every name she heard, and from her tone, Rose
knew immediately whether that person was Catholic
or not. And from that, whether that person was someone with whom the Desrosiers would associate or not.
Rose found herself smiling shyly at Collette.

"I'm sorry," she said in a near whisper.

Collette waved a hand, dismissing the apology, and
linked her arm with Rose's, half dragging her down
St. Benedict's stone steps and toward the trolley stop.

"We're new to Springfield and don't know a soul.
I see you here every Saturday and thought perhaps
next week we could take the trolley together. John—
that's my husband—thinks absolution is a wonderful
thing that all religions should embrace. What he
doesn't understand is that even if our consciences are
clear, we Catholics still feel guilty about our sins for
ages." Collette let out a musical laugh, and gave Rose
a sidelong look.

"Oh, goodness, I've offended you," she said, becoming serious.

Rose flushed. She had never heard anyone talk
about the Church and its teachings so lightly. It made
her uncomfortable and also a little bit . . . guilty. Yes,
guilty to secretly agree with Collette, to enjoy her
irreverence.

"Where do you live?" Rose asked to change the
subject.

Collette smiled and gave her arm a squeeze, as if
to say, "All right, I'll let you change the subject this
time, but next time you might not be so lucky."

"Just six houses down from yours on Mattoon
Street. We'll walk right by it. Why don't you stop in
for some tea? You can meet John and see how a sinful
couple live." Collette was joking—again—but Rose
sensed it was important that she visit her home, that
she would be hurt if she did not. Rose agreed, not
because she didn't want to hurt her feelings, but because in the short time since she'd met her, Rose de-

cided she liked Collette Taylor. Rose had not a single close woman friend, and her heart expanded just a bit thinking that this woman, who made her laugh at her own serious nature, might become her friend.

After departing the trolley, the two women walked companionably together, chatting about an upcoming church supper, unaware of the admiring looks from the gentlemen who strolled by, tipping their hats as they went. Collette, with her blonde curls, blue eyes, and petite figure, drew the most immediate looks. But those who took the time to shift their gaze from the curvaceous blonde found themselves staring at Rose's striking features. Rose's deep-brown eyes dominated a face that an artist would relish. With its graceful lines, lovingly drawn, hers was a face that invited an awed stare instead of a smile.

"Here we are," Collette said, standing outside an elegant brownstone in a line of brownstones along one of Springfield's most exclusive streets. "We rent, of course. But someday we hope to buy our own home."

Collette lifted the skirt of her sage-green wool day dress a bit and jogged up the four steps leading to the door, her hat tilting precariously before one gloved hand snatched it from her head altogether. "Wretched thing," she muttered as she opened the door for Rose.

Rose found herself in a marble foyer, where a simple chandelier hung overhead and a long hall stretched out before her. And from somewhere down that hall came a boisterous male voice.

"That you, Collette, all cleansed and ready for some more sinning?"

Rose blushed and bit her lip. She should be mortified by such talk, but instead she found herself wanting to laugh. Oh, if her mother ever heard anyone say such a thing! It would be the topic of suppers for at least a week. Imagine, standing in the house of a woman who had married a Protestant boy and wanting to laugh at his sacrilegious manner.

John Taylor, his head down and revealing a slightly balding pate, walked toward the two women, whistling a jaunty tune as he perused a letter. "Whistling is calling to the devil," her mother would say every time she heard someone whistle. And every time, a tiny part of Rose wanted to pucker her lips and blow out a tune. But she never, ever did.

Collette walked down the hall partway to meet her husband. "All pure," she said, laughter in her voice.

When they met, he swooped her up into his arms, burying his face in her hair, and shouted, "Let the sinning be—" And then he saw Rose. "—gin."

Collette turned, mischief dancing in her eyes, and introduced her new friend to her slightly embarrassed husband.

"Would you like to join us for tea, John?" Collette asked, her arm still about her husband. Rose watched them and felt a bit ill at ease, as if she were somehow spying on an intimate moment. John's hand caressed Collette's nape, an idle gesture, as if it were so common a touch, he was unaware he was doing it.

"No. I've got too much work to do, darling," he said, shaking the paper in his hand. "But it was a pleasure meeting you, Mrs. Beaudette. I hope you'll visit with Collette again." There was an intensity to his words that made Rose believe it was more than a polite invitation. Perhaps, like her, Collette needed a friend.

And then husband and wife embraced, kissing in front of Rose, making her shift her eyes away, her face heating with embarrassment.

"Let's have that tea and get to know one another," Collette said, again grabbing Rose's arm and leading her to the parlor. "I gave my maid the day off, so I'll make the tea and be right back," Collette said, leaving Rose alone in the sparsely furnished parlor. She wanted to wander about the long, narrow room, but instead she sat on a chair, folded her hands, and awaited Collette's return.

Collette breezed into the parlor minutes later carrying a black lacquer tray, setting it down with a little clunk. Collette, Rose noticed, seemed unaware or else uncaring that a good amount of tea had sloshed onto the tray, and she had to restrain herself from mopping up the brown liquid.

"Now. Tell me about yourself," Collette commanded.

The two talked for nearly an hour, before Rose, with some alarm, noticed the time. With apologies for her abrupt departure, she bade Collette good-bye with promises to see her again.

Collette closed the door with a small sigh.

"How did your visit go?" her husband asked from behind as he brought his arms around her trim waist. Collette turned from the door to face him, draping her arms over his shoulders and lacing her hands together behind his neck. Her blue eyes were troubled.

"She's . . . sweet, John. I like her."

John's lips curved into a smile that did not quite reach his eyes. "Don't get soft on me, love. It's him we want. Don't forget that." And he kissed away any protest that Collette might have made.

That night at dinner, Rose looked across the table at her husband of six months and remembered the easy way Collette and John had with one another. Luke had never kissed her that way, especially not in front of another person. He had never nuzzled his head against her hair or wrapped his arm around her to pull her closer. At least not during daylight and while they were standing up. And hardly at night either. At that thought, Rose dropped her head and stared at her peas.

"How is your ham?" Rose asked into her plate.

"A bit salty."

"I'll have to tell the butcher." Now that her thoughts were safely on the salty ham, Rose ventured a look at her husband. He sat slightly turned away from the table so that he could look over a legal brief without the threat of spilling some of his dinner upon it. His dark-blond hair, short on the sides and back, curled onto his brow, rebelling against a comb and an impatient hand that was constantly trying to tame it back. Rose's soft lips formed a smile. She loved those errant curls and wished she could casually push them back from his forehead. But nothing between Luke and her was casual, she thought with a frown.

"I have a new friend," Rose announced, the tiny bit of rebellion in her voice surprising both of them.

Luke looked up then, his dark gray eyes widening at her tone. "Good for you," he said, then turned back to his brief.

Rose sighed and stuck another pea into her mouth. She ate them one at a time, something that she knew bothered Luke. But that was the way she liked to eat them. One at a time. Piercing another pea, she said, "She's married to a Protestant boy."

She waited until he turned to look at her before popping the fork with its single pea into her mouth.

"You could get more peas at a time if you'd scoop them instead of piercing them," he said, then proceeded to demonstrate, his mouth curved down into a frown. "Are you expecting me to object?"

"About the pea?" Rose asked, purposefully misunderstanding him, though she could not have said why.

"About the Protestant boy."

"It wouldn't matter if you did. Object, that is."

When Luke put the brief down, Rose knew she had his full attention and was secretly pleased, if not a bit frightened. Out of sight, her hands fluttered nervously in her lap as she met her husband's rather stern gaze.

"Of course, it would matter to me if you were upset," she said quickly. "But I believe I would still want to be Collette's friend."

"Did you think that I would forbid you a new friendship?" he asked, and seemed so baffled, Rose was immediately ashamed.

"No, I . . . I suppose I did," she said finally.

"I would not." And he picked up his brief again, pointedly this time.

He's angry with me, Rose thought, studying his profile once again. What would he do if I went up to him, laid my hands on his shoulders, and rested my chin on top of his head? What would he do if I kissed his cheek and apologized for making him angry? If I kissed his lips . . .

A deep longing came over her as she looked at her husband. I don't even know you, she thought. I haven't the foggiest idea what you would do. Rose stared down at her plate, at a fork that held a single pea, and wondered why after six months of marriage, her husband was still a complete stranger to her.

2

Rose craned her neck to watch the last of the parishioners enter St. Benedict's for the eight o'clock mass, finally turning toward the front when she drew a frown from her mother who sat three pews away. Feeling like a chastised child, Rose sat quietly next to Luke, her hands folded dutifully on her lap. She had not seen Collette enter the church, though she knew her to attend this mass. Hadn't she said she would be here? It was silly, really, to look for a woman she'd just met the day before. But Rose had felt an instant affinity for her, a shared loneliness. Though they had chatted for less than an hour, Rose knew Collette was estranged from her family because of her marriage and she suspected it hurt far more than she let on.

"I've got John's family and that's more than enough," she'd said, laughing lightly. Collette had lost more than family, she had also lost lifelong friends to a bigotry that Rose could not understand. Collette and John had fallen madly in love despite their differences, despite her family's strident opposition when John began courting her. There had been ugly, soul-wrenching scenes with her parents, and a heart-breaking rift between herself and her sisters. After three years of childless marriage, Collette confessed to Rose that perhaps God was punishing her for going against her parents' wishes by not allowing them to have children.

"Nonsense," Rose had said fiercely. "God loves all children, especially ones made from love."

It seemed incredible to Rose that she had shared such an intimate conversation with a woman she hardly knew. But somehow it had come naturally, as if they had known each other their entire lives. In many ways, Collette reminded Rose of her own sister, Nicole. Collette was a brighter, happier, more vivid version of Nicole. She was the woman that Nicole might have been without their mother's strangling hold.

Rose loved her mother. But there were times, to her great shame, she hated her. Hated her for taking away every bit of joy that came their way, for shaping her daughters with an unyielding hand. Both daughters had failed her, for neither had the calling to become a nun as she had so hoped would result from their strict upbringing. But she was her mother, after all. And despite the harsh words and strict manner Rose knew the woman loved her and Nicole, for what mother did not love her own daughters? Rose would never forget the way her mother looked at her and Luke's wedding, or the tears that filled her mother's eyes as the newly married couple turned and faced the congregation. There had been no hugs, no kisses, just a straightening of Rose's veil outside the church and lips compressed so tightly, they seemed to disappear.

And of course there had been that excruciating conversation in her bedroom the night before the wedding. "Luke will demand certain . . . things of you in the bedroom. No matter how distasteful it is to you, you must submit. It is a duty, a burden God has placed on all women. Much like the curse," she said, referring to a woman's menses. "Offer the pain up to the poor souls of purgatory. It is all you can do."

It had been an extremely frightened girl who met her husband the night of their wedding. "Offer the pain, offer the pain," she'd told herself over and over. So nervous was she, neither had gotten much enjoyment out of the awkward consummation of their marriage. It had been, despite Luke's patience and consideration, a simply awful experience. Over the weeks and months of their marriage Rose stoically endured those infrequent nights, when Luke knocked on her door to find his wife huddling under the covers ready to offer her pain up to the poor souls in purgatory. Once, Luke had tried to take off her nightgown, his gentle hands urging the cotton material up over her hips and to the bottom of her breasts. Mortified, Rose had stopped him.

"Do you have to?" she'd asked, her voice small.

Luke had sighed. "No. I suppose not."

Suddenly, Rose realized where she was and what she was thinking about and her face heated scarlet. Mass had begun and her thoughts had been . . . Goodness, they'd not been on God, that was for certain! She looked up at Luke, who seemed engrossed in the missal, his lips moving as he uttered his responses. As if sensing her perusal, he turned to her and gave her the tiniest of smiles, a nearly imperceptible upturning of his lips. Beautiful, beautiful male lips.

Startled once again by her thoughts, Rose dragged her eyes back to Father Beaulieu just as he was lifting the Body of Christ to the heavens. Rose had daydreamed through half the mass, and about things she was better off not thinking about.

The mass ended with a collective sigh as parishioners tried not to look as if they were hurrying out the doors to enjoy a lovely spring day. Sunday was a day of ritual, of waking up early to a leisurely breakfast, donning Sunday clothes for church, and then departing for a round of visits. The Beaudettes, like scores of others, rarely deviated from their course and would have found it a bit disconcerting if they had.

Walking from the church, Rose smiled to find Collette waiting at the bottom step for her. Grasping her hand in pleasure, Rose turned to introduce her new friend to Luke, who was already looking impatient for them to be off.

"Luke, this is Collette, the woman I mentioned last night," Rose said, looking up at Luke with a smile lighting her face that made her beauty fairly dazzling.

Luke nodded. "I'm pleased to meet anyone who can provoke such a beautiful smile from my wife," he said, surprising Rose with his charm.

Collette, of course, responded with a smile of her own. "You may not be so pleased when you hear I'm going to try to steal your wife away tomorrow." She turned to Rose. "You will come, won't you? For lunch?"

"I'd love to."

Rose watched Collette walk away, feeling a bit sad for her having attended church by herself. At least when the Taylors had children, they could accompany her.

"I take it the husband didn't convert," Luke said, watching Collette pick her way among the milling parishioners.

"No, but he seemed very nice," Rose said, defending her friend.

Luke looked down at her, one eyebrow raised. "I was not criticizing her or her husband, Rose. I was simply making an observation."

"Oh." It was the second time in two days she had misunderstood her husband. She gazed up at the blue sky, wishing for the first time that they didn't have to go visiting, that they could take a stroll in Forest Park. It was something she had always wanted to do, walk arm-in-arm with Luke on a sun-dappled day. He had courted her during the hottest days of summer, when the mere thought of walking about in the heat was enough to send her into a swoon. How she had envied those rich folks who headed to Newport and its cool ocean breezes. Instead, they had sat in the tepid shade of her parents' garden under the watchful eye of her mother, and talked. They rarely even dared a kiss for fear she would catch them.

Luke proposed in September after a four-month courtship and they were married in December on a sharply cold winter day. Now May's soft breezes were pushing at Rose's skirts as she turned her face to the sun and breathed in the fecund scent of mud and growing things. They had met in May a year ago, and Rose had known within a week that Luke was *the* one. Her mother had told her so, after all. A good boy, a devout Catholic, a prominent Springfield lawyer. His parents were wealthy, perhaps a bit unorthodox, but they were good Catholics—important—and French-Canadian—vital. Once their parents had seen them together, they hadn't a chance of escaping matrimonial bliss. Not that they had ever wanted to.

"I just realized our anniversary is nearly here," Rose said, turning to face Luke who was giving her the strangest of looks. She watched as he swallowed and looked away, frowning.

"We've been married hardly six months," he said, his voice gruff.

"I meant the day we met. At the church social."

"Don't tell me I'm responsible for remembering more than one anniversary!" he said with mock outrage.

"Of course. *And* the first time we kissed," Rose said brightly, and happily started walking toward their buggy.

After a few moments, Luke followed. Their first kiss. It had been . . . magic. Not those tiny pecks he was sure Rose was referring to, but that one perfect kiss they had shared that hot summer day. After weeks of enduring her mother's eagle eye, he had finally gotten her alone on the pretense of looking at roses that thickly covered a trellis in the garden. The window where her mother sat knitting and in full view of the small garden was blocked by that wonderfully placed trellis. Luke wondered what had taken him so long to discover the darned thing. He enjoyed good conversations with a witty girl as much as the next fellow, but if he was about to propose, he'd be damned if he'd do it without at least truly tasting her lips.

She'd known, of course, why he'd led her by the roses, for as soon as they were safely hidden, she turned her lovely face up toward his and smiled in anticipation.

"I'm going to kiss you," he said unnecessarily, his lips nearly touching hers. He rested his hands on her shoulders and drew her near. The kiss started off innocently enough, for that was all he had intended. But then she tasted too good, her lips were too soft against his. And when he heard that little sound that came from the back of her throat that could only mean she felt as overwhelmed as he, he drove his tongue into her mouth. And she welcomed him. Rose was not experienced, he knew that immediately. But she responded with such honesty, with such wonderful abandon he nearly lost his head. Crushing her against him, he pressed the small of her back with one hand while the other made its way slowly down from her shoulder to the place where her breast just began to swell. When he cupped her breast, running his thumb over her nipple through the thin summer cotton of her dress, she deepened the kiss and pressed even closer, letting out a low moan that had Luke rejoicing.

And then her mother came upon them. Her face a mask of fury, she demanded that Luke apologize for making love to her daughter in her parents' garden. Luke apologized and found himself escorted out of the Desrosier home posthaste. He'd wanted to catch Rose's eye, to silently tell her that, although he'd apologized to her mother, he was not sorry, could never be sorry for the wonderful thing they'd just shared. But Rose's head was hung low, her body tense, her face rigid. He couldn't help thinking she looked too ashamed for being caught kissing.

After that, there were no kisses other than chaste pecks on pursed lips. After that, Rose's wonderfully passionate and innocent response was never repeated. He might have imagined that passionate woman, dreamed that wild kiss, but he knew he had not. And now . . . now they had been married for six months and he was still searching for that girl he kissed in her parents' garden. There were glimpses—a warmness in her eyes when she looked at him sometimes—but they gone so quickly he found himself wondering if he were imagining things.

Just that day in church, when he'd turned and smiled at her, she'd had that look. Damned if she didn't look at him as if she wanted him. The girl in the garden was there, hiding behind those brown eyes; he just didn't know how to find her.

3

Every Sunday, the Beaudettes had lunch with Rose's parents, then traveled to the opposite end of the Forest Park section of Springfield and had a more formal dinner with Luke's. The sequence never varied and was never discussed unless the weather was so inclement that travel was impossible. That the visits were usually decidedly unpleasant or brutally boring, or a horrid combination of both, also was never discussed. Sunday was a day for visiting and so they went.

Springfield's Forest Park section was divided by tree-lined avenues and graced by magnificent mansions. Dozens of carriages and buggies drove up and down Forest Park Avenue as Springfield's elite headed for the park. It was a source of great pride that F. L. Olmsted, the same man who designed New York's Central Park and Boston's Public Gardens, had also created the park in Forest Park.

Rose and Luke rode in their buggy, the top down to let the warm May sun in. A hint of summer's heat was in the air, so welcome after a snow-filled Massachusetts winter. The trees were already bright with new leaves and lilac bushes, their tiny purple buds still tightly bundled, giving proof that spring was indeed here. Rose held her opened parasol above her head,

even though her flat-brimmed hat with black and gray
ostrich features shielded her face nicely from the sun's
rays. She wore a dark gray silk gown with black velvet
trim and little black buttons running from her throat
clear down to her hem. The matching black velvet
jacket lay on the seat between her and Luke. Despite
the warmth, he'd decided to keep his jacket on.
Proper Luke.

The ride to Rose's childhood home was brief, a
mere fifteen minutes down a shaded avenue in Forest
Park. As Luke turned the buggy onto the circular
drive of the elegant home, Rose clutched her churning
stomach. She never told Luke how she dreaded these
visits. How awful for a daughter to not want to see
her parents or sister. Just seeing the house—with its
darkened windows, and the porch she was never allowed to play on—stirred an uneasiness in her heart.

Her eyes went up to the third-floor attic windows
and she shivered. Those endless days in the attic, Nicole would kneel at one end of the dusty, cavernous
room and Rose at the other; with heads bowed and
hands clasped, they would pray. So many times they
had silently walked up the narrow, uncarpeted attic
steps, their footsteps sounding loud and reluctant.
Rose would dart a longing look out through the octan-
gular window midway up those stairs. The attic was
suffocatingly hot in the summer and bitingly cold in
the winter. Their mother would admonish them to
offer their pain to the poor souls in purgatory, and
then disappear downstairs.

"What about *my* poor soul?" Rose had wanted to
shout. But she hadn't. She had dutifully taken her
place under the stern and watchful eye of Mother. She
would keep her back straight even after Mother had
turned away and the sounds of her footsteps on the
wooden steps had faded. Whenever Rose turned to
look at her sister, to smile or maybe even to whisper
something, Nicole was praying, praying, her eyes
squeezed tightly shut. Rose had always been awed by
her sister's devotion, and she had sometimes wished

she could be as devout. But after a few minutes of fervent prayer, Rose's mind would wander outside where she would run and run, her skirts flying about her. Carefree. In her mind she climbed trees and chased dogs and waded in cool ponds or stood before a bonfire, depending on whether the attic was scorching or icy. In that attic, as Nicole prayed, Rose did the things in her mind she was never allowed to do, though she longed to do them with a fierceness that sometimes frightened her.

"Your sister and Louis are already here," Luke said, jarring Rose from her memories.

"Hmm. I can hear Flora crying. Poor little thing. All she seems to do is cry." Because Louis wouldn't let Nicole comfort the little thing, she added silently. Her stomach gave an uncomfortable squeeze as little Flora let out another wail. Maybe Louis wouldn't let Nicole comfort the girl, but she'd be damned if she'd let him stop her, Rose thought.

As Luke gave the buggy up to Mr. Charest, the Desrosiers' all-around man, giving their horse a solid pat on his flank, Rose waited, teeth clenched hard. How she wished she could take Luke's hand and lead him away from this house, her family. She closed her eyes and lifted her face to the sun again, wishing, wishing.

"You'll get freckles," Luke said, his voice softly teasing.

"I've never had a freckle in my life," she said, resisting bringing her face down just yet. "The sun feels so good. I love springtime." Rose finally opened her eyes and turned her face toward the house.

"It will still be springtime tomorrow," Luke said, and placed his hand at her elbow as if sensing her reluctance to enter the house. Never had she expressed any hesitance about these weekly visits. Nor had Luke.

"Here they are," Louis boomed over Flora's cries. He strode from the parlor where the family gathered before the Sunday meal, his face flushed, Rose guessed, from wine he'd already consumed.

Lamps were lit in each corner; the Waterford crystal chandelier glinted in the gaslight that didn't quite brighten the oppressive room. Midnight-blue velvet drapes were drawn tight against the sun that entered the room only in sharp, narrow rectangles above the drapes. The frugality Rose's mother was known for did not extend to the gas that would not be needed if only she would open the drapes.

Rose's father sat in an upholstered chair looking as if he were about to fall asleep, his thin frame slumped, his head resting on the protective crocheted doily spread over the back of the chair. Rose's mother was constantly grumbling about how many times she had to change the doilies, all the while her father would point out he was using them for their intended purpose. How he could sleep with so much commotion had always been a wonder to Rose.

Louis slapped a handshake onto Luke as if it was the first time the two had met. After one of his firm and vigorous handshakes, Luke always wore a look of bemusement on his face as he flexed his injured hand.

"Someday, you'll just have to squeeze tighter than he does," Rose whispered in Luke's ear, and blushed when he let out a soft chuckle.

"Whispering is impolite, Rose," her mother, Aline, said from her spot opposite her father. Her fingers worked furiously on a bit of crocheting in her lap. Never had Rose seen her mother simply sitting. For as long as she lived, Rose would associate the familiar clacking of crochet and knitting needles with her mother.

"Good afternoon, Mother," Luke said with a polite smile. He nodded to Nicole and even to Rose's now-softly-snoring father.

"I noticed you looking about in church today, Rose. Father Beaulieu noticed as well."

I hate this, I hate this, I hate this. "I'm sorry, Mother."

Rose's mother shifted in her seat, her clacking needles never missing a beat. "Church is not a place for daydreaming or looking about."

Shut up. Shut up. "Yes, Mother." And she managed a small apologetic smile.

Rose turned her attention to her crying niece, who was sitting in the middle of the floor, her voice so hoarse the effect of her bawling had greatly been diminished. Going over to her, she bent down and heaved the one-year-old up and onto her hip. The crying instantly stopped.

"Spoiled. That's what she is. See how she stopped crying? Rose, we're trying not to spoil her. This constant crying is just a way to get attention. Am I right, Mother?" Louis, puffed out and pompous, turned toward Aline.

"Yes. And I've told Nicole as much. Rose, put the child down."

Rose didn't know where this unexpected rebelliousness came from, or rather the brazenness to exhibit her rebelliousness, but she clutched the little girl tighter and jiggled her a bit on her hip. "I don't mind holding her, Mother. If it makes her happy to be held, I don't see the harm in doing that. Is it a sin to be happy, Mother?" Rose's face flushed scarlet from anger and shame that she was purposefully provoking her mother.

"The sin," Aline said between thinned lips, "is in disobeying the wishes of the parents."

She could sense rather than see Luke bend his head slightly toward her. "Rose." Somehow he managed to suggest both a warning and understanding in that one word.

Rose let out a sigh. It was wrong to let a child cry, when all it wanted was to be held and reassured. Rose instinctively knew that she and Nicole had sat on that very same rug and cried their little hearts out, wanting only to be held. Ignoring the adults, Rose gently placed Flora back on the carpet, but stayed by her, holding her little hands between each index finger and thumb. Flora, her brown eyes still brimming with tears, smiled at her.

"An aunt is allowed to spoil her only niece once in a while," she said, smiling back at the little girl before looking defiantly up at Louis.

He stood there, gazing down at her, his thin mustache bending in an arc over his frowning mouth. At that moment, Rose hated him. Hated him for letting Flora cry, for making Nicole somehow believe he was right in doing it. For beating Nicole down with his constant criticisms and overbearing ways. Nicole was the most thoroughly unhappy person Rose knew. But her older sister would never admit it, would never even hint that anything was wrong.

Supper seemed interminably long to Rose, and her head ached from stopping herself from screaming to everyone to please, please be quiet.

"I've volunteered at the church for the Fourth of July picnic, Mother. Perhaps this year you and Father will join Louis and me?" Nicole asked, looking down at her plate.

"It's frivolous and a waste and therefore a sin. I have never understood what attracts people to want to eat outside in the dirt."

Louis cleared his throat. "I've said much the same thing to her, Mother. You and I are in complete agreement. Complete. I've told her this. And I've told her it isn't seemly for a woman in her condition to be seen in public. By the picnic, you'll be fat and no corset's going to hold you in. I will not have you gallivanting about in public, shamefully on display." He wiped his mouth and mustache with the linen napkin.

Nicole blushed red, her hands abruptly dropping her fork and knife and retreating onto her lap.

"Oh, Nicole, you're expecting? That's wonderful," Rose said across the table. But it hurt that Nicole had not told her herself, that apparently everyone at the table knew she was having a baby except her and Luke.

"When is the baby due?" Rose asked.

"This is not proper conversation for the supper table," their mother said. And that was that.

Years ago, Nicole would have mouthed the month and hidden a mischievous smile behind her napkin. And Rose, naughtily, would have giggled into hers. Rose stared at her sister's bowed head, willing her to look up and smile into her face. Anger welled up in her that she could not be happy about her sister's good news.

"When will the next christening gown be needed?" Rose asked stubbornly. Next to her, Luke was putting a biteful into his mouth and paused imperceptibly as Rose asked her question.

Nicole looked up at her then, and instead of a con-spirator's smile, she saw anguish and pleading in her sister's eyes. Rose darted a glance to Louis, whose mouth had become compressed, whose brown eyes glittered with anger. And then a change came over Nicole, a relaxing.

"November," she said.

Louis's hand clenched around his napkin. "My dear, I thought we all agreed this was not proper conversa-tion for Sunday dinner." Something in his eyes, some-thing in the way he said those words, caused Rose to shudder. When she looked at Nicole again, her sister's face was hidden by her bowed head.

Rose was silent on the way to Luke's parents' home, as she almost always was. He'd thought it was because visiting was tiresome, that so much discussion usually took place at the Desrosiers', Rose simply wanted to be quiet. He pulled on the reins, skirting a man and woman riding a bicycle built for two, and glanced over at his wife. Pale. She was so pale beneath her hat. One gloved hand clutched her parasol, the other lay in her lap, a balled fist. He wanted to put his hand over hers, to press gently onto her fingers and lay them open, but decided such a gesture might not be welcome.

"Are you feeling ill?" he asked finally.

Rose seemed to awaken to his words. "Oh. No."
She sighed, a sharp little huff. After a few moments,
she asked, "What do you think of Louis?"

He wondered if she was looking for the truth or
reassurance. "He's an ass," he said, opting for the
truth. To his surprise, she smiled.

"Yes." And it seemed after that, whatever had been
bothering Rose was put away. Once again, she
dropped her parasol and lifted her face to the sun. He
wanted to stare at her as she held her face serenely
to the sun, at her lips that she'd just moistened with
her tongue. Ah, Jesus, he thought, to have a wife so
beautiful he ached with it, to know he'd lie awake
tonight thinking of those lips, that tongue.

They pulled into the long drive that looked as if a
majestic house would sit at the end of it. But the truth
was the iron gate and stone-carved lions were much
more majestic than the house that they guarded. The
Beaudettes were rather well-to-do and lived on the
fringes of Forest Park, but they spent so much of their
money on clothes and travel and the pursuit of looking
wealthy that they hardly had enough left for real living. It had always been that way, money spent as
quickly as it came in, living on the edge of disaster.

He had spent his childhood moving from opulence
to near austerity, dangling close to oblivion but not
quite ever dropping off the edge and into poverty. His
father had been born with a silver spoon in his mouth,
which he used to fling his wealth around without regard
to consequences, or so it had seemed to Luke. When
his parents did not worry, he did. Soured investments
or soaring profits dictated whether the Beaudettes ate
potato soup or prime rib. And yet they never seemed
to care, never seemed to notice that their son watched
with solemn gray eyes as they lamented rather light-
heartedly about the fortune they'd just lost.

Old age seemed to have mellowed Luke's parents
a bit. They had lived in this fine Forest Park address
for several years. As he pulled the buggy around, he
glanced up at the pretty, pink-stone house and knew

before being told that it was deserted. The drapes were drawn, even on the second floor, and the first-floor shutters were closed. As he pulled the buggy beneath the great beech tree that provided shade in the drive in front of the house, his parents' butler came out to greet them.

"I'm sorry, Mr. Beaudette. Your parents have closed up the house and traveled to London for an extended holiday. They wanted me to tell you when you came for your visit and asked that I relay their regrets."

"Thank you, Mr. Ringler. When did they leave, please?"

"Tuesday, sir."

Tuesday. They'd been gone five days and hadn't sent word. Or said good-bye. Luke was surprised they bothered to instruct Mr. Ringler to tell him. And the more he thought of it, he decided Mr. Ringler likely took it upon himself to inform him that his parents had disappeared. Again. Ringler had been with the Beaudettes for more than fifteen years and had witnessed Luke Beaudette's abandonment on more than one occasion. Though a grown man now of twenty-seven, it still hurt to come for a visit and find them gone.

That look in Ringler's eyes, pity and anger and understanding, brought Luke back to another time, when he was twelve years old and returning home from boarding school so homesick he nearly cried when his schoolmate's father dropped him off in front of the Beaudette home. It was Christmas break, and the excitement of presents and of being home mingled together, filling him nearly to bursting with happiness. He ran all the way to the front door, eager to surprise his parents who apparently had forgotten he was due home. Luke hadn't given it a second thought; they'd forgotten to collect him before. Gripping the doorknob, he gave it a heave, and was shocked to find it locked.

It didn't register at first, of course. He just looked

at the door with a bit of confusion and tried the doorknob again, giving it a little jiggle as his brows knitted together. And that feeling, that familiar hollow ache, formed in his chest and he knew they were gone. They had left before but never on Christmas and never without at least hinting they might be off on one of their jaunts. Making a fist, he knocked on the door, ignoring the knocker, ignoring the little bell handle. He knocked hard, bruising his knuckles, tearing off a bit of flesh. Mr. Ringler had come to the door, solemnly letting him into the empty house. It was almost, Luke had thought as he cried himself to sleep, as if they'd forgotten they had a son at all.

That hollowness was back, even though he was no longer that little boy longing for his parents on Christmas Eve. "Thank you, Mr. Ringler. I'm sure I know how much they regret they are not here." He said the words with a self-mocking smile.

Understanding flashed again in the older man's eyes as he nodded and retreated into the house.

"Well, it looks as if we have the afternoon free," Rose said with false brightness.

Luke gave his wife a tight smile. *Goddamn* his parents. Each week he and Rose would arrive at nearly the same time, and his parents almost always seemed surprised to see them. One time, they'd caught his parents on their way out, as if they'd completely forgotten that their son and his wife visited like clockwork each Sunday.

"It's just as well. I've work to do," Luke said, not noticing Rose's disappointment. He snapped the reins gently, turning the rig around, and headed home.

4

Rose brought the delicate teacup to her lips, taking a dainty sip before replacing it silently onto its saucer. That silent placement was something she could do without conscious thought now, but it had taken hours of practice beneath the watchful eye of her mother. She frowned into her tea, seeing her murky reflection wavering in the cup. Taking another sip, she replaced it with the tiniest of clatters. And smiled. Rose looked at the eight-day clock once more just to be sure it was not yet time to leave for the Taylors. It wouldn't do to arrive too early. Rose clenched the hand that was not occupied with the saucer in an attempt to gain control of her excitement.

She had awoken Monday morning full of expectation, Sunday's springlike weather coursing through her veins, making her feel reckless somehow. One look at the darkened window told her it was raining and her icy-cold nose told her it was cold, as well. But she smiled anyway. Today she was expected to call upon Collette Taylor. By the time she was dressed and her voluminous hair swept high atop her head, it might have been the sunniest, warmest May day in history.

I'm going to visit a friend, she said to herself, trying to sound nonchalant. Other than her sister, Rose had never had a friend, a girl she could giggle with, share secrets with. They had been taught by a tutor at home, though Rose had longed to attend boarding school. She'd seen such lucky girls, wearing their gray uniforms with the little white collars, walking in the city, their teacher herding them in front of her. Rose remembered sitting in her parents' carriage, her nose pressed against the window, watching those girls walk by. How wonderful to have so many girls among which to pick friends, she'd thought.

Those discussions about boarding school had been the only time Rose argued with her parents, tearfully pleading with them. It was the closest she'd ever come to throwing a tantrum—a display that had meant long, long hours praying in the attic where she begged, not for forgiveness, but for her parents to change their minds. They did not.

She had women who called on her, of course; her card receiver rarely remained empty for an entire day. Women whose husbands belonged to the same club as Luke, who went to St. Benedict's, often called. But there was no one she could huddle close to on a sofa and share . . . oh, whatever it was that friends shared. Certainly they talked about more interesting things than the weather or the high cost of keeping servants. Collette might be my first friend, Rose thought. My only friend.

Rose walked the short distance between their houses, her gloved hand clutching her umbrella. She picked her way around puddles filled with dark-pink earthworms driven to the surface by the rain only to drown. It was raw and cold, but Rose loved walking in the rain and listening to the drops splatter above her. Sometimes she would just stand still and listen to the rain hit her umbrella simply because she could. Simply because it was something when she was a girl she could not do. Rose nearly walked by the Taylors' home, so lost was she in listening to the rain. Before she could put her hand to the knocker, Collette opened the door and whisked her inside.

"Oh, it's dreadful out, isn't it? And yesterday so beautiful. Oh, well, New England. I simply hate the rain, don't you?" Collette said as she handed Rose's umbrella and coat to a maid.

"Oh, yes," Rose agreed readily, without a single twinge that she'd just told a white lie.

Collette escorted Rose to the same parlor they'd sat in on Saturday, offering her tea that was already set up on a table. Collette sat back in her chair, looking relaxed, the teacup dangling precariously from her fingers as she talked. Rose sat on a sofa, near the edge, her saucer held beneath the cup as she took a small, noiseless sip. She wore her best blue wool day dress and her most sensible shoes. Collette wore a pink-and-white-striped silk skirt with a smart-looking white blouse with huge puffed sleeves, pink buttons, and pink piping. Rose's mother would have called Collette's outfit common, but Rose loved it.

As the two women talked, Rose found herself relaxing and scooted back on the couch until she rested, just slightly, against it.

"You and Luke must come to visit Friday night," Collette said in a good-natured command.

Rose frowned. "Luke attends his club each Friday evening. I'm afraid that is the only time he cannot visit. Perhaps Saturday?"

"Oh, no, that won't do. Friday is a tradition for John and me. We play cards. Poker actually. You'll simply have to come alone." Collette nodded once, as if that ended the conversation.

Rose seemed to snap out of her complacence. She sat forward, her back erect, once more in command of herself.

"Oh, no, Luke would never allow me to do *that*," she said, shaking her head.

Collette gave her one of those devilish smiles, showing straight white teeth and squinting her lively eyes. "You don't have to ask permission. He's not your father, after all."

"But gambling! It's so . . ."

"Fun," Collette supplied with a giggle.

"But I cannot lie to Luke."

Collette waved a dismissive hand. "We only play for chips. No real money. We need a fourth player and if I don't come up with one of my own, John will bring one of his own pals and then I'll be the only woman and that would never do. Where does it say 'Thou shalt not gamble' in the Bible?" Collette asked.

"It's not the sin of it, although it *is* a sin, and you cannot convince me otherwise. Luke is assistant attorney general. My goodness, if he ever thought of me *gambling* . . . I believe he'd be rather upset."

Collette crossed her arms and pouted. "It's not really gambling if we don't play for money. It's like playing bridge or hearts or any other perfectly innocent card game. But really, I do understand if you don't want to visit . . ." she said, letting her voice trail off.

Rose knew she was being manipulated, as Collette

was being almost comically obvious about it, but she didn't care.

Oh, imagine, Rose thought. Imagine sitting in their parlor playing *poker*. She wanted this, just for herself—to do something just slightly shocking. It was so wrong and yet . . . She bit her lip. She certainly didn't want her prudishness to mar her new friendship, and playing poker just for fun wasn't illegal and therefore must not be much of a sin.

"You're sure it's all just for fun?"

Collette's smile lit up the room. "Wonderful, Rose. I knew you had some gumption." She let out a sigh that almost seemed to Rose like relief and she suddenly felt awful for making such a big thing out of some innocent fun. Collette would find her a bit tiresome if she continued to act like such a do-gooder. She looked at her new friend, so lovely in her pink and white outfit. Rose couldn't imagine someone as pretty and vivacious as Collette not having a whole circle of friends surrounding her.

"I'll come for a visit, Collette. But I'm sure you have plenty of friends you could ask who perhaps wouldn't mind playing poker as much as I," Rose said, lifting her voice hopefully.

Collette's eyes turned down to her lap and her cheeks flushed prettily. "We've only been in Springfield for a few weeks. It's so hard to meet women my age when you don't have children," she said, ending on a wistful note. "In Boston, I had many more friends than here. I know it's not all that far by train, but I haven't made the trip once, and neither have they."

"You were in Boston? That's where Luke worked when he first graduated Harvard. Perhaps you knew some of the same people," Rose said, excited that she had found a reason for Luke to like her new friends. She instinctively knew that Luke would not like the Taylors, though she could not have said why.

"Oh, I'm sure not," Collette said hastily. "We had only a very small circle of friends and I doubt your husband knew any of us. Were you born in Springfield?"

Rose smiled, easily lured into another topic of conversation, completely unaware that Collette had drawn her dainty hand into a claw and squeezed her own thigh hard enough to leave a bruise.

"Friday night?" Luke frowned. "But that's the night I attend my club."

Rose stood before him, twisting her wedding ring round and round, looking decidedly guilty about something. Luke had seen enough guilty people in his career to know what one looked like.

"Yes. Well, I know that. Which is why I thought you would not object," Rose said.

Luke gave his wife a level look. "I have not objected," he said in that way Rose found thoroughly irritating, as if he'd just caught her in a lie. Which, if one were perfectly honest, he had.

"And you have no reason to. I'm just going for a visit."

He watched as she turned that wedding ring at a furious pace. His wife was lying, he realized with unfathomable surprise. Lying. He leaned back in his chair and put his hands behind his head, giving her his best prosecutor's stare, his gray eyes narrowed.

Rose looked at him almost angrily. "I won't be interrogated like one of your prisoners," she bit out.

Luke almost laughed and would have if he wasn't so unbalanced by the fact his wife had or was about to do something she knew he would disapprove of.

"I don't believe I have asked you a single question, Rose," he said, his voice measured. "Why don't you tell me why it is that you look like you've just murdered someone."

Rose sagged in defeat. "It's nothing, really. Now I've built it up so I suppose you think I'll be joining in a bank robbery. Collette invited me over to play cards," she said finally.

"Cards? And you thought I would forbid this?"

"Not just cards. Poker."

Luke let out a bark of laughter. "Poker? You, a member of St. Benedict's Ladies' Temperance Club, plan to gamble? Tell me, Rose, it is high stakes?"

Rose stopped fingering her ring and threw her balled fists to her side, but her voice remained calm. "It's no stakes. None. We're playing for fun."

Luke gazed at his wife standing before him, her color high, her eyes filled with what he could only call reluctant rebellion. "Rose," he said with palpable condescension, "no one plays poker for fun."

"The Taylors do. Collette assured me. Do you think I would even consider playing poker if we were truly gambling? She said it was just for fun. She's my friend, and . . ."

To Luke's dismay, it seemed as if Rose were about to weep. He rose from his chair to stand before her, slightly panicky at the thought that his wife was about to cry.

"Of course you can go to your friend's Friday night," he said, his eyes creased with worry. She had almost lied to him, would have lied if she hadn't been such an unqualified failure at it. He started to raise his hand to cup the side of her face but stopped, suddenly unsure of himself. Rose looked so damned woebegone all the time and he couldn't help but think he was at fault. And now she thought he was about to forbid her the first thing that had made her happy in months. How could she think so little of him?

"Rose, look at me," and his breath caught in his throat when she did. He would never get used to the effect those brown eyes had on him whenever she looked his way. "I don't want you to lie to me. But I also don't want you to feel you have to lie." He swallowed. How he wanted to draw her into his arms, to have her come willingly. To make love with a woman who wanted him as much as he wanted her.

"I'm sorry, Luke." She looked at his mouth and for a moment Luke thought she might kiss him there. Instead she pressed a hurried and clumsy kiss upon his jaw and he closed his eyes against the feeling that surged through his blood at that chaste kiss. If she knew what that innocent pressing of her lips upon his skin did to him, she would draw away, she would have that wary look in her eyes that left him feeling like some sort of despoiler of virgins.

"If you are wrong, if they are truly gambling, I want you to leave, Rose. It certainly wouldn't do to have a police raid and have the assistant attorney general's wife herded into jail in the roundup." He smiled.

"I promise." Looking vastly relieved that the discussion was over, Rose made to leave the study.

"And Rose."

She turned, a gentle smile on her lips, inclining her head in question.

"I'm truly not the ogre you think me to be." Rose made as if to argue, but he held up a hand. "Good night, Rose."

After she'd gone, he sat down heavily in his chair. His wife, his young beautiful wife, was afraid of him. He'd already known it, of course. During their first few months of marriage, each time he'd touch her, that disconcerting wariness would come to her eyes, as if she feared the most casual embrace would lead to the bedroom. And in those first weeks of marriage, that was what he wanted, true enough. Now, he'd do almost anything to not see that look. He stayed out of her bed as long as he could bear it. When he came to her, he tried to be gentle, tried to reawaken feelings he knew she had. His mind clung to that one kiss in the garden, to that passionate woman he'd held in his arms.

He looked up at the ceiling at the spot over which her bed lay and pictured her there alone, brushing her hair before her mirror. Long, languid strokes.

"Jesus, give me strength," he muttered as his groin tightened painfully. Somewhere in the house a clock began its mournful chiming. Ten o'clock. He thought of his bed, his cold empty bed, and headed to his desk to work.

5

By the time Friday evening came, Rose considered herself quite the expert on five-card stud. She no longer needed the little cheat sheet Collette had written out for her in her rather messy penmanship. But she had far more difficulty mastering her poker face. The sight of aces or a string of clubs was enough to make her brown eyes sparkle, coaxing gales of laughter from Collette. What fun they had, happily chatting endlessly about everything from dress patterns to the many local characters. How they laughed, to Rose's horror, about the unfortunate death of one of the area's most prominent citizens.

"I'm sorry," Collette said, holding her hand against her stomach. "But that Sadie Graves must be the stupidest woman the good Lord created. Imagine ignoring your physician and instead taking the advice of a medium."

"That medium ought to be ashamed of herself," Rose said, trying not to smile. "Or maybe the spirit who spoke through the medium is to blame. After all, it was the spirit who advised Mrs. Graves not to have the life-saving surgery. I do believe the woman never had a ghost of a chance." Rose giggled at what she thought was a wonderful play on words, but Collette groaned as if the poor joke caused her pain.

Their easy friendship had only one drawback—the guilt Rose felt that it should have been Nicole she was laughing with. The two women often remarked about the fact they had become so close so quickly.

By the time Friday evening came, Rose had stopped blushing furiously each time John came home and swung his pretty wife around in greeting, ending with the kind of kiss Rose thought couples reserved for the bedroom. Collette and John were a wonder to her. Never in her life had she witnessed such open affection between people. It was . . . depressing.

All that week, Rose sat across from Luke night after night, politely asking about his day. Rose wasn't sure if it was a new awareness that married life could be different, but it seemed as if Luke was becoming more and more withdrawn. Dinner was mostly a silent affair; more often than not Luke's attention would be on a sheaf of paper by his side as he distractedly ate. Rose didn't tell him about her daily visits with the Taylors. She didn't know why, but she wanted to keep this to herself, to hold it close, this happiness she found away from home that filled her with joy and a little bit of guilt. She sensed Luke's disapproval, no matter if he had given his hesitant blessing to the poker game.

"Tonight's the big night," Luke said, and his voice sounded overly loud and jovial.

Rose, startled to hear his voice cut through the silence, dropped her fork loudly against her plate. "Yes."

"It's just occurred to me, Rose, that you don't know how to play poker. That might pose a problem for you, even if no stakes are involved."

Rose's face flushed with guilt, knowing she had spent long hours being tutored.

"I played poker while at Harvard," Luke continued, unaware of Rose's discomfort. "I could give you a crash course in the game. Not that I was ever too successful, mind you. But I could teach you the rudiments."

Rose was almost stunned into silence, but recovered as Luke rose, ostensibly to fetch playing cards. "But I already know how to play," she said, and watched as Luke froze mid-stride. "Collette has taught me, you see. I'm quite good now, except I'm having trouble concealing that I have a good hand."

"A poker face," he said, strolling back to the table. He was smiling and Rose relaxed, feeling silly now to have hidden the poker lessons from Luke.

"Yes, poker face. It is a rather fun game, but Collette said she can tell what I'm holding the instant I look at my cards. It's rather disconcerting."

Luke's smile widened as he leaned against the dining table, close to his wife. "So you're an expert, are you?"

"Except for the poker face." She looked so adorably disappointed at her failure, Luke could not resist bending down for a kiss. But he stopped before their lips touched when he looked into her eyes.

"No. You never have been good at hiding your feelings, Rose. Have a good time."

Rose watched Luke leave the dining room with a crease of worry between her eyes. She'd sensed a bit of nastiness in Luke's tone and was baffled by it. Luke had never been angry with her and the thought that he might be was rather frightening. Throwing down her napkin, Rose hurried after her husband, catching him just as he was jamming his hat upon his head.

"You're angry with me," she said, clutching her hands together at her midriff. He was turned away from her and she could tell by the tilt of his head he was deciding whether or not to respond to her. "Luke, if you don't want me to go . . ."

He spun around. "I am not angry with you, Rose," he bit out, sounding very angry to Rose's ears. She stiffened and brought her chin up.

"I won't go," she said stubbornly.

Luke rubbed his eyes with the heels of his hands as if he was suddenly, overwhelmingly weary. "It has nothing to do with playing poker or the Taylors. I'm just tired."

Rose searched his face, knowing that he was not telling her all that was bothering him. She wanted to scream at him, to pummel her fists against his chest. She wanted to wrap her arms around him, to feel his arms wrap around her. Instead, she let out a little huff of air and shook her head.

"You're angry with me," she repeated softly, this time with certainty. "You can't tell me why?"

Luke gave her a hard, long look, his eyes lingering on her lips, and for a moment Rose thought he would tell her what was bothering him.

"No, Rose. I can't." He opened the door and

walked out into the night, leaving Rose staring at the
door, tears burning at her eyes.

6

"Lady luck's with you tonight, Mrs. Beaudette,"
Thomas Kersey said as he good-naturedly pushed the
small pile of chips toward Rose. She tried not to smile
too much at the compliment, but the muscles in her
face failed her and her mouth widened into a full-
fledged grin. Poker was such fun! Rose thought as she
eyed her growing pile of chips. She couldn't help but
wonder how exciting the game would have been had
the chips represented money instead of points, as Collette had explained.

Thomas Kersey was a rough sort of man, not at all
the kind of person Rose was used to associating with.
He was loud and brash and really quite disarming, she
thought. His reddish hair sprang about his head in a
charming way, and his winning smile and boisterous
manner made him so thoroughly likable, Rose felt
guilty for mentally acknowledging his lower social sta-
tus. He wore a yellow plaid vest, brown shirt, and
yellow pants, which had the effect of making him look
more like a circus barker than the friend of a respectable couple. But the Taylors took Thomas in stride,
never seeming uncomfortable when he was wickedly
off-color. Rather, they laughed and Rose joined in
with them after a few uncomfortable, red-faced
moments.

"Don't mind him," John said with a nod toward his
uncouth friend. "We only let him out into society on
Friday nights so he's a bit out of practice." He gave
Thomas a good-natured warning look, forcing Rose
to intercede.

"Really, I don't want to make Thomas uncomfortable during the only free night that he has," Rose
teased. "If he continues to make me blush, I'll simply
have to have more lemonade to cool my injured sensi-

bilities." She was inordinately pleased when the three other poker players laughed heartily. It was thrilling to be part of this lively group and wonderful that they found her funny, as well. Rose could not remember laughing more. Her stomach hurt and her face actually felt sore from smiling so much.

Hand after hand flew by as they talked and joked. The men drank whiskey and water, Collette and Rose drank lemonade, and as the night wore on they became louder and more boisterous and Thomas more careless with his bets.

"But who cares if it's just points, not cash—right, John?" he said with a devilish wink at Rose.

"You have lost a lot of points tonight, my good friend," John said with meaning. "I hope you have enough points at home to back it up."

Rose took a handful of her chips worth fifty points each and shoved them toward Thomas. "He can have some of my points," she said. For some reason, Collette and John thought the gesture hilarious. They laughed so hard, soon Rose joined them, clutching her stomach, eyes squeezed shut as tears streamed down her cheeks. She didn't noticed that Thomas didn't join in, that he sat there with a smile pasted on his face, his eyes, as they stared at John, filled with something close to fear.

When the laughter finally subsided, Thomas gave Rose her chips back. "A very gracious gesture, madam. But one I'm afraid I cannot accept."

"If you insist." Rose gathered up her chips and stacked them carefully in front of her. The mood at the table sobered after the earlier laughter, and suddenly it seemed as if the little group had been playing poker all night. Rose looked with shock at the mantel clock—it was nearly midnight.

"Oh, my goodness. It's midnight. It's . . . oh, my. I must get home." Rose stood in a fluster, a bit panicky it was so late. Surely Luke would be worried, or angry. She was reminded of the way he had left that evening; he'd been cold and unresponsive. She'd vowed not to let his foul mood ruin an evening she'd been looking forward to for a week. And she had not. But now she felt guilty for completely disregarding his feelings.

Collette hurried off to get Rose's coat, hat, and gloves while Rose paced madly in the parlor as she twisted her wedding ring round and round. As she paced, she passed by a door, open just a crack, that led to a hallway. Seeing movement from the corner of her eye, Rose stopped her pacing. John and Thomas were deep in discussion, and from the way they held their bodies, they almost seemed angry with one another. Then she watched as Thomas, with jerky movements, took out his billfold and slapped money into John's hands.

"Here you are, Cinderella," Collette said cheerfully as she entered the parlor. "I'll go get John to walk you home."

Rose put her coat on thoughtfully as she watched Collette leave the room. Had Thomas been paying John money lost in the poker game? A little worry crease formed between her eyes. Impossible. Collette had said the game was in fun. She believed her new friend, refused to think that Collette had lied to her. Of course she hadn't, Rose thought, smiling to herself. What possible reason could the Taylors have to only pretend to gamble for her benefit? Luke's comment that no one played poker for fun had made her think the worst of her new friends. Well, Luke didn't know the Taylors like she did. They were fun and nice. And most of all, they were her friends.

Once safely escorted home, Rose let herself into the front door feeling like a burglar. In her guilt-wracked mind, every tiny noise she made, from the excruciatingly loud turning of her key in the lock to the rustle of her skirts, was sure to bring Luke bounding down the stairs, pistol in hand, ready to face an intruder. The house was dark but for the low hissing of a gas lamp Luke had left burning. Seeing that light renewed her guilt. He'd cared enough to leave it lit, but she hadn't cared enough to arrive home on time. The servants, thankfully, were long abed, having been instructed to retire at the usual time—nine o'clock.

Lifting her skirts noisily, Rose began walking up the stairs, thankful that the thick carpet muffled her steps. At the top of the stairs, she gave a furtive look in the direction of Luke's room. A slice of light was visible beneath the door. He was awake. Darn. Rose stood at the top of the stairs, one foot still resting on the last step, her hand clutching the banister, and debated whether she should let Luke know she was home safe and sound. With a small grimace, she tiptoed to his door and tilted one ear to listen. Nothing. Biting her lip, she gave a tentative knock. Nothing. The crease was back between her lovely eyes. Oh, just go in, you ninny. And she did, very, very quietly.

The first thing Rose saw was the lamp, its flame low, beside her husband's bed. The next thing she saw was her husband's very naked body, face-down, on his bed. It was the first time Rose had seen him completely naked. Even when they'd made love, he kept his nightshirt on and Rose was always careful to keep her eyes averted from what was visible below his nightshirt. Her eyes wide, Rose moved toward the bed without thought, captivated by what she saw. He was . . . beautiful. The lamplight cast a soft glow over his muscled buttocks, making his flesh appear impossibly smooth, like satin. He faced away from her, so she could not see what her husband's face looked like in his sleep, and she was entirely too skittish to roam all the way around the bed to find out.

Rose's eyes went from his calves, sprinkled with golden hair, up to his powerful thighs, to his buttocks and the broad back that lifted and fell slowly with each breath. He lay with his arms slightly bent by his sleep-tousled head, the goose-down pillow discarded onto the floor. Rose's world tilted. I want to curl up beside you, she thought. I want to lay by you, naked, to feel your warmth and strength. Oh, Luke, I shouldn't feel like a stranger here, should I? In Rose's limited experience, all husbands slept separately from their wives. But right now she wanted his warm body beside hers.

Like a whisper of a breeze on a hot summer night, a feeling that Rose at first didn't recognize began drifting through her. She stood there for long, long minutes, drinking in the sight of him, learning him, wishing she could touch him. She was caught off guard by the feeling, a breeze that suddenly became something much, much stronger. The wanting swept through her so quickly, so unexpectedly, Rose nearly swayed from it. She thrust a hand to her mouth to stop the sound that threatened to erupt in the silent room. It was staggering, frightening.

It was wrong.

Wrapping her arms around her, Rose slowly backed out of the room. She silently closed the door, leaning her feverish head against it, trying to shut off those feelings that surged through her.

In the room, Luke turned, his eyes burning into the door as if he sensed she was still there, trembling on the other side.

Chapter Two

1

"Bless me, Father, for I have sinned. It has been one week since my last confession."

Rose already felt her soul being cleansed. For the first time in her life, she'd come to confession with true sins on her soul.

Something in Rose Beaudette's voice struck Father Beaulieu as odd. It was the sound of someone truly distressed. Leaning toward the little screen that separated him from Rose, he said gently, "Go on, my child."

Rose bit her lip. How awful this was. To think that just one week ago she'd had to practically make up a sin and this week, well, this week she had no shortage of sins.

"I think I may have gambled, Father." After giving it much thought, Rose decided that perhaps Collette, trying to protect her, told her a white lie just so she'd feel comfortable playing poker. Though she lied, Rose thought it rather endearing that her friend was so protective of her. And technically, Rose hadn't gambled. Only Collette, John, and Thomas had. Or maybe not. Maybe that money Thomas had slapped into John's hand had been something else entirely. Just to be sure, Rose believed she should confess.

"You *think* you have gambled." Father Beaulieu managed to keep the bemusement from his voice. Clearly, Rose was suffering from what she believed to be a grave sin.

"It's rather complicated, Father. But yes, I believe

I may have played high-stakes poker." Rose let out a little sigh. "And I almost lied to my husband."

Father Beaulieu had to bite down on his lips to stop from laughing. "Almost?"

"I was going to lie about playing poker. But I didn't. I did think about lying."

The priest prayed for strength. "I see."

"And I've one more sin," Rose said solemnly. "I committed the sin of lust." She whispered the last.

Father Beaulieu sat straight up hearing this one. Rose Beaudette seemed very sure of this sin, and it was a serious one at that. The Beaudettes had been married for such a short time—he had married the young couple himself—and he was surprised Rose would have looked with lust at a man other than her husband so quickly.

"Lust is a serious sin," Father Beaulieu said carefully. "For it is something that can lead to emotions much stronger, to sins that are much greater. Adultery comes from lust, my child. You must turn away and look toward God to keep you strong in your marriage vows."

Rose frowned. "Adultery? But Father, I was lusting . . ." Never had she been so thankful that Father Beaulieu could not see her beet-red face. ". . . after my husband," she finished.

Father Beaulieu shook his head and stifled another chuckle. "My dear child. Such feelings are not sinful within the confines and sanctity of marriage."

Rose was astonished. "They're not? By my . . . But I've always been told . . . Truly, Father?"

"Truly."

Father Beaulieu gave her penance for her "almost" sins, and though it was the heaviest penance she'd ever received, it was still fairly light. And her mind, try as she might, was not on her prayers, but on Father Beaulieu's revelation. A priest whom she respected, whom she was in awe of, told her that the feelings she had for her husband were not sinful. But her mother, whom she loved and feared and hated, had told her in scorching, endless lectures, that everything except begetting a child was sinful between a man and a woman. Worse than sinful, it was dirty and lowly.

She would never forget that last lecture, her mother's words, her distorted face. After discovering her and Luke in the garden, her mother had forced her to pray all evening, not in the attic, but in the living room where her mother could watch her as she knitted. She'd never forget that angry clacking of knitting needles that went on interminably as her knees ached and eyes burned from exhaustion. Rose had been truly ashamed. She had let Luke put his tongue in her mouth. Surely that was wrong. And surely it had been even more wrong to put her own tongue in his mouth. Red heat had suffused her face at the thought that she'd enjoyed that kiss, welcomed it, just as she had welcomed his hand upon her breast. As an unmarried woman she had been so terribly wrong to allow it. Kneeling there before her mother, Rose had felt she was as dirty as her mother told her she was.

Rose hadn't felt dirty last night as she stared at her husband. She'd felt . . . wonderful and a bit frightened. But not dirty. Rose was so lost in thought, she nearly ran into Collette.

"Hello, Rose." Collette wore a white shirtwaist with a green bow at the neck that perfectly matched the wide green stripes in her skirt. Her overlarge hat—which Rose thought would have looked ridiculous on *her*—looked enchanting on Collette.

"Oh, Collette, hello," Rose said distractedly as she continued walking out of the church.

"Well, I'm happy to see you too!" Collette said cheerfully as she hurried after Rose.

"Collette," Rose said, tilting her head a bit. "Do you and John share the same bed?" The minute the question was out, Rose could not believe it had passed through her lips. "Oh, goodness! I'm so sorry, Collette. Of course it's none of my business. Whatever possessed me to ask such a thing?"

Collette just waved a hand and smiled at Rose's

embarrassment. "You're obviously curious," she said with a laugh.

Rose sagged in utter distress. "It's simply that everyone I know does not and . . . I was simply curious because you and John seem so . . . oh, goodness, am I truly saying all this?" Rose placed her hands over her burning face.

Collette looked at Rose kindly. "Rose, we're friends. We can talk of such things. John and I seem so . . ." she prompted.

Rose swallowed miserably. "So affectionate."

Collette wriggled her eyebrows suggestively. "That we are!"

"You're awful!" Rose gave her friend a look of exasperation. Then she sobered almost comically. "Oh, I *wish* I could be more like you."

Collette looked away. "No, you don't, honey. Believe me." When she turned back, her smile had returned. "You and Luke have separate bedrooms?"

Rose nodded, shutting her eyes. She could not believe she was discussing such a thing.

Collette gave Rose's arm a squeeze. "That's not unusual, Rose. Just as long as, well, just as long as you have occasional visits." Now it was Collette's turn to blush scarlet.

"Of course," Rose said quietly.

Apparently sensing that Rose wanted to say more, Collette said, "You do have occasional visits, don't you?"

Rose took a deep breath. "Well . . ."

"I see."

"I'm not sure that you do. I'm not sure that I do."

Collette took Rose's arm and led her to a wrought-iron bench that rested in a little garden on the church's grounds. "Not all men have the same needs, honey."

"Oh, it's not Luke. It's me. It's definitely me. I don't . . . I didn't . . ." Rose covered her face again. She could not talk about this subject anymore.

"You don't like it," Collette said with a knowing look.

"No! I do!"

Collette shook her head in confusion.

"But I didn't think I was supposed to. So . . ."

Dawning comprehension showed on Collette's face. Rose looked down at her hands. "Now he doesn't even ask," she whispered.

Collette put her arm around Rose's shoulder. "Then you'll just have to ask him, honey."

From the look of dread on Rose's face, Collette might have told Rose to drink a gallon of fish oil.

2

Gray. Brown. Black.

Collette looked at Rose with dismay on her face as Rose's maid, Mildred, took each dress out of her immense walnut wardrobe one by one. "This is it? Tell me you have another wardrobe hidden somewhere. Oh, tell me, do."

Rose grimaced. "Is it that bad?"

Collette lifted one particularly drab brown sleeve between thumb and forefinger and shook her head. "Worse. What you need is an entirely new wardrobe. I know you think of yourself as a modern girl, but these mannish styles, with your height, will never do." Collette turned, her blue eyes wide. "Oh, dear. Are you in mourning?"

Rose eyed her gowns, skirts, and shirtwaists uncertainly. They did seem to be all black, brown, and gray. "I . . . No, I'm not. But I always thought the more subdued colors suited me."

Collette waved her hand, dismissing that notion. "You've thought nothing of the sort. Why, with your coloring, I believe . . ." She tilted her head and gazed at Rose critically. ". . . a soft butter yellow, and rose, of course. Certainly rose should be your trademark color."

Rose let out a delighted laugh. "Wouldn't that be a bit egocentric of me to go about in my namesake color?"

"I think it would be saucy and very modern. It's 1896, Rose, nearly 1900. Women can do whatever they please. I plan to purchase bicycle bloomers, but I know you're not quite ready for that."

Rose's eyes grew large. "For beneath your skirt, of course."

Collette tilted her head and appeared quite mischievous. "I did see a picture of a lovely velveteen bicycling outfit where no skirt was worn. It was quite dashing. But I suppose you're right, it would never do to wear such a daring outfit. I don't have a bicycle in any case." She pouted and Rose laughed again.

Collette tapped a finger against her rosebud mouth. "We should make a list of what you need. Skirts, of course. Yours are much too wide in the hip. See how mine fall?" she asked, twirling her snugly fitted skirts back and forth. "And your shirtwaists are rather drab. I'm afraid your gowns are horribly out of style. Why, these look to be two years old."

"No. But I simply can't make myself wear those ridiculous puffy sleeves. I'd feel rather like I'm about to fly off."

Collette shook her head sadly. "My dear girl, you must obey fashion. It is the one rule of life I live by," she said solemnly.

Rose gave an inward grimace. She'd never thought about clothes before. Oh, she'd thankfully given up her bustles and good riddance to them, but she'd never let Paris dictate her taste in clothes. With a little sigh of resignation, she realized that what Paris could not do, Collette certainly would. She ought to simply enjoy herself. Still, she couldn't completely hide her dismay as Collette rifled through her bureaus and wardrobes, casting nearly everything she owned, including her unmentionables, aside with a little derisive snort.

Finally Collette lifted her hands in mock despair. "It's as if you don't give a whit about what you wear."

Rose could only tilt her head and give Collette a little self-deprecating smile.

"Well," Collette announced, "we have our work cut out for us. First we'll go to Hayes and perhaps Forbes and Wallace and buy you some ready-mades to get started. Just a few day dresses, skirts, shirtwaists, et cetera. I imagine you'll want your gowns to be made by a seamstress. We'll visit one tomorrow and see what we can have done immediately. Honestly, Rose, one might think you were an old spinster, not a beautiful young bride."

Rose blushed prettily, but her pleasure was short-lived. "Your maid needs a lesson from mine on hairstyling."

Mildred, a middle-aged woman who had worked for her mother before coming to work for her, flushed and Rose patted her arm as an apology as she gently dismissed her.

Collette continued, completely unaware she had hurt the maid's feelings. "You could use a bit of rouge . . ." She stopped as Rose frowned. "Honey, don't misunderstand. You're the prettiest girl I've ever seen but you'd never know it."

Collette dragged Rose over to the mirror hanging above her bureau. "Look at those eyes. God, what I wouldn't give for lashes that long. And . . . hey." Collette stopped as if surprised to discover it for herself. "You really are quite lovely. You simply don't *act* pretty."

"Vanity is a sin," Rose said distractedly as she studied her reflection. I am pretty, she thought, and smiled.

"There! See? You know you're pretty."

Rose bit her lip. "Oh, Collette, I honestly never gave it much thought."

"I certainly believe you. Why, with some new clothes, a new hairstyle, some rouge . . . Luke won't be able to resist you."

A week ago, Rose would have been mortified by such talk. But now, she looked at herself in the mirror, her eyes sparkling, and nodded. "Let us begin to turn me into a butterfly."

It wasn't until Wednesday that Rose's metamorphosis was begun. Her thick, full hair, once hanging down nearly to the small of her back, was cut to her shoulders. Curls once weighed down now sprang free, framing her lovely face in a way that even Collette couldn't have imagined. Rose was exquisite. She was wearing her new apple green skirt with a white shirtwaist and an apple green bow at her throat, turning around in front of the mirror. The white and green bow at her back gave the outfit a rather dashing appearance and Rose kept looking behind her shoulder in the mirror to see the effect. The narrow skirt required extra cinching of her new corset, making her waist appear tiny.

"Oh, Collette, I look so . . . nice," Rose said, smiling broadly.

"Pah. You look beautiful and you know it."

"I do. I look beautiful. I can't wait until Luke sees me," Rose said without vanity. "Thank you. You're the dearest friend I've ever had."

Collette looked away from the mirror then and Rose thought she'd embarrassed her. She was too happy to see anything but modesty in Collette's flushing features.

"I can't do it, John. I just can't. You should have seen her. She was so darling. And innocent. *Innocent.*" Angrily Collette threw her small bag onto the couch and brought her hands to her hips. John, feet up on his desk, face buried in the *Springfield Union,* held up one finger to his ranting wife. When he was finished reading the article, he calmly set the paper down, brought his feet down, and approached her.

"I will not discuss this with you," he said, rather

roughly grabbing her chin between his thumb and forefinger.

Collette jerked her head away, unaffected by the rough treatment. "Why can't you just go after him? Why her? She's nice. I like her." With an exasperated groan, she said, "She trusts me, John. Like a little puppy, she does everything I say. It's too easy. It's cruel."

"It is no concern of mine if the little brainless ninny jumps off a cliff if you tell her to. In fact, darling, you have just proven what a wonderful job you are doing forming her unformed mind." He kissed her then, soft little nips that made her frown turn into a grudging smile.

"Stop that," Collette said lightly. "Rose is no dummy. She's just lonely and needs a friend. And I'm feeling a bit guilty taking advantage of her. Oh, John," she sighed, returning his enticing kisses. "Why *can't* we just go after him?"

John withdrew sharply. "Sure, go after the assistant attorney general. Of course, Collette, I wish I would have thought of that. Now, my genius wife, how do you propose we do that? How do you propose we ruin a man surrounded by the law, a man who's incorruptible?" He waited a few moments before continuing his derisive speech. "I didn't think you had any ideas. We have to go after her. So much easier, don't you think? And you've already proven how pliable she is, how vulnerable."

Collette looked at John with distaste. "You can be so nasty."

"Thank you."

She couldn't help but laugh at his blasé response. "You really are a cad," she said, tilting her head back a bit as if studying him. "It's a good thing I love you so much. Which reminds me, our little couple is a bit lacking on that front."

John moved back around his desk and sat negligently in his chair, raising his eyebrows in question.

"Oh, don't worry. I'm acting as Cupid and the poor

little twit is following my advice to the letter," Collette said, her voice tinged with anger.

"Little twit, is she now?"

"I like her. I don't want her hurt, so sometimes I want to shake her for being so damned compliant. At the same time, I want her to be so compliant."

John chuckled at his wife's odd dilemma.

Collette, pouting prettily, walked over to her husband and sat in his lap. "It's not funny. It's horrid."

"And just a little bit fun seeing how far you can go?"

Collette wrinkled her nose. "Just a little. But mostly I feel horrid."

John gave her a wicked kiss. "Like taking candy from a baby?"

"That's it exactly."

3

Michael Farwell, Springfield's chief of police, took out a cigar, mutilated and wet at one end, and pointed a pudgy finger at Luke. "Don't tell me we haven't got enough evidence. Don't tell me that, Beaudette." Chief Farwell leaned forward in his chair, his big belly falling between his knees, making it appear as if he were about to topple over.

Luke sat back in his burgundy leather chair, his elbow on the armrest, his chin planted on one thumb. His index finger, driving his brow upward, made him look even more skeptical than he was. Luke's apparent lack of concern for the chief's complaints only served to anger the officer more, something that Luke didn't seem overly concerned about.

"You!" And he turned his portly face toward Luke's friend and fellow attorney, Arthur Ripley. "You told me two weeks ago we could bring charges. Two weeks ago. Who the hell's in charge here? Don't make me go to your boss over in Boston. I'll do it. You two pups wouldn't know evidence if it was sitting right here on his desk." And he pounded Luke's meticulously neat desk with one beefy fist.

Arthur passed Luke a look he knew well, one that said, "We don't make enough money for this kind of horse manure."

Chief Farwell saw the look and his red face became redder. "I know what you're thinking. If the police had done their job, this case would be over. I say go to the grand jury. Let them decide if there's enough evidence. We've got witnesses. We've got that signed affidavit. Indict Mr. Cardi. Close down that so-called Supper Club. You two just sit on your arses all day shuffling paper. We've given you evidence, goddamn it!"

Luke shot a warning glance to Arthur just as he was about to open his mouth to argue with the chief. In a voice calm and measured, in a tone that drove the frazzled and blustering souls who entered his office mad with frustration, Luke explained clearly why the state did not have enough evidence and why the evidence they did have wouldn't lead to anything except Guido Cardi's freedom.

"You know as well as I do that by the time we get to your witnesses, Cardi will have persuaded them that they were mistaken by whatever they saw in the Supper Club. Or they will be conveniently out of town visiting a sick aunt. Or they will have mysteriously disappeared. We need hard evidence, Chief. We need the books, or at least a reliable witness to affirm that Cardi is using his gambling proceeds to import opium. Right now, we can't even prove he's running an illegal gambling establishment."

While doctors had readily prescribed opium for years for a variety of maladies, only recently had illicit and extremely potent opium found its way to some of Springfield's middle-class homes. Unlike the opium dens on the West Coast that drew the poorest and weakest sorts, Cardi was apparently targeting average citizens who were unable to convince a physician to prescribe the drug.

"I know the mayor's hot about this one," Luke said. He suspected the mayor's son had gotten caught up in Cardi's web of gambling and opium addiction. "But if we're not careful, we'll get nothing."

By the time Luke was finished, Chief Farwell's face was thoughtful as he chewed on the end of his cigar. He let out something that sounded much like the growl of a frustrated bulldog.

"So you see, Chief . . ."

Chief Farwell stood abruptly. "Yeah, yeah. I see. I see you two are a couple of cowards." But his words held no malice this time, and Luke smiled.

"I have one of my own men investigating," Luke said. "He couldn't have gotten as far as he has without the fine work of your police department."

Chief Farwell stuck out his bottom lip. "You just keep me apprised of your so-called investigation," he said, adjusting the wide black belt that wrapped around his expansive belly. Jamming his hat on his head, Chief Farwell headed for the door. He was about to close the door when he stuck his head back in the office. "John Haxton would have prosecuted."

When the chief was gone, Luke wearily rubbed his hands over his face.

"Haxton was an idiot," Arthur said, eyeing his friend with concern.

Luke shook his head. "He was a damned good prosecutor," he argued. "Hell, Haxton probably would have gotten an indictment."

"And also would have ultimately lost the case. You know that, Luke. That's why you're the Golden Boy around here."

Luke grimaced at the nickname. It was true that his conviction rate was better than any other attorney's in the office, but he rather thought it was because Boston tended to attract the better defense attorneys than Springfield. "This Golden Boy doesn't feel very good about this particular investigation."

"I'll let you in on something. Sully didn't want to tell you until he was certain, but he's pretty sure Cardi is bringing a load of opium through soon. He's been cleaning up that old warehouse of his by the river and having meetings at the Supper Club with some pretty shady characters from Providence and New York."

Luke gave Arthur a dark look. "When was Mr. Sullivan planning to let me in on this information?"

Arthur cursed under his breath. "It's not good information. Yet. That's why he didn't want to tell you. It's why I shouldn't have opened my big mouth to tell you. Sully's got this guy on the inside, a real talker, but he can't believe half of what this fellow says. But Sully told me he thinks the guy is spouting steam. We can't plan a raid based on his information."

Luke shot his friend a look of disgust. "You're right. You shouldn't have told me anything. Sullivan usually doesn't report his findings until he's sure about them."

Arthur smiled broadly. "You're wrong there, Mr. Prosecutor. He doesn't tell *you* his findings until he's sure. No one wants to face your wrath when you prove them wrong. Everyone in this office knows that unless you see it with your own two eyes you don't believe a word of it."

Luke shrugged good-naturedly. "You and I both know that if I didn't, there'd be plenty of overturned convictions."

Luke knew of his reputation as a stickler. But he'd be damned if his office sent an innocent man to prison because their investigation wasn't thorough enough. He thanked his parents laissez-faire attitude toward life for ingraining in him a sense that he could never be thorough enough. At age twenty, he'd saved his parents from financial ruin because he'd taken the time to read up on tax laws. His stern lecture to his parents had amused them both and drove him nearly mad with frustration. It was almost as if they expected someone, somehow, to resolve all their problems for them. The thing was, someone almost always did.

"What time is Mr. Sullivan expected back this afternoon?" Luke asked.

"He may not be back at all. He's hot onto something. I wouldn't be surprised if he got enough for us to conduct a bit of a raid by the weekend."

Luke raised one eyebrow. "I'll believe it when I see it."

4

The last time Rose had been so nervous was her wedding day. Luke arrived home just minutes ago and went directly to his study, asking to be called when dinner was ready. Rose knew this because she hovered at the top of the stairs and scurried out of sight when he walked past the staircase. I won't put too much importance on this, she told herself. He'll notice and I'll act surprised. "Oh, my hair? Yes, I did have it cut. Do you like it? And my dress? Well, it is springtime, after all. Just because I haven't bought anything so lively and colorful my entire life isn't reason to think I'm up to anything." Rose giggled.

Collette had said Luke's eyes were going to pop out of his head. He was going to sweep her into his arms and soundly kiss her. Collette hadn't said anything more, but Rose had filled in the rest. This time would be different. This time she would welcome all those delicious feelings that flooded her whenever Luke kissed her. This time she knew it wasn't dirty or sinful. This time, oh, this time would be perfect. And from now on when Luke came home she'd throw herself into his arms and he'd hold her close and swoop her around in a circle. They'd sit by the fire on long winter nights, nestled close. They'd stroll along the city streets arm in arm and very proper until they found a shadow where they'd steal away and lose themselves in each other for a long moment.

Rose let out a long, lingering sigh. How wonderful it was going to be. Still glowing from her daydream, she was startled by the tinkling of the crystal dinner bell. She hurried to her room to check her dress and hair one last time before heading downstairs, her stomach fluttering nervously. She simply could not wait for Luke's face to fill with wonder, as Collette said would happen, when he first laid eyes on her.

Luke was already at the table, which was spread with a flawless white linen tablecloth and two gleaming place settings, when Rose arrived. She had a silly grin on her face and knew it but just couldn't help it.

"Hello, Luke. How was your day?" she asked as the maid silently placed their meal of roast chicken, turnips, and scalloped potatoes on the table. The Beaudettes on these informal occasions served themselves once the meal was brought.

"Busy," he said, lifting his head briefly before looking again at some legal document laid out beside him.

Rose's grin faded momentarily. "Must you work through dinner? You've been working so hard lately. Some big case, I presume."

"Hm-mmmm," he mumbled as he chewed some chicken.

"Care to tell me about it?" Rose asked, a bit brittlely. She refused to tell him to look at her.

He waved a hand at her without looking up. "Nothing interesting. Just a lot of research. All boring stuff."

Rose swallowed some potato past the lump in her throat. Part of her screamed at her to make Luke look. But the other part almost wanted him to fail. See? He doesn't even notice you. He doesn't care a whit, you stupid, stupid woman! Then and there she resolved not to say another word throughout dinner unless he spoke to her. If he noticed, fine! If not, then, well, damn him then, she thought, blushing at even thinking a curse word.

He didn't. Enmeshed in his work, Luke was not even aware he was eating, never mind ignoring a wife who was by now on the verge of tears. When she got up to leave just before dessert was served, he barely heard her say good night, not absorbing how odd her voice sounded, how constricted. Almost as if she'd been crying. Absurd thought. Why in the world would Rose cry? The chicken wasn't *that* overcooked. Hours later, just as he was getting into bed, his eyes burning from reading, he thought of Rose. Something nagged at the edge of his mind. Something, something . . . Ah, hell. Maybe it will come to me in the morning, he thought tiredly, pulling up the covers he'd be certain to kick off as soon as he was asleep.

It took Luke until Thursday to notice half his wife's hair was missing and she'd gone from wearing subdued grays and browns to wearing more stylish clothes. By then, Rose was so angry she could hardly bring herself to speak to the man at all.

On Thursday afternoon, she was visiting with Collette and Nicole in her sunny little sitting room, the windows left open to allow in the sweet spring air. It was, perhaps, a bit too cool for those open windows, but Rose loved to watch her sheer curtains blowing softly in the breeze. She wore her latest purchase, a butter-yellow dress with ivory lace trim, a lovely contrast to her dark hair, which was left down and curling about her face.

Collette wore a striking royal-blue skirt and white shirtwaist with royal-blue cuffs and collar that made her eyes appear even bluer than they were. Nicole, wearing a serviceable brown wool dress, looked like a moth among butterflies. Rose couldn't help but think that just a week ago, she would have been dressed like Nicole and have thought nothing of it.

It was thrilling to wear pretty clothes, to look in the mirror and see someone vibrant and alive peering back. Rose found she was woefully ignorant about current styles, but under the careful tutelage of Collette, she was quickly learning the intricacies of appearing at one's best at all times. Now, just three days after her metamorphosis, she was painfully aware of Nicole's drab dress. She looked over at the sister with whom she had shared so much, and felt the uncomfortable stirrings of pity. Collette and Rose delighted in each other's conversations, giggling and exchanging knowing looks that, without intent, cut Nicole from the happy chatter. Rose had invited Nicole over to visit with her and Collette, hoping to drag her sister out of her blue mood. She had seemed so lifeless lately, and Rose wondered if it were more than that she was pregnant.

Collette had Rose in stitches telling stories about her time in boarding school. Wiping a tear from her eye, Rose glanced at her sister to see if she were also laughing, only to find Nicole staring out a window.

"Nicole," Rose said, trying to draw her sister into the conversation, "remember how I begged Mother and Father to let me go to boarding school? I sure got sore knees praying in the attic that time. At least, Mother *thought* I was praying. I was actually thinking up ways to sneak something ghastly into her tea. But I never did work up the nerve." Rose laughed, for the first time seeing something humorous, not tragic, in the sisters' harsh upbringing.

"But you always prayed, didn't you, Nicole?"

Nicole turned to her smiling sister, her lips turning up just slightly. "I prayed," she said softly. "But not for what Mother wanted us to pray for."

"What did you pray for?" Collette asked. "If it was anything like what Rose prayed for, I'm not sure if I want either of you near my tea."

Nicole smiled, but Rose saw that her deep-brown eyes were hiding a sadness that made Rose wish she had never brought the subject up. She'd always thought of Nicole as the dutiful daughter, and that Nicole had liked her role. But she had the uncomfortable feeling that perhaps Nicole had simply hidden her rebelliousness better than Rose had, that even now there was something surging inside her older sister.

"I just prayed," Nicole said softly, ending the conversation.

"I plan to never have my children pray in an attic, knowing what we prayed for," Rose joked. After that, the talk turned superficial and silly, the three women thoroughly enjoying each other's company. Until Luke decided to see what all the commotion was about.

Curious to hear such carefree sounds coming from his wife's sitting room, Luke made his way toward the happy noise. His eyes darted from a pretty blonde to an even prettier brunette, and finally to his wife whose back was turned toward him. He was about to talk to the woman wearing the brown wool dress when his eyes snapped to the brunette sitting across from him, her glorious brown eyes spitting fire.

"Sweet Jesus," he whispered. Recovering his shock, but not his composure, he blurted, "What the hell have you done with yourself, Rose?"

Not what Rose had expected. Not even close to the moon-eyed look she'd imagined Luke would give her. Stiffening in her chair, Rose glanced first at Collette, who had the gall to be obviously repressing laughter, then at Nicole who seemed equally as mirthful.

"Nicole," Collette said, sounding chirpy, "why don't I walk you to the trolley." The two women vanished from the room, leaving Luke and Rose staring at each other.

Rose crossed her arms, nonplussed—at least on the outside—by the look of bafflement on Luke's face. "I've cut my hair and bought some new dresses."

Luke opened and closed his mouth. "Yes. I can see that." He found it rather confounding to walk into a room and not recognize his wife. But he looked at her now, took in her color, her flashing eyes, the way the dress made her waist appear so tiny and found himself knocked off kilter. Her hair, normally knotted tightly at her nape, curled about her face and shoulders, making her look . . . ah, Lord, Luke did not want to think about what that hair made her look like. That tousled hair, combined with her flushed cheeks, gave her the look of a woman who had been well loved. And that, more than anything, produced the scowl that formed on his face.

Rose stared at Luke, hurt and angry. "It will grow back," she said.

"No, I . . . I think it's nice." A vast understatement, he thought morosely. He took a step forward, his gray eyes softening as her disappointment in his reaction finally registered. "Rose. You look fine. I was just surprised to come home and find a completely different wife than the one I left this morning." Luke thought his words would have brought a smile to his wife's lovely mouth, but instead, they turned downward in a frown.

"I got my hair done yesterday."

It was Luke's turn to frown as he tried to recall what his wife had looked like. He brightened. "But you had it up yesterday, no?"

"No."

"Oh." They'd had supper together, he was sure of that. Hadn't they?

Rose stood there, watching her husband's bewilderment grow as he tried to recall seeing her the day before. "It doesn't matter when I had my hair done, Luke," she said tiredly.

"No, I suppose not," he said, but could tell he'd disappointed her again with his response. What the hell was going on? he thought with the tiny bit of panic all men feel when they realize they haven't the foggiest idea what makes the woman they love tick. He didn't like this one bit. Rose was not a woman who primped and expected wild praise about her looks. Rose wore her hair up. Her dresses were nice enough, weren't they? He had married Rose because she had seemed so steady. Having grown up in a home with two whimsical parents, he wanted nothing more than to know that the wife he left in the morning would be the same one he returned to at night. And Rose had seemed to perfectly fit his ideal of the genteel, gentle, unchanging woman he'd hoped for. Until now.

She lifted her chin up a notch, stopped fiddling with her wedding ring, and planted a fist on each hip. "This is the new me," she said with utmost sincerity.

It was her chin that gave her away. Luke, standing

there staring at this vision of strength and beauty, felt that male panic grow in his gut, until he saw just the tiniest quiver in that proud little chin. That's better, he thought with relief. Tears were something he understood. His heart, already mush when it came to this wife of his, melted. He went to her and took her hands in his, thinking wildly of what he could say to make her smile.

"I thought the old you was just fine," he said. He knew from her expression he had not said the right thing. She dropped his hands.

He didn't like it, not the hair, not the dress, Rose thought. He liked the old her, the meek one who wore brown dresses and put her hair in a knot that gave her a headache every day, the woman who didn't play poker or giggle with a girlfriend. He liked the wren when all Rose could dream about was being a bluebird. This past week, Rose had felt as if she'd been set free. This girl, the one who wore buttercup yellow dresses, had been inside her the whole time. She was not Collette's creation, but Collette had simply peeled away the layers and uncovered her. She could not, would not go back to the way she had been.

"You don't like it at all?" she asked, fluffing out her dress.

Luke looked at her, his eyes traveling up and down, his expression grim. She was so damned beautiful, all he could think was that he wanted to carry her up to his bed. She looked like a woman who would welcome him, who would lie on his bed, skirts flying about her, eyes sleepy with want. But he knew better, and his body, God, his body clenched tight with that bitter knowledge.

"No," he bit out. "I don't like it. You look . . ." He couldn't finish, couldn't talk about what he thought when he looked at her. I'm a cad, he thought as he looked at Rose's stricken face. But he could not bring himself to apologize. Luke knew he could resist the woman who wore those shapeless, matronly dresses. But this woman? Ah, no. He could not. She would drive him mad, and he would want to love her, and he would see her eyes fill with fear. And then the agony of loving a woman who did not want to love him would crash down upon him, leaving him remorseful and ashamed. And angry.

Rose pulled her head up with an angry jerk. Grabbing her skirts, she tugged them sharply so that they might not brush his trousers. Rose hurried from the room, mortified that she would be unable to keep the sob that was growing in her aching throat from escaping.

5

Luke's study was a decidedly masculine place, with gleaming mahogany wainscoting below rich wallpaper depicting an English fox hunt. His desk was a huge affair carved from walnut, its legs wood sculptures of lions forever frozen in a savage lunge for unseen prey. The floor was covered in a thick carpet of such a dark red, it almost appeared black in the room's shadowed corners. Gold drapes covered a set of long, narrow windows that overlooked the cramped alley that separated the Beaudettes' brownstone from the one next door. It was one of the few houses on Mattoon Street that did not share walls with its neighbors.

The furniture in the study was big, dark, and hulking, and faced the room's Italian marble fireplace in which a cheerful fire now danced. For all its masculine decor, Rose loved the study. It smelled like Luke—of leather and cigars, of paper and ink. At first it had struck Rose as odd that a man who did not hunt would surround himself with symbols of that sport. But as that room became the gathering place for men after dinner parties and for meetings with other attorneys, she realized it did not reflect her husband's personality or demeanor, but rather his practical side. Men would be comfortable here, away from lace and delicate furniture. Everything in that room nearly shouted of masculine power and control. Except for one tiny corner, hidden behind a massive mohair chair.

There Luke kept his collection of mechanical banks. Well-dusted and sitting on a round pedestal table were twenty of the things, all with a coin at the ready. Her favorite was the bucking bronc with a cowboy atop and ready to be thrown forward so he might deposit the coin into a water trough. It was a whimsical collection of a practical nature. She wondered if Luke, serious and stalwart Luke, could possibly enjoy the fanciful nature of his collection. She imagined he must, else why gather them, why put them on display but in a hidden part of the room?

She wandered to the collection and pressed the lever, sending the cowboy flying from the horse. As always, when the coin hit its mark, Rose let out a happy laugh. Then she looked about the room nervously, smoothing her dress with fingers that shook. She had good reason to be nervous this evening, she thought. Tonight she planned to seduce her husband.

After rushing from her sitting room the day before in bitter disappointment over Luke's reaction to her new clothes and hair, Rose calmed down enough to realize that perhaps his reaction hadn't been entirely negative. At first, he'd seemed stunned, but not in an unpleasant way. At least Collette had convinced her of that.

"My goodness, Rose, he looked like he wanted to ravish you then and there," Collette had said.

Wiping her red nose with an embroidered handkerchief, Rose said, "Do you really think so?" Never one to weep about such silliness, Rose found she couldn't stop crying over Luke's callous behavior. After much argument, Collette had convinced her that Luke had liked the change in his wife—he just didn't know it yet. Rose, still skeptical, listened as Collette expounded the wonders of a bit of alcohol to fortify one's courage.

"I have never touched a drop of alcohol in my life

and I'm not about to start now," Rose said, crossing her arms.

"Then you'll simply have to seduce your husband without the aid of a bit of wine. You know yourself better than I do. I'm sure you'll do just fine."

And with that, Collette had pulled on her lacy gloves and walked from Rose's drawing room, stopping only to place her hat on her head as she peered critically into the hallstand's beveled mirror. Rose had stubbornly remained seated in the drawing room, knowing that Collette was simply testing her and refusing just this once to be swayed by her argument.

Now, though, as she glanced at the clock ticking relentlessly atop the mantel, she felt any courage she had slowly draining away. Luke would be home within the hour and she was certain that he would investigate the light coming from his study. Just to be sure, she raised the gas flame a bit more on the fixture near the door. She stood there, biting one knuckle, her eyes inevitably moving to the crystal decanter of brandy resting on a small table behind the sofa.

He is my husband, she told herself. It is not as if I do not know what will happen, as if I am a virgin, she thought. But she felt that queasy sickness come over her at the thought of what she was planning and she let out a frustrated huff of air. "It is not a sin," she whispered. She closed her eyes and pictured Luke lying in bed, his beautiful body stretched out before her, and she found herself smiling. Smooth skin, satiny. Her smile widened as she mentally traveled over her husband's body. Naked. Masculine. Hard.

Her eyes flew open and the first thing they focused on was that crystal decanter filled with amber liquid. Maybe just a tad, a sip to calm my nerves. She walked to the small table, head held high, her mouth set with determination. She gripped the decanter's neck, and the cool hard crystal was somehow comforting beneath her hand. She removed the stopper with forced nonchalance. Taking a deep breath, she poured a bit into a glass, a thimbleful that wouldn't have gotten a kitten tipsy, she reasoned. Rose brought the glass to her lips and allowed the tiniest bit to seep past her lips and onto her tongue, where it burned slightly. She swallowed, wrinkling her nose.

Then she waited to see what would happen. She waited for that nice little bit of relaxing warmth that Collette had described to hit her. Nothing happened. Frowning, Rose poured more into the glass, about the width of her thumb. Holding her nose, she gulped the entire amount, coughing as her throat closed up around the burning liquid.

"Ugh!" Rose sputtered, putting the glass down with finality. Now that the brandy was down, the pleasant warmth spread from her throat to her stomach and Rose realized that this was what Collette had been talking about. It really was rather nice, she thought, closely examining every little change the alcohol made. She wondered if a bit more would make her feel even better. Maybe just one more thumbful, she thought. She really hadn't had more than a sip so far. Rose poured slightly more than a thumbful in this time. She raised the glass to eye level, looking at the brandy as if she were challenging it to do its duty. Holding her nose once more, she threw her head back and gulped it down.

A few minutes ticked by and Rose began to think that brandy truly was a wonderful thing. In fact, everything was wonderful. This room, her husband, the world. Wonderful wonderful. Rose turned to look at the clock and was only slightly alarmed when it seemed to spin away from her sight before she brought it into focus. Luke would be here any minute. Suddenly, her stomach gave a nervous twist and Rose knew the brandy hadn't done its job. Yet. More brandy splashed into her glass. And more. And then Rose wasn't nervous at all. Not one little bit. Just terribly, terribly sleepy. She looked at the couch, at the embroidered pillow that looked so inviting and decided she might as well lie down and wait for Luke to come home. Her head felt funny, thick and numb.

"I can't feel my lips," she said aloud, and giggled. She sat heavily on the couch, feeling as if someone had taken all the bones out of her body, and laid her head on the pillow. Just for a minute. "How can I s'duce you when you're not even here?" Rose grumbled just before she fell asleep.

Luke eyed the light coming from his study with uncertainty. He suspected Rose was waiting up for him and truly, he was too tired to deal with an overwrought woman right now. He wanted to open that door and find Rose sitting sedately by the lamp, a bit of embroidery in her hands, perhaps something for Nicole's new baby. He wanted her hair knotted at her nape, her tempting body draped in something brown or gray. But he knew, somehow, that when he walked into the study, that was not what he would find.

He opened the door without knocking, eyes searching for Rose, finally resting on her still, sleeping form. His face, lined with tension, relaxed as a soft smile came to his lips. That smile slowly faded as he took in the rest—the empty glass, the half-empty decanter, and the soft drunken snores of his heretofore teetotaling wife. He shook his head and let out a small huff of laughter. What the hell was Rose thinking? he thought as he walked over to her sprawled form.

He stood over her. "Rose." He watched as her eyes slowly opened and a huge silly grin came over her face.

"Hello, Luke." Rose struggled to sit up. She scratched her head with one hand, tousling her already tousled hair, and tried to swallow past the dryness in her mouth. "I feel decidedly . . . different," she managed.

"I think what you feel, Rose, is decidedly drunk," Luke said, forcing a sternness to his voice that he didn't feel. She looked too adorable to get angry at.

"Mmmm. I s'pose." And then, as if suddenly realizing that Luke was standing over her and she was carrying on a conversation with him, Rose straightened and tried to smooth her wrinkled skirts. "Luke, you're home!" she said, pretending surprise.

Luke had to bite his lip to stop from laughing aloud. "Indeed I am."

Rose threw her hands in front of her face. "Oh. I wasn't s'pose to fall 'sleep," she slurred, shaking her head in mortification.

"You weren't?"

She brought her hands down, expecting to find Luke still standing above her and surprised to see him sitting by her side. "There you are," she muttered. "It was supposed to be a surprise."

"What was?" he said indulgently.

"Me." She let out a heavy sigh as if a great weight had been lifted from her, but Luke was no closer to knowing why his wife was in his study inebriated than when he walked through the door.

"Well," he said. "You certainly have surprised me."

Rose suddenly deflated and sagged against his shoulder. "You don't un'stand," she said dispiritedly.

Luke sat there, enjoying the weight of her against his side for a few moments as he stared into the fire's glowing embers. When he finally looked down at her, he noticed his jacket was splotched by tears that plopped silently from her chin.

"Ah, sweetheart, don't cry. You can surprise me some other time." He gathered her onto his lap, a boneless heap of skirts and petticoats. Rose nestled her mouth against his neck and he could feel the cool air on the tears she left on his burning skin. He clenched his jaw against the desire that swept through him at the touch of her soft, soft mouth, at the feel of her body draped across his.

"You taste good," Rose said.

Luke closed his eyes. Oh, God, was that her tongue on his neck? Give me strength, he pleaded to no one in particular.

"I want to kiss you everywhere," Rose said as she nestled against him, her behind pressing suggestively against his arousal.

"Sweet Jesus," he whispered. And then louder: "Rose."

"Hmmm?" came the sleepy reply.

"Do you . . ." He squeezed his eyes shut. "Do you know what you're doing?"

Her teeth grazed his neck where her tongue had been before she answered. "I'm s'ducing you."

Luke breathed in and out a ragged breath. "So you are." He swallowed. To take her now, when she was so drunk, would be wrong. Wouldn't it? But maybe she wasn't as drunk as she appeared, he reasoned with a fevered mind. Rose kissed him along his jawline, one hand holding his head as if he might try to escape. She kissed the side of his mouth, and Luke, sitting as still as a statue, turned his head just slightly toward her, knowing he was nearing the end of his endurance. He let her kiss his lips, but he had not yet responded.

"Kiss me, Luke."

With one last look up to heaven, Luke admitted defeat. With an animal sound, he brought his lips down onto hers, teasing her mouth open with his tongue. He left himself go, he let himself kiss her, ravage her mouth with his as his hands pulled her against him. She responded with abandon, with something Luke could only think was joy, letting out pleasure sounds that had him wanting to rip her clothes off and lay her down on the soft carpet. He brought a hand to her breast, half fearing she would push him away. Instead, his wife, his beautiful wife, pushed herself against his hand, letting out a sound of frustration that could only mean one thing.

Luke pulled away, catching his breath. "Let's go upstairs, Rose. Is that all right?"

Rose, lips red from their kisses, smiled sleepily at her husband. "Yes. Upstairs."

She was like a rag doll in his arms, her arms draped about his shoulders, her head resting heavily against his neck as he carried her up the stairs. At the top of the landing, he hesitated, unsure whose room to go into.

"Where, Rose? Where do you want to go?"

No response.

"Rose?" But he knew, without looking, that Rose was in a drunken slumber. Luke let out a self-deprecating little laugh. "Hell." He stood there, his conscience warring with a part of his body that was hard and pressing almost painfully against his pants. One more try. "Rose?" he said rather loudly, and then muttered a curse when she continued to sleep, oblivious to his frantic need.

He laid Rose in her bed on her side and undid the tiny buttons in the back of her gown, parting just enough to reach the laces of her corset. He loosened them, then debated whether he should continue. His eyes traveled to her creamy back, exposed above her chemise, and decided his physical reaction to that bit of skin helped his brain win the debate over that other part of him that ached to see more perfection. Though it might be the only opportunity he would have to see his wife completely nude, he settled, rather begrudgingly, on removing her shoes. He even left her stockings on. When Luke was finished, he tucked a blanket around her and kissed her cheek. Before leaving her, he gazed at her flawless profile, at those lips that had opened for him with such abandon. And he smiled.

He bent down to whisper in her ear. "I knew you were in there somewhere."

Chapter Three

1

"Bless me, Father, for I have sinned. It has been one week since my last confession." Rose's voice came out oddly strained. It was three-thirty in the afternoon, confessional was over at four. She had waited as long as possible for her stomach to stop churning, her head to stop pounding, and her courage to give her the strength to tell Father Beaulieu what she needed to tell him.

Rose still could not believe how horribly she had felt upon waking that morning. Her mouth had been dry and nasty-tasting, and her eyes, when she finally pried them open at nine o'clock, hurt. At first, finding herself in such a state, she was momentarily confused. Then she remembered. The study. The couch. The liquor. The kisses.

"Oh, Lord." Rose wanted to go back to sleep and wake up a thousand years from that moment. She lay there, thirsty and wretched, and trying to recall, her brain pain-wracked, exactly what she had done the previous evening. She was rather certain that she had not succeeded in seducing her husband, if her clothed state was any clue, she reasoned. She laid a drooping hand on her forehead. It was all foggy, these recollections that only made her head pound harder. She remembered—at least she thought she did—sitting upon Luke's lap. They had kissed, of that she was certain. And then . . . a blank. A big, horrible, muddled blank.

Nature's urgings finally forced Rose to sit up. She clutched the bedsheets, trying to stop the room from spinning. And that was when her stomach decided to complain. In a mad rush, Rose threw open her door and ran across the hall to the bathing room where she nearly fell upon the toilet and promptly emptied the bitter contents of her stomach. She laid her head against her arm for several long minutes afterward, faintly amazed that a head could pound so hard and not explode. That was how Luke found her, still leaning against the toilet, letting out rather pathetic little moans, swallowing desperately in an effort to not lose the rest of the contents of her stomach into the bowl.

"I was going to check on you to see how you were, but I suppose now I know," Luke said dryly from the doorway.

"Oh, Lord. I'm dying, Luke. I'm truly, truly dying."

He had the audacity to chuckle. "You only feel like you're dying. But unfortunately, you are very much alive and will likely feel this way for a good many hours."

Rose let out an agonized moan, making the damn man laugh again. She lifted her head a fraction, just enough so she could glare at her smiling husband. "This is not funny."

Luke bit his lips in a hopeless attempt to look solemn, then walked over to his wife to help her up. She still wore her gown in the same state of undress as he left her the night before and he couldn't help but admire her slim back. And that led to thoughts of those wonderful kisses from the night before, kisses his wife, no doubt, had little memory of.

"Here we go," he said, putting his hands beneath her arms.

"Do I have to move?" Rose managed to say.

"I'm afraid so." Once standing, she leaned heavily against him, one hand clutching the front of his shirt for support, the other searching for the toilet's chain-pull dangling just out of reach. Luke pulled it for her and she mumbled her thanks. They took two shuffling steps before Rose said in a panic, "Oh, Luke. I think . . . I think . . ." She tore away from him and fell toward the toilet. Luke frowned and shook his head at the sight of his wife vomiting before him.

"No more drinking for you, my dear," he pronounced.

When Rose recovered, she looked up at Luke, swiping a strand of hair from her face. "If I ever drink again, you have permission to shoot me." She said it with such grave conviction, Luke barked out a laugh. Rose shuffled to the sink where she made a half-hearted attempt at brushing her teeth, all the while praying she would not become sick again.

"What possessed you to drink, Rose? As far as I know, you've never touched a drop," he said as he helped her out of the bathing room.

Rose blushed and her head pounded anew with mortification. She hurt too much to think of something witty to say to deflect his question and so she kept silent.

"Do you remember what you told me last night?" Luke asked, and she could hear the laughter in his voice.

"Surely you wouldn't pay attention to the ramblings of a drunken woman," Rose said, hoping that would end this excruciating conversation. Whatever it was she'd said to Luke, she did not want to know.

"Hmmm. You were quite clear on this point."

Rose sat down on her bed carefully, fearing her head would certainly topple off her shoulders if she were to move too quickly. She began panting as her stomach turned over and squeezed her eyes shut. "Oh, stop torturing me, Luke! Can't you see I'm dying? What did I say, for heaven's sakes!"

Luke looked down at his mussed-up, hungover, half-undressed wife and smiled. "You said you wanted to seduce me."

Rose became very still. "I said . . . No, I couldn't have." She buried her face in her hands. "I did. I did say that. I remember now. Oh, God," she groaned.

Luke was amused, but also a bit perturbed by her reaction. "It's not as if you told me you wanted to kill

me. That would be something to be upset about,
Rose."

But Rose simply shook her head, horrified by her
behavior the night before. What must Luke think of
her, finding her in his study so drunk she could barely
walk, announcing that she was bent on seducing him?
That certainly had not been part of the plan. She was
to drink a glass of wine to relax, not down half a
bottle of brandy and get completely foxed. The seduction was supposed to have been a subtle thing. She
felt like such a wretch. "I'm so sorry, Luke. It was
horrid of me. Unforgivable."

"You're sorry." Luke had been smiling, but now he
looked down at his wife with an expression far colder
than the one he had been bestowing upon her before.

"Oh, yes. So sorry," Rose said with heartfelt honesty. "I never meant to do that."

"Of course," Luke said, all warmth gone from his
voice.

Rose grabbed her head to hold the horrible pounding at bay. "Luke, please don't be angry with me."

"I'm not angry."

Rose closed her eyes against his lawyerly tone and
squeezed out two tears. "Oh, you are! You're always
disappointed. Don't deny it, I know you are and I
tried to do something about it but I'm constantly making mistakes. I thought you'd like"—she stopped to
let out a sob—"my hair but you didn't. I thought
you'd like my new dress," she said, lifting the wrinkled
mess with disgust. "I can't even seduce my own husband right," she wailed, turning away from him and
burying her face in her pillow.

Luke had felt panic grow when he saw her tears, as
certain that he was a complete cad as he was uncertain
what the damned tears were about. Until the last
wailed lament. She didn't feel sorry for trying to seduce him, he realized, she felt sorry for the *way* she
had tried. He sat down cautiously on the bed, and
went to pat her shoulder until he realized it was naked
but for the thin band of her chemise. He hesitated,

then laid a warm hand there anyway, his heart swelling inside.

"You don't have to seduce me, Rose. I'm already seduced. Believe me."

She shook her head, her muffled sobs becoming louder. Finally she lifted her head and sat up. "No. I botched the whole thing, don't you see? I wasn't supposed to get drunk. I was supposed to relax and then . . . and then . . . Well, you do understand, don't you, Luke?"

Luke let his hand travel to the back of her neck. "I think I do."

Rose sniffed loudly and winced. "Oh, my head hurts so much." She shook her head, suddenly embarrassed again to be discussing such a thing with her husband.

"Can you tell me what brought all this on?" Luke asked as his thumb stroked her jaw just below her earlobe.

Rose looked down to her lap where she fidgeted with her wedding ring. I want you, she thought. I need to lie with you, to feel you curl around me at night, to wake up and kiss your lips. I need to have you inside me, I burn for you, Luke. But as those thoughts entered her head, she flushed hotly beneath his gaze. She could never say that! He'd think her depraved.

"I want to have a baby," she said finally, relieved to have found a plausible explanation for her behavior. It was true enough. She longed for a sweet little baby made from their love.

Luke told himself he was glad for that. Glad she wanted a child. But he found himself strangely disappointed in her response. She wanted a baby so much, she was willing to allow him into her bed. She wanted a baby so much, she'd drunk herself silly so the thought of making love with him wasn't quite so repugnant to her.

"I see." He swallowed that disappointment and forced himself to smile. "I want a baby, too, Rose. We'll begin trying. Would that be all right?" He kissed her softly on her cheek.

"Yes."

Luke frowned as he tried to ignore the bitterness he felt to hear the fear in that one small word.

But Rose felt no fear, just an inexplicable sense of loss. Of course she wanted a baby. But what she really wanted, what she truly needed, was Luke.

Hours later, sitting in the confessional, the entire morning rolled through her mind, which was still a bit befuddled by the alcohol. She had taken some baking soda in water and her stomach had finally settled down enough for her to eat some dry toast, but her headache lingered despite the headache powder she'd taken. The confessional felt suffocating, the smoke from the incense thick and choking even though there was no more than usual.

"Last night I got drunk, Father. Very drunk. And I suppose I've been a bit vain lately." Rose wanted to cry for no apparent reason. She felt desolate, not because her sins were terrible, but because she didn't truly care that they were. *What is happening to me?* she thought. *No wonder Luke looked at me so coldly. Who would want such a pathetic creature for a wife?* For a short while, Luke had seemed almost amused by her adventures with a brandy bottle. But by the time he walked from her room, he was once again the distant, polite man he'd been since they'd been married.

Rose had realized with a jolt while walking to church that distant and polite wasn't good enough anymore. She thought of her parents, of Nicole and Louis, of her own marriage, and she just wanted to shriek. Surely this was not the best she could hope for, surely all those romantic tales she'd heard and read since she was a child could not all be lies. Rose thought if she uttered another polite inquiry about Luke's day she would surely scream.

As she'd reached the steps to the church, she realized if her marriage was going to change it would have to be up to her. She was living a life she hated. She was not the prim, straight-backed, pure girl everyone saw, and the thought of keeping up the charade one more minute was immensely depressing. She wished Collette was here but knew she'd no longer be at confessional since they both usually attended much earlier. Collette would understand, for hadn't she struck out on her own, snubbed her nose at convention and done what she'd wanted? The thought of Collette made her smile. A part of Rose wondered whether Collette had fostered these feelings of discontent, but she immediately dismissed such thoughts. Collette had not brought about this change, she had merely set her free. Why gravitate to such a lively, carefree woman if she were not aching to let that part of herself out?

Rose realized, standing outside the massive church with its spire jutting into the sky, that she was still that little girl in the attic who pretended to pray but daydreamed about chasing butterflies. She'd been living a lie for years, trying to be the woman everyone wanted her to be. For isn't that what women of her class did? They left calling cards on little silver trays, they never swore or drank or talked politics in any earnest way, they visited and talked about children and husbands and servants. They never slouched in chairs, laughed too loud, or lifted their skirts higher than their ankles. They never, ever ran into their husband's arms and pressed a passionate kiss against his smiling lips. They never talked about love. Rose was beginning to suspect it simply didn't exist in any meaningful way for the women she'd been associating with her entire life. But it existed in her, she knew it did, and she wondered if that meant she was some sort of oddity.

She wanted to run in the rain, to climb trees, to ride a bicycle. And she wanted Luke there beside her.

So that was why, when Rose Beaudette confessed one of the worst sins of her life, she couldn't bring herself to truly feel sorry for what she'd done. As if sensing that, or perhaps because he was exhausted from a day of hearing endless sins, Father Beaulieu

gave her no lecture. Instead he gave her the heaviest
penance she'd ever received—two rosaries.

Rose left the confessional, glad to be out of the
dark booth, and knelt in the nearest pew. The rosary
beads felt cool and familiar in her hands. For the longest time, Rose knelt there holding the beads, letting
them dangle from her fingers, saying no formal
prayers.

"God," she whispered so softly that the old woman
draped in black kneeling nearby did not hear her,
"please give me the strength to be happy." A single
tear plopped onto her folded hands. Until that moment, Rose had not known she'd been unhappy. She
stared at that single drop as it shimmered at the base
of her thumb and finally slipped down her wrist, disappearing into her sleeve. By the time she finished saying
her rosary, all traces of that tear had disappeared.

2

Rose was in a snit, Luke was sure of it. He'd never
seen her this way—sullen and argumentative. When
she appeared for their dinner party wearing one of
her old gowns, he'd given her an approving look.
Wrong thing, old boy, he told himself when he saw
Rose's dour expression.

"I suppose you like this dress," she'd said, jerking
her chin high as if challenging him to lie.

"Of course I like it," he'd said, perplexed by her
belligerence. "It suits you perfectly."

Her delicate nostrils had flared at what Luke had
thought was a compliment. What the devil was going
on with his wife lately? he thought with bewilderment.
She was cutting her hair and wearing fashionable
dresses one moment, getting drunk and trying to seduce him in the next, then getting angry over a perfectly fine compliment.

"It does not suit me, Luke Beaudette. Not one little

bit." And with that, Rose had brushed past him and headed to the carriage he had hired.

Dinner was at the Trumbells' that evening. Ralph Trumbell was an up-and-coming defense attorney who managed to stay on good terms with his nemeses in the courtroom—prosecutors. The dinner would mostly be made up of lawyers and their wives, but Luke knew Judge Samuel Mitchell was also invited to attend. Mitchell was a tough old coot whom Luke respected immensely. He had looked forward to this evening of talking with Mitchell and other attorneys, away from the courthouse, about topics other than law. It was a rule that Trumbell laid down at all his dinner parties— no shoptalk. If anyone brought up a case, he was immediately expelled, rather good-naturedly and with a delightful amount of fanfare, from his home on Maple Street.

Luke sat beside Rose, who had squished herself against the side of the carriage, and looked at her warily.

"Are you feeling up to this?" he asked.

Rose looked straight ahead. "I'm feeling fine, Luke. Wonderful, in fact."

Luke's uneasiness grew. Rose was acting rather peculiar, so un-Rose-like, he wasn't certain what to do. "Are you sure . . ."

Rose glared at him. "I'm fine," she said, cutting him off. But Rose knew she was not fine and she also knew she was being completely dreadful to Luke. She'd never felt so out of sorts in her life, as if she were detached from herself, as if she could see herself clearly for the first time. As the wife of a prominent Springfield attorney, Rose had dressed in a manner that was expected of her. Her brown dress with ivory lace at her throat, wrist, and hem was pretty enough. It was even flattering, Rose had thought when she gazed at her reflection in the mirror, accentuating her small waist and trim figure. It was completely appropriate and respectable. It was exactly what the wife of a prominent Springfield attorney would wear.

I hate this dress, she thought, fully realizing that just two weeks ago it had been one of her favorites. I hate these dinners where the men go off and smoke and drink and play billiards and the women sit and chat about . . . nothing. I want to play billiards. I want to talk about the latest, oh, whatever the men are talking about. A bicycle race, perhaps. Or maybe the new trolley line that goes all the way to Connecticut. Oh, Lord, I want to talk about anything but how well lemon cleans windows or how Mrs. Richardson's goiter is getting bigger than her head.

Oh, what is *wrong* with me? Rose twisted her hands in her lap, her gloves making it impossible for her to fiddle with her ring. In that moment, Luke reached over and laid a hand over hers and gave it a firm, reassuring squeeze, as if he somehow knew she was being torn apart. That gesture only made Rose feel worse. She'd been awful to Luke all evening, churlish and downright childish.

"Luke?"

He was gazing at her with a strange intensity and Rose felt her stomach flutter.

"I'm sorry I've been so disagreeable today. Perhaps it's the aftereffects of the alcohol. I'll try to enjoy this evening. Truly."

It was an impossible feat. For the first time in her life, it seemed, Rose found herself bored to tears. She'd been bored before at endless dinner parties and interminable chamber music concerts that were supposed to inspire but only acted as a sleeping potion. She'd just never acknowledged it before. It was that acknowledgment that made the boredom press down on her.

Dinner was a lavish affair at a long table that seated twenty. Luke sat on the same side, but several seats away, something the hostess planned in order to encourage conversation between her guests. Rose supposed had husbands and wives been placed side-by-side, they wouldn't have uttered a word and the dinner party would have been a complete failure. Rose sat next to a Mrs. Randolf Hurley, who told Rose, in great detail, about her trip to Italy the summer past. It should have been an interesting conversation, but Mrs. Hurley was fascinated by Italian architecture. In excruciating and tedious detail, she intricately described the Villa Medici and the Farnese Palace, two places Rose had never heard of but was quite sure she would now recognize if she ever traveled to Rome.

She smiled politely and nodded, while in her mind she screamed for the older woman to be quiet. *If you say one more thing, one more, my head is going to explode. Boom! There it goes, all over this beautiful table. See? I've ruined that lovely Waterford crystal bowl.* Rose found herself smiling at her inner musings, which only served to encourage Mrs. Hurley even more. Rose tried to catch Luke's eye, but it was quite impossible and he seemed engaged in a lively discussion with the man seated next to him, Judge Mitchell.

Rose looked about the table and she realized that, had she not known who was married to whom, she never could have put mates together. There were no secret smiles, no longing gazes, no silent messages sent through a look or a shrug. Rose found herself spending an uncommon amount of time trying to catch Luke's attention only to find that throughout the entire meal, he never glanced her way. Not once.

After the meal was ended, the men, as Rose knew they would, headed to Ralph Trumbell's well-appointed and very male billiard room. He had installed special electric fans to disperse the cigar smoke since the last dinner party and was anxious to try the system out with a roomful of smoking men. Though Rose loathed cigar smoke, she watched the men depart with envy. Surely they were going to have more fun than the women, who were already heading sedately to Agatha Trumbell's comfortable drawing room.

Conversation was interminably dull. Rose's one attempt to bring something lively into the conversation failed miserably. She recalled how much she and Collette had laughed over the unfortunate Mrs. Graves, and brought up the subject of the lady's demise at the hands of her greedy medium. Mrs. Trumbell immediately brought out a pristine handkerchief, dabbed her eyes, and said, "Oh, yes. Sadie was a grand, grand friend of mine."

Rose said a quick prayer of thanks that she had not said something irreverent and experienced a tiny twinge of guilt that the woman had been the object of such mirth. After that, Rose nodded at appropriate times, but added nothing to the *fascinating* discussion about the wonders of Vaseline. Finally, the loud voices of the men, fueled by camaraderie and brandy, filtered into the drawing room and Rose breathed a sigh of relief. The evening was nearing its end.

"Ladies," Ralph Trumbell said loudly upon entering the room. The ladies nodded their heads, dropping their discussion as they watched the men enter. Rose watched as the husbands moved to stand by their wives. She looked for smiles, a touch, but saw nothing but well-dressed men standing next to well-dressed ladies conversing politely about nothing. When Luke took his place beside her, and said, "I hope we didn't interrupt your conversation," it was all Rose could do not to stand up and shout in frustration. Instead, she smiled tightly and said, "We were just getting to the part where Vaseline can be used to quiet a squeaking door when you walked in. I was on the edge of my seat in anticipation."

Luke looked down sharply upon hearing his wife's acerbic tone. His gut twisted as his eyes made a quick sweep of the room to ascertain whether her remarks had been overheard. These people were important to him. Rose knew that. Now why in hell would she choose this moment to assert her dissatisfaction with the topic of conversation?

"Rose." His voice held a note of warning, which Rose chose to ignore.

"Have you noticed, Luke, that not once has anyone laughed aloud?"

Luke glanced around at the men and women, who

had broken into small groups. There had been plenty of laughter in the billiard room, and he told her that.

"Of course there was," she said, her voice just loud enough for Luke to hear as he bent his head toward her. "But do you notice that there is none now? That not one of these men has touched his wife all evening? It's as if they don't know each other. Or at least as if they don't like each other."

Luke smiled. "Many of them don't."

His glib remark only depressed Rose further. To her disgust, she felt tears burning in her eyes and she swallowed determinedly to keep them at bay.

"I think that's just awful. Don't you?"

Luke straightened and put his hands behind his back as he perused the room. Rose was right, but he was not surprised by what he saw. "It's the way it is, Rose. It's nothing to get upset about."

She turned to him then, anguish clear in her brown eyes. "But don't you see, Luke? We fit in. We're just like them. We make polite conversation, we inquire about each other's day." Rose knew she was on the verge of committing the greatest social sin—she was on the verge of calling attention to herself. She swallowed again and collected herself as she had done thousands of times before. "I'm sorry, Luke. I was simply babbling on. You know how I do that," she whispered, and her expression was once more bland and polite.

After a long look at his wife, Luke sighed with relief, glad that apparently Rose had resolved whatever had been bothering her.

3

It was an unusually hot day for the Berkshires, giving Springfield's residents a glimpse of the summer to come. The air had that summer-heat smell that made old men wish they were seventeen and young boys wish they were twenty. Rose watched a swarm of tiny gnats as they swirled in an ever-changing cloud outside her window. Spring fever was really hitting her, this day. She felt like singing, like running about barefoot. Moving her skirts aside, she let out a happy bubble of laughter. She was indeed still barefoot even though it was mid-morning. Earlier that morning, she had been about to don her stockings and shoes when she'd stopped. She didn't want to put on those suffocating leather things. So she hadn't.

"The rebellion has begun," she'd said, making a fist and waving it high, as if she were about to attack the Bastille. Her skirt was a bit too long without her shoes and made walking slightly more challenging, but Rose didn't care. It felt like summer and she felt like a young girl, and if she didn't want to wear her shoes, well, she just wouldn't.

A knock on her door interrupted thoughts of rebellion. "Telephone call, ma'am," her maid announced.

Rose pulled herself away from the window. "Do you know who the caller is, Mildred?"

"Mrs. Taylor, ma'am."

Rose hurried to the telephone, mounted on the wall near the kitchen. "Hello. Collette?"

Collette's voice came through over the faint noise of other conversations on the line. "Yes. It's Collette. John and Thomas Kersey—you remember him from poker night—and I are planning to go swimming at the park. We were wondering if you'd like to join us."

Excitement filled Rose, but as quickly turned to disappointment. "I don't have a bathing suit," she said.

"I have one you can use, I'm sure. Be at our house at noon. Bring Luke along if he wants. John's been wanting to meet him."

Rose bit her lip. She knew she wouldn't have nearly as much fun with her friends if Luke came along and that thought brought with it a wave of guilt. "I'll ask Luke, but I'm sure he won't be able to get away from the courthouse." After Rose hung up, she called the operator and had her ring Luke's office number, a part of her hoping he could not break away from work. Minutes later, she heard his voice.

"Rose, what's happened?" He sounded alarmed that she had called, Rose thought, cringing a bit. She really shouldn't have bothered him about such a silly thing as an invitation to swim.

"I'm going swimming in the park with some friends and, well, I'm sure you're too busy, but I thought I'd see if you could come along."

"That's why you called?"

Rose swallowed. "Yes. I'm sure you can't. I was unsure about calling about something so small, but I thought . . ."

"No. That's all right. Who are you going with?" He sounded perplexed more than annoyed, Rose thought.

"Collette and John and another friend of theirs."

"I see. Well, I doubt I can, Rose." The line was silent except for a soft crackling noise. "Collette and John, you say?"

"And another friend." Rose had no idea why she didn't come right out and say the other friend was a man, except that perhaps she knew Luke would then disapprove. And if he'd disapproved, Rose would have felt guilty going against his wishes, and she probably wouldn't have gone at all. For some reason, at that moment she wanted to go swimming more than anything she'd ever wanted before.

"I'll try. But if I do go, it will probably be later."

"I'll look for you. But don't worry if you can't make it. I understand."

Luke stared at the phone as if it would offer up answers to his wife's odd and obviously reluctant invitation. Swimming. In the middle of the week. With Collette and John. And a friend.

"Charles," he called to his secretary. Charles poked his head through the door and entered Luke's office when he was motioned in.

"Do me a favor. Go down to Forest Park today, to the swimming pond. You know where I mean?" At his secretary's nod, Luke continued, squashing down his unease at checking up on his wife. "There'll be a party of four there this afternoon. Two women . . ." He hesitated. ". . . and two men. I just want visual confirmation that the group is there."

"I'm to assume you do not wish me to make contact with them?" His secretary seemed to take the request in stride.

"You assume correctly."

Two hours later, Charles Cutter returned. "Two couples were at the lake, as well as several mothers with their children. Will there be anything else, sir?"

"No. Yes." Luke closed his eyes briefly. "What were they doing?" he asked calmly, as if his gut wasn't twisting. Rose hadn't lied, but she'd come damned close to that by her omission. Unless she hadn't known that the Taylors' friend was a man.

Charles smiled despite himself. "They were having a grand time, laughing up a storm, splashing around like a bunch of kids. I felt like joining them. It's a hot one today, sir. Will that be all, sir?"

Luke swallowed. "Yes. Thank you, Charles."

Luke pretended to get back to work until his secretary left the room. When the door shut, he dropped his fountain pen and leaned back in his chair. There must be an explanation why Rose hadn't told him. He felt physically ill at the thought of Rose with another man. Was this what had caused the change in her? Interest in a new man? Luke's eyebrows drew together over his troubled gray eyes. Impossible. Not Rose. At least, not the Rose he knew. That thought stopped him cold. Maybe he didn't know Rose at all.

4

Rose felt glorious and wondered when she'd ever been so happy as she flounced into the entry hall, cheeks flushed from the sun, hair piled in an artless tangle atop her head. She hurried toward the dining room, aware that she was late from her outing at the lake. She still felt sand that she'd been unable to brush off from the bottom of her feet prick her skin and one ear was still a bit deaf from the water. Collette had showed her how to shake it out, but so far she'd been unsuccessful. Just before entering the dining room, she banged her head against the heel of her hand and was rewarded by a warm tiny rush of water.

"Luke! There you are," she said, wiping away the water from her fingertips. Luke sat at his place at the end of the table looking rather stern, but Rose thought he'd never looked so handsome. He wore a dark blue suit that looked well with his stormy gray eyes and blond hair, but she rather wished he'd take the suit jacket off, along with that choking collar and necktie. So full of good cheer, she didn't notice Luke's shuttered look as she grabbed her plate and utensils from their place at the head of the table and brought them with her as she sat with a little bounce next to her husband.

"Oh, Luke, I had such fun today," she said as she carelessly deposited her plate and silverware. "I can't remember laughing so much."

"You are late," Luke bit out, trying not to be charmed by his bubbling wife—a wife that never in his recollection had bubbled before. Quite a different wife, he thought, from the one who'd been glum and distant the night before at the Trumbells' dinner party. Rose wrinkled her nose at him playfully, apparently choosing to ignore his dark tone.

The maid placed a large platter between Luke and Rose and, without a glance to what the fare was that evening, Rose began piling up her plate as she gushed about the day. Luke couldn't help but notice how bright her eyes were or that the sun had left her lips a bit red. The thought that another man was responsible for her glow made him almost faint with jealousy and rage—two emotions Luke had never in his life experienced.

"Oh, I know I'm late, Luke. I hurried as fast as I

could. It seems I'm the only one of us who worries about the time. They all seem to have no obligations at all."

"How many of you were along on this great adventure?" Luke said, keeping his tone light.

"Just the four of us. Collette, John, their friend Thomas Kersey"—she paused to take a bite—"and myself."

Rose's response was so ready and innocent, he immediately cast aside what he now believed to be ridiculous suspicions. It felt as if a cool breeze enveloped his body at her easy explanation, so great was his relief. But he was still curious.

"Kersey?"

Rose nodded. "Thomas Kersey. Oh, Luke, he's not the sort of person we ever associate with, but he's so charming. So very amusing in a rough sort of way." She stopped to take another bite, chewing quickly so she could continue her monologue about the day's events. "He made relentless fun of my lack of swimming prowess," and Rose laughed at some remembered joke. She popped another morsel into her mouth.

"Oh!" she said, laying a hand on Luke's wrist. "I know how to swim now. Well, almost. Collette showed me how to tread water. I do it quite well now. I only almost drowned once." At Luke's startled look, Rose laughed. Oh, how happy she'd been today. "I was only in four feet of water. All I had to do was stand up. Of course, I didn't know that at the time and made quite the idiot of myself. I'm afraid Mr. Kersey had great fun at my expense with that. He kept thrashing about, pretending to drown, then standing up to show me how it was done." She stopped to saw off another piece of food. Gesturing with her food-laden fork, she said with complete honesty. "I wish you had come, Luke. It was such fun." Rose's eyes grew wide with alarm as she focused on a black bit of something dangling from the end of her fork.

"Goodness! What have I been eating?"

"Blood sausage," came Luke's dry reply.

Rose covered her mouth with one hand and dropped her fork, looking at the offending instrument with horror.

"I didn't have the heart to tell you that the food you were eating with such relish usually makes you physically ill at the mere sight of it," Luke said, a smile twitching on his lips. "I'm sure there is something you'll find a bit more edible at the sideboard."

Rose burst out laughing, a pleasing sound, Luke thought.

"The sun and a swim certainly have done wonders for you, Rose," he said, leaning back as he looked at his wife anew. She was quite lovely, wearing a soft pink dress with wide bell sleeves that ended just above her elbow. The skin on her forearms was pink from the sun. He was struck by a familiar longing that he could draw her into his arms and she would come willingly. She was just too damned beautiful, he thought.

Rose let out a long, melancholy sigh. "I've never had a day like this, Luke. It was the very first time I've worn a bathing suit, the first time swimming. The water was so cold but it was wonderful. And the bottom of the lake was muddy and squishy between my toes." She wrinkled her nose and Luke smiled at her. "You've probably been swimming a hundred times, but I've only gone in my imagination. There's so much I want to do. My whole life . . ." Rose stopped, not wanting to become maudlin when she wanted to keep this wonderful feeling and wrap it tightly around her.

"You truly enjoy these people, the Taylors." Luke wasn't sure he liked the fact that another couple seemed to have so much influence over his wife. And yet she was so happy today. Happier than he'd ever made her.

"Oh, yes, Luke, I do. I know they're not the kind of people you're used to. Or that I'm used to, for that matter. Maybe that's why I like them so much. Last night at the dinner party . . ." Rose flushed, not wanting to criticize Luke's friends.

"It can be a bit stuffy at times. I know that."

Rose gave him a look of gratitude. "So you don't mind that I've invited the Taylors to dinner tomorrow night?"

Luke narrowed his eyes good-naturedly. "Ah, I see your ploy now, my dear! I should have seen it coming."

"Good. They will arrive at seven o'clock. Will that give you enough time to finish your work?"

It wouldn't, not with the police and his office planning a raid on the Supper Club Friday evening, but he didn't have the heart to disappoint Rose. Not when she looked so hopeful and happy.

"I'll be here," he said. He'd be glad to get a look at the Taylors firsthand. That brief meeting with Collette outside church had told him nothing. He just couldn't shake the uneasy feeling he got when he thought of their friendship with his wife. *Maybe I'm just jealous,* he thought. *Maybe it bothers the hell out of me that I can't make my wife as happy as two strangers can.*

5

John Taylor pulled on his wife's laces until she let out a little squeak of pain.

"That's tight enough," she managed to say through compressed lungs. He gave one more sharp pull before tying the laces with jerky motions, and she looked back at him with a frown.

"I don't see why you're so worried about having dinner with the Beaudettes. It's not as if the husband knows you. He knows your father and that was years ago."

John moved in front of Collette. "I just don't want to take any chances. I'm this close," he said, holding up his thumb and forefinger. "This close to ruining him. God, it's sweet. I can taste it already."

Collette sat, pouting at her reflection in her silver hand mirror. She pulled at a couple of curls, then turned her head this way and that to see if she cared for the effect. "You're sure we won't get arrested? I know I asked you before, but I have no desire to end up sharing a cell with Miss Goody-good." Collette lowered the mirror to scowl at her husband.

He gave her his most charming smile. "Everything's set. The raid is scheduled for exactly ten o'clock. At ten minutes before the hour, you and I slip out the back. Miss Goody-good will be caught red-handed. I think roulette might be a good game for her. Or perhaps twenty-one," he mused. "And just in case her influential husband decides to hush it up, there'll be a reporter from the *Union* who'll just happen to stop by the jailhouse that night. He'll have the story half written before anyone rouses Beaudette with the news his wife has been arrested at an illegal gambling joint." He rubbed his hands together, unable to contain his glee. "You're sure you can convince her to go?"

"Oh, I'm sure. I think I could get her to do just about anything by now," she said with derision.

John laughed at his wife's sour expression. "You've done a wonderful job, darling. I couldn't have done it without you. Luke Beaudette is not an easy man to get to, but his wife dove right into the boiling pot."

Collette let out a heavy sigh. "After Friday night, it's over, right? Then we can get the hell out of this town and go back to Boston, right?" she asked as she jerked on her dress.

"You bet, darling. Why? Getting a little tired of all this?" he asked, waving his hand at their extravagant apartment.

Collette sidled up to John, draping her arms over his shoulders. "Believe it or not, I do miss our little tenement. It's the game. Rose is just too damn perfect."

"Annoying as hell, isn't it?"

Collette nodded slowly, then kissed her husband's smiling lips. "It wasn't at first, but the more time I spend with her, the more annoyed I get. How can a woman be so damned perfect? It's got to be an act. 'Oh,' " she mocked, to her husband's delight. " 'The water's so cold! The bottom is so squishy! The sky is so blue!' She's so damned appreciative of everything. It makes me feel . . ."

"Guilty as hell," laughed John. "See, darling? You're just as good as she is, you just haven't had everything handed to you on a silver platter." He moved behind his wife and began buttoning up her dress far more gently than he had tightened her corset.

"It doesn't make me feel guilty," Collette said harshly. "It makes me feel sick. I've had enough. At first it was fun, but it's not anymore. I'm just glad it's almost over."

John finished buttoning her up and he turned Collette around. "You're lying, sweetheart," he said softly, not quite with menace. "I know you don't want to go through with this, and you're putting on a show for my benefit. Oh, I know you are a bit annoyed, but more than a little guilty, too. Just remember, it's for my father."

Collette bit her lip. "I know, John. I'd never do anything to ruin things for you. You know that, don't you?"

"God help you if you do, Collette. You think what I'm doing to Luke Beaudette is bad? If you cross me, if you betray me, it'll be much worse for you. Much worse."

"I know," Collette said, with a tremulous smile. "That's why I'll be good, John, I promise." She kissed him and he drew her to him with a hard fierceness that made Collette pull back.

"Oh, John. You know I'd never betray you," she said, all fear gone from her voice as she sensed the near desperation of his embrace. "I'm so proud of you, darling, you must know that. You could have killed Beaudette outright. I know you wanted to." She leaned back, completely in control as she watched John flush with pleasure.

"This is better. His ruination," Collette purred. "The newspapers will find the whole sordid episode wildly intriguing. Imagine, the attorney general's favorite attorney's wife arrested at the Supper Club. It's delicious," she said, laughing at her witty pun.

John did not appear amused and his expression suddenly became cold. "It's not enough, this plan. It's not." Closing his eyes, he took two sharp breaths. "But it will do. It has to do, right, love?"

"It's a wonderful plan. Brilliant. Just like you," Collette said, stepping back to give her husband a critical eye. She pronounced him handsome as well as brilliant and the two headed for their dinner with the Beaudettes chattering happily.

6

Luke had an instant and unreasonable dislike of John Taylor. He was too damned friendly, with a smile that didn't reach his eyes and an overloud voice that grated on his nerves. He found his broad Boston accent irritating and a bit overdone, like a Harvard man gone awry. John Taylor was no Harvard man, but rather, as Taylor had graciously and vaguely volunteered, a business manager. He had refused to give more details, saying only that talking of it would give him a headache, and with a warning look from Rose, Luke let it go at that.

Luke was not a man who made instant judgments, and that had made him suspect his own misgivings. He spent the first few minutes of their acquaintance trying to come up with a solid reason for his dislike. Jealousy? Possibly. He could not help but notice that as soon as the pair entered the house Rose became animated and lovely. She fairly sparkled when she welcomed them into their grand hallway, which still smelled of the beeswax she had instructed their servants to rub on the massive amount of walnut woodwork in the entry hall.

The pair seemed nervous, Luke thought. Intimidated and out of their element, looking about like children do at a museum, taking in all the lovely things but knowing they can never touch them. Luke was not a snob; he could not be when he knew the rich and the poor could be equally immoral. So, it was not snobbery, or, he decided, jealousy. Because he found himself looking at Rose like an awestruck schoolboy, and wishing suddenly that the Taylors could go home so he could ply his wife with some brandy and let her try her hand at seducing him again.

But there was something . . . something about the man. Ah, he thought with relief as he realized what it was about Taylor that had him so uncomfortable. He reminded Luke of the disagreeable bicycle salesman who had confronted him nearly every day last summer as Luke walked by his shop. The man had stood outside, fiddling with a ridiculously large mustache, and straightened as he saw Luke, giving him a wide smile of greeting as if Luke were an old war buddy he hadn't seen in years. Each day, Luke would tell the eager salesmen, firmly and politely, that he was not in the least interested in buying a bicycle. And Luke secretly thought at the time that even if he had wanted a bicycle, the last place he would buy it was from that particular shop. It was a morbidly hot day when Luke finally confronted the man.

"If I wanted one of your goddamn bicycles, I would have bought one by now, don't you think, sir? My God, man, do you not understand English? I have told you more times than I can tally that I am not interested. Do you have a brain deficiency? Is there any way I can be more clear?"

The salesman at first had the look of an innocent man being accused of a ghastly crime. Then he had jerked down on his vest, a gesture that judging by the wrinkled edge of the garment was done on a frequent basis, and compressed his mouth into a tight line.

"I do beg your pardon, sir. You can be assured that I will not bother you again."

"Good. I would be most gratified!" And Luke had continued on his way, feeling only the slightest nudge of guilt that he had lost his temper.

Each day since, the salesman had stood outside the door and watched with a strange intensity as Luke approached. He never said another word, but kept eerily and malevolently silent. It was damn disconcerting, that look. It made the back of Luke's neck tingle each time he walked past. Ridiculous to fear the man, Luke reasoned. But something in the salesman's eyes went beyond irritation, to something dark and corrupt.

John Taylor was like that man. All smiles and cold eyes. Too friendly. He made Luke exceedingly uncomfortable with his overdone praise of their home. Taylor had a glad and boisterous comment about everything, as if Luke himself carved his elaborate desk and cut the fine crystals in their Waterford chandelier. Luke glanced at Rose to see if she felt the same, but she appeared oblivious, so happy was she to share her home with her newest and greatest friends.

After an agonizing hour in the study, in which John, Collette, and Rose seemed to recap every adventure they'd so far experienced together, the dinner bell was rung. Luke bolted from his chair.

"If I could interrupt, I believe I have heard the dinner bell," he said. The three looked at him as if he'd been hearing things. "May we?" And he gestured toward the door. Rose placed her hand in the crook of his arm and they stepped back to allow the Taylors to precede them. As they passed, Luke was quite sure Taylor leaned over to his wife and whispered, "Ah, the dinner bell. We *must* get one for ourselves."

Rose would have blamed the wine for her euphoria had she imbibed more than the tiniest sip, and even that made her shudder. She gazed around the table, taking in the smiles on John and Collette's faces that told her all was going well. The sea bass was succulent—or so said John—and Rose promised to inform the cook. Conversation was light and witty and Rose felt so wonderfully a part of it. She heard laughter when she tried to be droll, gasps of outrage when she was trying to be outrageous. The dinner was everything Rose had hoped it to be. Certainly Luke could understand now why she spent so much time with this unconventional pair. Who could not be charmed by them? She glanced over at Luke, hoping to share her enjoyment of the evening with one of those secret little looks that John and Collette were constantly sharing, and felt her heart plummet. Luke was, well, not quite frowning, she thought, glancing down at her plate quickly. But he certainly didn't have the expression of a man enjoying himself. Luke stared at John as if he had just put something quiet disagreeable into his mouth and was trying to hide the fact.

"Luke, did you know that John lived in Boston at the same time you graduated from Harvard?" Rose said, slightly desperate to involve Luke in the conversation.

"Really?" Luke said in a tone that bordered on boredom.

"Yes. Isn't that right, John?"

Collette began answering. "Why, um, yes, Rose. I believe it must have been '92 or '93." She stopped abruptly, letting out a tiny screech and putting an odd little smile on her lips. If Rose didn't know better, she would have thought John had kicked Collette beneath the table.

"No, darling," John said smoothly. "We didn't move to Boston until just last year. Right before we moved here. We were in Providence before that."

Collette gave her head a jerky little shake. "Oh, of course. Providence." She turned to Luke and flashed him a blinding smile. "You must have been in Harvard while we were in Providence. We just missed you."

Luke had the oddest expression on his face. Rose didn't like it at all. "We might have been neighbors after all," Luke said pleasantly. "I was an undergraduate at Brown and didn't transfer to Harvard until the fall of '92. What a coincidence."

John gave him a wide smile. "You don't say. Why, we seem to be following each other around," he said in his usual friendly manner. "Where do you plan to live next? I'll make sure I start house-hunting."

The table erupted with laughter and Rose noticed that even Luke smiled. Barely.

"And what sort of work were you doing in Providence? Family funds were a bit low at the time and I worked much of my way through Brown. With all these grand coincidences, perhaps we even did similar work."

Rose relaxed. Luke finally seemed to be trying to get along. She looked at John expectantly.

"Well, I was . . . at the time I was just beginning in business." John gave a satisfied nod, but his cheeks were ruddy and Rose was certain he was embarrassed to say what his first job had been.

"Business," Luke said dryly.

Rose darted her husband an angry look. Oh, she thought, he could be so obtuse at times. Couldn't he see how John was not proud of whatever he did? That perhaps all this talk of Brown and Harvard only reminded John that he had not gone to college? Rose did not know for sure, but she suspected as much. Luke and John were fairly glaring at each other.

"Anyone for dessert?" Rose said in an odd chirpy way that had Luke giving her a look of wry amusement. She motioned frantically for the maid, who disappeared only to return moments later with a tray filled with steaming apple cobbler. Thankfully, everyone's attention was diverted from conversation and onto the cobbler.

The rest of the evening went quickly. By the time the Taylors bade them good night, saying what a wonderful time they'd had, Rose knew they hadn't had a good time at all. They appeared to be almost frantic to get out the door, she thought unhappily. When the door shut behind them, Rose turned, hands on hips, and glared at Luke.

"You didn't try even a little bit," she accused.

"I tried as hard as you do at my friends' gatherings."

Rose let out an angry huff of air. "You knew how much this evening meant to me. I believe you went out of your way to appear bored and belligerent."

"No," Luke said with insufferable honesty. "I was truly bored. To be honest, I cannot believe you hold those two in such high esteem. They are nothing like us."

Rose narrowed her eyes. "Perhaps they are not like you. But they are like me. Or rather, I am like them. I have fun when I am with Collette. I laugh until it hurts. Certainly there is nothing wrong with enjoying oneself. Or would you rather I be like you, like some . . . some . . . stick in the mud. All frowns and hmphs and ahems."

To Rose's disgust, Luke appeared to be trying to hold back a smile. "I had no idea I was such an old stodge."

"You are." She bit her lip. "Sometimes. Tonight you were."

"Perhaps," he said in that dismissive way that Rose loathed, as if she was a disagreeable witness on the stand who had just given him an answer he clearly did not believe. When he turned away, putting the final period on their conversation, it was all Rose could do not to run after him down the hall and force him to admit he'd been a complete cad all evening. Instead, she walked very, very quickly.

Tugging on his arm, Rose forced him to stop. "Luke," she said, lifting her chin several notches. "I believe you should apologize."

Luke turned, the flickering gaslight making him appear more angry than he was, his dark gray eyes turning black. "I will not apologize, Rose. Those people are rabble."

Rose opened her mouth in disbelief. "Rabble! You know nothing of them!"

"I know enough. A woman who dresses like a trollop, with hair that is suspiciously rather too blonde. A man with no apparent source of income, who can't look a man in the eye. I know that they've turned my wife into something I don't recognize. Look at you!" And his eyes swept to her modest neckline that exposed nothing more than some creamy flesh, now flushed with anger. "Look at you," he said more softly this time, and his eyes strayed to her mouth.

Confused, Rose only shook her head. "Look at me?" She knew her dress was modest, far more modest than Collette would have had her wear. But, she thought, far more daring than what she usually wore.

"Yes." Luke grasped her arms and drew her beneath the gaslight, pulling her closer. His eyes wandered over her, taking in her hair, drifting downward to a throat that was rarely exposed, lingering at her breasts, and finally returning to meet her troubled gaze. "Where did this come from, Rose? Not from me." There was no anger in his voice, but instead a latent sadness.

Rose shook her head. It was all for him, she thought. All of it. She felt his hands on her arms, warm and strong, and she leaned forward as if she no longer could stand on her own. Oh, this man, with his solid heat that turned her to liquid just by holding her so innocently. Rose moved her hands to his chest and up to his shoulders, ignoring the fact that his body stiffened beneath her palms. Feeling daring and strangely yielding, she lifted herself onto her tiptoes and pressed a kiss upon her husband's lips. Rose felt a rush of freedom with that touch, a frightening wildness that she'd always kept barely contained but which was now clawing to escape. She heard his sharp intake of breath and pulled away, fearing that she'd shocked him. But as she pulled back, Luke came closer, as if he could not allow her to separate her lips from his.

Please, she prayed to herself. Please, please, let me love him.

With a little sound, she surrendered and let him pull her close, let him press his lips against hers, let him lick her lips. Please please please.

7

Luke started slowly, like a man holding his hand out to a frightened doe. Little kisses, slightly more than chaste. His whole body ached to draw her tight against him, to let her feel how much he wanted her. Instead, he kissed her lips, mouthing her, reveling in the tiny little sounds of pleasure he heard. His mind screamed for him to go slowly, but his body, his poor love-starved body, was screaming just as loudly.

My tongue in her mouth. Try that. See what happens. If she pulls away—oh, God, don't let her pull away. But if she does, it will be all right, I'll just smile and go back to those other kisses. He licked her lips, sweet, sweet. "Rose, darling, please, let me. Let me." And he told her with his mouth and tongue what he wanted her to do. At the first touch of his tongue against hers it took all his will not to crush her against him, but he maintained his control. Beautiful mouth, lovely and soft and wet. At first she was tentative, her tongue darting for a little taste, but then she turned her head just slightly and her grip on his shoulders grew fierce, and he knew she was lost. Thank you. Thank you.

Still he held back, moving his hands slowly from her arms to her waist, drawing her closer, reveling in the sensation of her body pressed against his. His hands shook as they moved over her back, up and down, in a smooth caress that tested his control. And then he cupped her round little buttocks, pulling her up against him. Hard. He heard a sound, not quite a pleasure sound, but not a protest either. He pulled back, afraid he had been too rough, that he had shown her just how much he wanted her. If she knew, Luke was certain she would have pulled away.

"Rose, darling," he said, breathless, kissing her flushed cheek. "We can go upstairs. Would that be all right?"

"Yes." But Rose knew. She *knew* she was about to fail him. It's not a sin, it's not dirty. It's Luke, my husband. I want to love him. He began kissing her again and she tried with all her being to respond, to fake a response when it became clear to her that she could not, but when he touched her breast, she cringed. And her heart broke.

"What's wrong." His voice was flat.

"I'm sorry, Luke. Kiss me again. Please." Even to her own ears Rose sounded desperate. She began pressing kisses against his unresponsive lips, she threw herself against him as tears slipped down her cheeks. Luke jerked his head away, and thrust her away from him. "Luke. Please!"

"No, goddammit. I will not rape my wife. I will not."

"But you don't . . . do that." Rose shook her head, tears streaming down her face anew at the horribleness of his words.

He looked at her with pain and desperation in his eyes. "I do, Rose. Every time I touch you I feel like I'm forcing you. As if my touch is abhorrent. I don't understand. You were there for a while. Or were you just pretending the entire time? My God, Rose, don't pretend to enjoy my touch." He squeezed his eyes shut. "What the hell is going on?"

Rose could only stand there dumbly.

"Is it me?" The words sounded as if they'd been wrenched from his throat. How many times had he gone to her and seen her cringe, how many times had he wanted nothing more than to hold her against him but didn't, fearing she would stiffen and pull away? As if he were abhorrent. As if he were something to be barely tolerated.

As if she didn't love him.

"Oh, no, Luke. It's not you," she said through the thickness in her throat. She reached for him, but he backed away. The way Luke looked at her, Rose felt he almost hated her.

"You responded. I know you did. I knew exactly when you stopped feeling."

"I didn't stop feeling," Rose said, loudly, desperately.

"Goddammit, don't lie to me. Don't you dare! You act as if . . . My God, you act as if you're imagining I'm someone else. And then when you realize it's me . . . Is that it, Rose? Are you pretending you're with someone else?"

"Don't, Luke. Please." Rose covered her face with her hands and shook her head. "How could you think that? How could you say it aloud?"

"How could I not?"

Rose felt chilled by his frigid words.

Luke let out a sound of disgust. "I apologize, Rose. The question was uncalled for."

Rose brought her hands down and wanted to turn away from the coldness she saw in those beloved gray eyes. They stood silently for agonizing seconds before Luke turned away and spat. "I'm going out."

Fear clutched at Rose's throat. Never had Luke gone out without her during the week. He was a man of strict schedules. Friday he went to the club. Saturday he and Rose went to the theater or some other such social event. Sunday they visited family. On rare weekdays, they attended a dinner party or a concert. Rose knew other husbands often left their wives at home to visit their clubs, but Luke had not been one of them. Grabbing his hat from the hallstand, he turned to leave and would have made it out the door if Rose had not done something she hadn't done since she was a girl. She lifted her skirts and ran as fast as she could to intercept him. The look on his face was one of disbelief when he went to open the door and instead saw the determined face of his wife glaring up at him.

"You can't leave until I explain."

With an ease Rose found inordinately discouraging, Luke lifted her out of the way. "Watch me." And he stepped through the door without looking back.

8

The day matched Rose's mood: gloomy, raw, cold. She glanced down with detachment at her skirt, half-soaked from the rain that swept unhindered into the trolley. Passengers sitting near the edge of the unprotected car found the bottom half of themselves quite wet. She shook out the dark blue skirt, wrinkling her nose at the disagreeable odor of wet wool. By the time she reached her sister's home, her skirts would be heavy with water and decidedly uncomfortable. Somehow, Rose couldn't gather enough energy to generate more than a slight feeling of irritation that the city fathers hadn't wanted to spend the extra money to install windows on the new trolleys.

The car clattered down Main Street, stopping frequently to let passengers on and off, finally entering the finer neighborhood of Belmont Avenue and Forest Park where Nicole had lived with her husband on his family estate for four years. Nicole lived just a half mile from their mother's home on Sumner Avenue, and Rose had always been grateful that Luke decided to move away from Forest Park to the newer homes on Mattoon. Their brownstone was not nearly as fine as some of the mansions on Sumner and Belmont, but Rose would not have traded their home for any in the Park.

At her stop, Rose snapped open her umbrella and stepped down from the trolley, unsuccessfully maneuvering around an enormous puddle. Shaking out her shoe, Rose had to swallow back the tears that had been threatening all day. She had not seen Luke since he stormed out the door the previous evening. If she hadn't seen the remains of his breakfast before the maid cleared them away, she would not have known whether he returned home at all. Rose had tried to stay up, hoping to talk to him before he retired for the evening, but as the clock struck one, she slumped over onto her goose-down pillow and fell fast asleep. Rose cringed in self-loathing each time she thought of the previous evening. How she had hurt Luke! For him to actually believe she thought of someone else when she was kissing him. She wanted to scream at him that he was an idiot. How couldn't he know how much she loved him, how much she wanted to make love to him?

But Rose had her answer in that awful tightening, that fear that came upon her, sneaking up before she could stop it. As angry as she was at Luke for believing such an awful thing of her, she understood why he believed it. It was absurd, truly. If he only knew how much she loved him, wanted him. But he couldn't know. He only knew a wife that pulled away. It hadn't struck Rose until last night how she had been hurting him. Knowing that she had hurt him countless times was devastating. Luke had always been understanding and gentle. But now Rose knew that those times she pulled away with a tight smile on her face had been a blow to his heart. She had bruised and battered him without knowing, and she could only pray that she had not hurt his heart beyond repair. Rose simply felt dreadful.

Two weeks ago, Rose had believed she had a happy marriage. Now she knew they had been existing, living in the same house like two polite strangers not truly knowing what the other felt, what the other wanted. It was shattering to realize they were dangling on a yawning edge that led to a life of routine and cold distance. Rose didn't need new dresses and shorter hair. She knew only one thing could drag them away from the edge: She needed to love her husband.

And she couldn't. Oh, God, Rose thought as she stared at the rain-pocked puddle at her feet, what is wrong with me? She needed to talk to someone, needed to be reassured that she could salvage her marriage. For some reason, Rose didn't want to turn to Collette. Collette would say something ridiculous to make Rose laugh, but Rose believed that Collette with her happy, cheerful existence, couldn't fathom this kind of sorrow. Instead, Rose was turning to Nicole, though she could never discuss with her sister what was happening. Nicole was so solid and good. She wouldn't harangue Rose into telling her the particulars of why she was so blue, she would simply accept it with a kindness that was healing. That was what Rose needed. A hug from her big sister, her unconditional love.

Nicole's heart fluttered wildly in her breast, though she forced herself to calm down as she walked toward her kitchen. The large room was empty now as her cook didn't arrive until ten o'clock each morning. Louis had breakfast at his club, saying it was the best time for him to meet with business associates. Nicole never had an appetite in the morning anyway, so never missed having a large breakfast. A bit of tea and some toast were more than enough, particularly with her nagging morning sickness.

She loved her kitchen and tried to let only happy things happen there. The entire back wall was a bank of small windows that the servants cursed, for they were tedious to clean. But they let in glorious warm sunlight in the mornings and even on this gloomy day cheered her by letting in weak gray light. The rest of the house was dark with Oriental furnishings, deep reds and golds chosen by Louis. Nicole found the decor oppressive. The kitchen, however, was hers. Had Louis known how much time she spent there, talking with Mrs. Freebody and her helpers, he would have forbidden it. It was the only place in her home that *felt* like home—the home she had always dreamed of, anyway. Even without the bustling activity of Mrs. Freebody and her "girls," it was a welcoming place, she thought as she pushed open the door.

Nicole smoothed her hair and smiled as she saw a man's familiar outline through the curtain hanging on the kitchen's back door.

"Come in, Mr. D'Angelo," she said as she opened the door, letting the damp freshness of the air invade her kitchen. Her heart hammered in her breast at the sight of him. His dark hair was damp and curling, making him appear even more boyish, more endearing. He wore white overalls on his long, lean form, and in his hand he carried a metal basket that held a small bottle of cream and a pot of butter. As Anthony D'Angelo entered the kitchen, he nodded politely, then flashed her a smile exposing straight white teeth. Nicole's heart flip-flopped when she saw that smile, and she backed away to let him pass and enter the house.

"Would you care for some tea? I've just made some and it will warm you up. It's so cold today. I thought we wouldn't be turning on the furnace again this year, but I was wrong. I'll be ordering more coal . . ." She stopped. Always she tried to pretend he was simply Mr. D'Angelo, the man who delivered milk. But he was not. He was Anthony, her friend, her heart. They both knew it and ignored it, but sometimes, they would forget and let their eyes soften and their lips form a smile that went beyond polite. And then pain would flash, their smiles would turn regretful, and that would be that.

Anthony was looking at her now like that, his thickly lashed chocolate-brown eyes warm and happy. "Tea would be nice, Mrs. Baptiste," he said in his wonderful Italian accent.

"Please sit down, Mr. D'Angelo. I'll bring you that tea." This morning Nicole was determined to maintain her distance despite her traitorous heart. It was frightening and wonderful to have this man to think about when she was knitting in her cold little parlor waiting for Louis to come home from work. It was quite another to encourage him or herself into thinking for a moment that they could ever do more than smile warmly at each other.

Anthony sat down at a table tucked into a cozy little corner that the servants used for their meals. Its green-and-white-checked tablecloth looked cheery, a splash of color on a gray day. "You look beautiful this morning. *Bella,*" Anthony said, ignoring her businesslike tone. He always did. He liked to see her blush.

"I'm not beautiful, I'm fat and getting fatter," she protested good-naturedly. "And do you truly think this green pallor suits me?" She turned away, blushing fiercely, and her hand strayed to her stomach.

"You are with child." It was not a question.

She looked at him with wonder that he could have guessed, and he shrugged.

"You have been green for weeks," he said, and she laughed. It was true. One morning she was retching into the sink just moments before he arrived and Nicole had wondered whether he had heard the disagreeable sound. Now she knew that he had.

"Yes, I . . ." Nicole looked away, feeling embarrassed to talk about such an intimate thing with a man. Particularly this man. For there was only one way for a woman to become pregnant. "I'm hoping for a boy."

He stood abruptly, causing the teacup she had just placed before him to rattle. "Then you'll want for me to bring more milk, no?" Anthony, always so sure of himself, suddenly appeared quite unsure of what to do. "This is good news. I will light a holy candle and pray you get your wish of a strong son."

Nicole wiped up a bit of tea that had splashed over the edge of the teacup and onto the table, and he glanced at the cup with uncertainty. "I'm running late. I got so many orders today. It's Wednesday, no? Everyone runs out of everything by Wednesday."

Nicole stared at his teacup as he gave his short explanation. "You won't drink your tea?" she asked weakly.

He looked at her as if she were crazy, then his troubled brown eyes looked at the tea. "I don't even like tea," he said angrily.

Nicole looked stunned. "But all this time . . ."

"Yes," he spat. "All this time I drink your tea. I drink your tea every day and I don't like it." His eyes softened as he took in her stricken expression. "I don't sit here for the tea. You know that."

Nicole turned away and walked stiffly over to the sink, keeping her back toward him. "I know," she whispered.

He walked up behind her, lifted his hand, but withdrew it without touching her. "I think I should go now," he said, his accent thick. He didn't move. When she didn't respond for several long moments, he turned away and walked to the door. But before he walked through it she spoke, stopping him as his hand curled around the doorknob.

"I want a boy. Because then he'll be satisfied." Her eyes were closed as she listened to the silence, praying he understood what she said. And praying he would not.

"Don't say that," he said harshly. "Nicole. Please don't." Clever Anthony. She should have known he would understand that a boy would mean she would not allow her husband again into her bed. It was a cruel thing to say to him, she knew.

Nicole turned to him, biting her lips to stop the tears that burned in her throat. "I'm sorry," she managed to say. They stood looking at each other, bitterly acknowledging life's truths.

When the door to the kitchen swung open, they both cast startled, guilt-ridden looks at it, jerking their bodies as if they had been inches apart instead of several feet.

Rose gave a curious look at her sister and the milkman who stood at the door as if he were about to leave.

"Hello."

Anthony nodded politely. "Friday is the next delivery?" he asked Nicole.

She gave the man a jerky nod. "Yes, Mr. D'Angelo. Have a nice day."

After the milkman departed, Rose's eyes went from the untouched tea sitting on the table to Nicole's back. Her sister and the milkman had been looking at each other like two actors in a Shakespearean tragedy. It was . . . startling, that look.

"You can drink the tea there," Nicole said, turning to face her younger sister. Rose gave her a searching look and relaxed when she saw nothing unsettling in her sister's face. "I sometimes give Mr. D'Angelo some tea, but he didn't want any today." Nicole's eyes strayed to the door. "He doesn't like it," she said with a touch of irony. "All this time . . ."

Rose's brows creased as Nicole's eyes clouded. "All this time?"

Her sister took a deep breath and returned from wherever she'd been. "Yes," she said with a little laugh. "Can you believe it? For four years he's been our milkman and every so often I'll give him some tea. Every time he's drunk it down without a word. And today, he tells me he doesn't like it." Nicole's voice sounded almost too bright.

"How very gallant of him," Rose said, not knowing how to respond.

"We're all gallant in our own way." Nicole grabbed her own teacup and sat down at the table, nodding for Rose to do the same.

The two sisters sat companionably sipping their tea, each lost in her own thoughts. This was just what Rose wanted—something normal.

Nicole broke the silence. "You're not wearing one of your new dresses."

"No. The rain . . ."

Nicole nodded her understanding. "How is Collette?"

"Oh. Fine."

"And Luke?"

Rose tensed a bit. "Fine." She hesitated before adding. "We had a little tiff last night. I suppose that's why I'm here. I wanted a shoulder to cry on." At Nicole's look of concern, Rose rushed to reassure her. "Oh, it's nothing serious. Just our first fight. Everything will be back to normal by tonight when he comes home from the office." Somehow, going back to "normal" sounded immensely depressing to Rose.

Nicole looked out the window for a long moment. "Do you remember that dollhouse Aunt Flora gave to us? The one we couldn't touch or play with?"

Rose gave her sister a curious look, then smiled. "Of course I do." She hadn't thought about that dollhouse in years, but now Nicole's mention of it brought it back to her. The dollhouse had been . . . magical. Rose had been ten years old when Aunt Flora had sent the dollhouse as a gift. Rose and Nicole had loved it on sight, their fingers itching to rearrange the tiny figures and furniture. Rose remembered thinking that if she stared long enough at the dollhouse, she could feel herself entering those tiny rooms, with their ornately carved paneling and pretty flowered wallpaper, where no one cried and no one shouted.

It sat upon a gleaming rosewood table and was really too nice to play with, so she'd been reminded time after time. Sometimes Rose would tiptoe up to the dollhouse, wanting so much to rearrange the elegant rooms, and would stare and wish and wish that it was where she truly lived. Rose wasn't certain why, but thinking about the dollhouse brought forward another memory, an ugly confrontation between Nicole and Mother. Ten-year-old Rose had stood near the table, very careful not to get too close so there would be no chance she'd be tempted to lay her hand on the table, leaving behind telltale fingerprints, when the shouting began. As she had done before, Rose escaped into those tiny rooms where no one shouted and no one cried. Although she played pretend with the dollhouse nearly every day, she never touched it. Well, not so anyone would notice. Not even Mother.

She liked to pretend that the house with its gingerbread trim and magnificent turret was truly her own home, that the beautiful little mother doll, with her nicely bustled yellow silk gown and elegant lace collar and cuffs, was her own mother. The man, with his jaunty top hat and smiling mouth, was her father. Of course, Rose had liked her sister Nicole just fine and didn't change a thing about her. So the sister doll with her real human hair was Nicole, just as she was. And the smaller doll, really much too young to be herself, was Rose by default.

"You're the most beautiful daughters in the whole world," Rose whispered for her doll mother. "I love you very, very much." Then Rose frowned and gave the door of her and Nicole's room a wary look, thinking she'd heard Nicole sob.

"I love you too, Mama," Rose said to her doll mother, resolutely ignoring whatever was happening, even though she began to feel sick to her stomach. She called her real mother "Mother," proper and respectful and almost always preceded by an "If you please," or a "Thank you." Below stairs was suddenly quiet and she relaxed, hoping that whatever the shouting and crying was about was over. She wished with all her heart that her mother could be more like the Mama doll of her imaginings.

Ungrateful girl, Rose chastised herself. I'll have to tell Father Frenier about my hateful thoughts in confession, she told herself sternly, and immediately said a Hail Mary to lessen the great sin of breaking the commandment about honoring thy mother and father, even if she broke it just a little bit. Rose had been halfway through the prayer when she heard the scream.

Nicole! Oh, Nicole, Nicole, what have you done now? she cried to herself as she pressed her hands over her ears. The screaming stopped, replaced by a more horrible keening cry, and Rose gathered up her courage to see what had happened. She marched over to the door, her steps muffled by the thick carpet, and grasped the crystal doorknob. And there, her courage failed her. She stared at the door, momentarily transfixed by the swirling designs of the wood grain, until she heard another cry. If she didn't go, her mother would call her to witness her sister's sin, and that was somehow worse for Nicole, to be held up formally before her younger sister as something sinful. Rose crept down the narrow back stairs, the ones that were traversed by the servants.

Rose's heart cried out for her sister who continued to wail. She would not be able to hug her yet. That would come later when they were abed and the house was quiet. Nicole would let the tears come again then and Rose would hold and rock her. The cries were coming from the kitchen and Rose swallowed a lump of bile that formed in her throat. The kitchen held such awful things—her father's old leather strap, the wooden spoon, the lye soap.

Rose had entered the kitchen softly, her brown eyes wide in her pale little face as she looked at Nicole who clutched her beet-red hand against her chest. Her mother, enveloped by steam from hot water, was scrubbing a pot furiously at the sink. Helga, their cook, was nowhere to be seen. Rose's eyes went from Nicole's reddened hand to the pot and back to Nicole who, with a tiny nod, confirmed Rose's suspicions. Mother had scalded Nicole's hand in whatever had been in the pot. Though Rose thought she'd been particularly quiet, her mother turned to see her quaking by the door. Grabbing a towel and drying her hands with efficient pats, she straightened and glared first at Rose and then, with pure disgust, at poor Nicole. While her mother was staring at Nicole, Rose lifted a quick finger to her nose to wipe it before her mother could see any evidence of her distress. She was about to get a "lesson" and no tears were ever allowed during one.

"Your sister," her mother started, and then stopped, as if it were too much for her to say. "Your sister was touching herself."

Rose's brows came together. Touching herself?

What was sinful about that? Rose looked at her mother and back at Nicole, confusion clear in her face.

"Down there!" And her mother pointed to Nicole somewhere below the waist of her pretty forest-green skirt. Rose bit her lips, fearing her mother would still see that she hadn't understood what great sin Nicole had committed.

"If I ever catch you touching yourself *down there,* your punishment will be more severe, Rose, for you know now what a great sin it is. Your sister"—and she cast Nicole a look of pure distaste—"is a dirty, dirty girl. I will not have such filth in my home. She is dirty." And she shuddered real revulsion at the thing that Nicole had done.

Rose glanced at her sister, whose face turned nearly as red as her scalded arm, which was still clutched against her chest. Whatever Nicole had done, Rose thought, it truly must have been awful. She had promised herself she would ask her sister about it so she might never, ever commit such a terrible sin.

Rose frowned at the unhappy memory and gave herself a mental shake. She hated that one of the happier memories of her childhood, that wonderful dollhouse, had been tainted.

"I used to stare at it for hours and move the dolls and furniture around in my imagination," Rose said, trying to banish the ugly memory. "I used to pretend . . . well, that you and I were the little children dolls and the mother and father dolls were someone other than Mother and Father. Is that terrible?"

Nicole laughed. "No. We were children. We wanted to play and we had parents who preferred solemn little children who didn't make noise."

"It wasn't that bad, was it?" At Nicole's look of disbelief, Rose smiled. "You're right. It was that bad. When Luke and I have children, there will be one rule in the house: Have fun."

Nicole had been smiling, but suddenly the smile was gone and Rose was startled to see tears glistening in her sister's eyes.

"Nicole?"

She shook her head. "I used to stare at the doll-house, too. But I used to imagine I was the Mommy doll and the two children were mine and the Daddy doll was this wonderful husband who made me laugh." She stopped, her eyes still staring through the rain-spattered windows.

"I hate him," Nicole said in a toneless way, as if she had said something as innocuous as "It's raining." She turned to look at Rose, her eyes strangely devoid of emotion considering the words she'd just uttered.

At first, Rose was uncertain who she meant. But then she knew Nicole meant her husband. It was un-thinkable. No one could hate her husband, and if she did, she could never admit it, could never say aloud words that could never be called back. But they were there, hanging between them, ugly and unretractable. Rose immediately made a sound of protest, for wasn't it her duty to tell her sister that she could not hate Louis, she should work through whatever it was that was wrong? She opened her mouth to give Nicole a lecture on marriage and wedding vows, but snapped her mouth closed when she saw the look of pure de-spair on her sister's face.

"I hate him, too," Rose said in a rush, then gave a hysterical little laugh.

Nicole looked stunned and Rose thought perhaps she'd made a mistake, perhaps she should have launched into her lecture about marriage vows, that perhaps a lecture was what Nicole truly wanted to hear to set her straight. When Nicole burst out laugh-ing, Rose knew she'd said the right thing after all. Still laughing, clutching her middle with her mirth, Nicole stood and hugged her little sister. Their laughter soon turned to tears, so raw were their emotions. After slobbering on each other a few minutes, the sisters broke apart, took in their red, swollen eyes and their wet faces, and laughed again.

"Oh, we're insane!" Rose shouted.

Nicole sat across from her again, covering her

mouth with the tips of her fingers and shaking her head. "What am I going to do?" Fresh tears coursed down her face. She answered her own question. "Nothing. There's nothing I can do! Oh, Rose. I'm so unhappy. Why did I marry him? I knew then. I knew it was wrong! But I let everyone convince me he was wonderful. A banker, older and wiser. A good provider, a good man." She shook her head again.

"Does he beat you?" Rose asked softly, thinking back to that Sunday dinner when Louis seemed to threaten Nicole.

Nicole let out a bitter laugh. "No. He's never hit me. It's difficult to explain what he does. It's constant . . . belittlement. He makes me feel as if I'm the fattest, laziest, dumbest female God created. At first, I couldn't believe he was saying such awful things to me. How could he if he loved me? But I know now he doesn't love me and probably never did. It wasn't so difficult before Flora was born."

Rose's heart nearly stopped. "Flora?" If he was hurting Flora, she'd confront the man herself.

"He won't let me be with her. You've seen how he is when she's crying. I want to hold her. It breaks my heart, Rose, to hear her little cries. And now she says 'Mama, Mama' over and over, screaming sometimes. And he won't let me go to her."

"Oh, Nicole," Rose said, reaching for her sister's hand.

"One night, Flora had been crying for, I don't know, a quarter of an hour. We were in the parlor but I could hear her. He's ordered the nanny not to go to Flora once she's put to bed. Says he doesn't want to spoil her," Nicole said with disgust. "I started to get up, ready to defy him. But all he had to do was *look* at me and I sat back down. Like a well-trained dog." She let out a long sigh. "When he's not here, I do spoil her, to try to make up for all those times when I can't. She's just a baby, Rose!"

"I know," Rose murmured.

"When I say it out loud, it all seems so petty."

"No, it doesn't."

"Yes. It does. But I can't help it. I loathe everything about him. Everything!" She shivered in revulsion, then lay a gentle hand on her stomach. "If this is a boy, Rose, I won't suffer it. He'll have his namesake. I won't, Rose. I can't."

Suddenly, Rose's worries seemed so insignificant. Her sister had been suffering for years in an unhappy marriage, forced to let a man she loathed touch her like that. Rose's life looked blissful in comparison. She loved Luke and he loved her. Oh, it was not the all-consuming, heart-wrenching love described in novels and poems, and perhaps it never would be. But at least she had a chance for that kind of love. Nicole did not.

"I'm sorry," Nicole said with a small smile. "You came here hoping that I would cheer you up and all I've done is complain about my life. I have a lovely home, a beautiful little girl. I have more than most."

Rose looked thoughtful. "I've decided something, Nicole. Just because you know someone somewhere is suffering more doesn't mean you aren't entitled to feel sorry for yourself a bit. I don't think God minds a little self-pity once in a while."

"Truly?"

Rose nodded decisively, as if she were the authority on the matter.

Nicole gave her sister's hand a little squeeze. "I'm glad you decided to visit."

"Perhaps next time I drop by we can do a little less crying and a bit more laughing."

A noise at the kitchen door distracted them; Mrs. Freebody had arrived, marking an end to their visit. But they knew as they said their good-byes that the distance that had inexplicably sprung up between them had been bridged. They had shared something that brought them back together, made them sisters again.

9

Luke watched as the rain fell in rivulets down his office window, following the trail of a single drop as if it were the most fascinating bit of nature he had ever seen.

"Luke, are you listening?"

"You were explaining to me about the raid," Luke said, his eyes still on the window.

"Yes, I was. Five minutes ago. Now I'm discussing the Windmill Hill case. It looks like it will go to court after all. I'm not certain Byer has had enough experience in the courtroom. This is a big, complicated case. What do you think?"

"Yes."

Arthur sighed. "It was not a yes-or-no question, Mr. Beaudette."

"Hmmm?"

"Luke, go have lunch. I'll meet with you at, say, two o'clock. Do you have anything scheduled?"

"No. That would be good. Hell, I apologize, Arthur. I'll be here at two. All of me," he said with a smile.

"Are you quite well?" Arthur had never seen Luke so distracted. Nothing could draw him away from discussion of an interesting case and the Windmill Hill case was damn interesting.

"Of course. I'll see you at two." Luke watched Arthur depart, a frown marring his face. Then he turned to watch the rain, his thoughts going once again to his lovely, frustrating wife. He was acting like a lovesick boy, not a man who'd been married for six months. But that was exactly what he felt like. He couldn't stop thinking about her. Luke chuckled bitterly. He was becoming obsessed with his wife! A part of him longed for the way it had been—quiet, uneventful. They'd had the kind of marriage he'd longed for. After the instability of his childhood, living with parents who were irresponsible and insouciant, all he'd wanted was something ordinary. He'd told himself he could live without the passion he'd tasted in that garden; most men did. Rose was an ideal companion—smart, beautiful, serene, pliable. Perhaps a bit boring. But that's what he loved about her, damn it! He didn't want a wife who sent him off-kilter, who raged one moment and begged forgiveness the next. A wife who with one look could make him want to drag her up against him, a wife who with one touch could make him want to cry with need. And yet . . .

Luke shook his head. Perhaps, he thought, that was exactly what he wanted. Why else would he be sitting in his office in the middle of the day thinking about her when he should be meeting with Arthur and discussing whether or not a green attorney could handle one of the biggest real estate cases to cross his desk? Of course Byer could not handle the damn case! With an impatient hand, he pushed his sandy hair back from his forehead. If not for Rose plaguing him, he could have made a decision. Instead, all he could think about was how warm her lips were, how she tasted. Of those maddening little sounds she'd made when he pleased her.

And then he would think of her pulling away, his body hard and straining. God, how he wanted her. It seemed the more she became what he thought he didn't want, the more he wanted her. With sickening realization, Luke discovered he was falling in love with his wife. That he'd already thought he loved her made this new feeling seem even more abhorrent. Luke realized he'd admired Rose, been pleased by her wit and charm, happy that she fit exactly into the mold he'd manufactured for a wife. But love? No, he had not loved her. Not like this.

He muttered a curse. It would only be worse now, the wanting and not having. He didn't want to love Rose in this all-consuming way. It made him feel like that little boy coming home for Christmas only to find his parents gone. His heart was exposed for the first time in years, and he hadn't the foggiest notion of how to cover it back up. Or whether he wanted to at all.

"Jesus," he whispered, a prayer and a curse. "How did I let this happen?"

Luke walked through the door that night, his heart in his throat. He hadn't seen Rose since he'd stormed out the night before, and now he regretted his harsh words, his crazy accusations. He glanced up the stairway, then down the hall toward the kitchen and dining room, listening for her. Hearing her voice coming from the back of the house, he threw his hat and coat on the hallstand, stopping to look in the mirror to take a swipe at his hair, and froze. He didn't like the look in his eyes, that bright hopeful look that made him feel laid bare.

Rose walked from the kitchen, her head slightly bowed as she gave instructions to a maid. Glancing up, Rose saw Luke standing there, but continued to talk to the maid, ignoring the mad beating of her heart.

"Hello, Rose." Just the sound of his voice did riotous things to her insides. She let the maid go about her job, stopping in the hallway directly beneath the gaslight fixture where she and Luke had shared their passionate kiss less than twenty-four hours before.

"Hello. Did you have a good day?" Rose was proud she was able to keep her voice so steady. What she wanted to do more than anything was throw herself into his arms. But with his cool gray eyes impassively assessing her, he seemed as he always did: formal and distant. And wonderfully handsome. Without a word, he came up beside her and laid a gentle hand at her elbow, guiding her to his study. Rose went with him reluctantly, glancing uncertainly up at his stern profile, trying to gauge his mood. Oh, she thought with awful disappointment, he's still angry. Her stomach twisted nervously.

"Actually, I did not have a good day," Luke finally said as they entered the room and he released her. Rose watched, her brows furrowed, as he walked over to the cold fireplace. "I don't like . . . arguing with you."

Rose's heart picked up a beat. "I don't like when you argue with me, either," she said, smiling expectantly at her little joke. She watched with surging hope as Luke's lips quirked upwards. He took a deep breath and turned toward her and Rose grew alarmed at the seriousness of his expression.

"I'm so sorry, Luke . . ."

He held up a hand to stop her. Thrusting his hands behind his back, he walked toward Rose, stopping an arm's length away. "When we were married," he began, his eyes on the far wall, "we promised to love one another, to cherish one another." He took a deep breath and swallowed.

Oh, God, Rose thought, he's going to say something awful. He's going to say he doesn't love me. "Well, yes, we did, Luke. And . . ."

Again he halted her mad attempt to stop him from saying more. In a terrible rush of pain, she knew she could not bear it if he did not love her. Her legs suddenly felt like water beneath her and she barely made it to the sofa before allowing herself to collapse onto it. Though her throat felt as if someone was squeezing it closed, she managed to choke out, "You don't have to say it, Luke. I know how you must feel about me. Please. Can't we just go on?" It was a cowardly thing to say, but Rose knew she would die to hear such words from him.

Luke suddenly looked angry; his eyes burned her with some emotion he obviously was barely keeping in check. "I do have to say this, Rose. For my own sanity." As if realizing he was shouting to her, he closed his eyes and took another breath. "Please do not interrupt me again. This . . . is not easy for me. You must know that."

Rose wrapped her arms about her waist, a vain attempt to keep this terrible pain at bay.

"When we were married," Luke began again, "I did not love you." Rose's head snapped up. Luke cursed and drew a fist hard against his thigh. "I'm not saying this right. Of course I loved you when we were married," he bit out, then gentled his voice. "Rose. Look at me." He sat down beside her and forcibly drew her hands from her waist into his warm grasp. Rose stared at the carpet, her breath coming in shallow little gasps.

"What I am trying to say in the most inept of ways is that I . . ." He stopped again, torturing himself as much as the woman who sat next to him looking completely stricken. "Jesus! If this were a courtroom I would have spat it out by now! What I am trying to tell you, Rose, is that I love you. With all my heart, with all my being. That emotion I felt before was . . . nothing compared to this terrifying thing I feel now." He had nearly been shouting, but he finished softly, "And I . . . I'm lost, Rose. I don't know what to do with it." He stood abruptly, letting out another curse. "You have to understand that I didn't mean for this to happen." He sounded so angry about it all, Rose nearly laughed, and her heart swelled so much at his words she wondered how it was still inside her breast.

"You didn't want to love me?" she asked with bewilderment.

"No! Goddamn it! Not like this."

"Whyever not?"

Whyever not. Luke looked at Rose, all the love he felt for her there in his eyes to see. "Because it hurts like hell."

Rose's smile broadened. "It does, doesn't it?"

Luke knelt before her, again taking her hands in his. "Are you telling me . . ."

Rose laughed, leaning forward and peppering his face with little kisses. "Of course I love you, Luke. Where did you ever get the notion that I did not?"

He crushed her to him then, his face nestled against her neck. "I do love you," he whispered against her ear. They held each other for a long moment, reveling in the feel of their arms wrapped so tightly around one another. Luke was the first to pull away, and

Rose's heart broke upon seeing the uncertainty still in his beautiful eyes.

"Why won't you let me love you, Rose?" He could almost see her tightening and pulling away though she didn't move. She bit her lips, then laid her head against his chest, her arms still wrapped about him.

"Give me time, Luke. Please. Just a little more time."

10

Flora laughed, a joyous sound that filled Nicole's heart—as did the man who made her little girl laugh. Anthony lifted Flora above him once again, letting her soar high above him, her giggles filling the sunny kitchen. When he finally set her down, she gave a little sound of protest, then toddled happily to a growing pile of pans set there on the spotless tile floor for her to play with. Nicole gave Anthony a grateful smile for making Flora so happy.

The first few moments of his visit had been unbearably awkward until Nicole presented him with a steaming cup of strong black coffee. The smile he gave her was dazzling. "You are a quick learner, Mrs. Baptiste."

They had sat at the table as they always did, across from each other, and talked about inconsequential things, letting their eyes meet occasionally. Anthony had been about to leave when Flora came toddling in, trailed by her harried nanny.

"It's all right, Miss Moreau, I'll watch her for a while." The nanny gratefully disappeared, knowing it would be hours until she would have to perform her duties again. Flora had walked directly to Anthony and wrapped her arms about one leg, craning her head back and beaming him a big smile.

"Ah, Flora, you wrap yourself around my heart when you look at me like that. Will you marry me, *amore mia*?" My love. He always called Flora that, his brown eyes gentle, and Nicole had no doubt Anthony loved Flora. After playing with her for several minutes, he let out a long sigh.

"I must be going. But I'll see you . . ."

"Monday." Nicole flushed. She always kept her dairy orders ridiculously small to ensure frequent visits from Anthony. It was these tiny orders that had finally made Anthony realize Mrs. Baptiste actually looked forward to seeing him as much as he looked forward to seeing her. "Let me get you what we owe," Nicole said, turning toward the cupboard where she kept the cash she used to pay for deliveries.

"What is she doing in here?" Nicole spun around at the sound of her husband's harsh voice. Her hands clutched the counter behind her, an unconscious gesture that bespoke her fear.

Louis gave Anthony a dismissive glance before speaking again. "How many times have I told you I don't want Flora in this dirty kitchen? She belongs in her nursery with her nanny. It is what we pay the woman for, is it not?"

Nicole darted an agonized look to Anthony, mortified that he should witness her humiliation. His beloved face as he gazed at Louis held a look of pure puzzlement, as if he couldn't quite fathom what he was hearing.

"Yes, Louis."

Louis gave her a sneering look. "Yes, Louis," he mimicked cruelly. "That's all you say. Yes, Louis. No, Louis. But you don't listen." He jabbed his head with his forefinger and glanced at Anthony so he could share his little joke. Nicole was afraid to look at Anthony, afraid of what she might see.

"Must I write things down for you? Would that make things easier to understand? It is not so difficult, is it, Nicole? Certainly you have the intelligence to understand me. But perhaps not. I ask that the girl stay in her nursery and I find her here in the kitchen. Twice. What is it about my words you find so difficult to understand? Because I know you would not defy me." He took a step closer. "Don't I?"

Nicole swallowed painfully. Oh, why did Anthony have to witness her shame? Why? "I'm sorry."

Louis lowered his head so he could look up at her, a movement that silently told her how little her apology meant. It made him look mean and ugly. "We'll talk about Flora's care this evening." He shot an impatient look toward Anthony. "What the hell are you gawking at?"

Nicole had never seen such an unfathomable expression on Anthony's face. He looked for all the world as if what he had just witnessed meant nothing, but Nicole knew that he was a breath away from doing something irrevocable. The hands at his sides were unclenched, but they shook slightly, the tendons taut as if under a terrible strain.

"He's just waiting for me to pay him, Louis."

"Well then, pay him, my dear. Or do you want me to do that, too?"

Nicole was silent. She could not trust herself to speak.

Louis patted her on the cheek, an unloving gesture. "Try to do what I say. Will you? If I hadn't forgotten my report at home . . ." He shook the papers in front of her in a faintly threatening manner. "I'll see you tonight, then, dear."

Nicole held herself rigid until she heard the front door close. She did not look at Anthony, who continued to stand by the kitchen door. The distant sound of the door slamming seemed to release them both. Nicole spun around, away from Anthony's inscrutable gaze, and covered her face with her hands. In three long strides, he was behind her, so close Nicole could feel the heat of him.

"Does he strike you?"

Nicole could only shake her head. She tried to be silent, but finally a sob burst through her hands pressed painfully against her mouth. And finally, finally, she felt his warm hand on her shoulder. It was too, too much, that kindness, that simple touch. Her hands still over her face, Nicole turned and leaned into his chest, letting out a sound filled with anguish.

Anthony stood still, looking down at the top of her head, at the uneven part and her white scalp, at anything that would stop him from taking her into his arms. For he knew if he did, he could never come back, that this woman, so much a part of his heart, would become embedded in his soul. But she was there, against him, her heart breaking. His resolve lasted perhaps ten seconds before he laid a hand against the back of her head and pressed her to his heart.

"Ah, *amore mia. Cuore mio.* Don't cry." He felt her shake her head. "You are so strong. My brave little one. You must continue to be strong."

She dropped her hands and wrapped her arms around his waist. "I'm not strong," she said against his coverall.

He placed a hand on each side of her face, forcing her to look at him. "You are strong, *amore mia.* Remember that. You love a man who you should not. And he loves you. And yet you stay here, as your vows insist that you do. You know that you will. Don't you?"

Fresh tears fell from Nicole's love-filled eyes. "I know," she whispered. "But it hurts. It hurts so much."

Anthony drew her against him, swallowing past the sudden thickness in his throat. "You know that I cannot come back here."

She knew. Oh, God, she knew. He pressed his lips against her temple, his hand strong and warm on her cheek. It was perhaps the agony Nicole felt in that kiss that gave her the strength to pull away.

Nicole sat in the kitchen for the remainder of the day, watching with numbed detachment as Mrs. Freebody, Millie, and Georgette bustled about the kitchen. At midday, milky clouds began to obscure the sun, causing little squares of sunshine to fade in and out on the kitchen floor. Nicole stared at those squares of light with the hint of a smile touching her lips and remained silent. The kitchen staff through an unspoken agreement let Mrs. Baptiste sit there, not minding as her eyes followed them about the room. The four of them were comfortable in each other's company and no word need be said aloud to tell the workers that Mrs. Baptiste wanted to be alone in their company.

The sound of a wagon brought Mrs. Freebody to the kitchen door. "Mr. Zamperini is here," she announced as she pulled back the curtain. "Late as usual." She swung open the door, letting in the sharp air, cool and mud-scented, a precursor of rain. "You're late, Mr. Zamperini. Perhaps Brouski's Grocers could be more prompt." It was a weekly ritual, their sparring, one that the two seemed to enjoy immensely.

"That Pollack, his flour got beetles. I heard from Mrs. Hull down on State Street. She had to bring it back and she call me where she know she can get good flour. You wanna flour on time or flour with beetles?" Mario Zamperini marched through the door, a tiny dark man with a huge voice. He barely topped five feet tall, even with his hat, and his sharply lined face, blurred by two days' growth of beard, was dominated by lively dark-brown eyes that seemed to smile even when he was grumbling. He wore a collarless shirt and an ever-present and always-clean white apron. Nicole often wondered if he kept a stack of clean white aprons in his wagon. As he unceremoniously handed Mrs. Freebody a sack of flour, he glanced over to the table and flashed Nicole a smile.

"Ah, Mrs. Baptiste. So good to see you," he said with a little bow. "I'm only a little late, yes? No big deal."

"Bah." That from Mrs. Freebody who produced her list to match against the order from Zamperini's Grocers. "I hope you remembered everything on the order. This time," she added pointedly.

Mr. Zamperini looked as if she had just called him a thief, so shocked was his expression, and Nicole had to smile. Dramatically shaking his head in time with his wagging index finger, he pronounced, "I never forget an item. Never. *Donna* you say that, Mrs. Freebody."

"Sugar."

"That was two years ago!" He turned to Nicole to explain. "We got a bad shipment of sugar. It was no good. I could not sell it to my customers. You tell me, Mrs. Baptiste, what should I have done? Bring in that bad sugar? No! But this . . . woman, she thinks I should give you the bad sugar." He let out a sound of disgust to which Mrs. Freebody responded with her typical snort.

Mr. Zamperini's visit had scraped away some of the numbness that had enveloped her body after Anthony had left. She supposed it was his wonderful Italian accent, which was much more pronounced than Anthony's but still so painfully familiar. She listened with amusement as Mr. Zamperini and Mrs. Freebody continued to exchange barbs as each item was brought in, her hands around a cup of tea that had long since grown cold. When the last item was delivered and paid for, he headed for the door.

"Mr. Zamperini, would you mind translating something for me?" she asked, her heart hammering in her throat. The grocer looked at her expectantly. "*Cuore mio.* I'm not sure I'm saying it right. *Cuore mio.* What does that mean?"

The little man tilted his head and smiled. With both hands over his heart, he said, "It means 'my heart.' *Cuore mio.* My heart."

11

Rose was still mulling over the note Collette had sent her that afternoon, suggesting she wear a particular gown, when she knocked on the Taylors' door Friday night. As Collette suggested, she wore her newest and most daring gown, which bared nearly her entire upper chest. Its soft silk, the color of palest rose, looked lovely with her dark hair and eyes, and gave her creamy skin a rosy glow. The only thing that marred the gown was the look Luke had given her and the words he had said that evening before he left for his club. At first, his eyes had held the unmistakable warmth of a man who is pleased with what he sees. But that was before he realized she had dressed that way to play cards at the Taylors'. Rose realized he hadn't truly been disagreeable until she mentioned Thomas Kersey would also be visiting the Taylors. He'd acted like a man fighting jealousy, which Rose would have found wonderful if Luke hadn't been so ill-mannered about the whole thing.

"I see you've decided to show complete strangers what your own husband has not seen." With that, he walked through the door. If Rose had anything in her hand, she would have thrown it at the door. Stupid man. Didn't he know that when she selected this gown, she did so with him in mind? It was as if those beautiful words of love he had uttered were figments of her imagination.

Rose pushed thoughts of Luke away as Collette answered the door. "We sent the housekeeper home early," she said, explaining why she was performing the duty of ushering Rose into their brownstone.

"Now. Please explain why I am dressed like this," Rose said, indicating her gown.

Collette clasped her hands together. "It's a surprise. You've heard of the notorious Supper Club?"

Rose nodded. She'd heard it discussed only in whispers, and knew it was not a place where people of her set usually went. Rose knew nothing about why it had such a nefarious reputation, but she knew a shroud of indecency hung over the place.

"Well, guess where we are dining this evening?"

"Oh, no, Collette. I couldn't." But she was smiling

and the curl of excitement in her belly told her that suddenly there was nowhere more she would like to go than the Supper Club, a place that everyone she knew would disapprove of.

"I know that look," Collette said, grabbing her arm in her excitement. "I'm a bit nervous as well. But John is such the adventurer. If it was up to me, we'd never do anything thrilling. I'd spend my Friday evenings doing cross-stitch or some such other tedious activity."

Despite her excitement, Rose was still skittish, her well-imbedded cautiousness warring with this newfound daring. She pushed down her trepidation, telling herself that eating in a restaurant would harm no one. What could be improper about an eating establishment?

Rose found she was faintly disappointed when they stepped out of their hired carriage in front of the Supper Club. It seemed extraordinarily ordinary, like any number of fine restaurants she had frequented with her husband. A smartly dressed doorman opened the carved wood door, bowing in a wonderfully old-fashioned way as they stepped through the entrance. Inside, several chandeliers glittered above the dining area where well-dressed patrons sat. Tables, draped with white linen that fell gracefully to the red-carpeted floor, sparkled with fine crystal and silver settings.

Rose silently chastised herself for her disappointment. What had she expected? Dancing girls?

A man greeted John by name, treating him in a deferential manner that both intrigued Rose and left her faintly curious. Perhaps this visit to the Supper Club wasn't as unusual for the Taylors as Collette had inferred. They were about to sit when Thomas Kersey arrived, apologizing heartily for not being able to accompany them in the carriage.

"I've already eaten," he said, patting his vest, "so I'll let the three of you spend your hard-earned cash on this fine fare."

John smiled. "Losing again, are we, friend?"

Thomas's grin only widened. "Will the three of you be joining me downstairs?" he asked, ignoring his friend's verbal jab. At John's nod, Thomas left them, walking off, his steps light, a man without a worry in the world. As Rose watched Thomas make his way from the dining room, her gaze moved to a man watching from what Rose guessed was the kitchen entrance. The man seemed vaguely familiar to her and she continued to stare at him until she became suddenly aware that the man was also looking at her. She quickly brought her eyes down to the table, and when she dared look again, the dark-haired man had disappeared into the kitchen. He obviously was a restaurant worker, and Rose, feeling vastly relieved, decided she could not know the man.

The food was plentiful and wonderful. Rose, who had never had shrimp in her life, was feeling especially daring that evening, and so tried a dish with the small, pink sea creatures. She took one bite and wondered why she'd allowed twenty-four years of her life to pass before trying such a delicacy. Shellfish always had looked too much like insects to her, and she had steered clear of them. But tonight she was feeling decadent and adventurous.

To Rose's dismay, dinner conversation was stilted. Collette in particular was unusually quiet and seemed to want to avoid all conversation. The excitement she'd displayed over going to the Supper Club had vanished entirely, leaving Rose wondering if Collette truly was uneasy about being at the restaurant. Each time she tried to look at her friend, Collette darted her eyes away.

"This really isn't such a daring escapade as I thought," Rose said, thinking to put her friend at ease.

"The night is still young," John said, and Collette shot him a pained look.

As their bill was paid, Collette leaned toward Rose. "How adventurous are you feeling tonight?" she whispered.

Rose, getting caught up in Collette's sudden excitement, bit her lips. "Very," she fairly burst out.

Collette stood, grabbing Rose's hand and nodding

to John, and then they left the table and headed toward the restaurant's entrance. But instead of walking out of the door, Collette and John led her down a hallway lit only sporadically by lamps hung on the walls. It appeared the hallway led to nowhere, and when they stopped before a blank wall, Rose's confusion was nearly as great as her trepidation. Suddenly, the wall at the end of the hall disappeared, sliding to the right and revealing yet another, shorter hallway. A large man stood at the end of the hall, his beefy arms crossed over a barrel chest. His head was tilted back and he looked at the group through eyes made into slits. He barely looked at John and Collette, but turned his eyes to Rose. She could feel those eyes on her even though they were so dark and so slitted, she couldn't say for sure the man was indeed looking at her.

"She's all right," John said, and the man moved out of their way. John opened the door, gallantly waving the two ladies in front of him.

"Where are we going?" Rose whispered, eyeing the steep set of stairs before them.

"On a grand adventure," Collette whispered back, then clutched her arm, as if she, too, were a bit frightened by what they were doing. At the bottom of the stairs, John heaved open a thick door that almost appeared to be made out of some kind of metal, and released the sounds of a large crowd and the biting scent of cigars.

Rose couldn't believe her eyes when they walked through that door. She felt like Alice walking into Wonderland, so unexpected was the vision before her. She knew instantly what she was looking at, although she had never seen one before in her life. It was a gambling hall. A well-attended, exceedingly large, and almost grotesquely opulent gambling hall. Everywhere she looked were men and women—though the men greatly outnumbered the fairer sex—standing by tables, shouting, cheering. It was madness to find herself standing in the midst of such activity. Such *sinful* activity.

Rose immediately turned and headed back to the door, only to be stopped by Collette. For an instant, she thought she saw anger in her friend's eyes, but Collette's words were anything but angry.

"Isn't this insane? I can't believe I allowed John to convince me to come here. I'm so sorry I tricked you, Rose. But I knew you'd never agree to come here and I was so afraid to come by myself."

Rose was too rattled to point out that Collette would have been with her husband and did not need Rose there.

"Please be a friend and don't move an inch from my side! I mean it, Rose. I'm scared to death!"

And then, Collette's eyes sparkled with mischief. "Isn't it exciting?"

Rose felt sick inside. This was certainly not exciting. She looked about the room, terribly afraid she would see someone she knew. No one in the crowd looked even vaguely familiar, and Rose began to relax. How angry Luke would be if he knew she was here. As if reading her mind, Collette said, "No one will ever find out, Rose. I can guarantee you that no one in our circle frequents this establishment. Most of these people come here from Boston and Providence. It's almost famous!"

"If everyone knows about it, how can it continue to operate?" Rose asked. She wondered how Collette knew so much about the secret gambling hall, and also found herself, to her shame, uncomfortable with Collette including herself in Rose's circle. It should not have bothered her, but she found, oddly, that it did.

Collette flushed at Rose's question. "I suppose people who gamble like it so much they make sure it stays a secret from the police."

Rose nodded. The Supper Club certainly had gone to great lengths to hide the existence of the hall, but she was still amazed that such a place operated in downtown Springfield, not four blocks from police headquarters—and just slightly further away from where her husband worked upholding the laws of Massachusetts. She wondered if Luke knew about the hall, and decided he must not. For if he did, surely he would have had it closed down. Certainly Rose could not be the one to tell him about it. After all, how would it be possible for her to know of such a place unless she had been there? It was too awful to even contemplate. A little spark of anger flared at the thought of how inconsiderate Collette had been to bring her here. Didn't Collette know how very inappropriate it was for the wife of an assistant attorney general to visit a gambling hall?

John had found Thomas and was waving at Collette and Rose to join them. Collette moved forward immediately, but Rose continued to hang back. She couldn't shake the feeling that Collette was far more comfortable moving about the hall than she was. Perhaps, she thought, it was because her husband was here. Rose let a hysterical bubble of laughter erupt at the thought of her own husband being by her side. Luke would be apoplectic!

Thomas sat at a table with a few other men, cards held in front of him. A man John explained was the dealer fed Thomas a card, which caused him to thrown down the rest of his cards with disgust.

"Vingt-et-un is not your game, my friend. You've lost more money at the blackjack table than anywhere else. Why don't you try something else?" John said, placing a companionable arm about Thomas's shoulders.

"Mind your own business," Thomas said good-naturedly, with only the slightest bite to his words.

"Shall I explain this game to you, Rose?" John asked.

Rose shook her head. "I'd rather not know."

Ignoring her, John explained that the dealer and the players were each trying to get as close to twenty-one as possible without going over. "It's as simple as that," he said. "But there are certain nuances of the game that seem to be lost on Thomas."

Thomas leaned back, allowing a hand to be played without him. "Is that so?"

"You see, Thomas here likes to take chances. I've seen him take a card when he's showing a seventeen. Now, what are the chances the next card won't put him over twenty-one? But he'll do it. He'll gamble."

"I only take a card if the dealer's showing a friendly up card," Thomas grumbled.

John pursed his lips. "How much have you lost tonight with your grand strategy?"

"None of your business," Thomas said rudely, not bothering to take the edge off his words with his customary grin.

"That bad, hmmm?"

"Go to hell."

"Thomas!" Rose exclaimed, surprised at his rudeness.

"What the hell did you bring her here for, anyway? You know she don't belong."

Rose looked at Thomas as if he'd slapped her and he immediately looked chagrined. "I'm sorry, honey. I just get churlish when the cards don't fall my way. How about I give you the grand tour of this little establishment?"

Accepting his heartfelt apology, Rose allowed Thomas to lead her through the hall, John and Collette trailing behind them. They stopped at various games—baccarat, poker, dice games of hazard and craps, finally stopping at the roulette wheel. For each type of game, other than poker, people gathered around the tables, some cheering and some so solemn Rose found it disturbing. Thomas explained that some people lost everything at the gaming tables, only to win it back with the single roll of dice. Rose was saddened by such stories and was dismayed by the edge of excitement she heard in Thomas's voice.

She was most fascinated by the roulette wheel. It seemed the most fun and easiest to understand of all the games in the hall. Seeing her interest, Thomas asked, "Like to take a try?"

"Oh, goodness, no. I'll just watch."

"I think I'd like to try," Collette said. "John, give me some chips."

He gave her a small handful of colored discs without hesitation, and again Rose wondered if the two hadn't frequented the gambling hall before. "You play roulette. I have to go speak with someone."

Collette gave her husband a little distracted wave, her attention already focused on placing her disc on the table. Turning to Rose, she said, "Which number?"

Rose shook her head, not wanting to participate at all. Wave after wave of anxiety washed over her. I should not be here, she thought. Whatever am I doing here? Thomas was right. I don't belong. "You choose," Rose said, trying to keep her voice light. She didn't want Collette to get angry with her, but she would have to leave—and soon. The excitement of doing something entirely out of character was dissipating, leaving Rose feeling slightly ill.

Still, when that wheel began spinning, some of the anticipation that showed clearly on Collette's animated face was contagious. When she won, Rose surprised herself by clapping loudly and letting out a squeal of delight that was drowned out by Collette's happy screech.

"I won! Oh, you must try this, Rose. You must. Here. Use one of my chips and put it on any number." Rose looked at the chip as if Collette was offering her moldy bread. She shook her head.

Collette let out an angry huff. "Oh, really, Rose. You are simply too good to be true. God will not strike you dead if you place a dollar wager on the roulette wheel. Honestly, I've never met anyone quite like you."

"Leave off, Collette," Thomas said. "If she doesn't want to gamble, she doesn't have to."

Dismayed that she had somehow caused a rift between the two friends, Rose stepped forward. "I will. It's okay, Thomas. Collette is right. I'm just being a ninny." She placed a chip on the number three spot and stepped away as if it might leap back at her. "See? Nothing to it." The croupier set the wheel spinning and Rose tried not to watch the wheel.

"Oh, too bad," Collette said. "Here, try again."

With a feeling of resignation, Rose placed another bet, trying to push thoughts of Luke away, of how disappointed he would be in her. She tried to tell herself she was having fun, that she was a grown woman who could do as she pleased. But her heart wasn't in it. Even as the wheel stopped on her number, she could only manage a smile while Collette jumped up and down, celebrating the win.

"See? Wasn't that fun?" Collette said, smiling at Rose and giving her arm a little squeeze.

"I suppose."

Thomas chuckled at her unenthusiastic response. "I'm afraid our dear Mrs. Beaudette is not destined to become a gambler," he said with affection. Rose gave him a smile of gratitude while Collette rolled her eyes in disgust.

"Try again?" Collette said, her voice sounding brittle. Rose shook her head, not caring if she disappointed her friend. She couldn't understand why Collette was acting this way, almost as if she didn't like her at all.

John approached them, a scowl on his face. "Let's go. Our evening is over."

Collette looked startled. "Go? You want *all* of us to go?"

"Yes," John hissed, grabbing his wife's arm none too gently. Collette put on a bright smile that was so obviously forced, Rose felt intensely uneasy. Something had happened, but it was obviously between Collette and John and she didn't want to interfere.

"I think I'll stay a while," Thomas said, looking with curiosity from Collette to John.

"Suit yourself," John bit out. He and Collette began

walking quickly, as if they couldn't get out of the hall fast enough, Rose trailing behind them, a frown marring her face.

An uncomfortable silence permeated the carriage during the ride back to Mattoon Street. The night, which had begun with such promise, had deteriorated, leaving Rose bewildered and unsettled. After she stepped from the carriage with John's assistance, she stuck her head back in.

"Will I see you tomorrow at confessional?" Rose asked, knowing she somehow sounded censorious, as if by asking such a question she was pointing out Collette's sins.

"Of course."

Rose entered the house quietly, looking immediately to the ornate grandmother clock near the stair's newel post. It was only ten o'clock, but Rose felt as if it should be much later. She was mentally drained and generally miserable. A small part of her fought with her feelings of guilt, rationalized what she had done wasn't so bad and had hurt no one. But so much of what happened that evening disturbed her. A glance at the empty hallstand told her that Luke was still out, and for that she was glad. She didn't think she could see him without blurting out where she had been that evening. She made her way upstairs, her hand heavy on the railing, her thoughts troubled.

There was something so strange about the evening, she thought. She just couldn't figure out what it was that bothered her so. Rose tossed and turned until she heard Luke's footsteps; the sound of his boots on the carpet in the hall seemed to pound into her heart. I should go tell him where I've been tonight, she thought frantically. Now. Go! But her body remained paralyzed even as she silently screamed to herself to let Luke know. For she knew that if she didn't tell him now, she might never have the courage later. Rose remained abed, her hands clutching her blankets, until exhaustion finally overcame her.

The next morning, she entered the breakfast room

with a bit of dread, the smell of eggs and ham making her slightly nauseous.

"Good morning," she managed to say through a throat that felt like a whole sausage was stuck in it.

"Good morning, Rose," Luke said, his eyes resting warmly on her. "I wanted to apologize for my short words last night. You looked lovely and I should have told you then."

"Oh." Rose's hands fluttered nervously, her guilt compounding with each kind word Luke uttered. "I . . . It . . . Thank you," she finally said, miserably.

He gave her a quick smile. "How was your poker game last evening? Would we be rich if cash were involved?"

Rose felt she was going to be sick. Truly, truly sick. Tell him, she shouted to herself. Luke was looking at her expectantly, a smile still on his beautiful lips, and she knew she couldn't do it. Couldn't say anything that would take that smile away, that would take his faith in her away.

"I'm afraid I'm not a cardsharp just yet," she said, hoping that her evasive answer was not technically a lie but knowing in her heart that it was.

"Perhaps you and I could practice later this afternoon," he said, and Rose thought she'd faint on the spot. He was being too darned nice! Why, of all days, did he have to be so agreeable? If he had been cranky, if he had started in again on how inappropriate her dress was for a night of card-playing, she might have told him that not only was her dress inappropriate, but so were her activities.

"That would be lovely," she managed. Just lovely.

Chapter Four

1

"Bless me, Father, for I have sinned. It has been one week since my last confession." So many sins. So many! Rose could not believe the words she was about to utter, did not have faith that God would truly forgive her simply by her saying aloud to a priest all that she had done.

"I fear I have a great many sins this week, Father," Rose began. She wanted to cry and it was only the comforting familiarity of the church that gave her strength. Thank goodness the inside of the confessional was so dark, as if it could suck the sins from her blackened soul and then allow her to reenter the light of the church.

"I lied to my husband. And I truly gambled this time. I knew it was wrong, but I did it anyway."

Father Beaulieu, as alarmed as he was to hear Rose Beaudette confess to such serious sins, couldn't help but smile gently at the obvious remorse he heard in her voice. Still, he was becoming concerned that this woman, whose greatest sin heretofore had been that she had "bad thoughts" about certain people, was now committing sins with disturbing regularity. One of the Lord's lambs had slipped further from the protection of the church and he was deeply troubled to find the lost lamb was Rose.

"Lying to your husband is quite serious," he said.

Rose closed her eyes. "I know," she whispered.

"You must tell him the truth, child. Although I ask the Lord to forgive you, it is only by telling the truth that God can truly forgive such a sin."

"Oh, but I cannot, Father. At least not yet. I will. I promise, but . . ."

At her argument, Father Beaulieu's bushy eyebrows shot up in surprise. "There are no 'buts' about it," he said, making his voice hard. Perhaps this lamb had strayed farther from the flock than he imagined.

"Yes, Father," Rose said, but she knew in her heart she could not tell Luke where she had gone and she felt her soul grow a big black mark that would never be erased.

Her penance was three rosaries, but Rose said four just in case God was counting. When she finally rose, her knees hurting slightly, she looked about the church, seeing entirely new faces from when she'd entered. Her penance had been so great, parishioners had come and gone while she prayed. She couldn't help but think back on the Saturday when she'd had so few sins she'd been embarrassed by her lack of penance. Collette was not among those kneeling in the pews, but as she made her way to the holy water, intending to wet her finger thoroughly, she saw a flash of blonde hair and bright pink coming from the confessional.

Collette walked quietly over to her. "Wait in the vestibule. I'll only be a minute."

A *minute*! How could that be? Rose wondered, knowing at least one of the sins Collette had to confess. Unless she didn't confess that particular sin. Rose, in a new spirit of forgiveness, decided it was none of her business what Collette confessed to. As she waited in the vestibule, chewing her lip in a way that would have made her mother frown severely, Rose's mind whirled with angry thoughts—not all directed at herself. How could Collette be so cheerful, so blasé about what they had done the night before? She realized that Collette's complete lack of concern could only mean one thing: The two women were further apart than Rose had imagined.

After only a short time, Collette joined her, grabbing her arm with enthusiasm and tugging Rose toward the church's heavy doors, one of which had been left open to allow the sweet spring air into the musty building. Despite herself, Rose found herself smiling instead of scowling at Collette.

"Don't you have any remorse at all, Mrs. Taylor?" she asked, shaking her head.

Collette was momentarily surprised, but recovered quickly. "You mean about last night? Well . . ."

"You don't, do you!"

"I thought it was fun," she said simply. "But I'm sorry to put you in such an awkward position. I didn't realize until I got home last night that you are possibly the last person in this city who should be frequenting secret gambling halls."

Rose let out a sigh of relief. Collette had understood, after all. "I was mortified! But it was my fault. I could have absolutely refused to stay. And no one forced me to make a wager on the roulette wheel."

"That's true," Collette said, waving a finger at her. "Naughty, naughty."

Just like that, Collette had Rose laughing. Just like that, all was forgiven and any misgivings she'd had about her friend's odd behavior were swept away, leaving Rose wondering why she could have had any doubts about their friendship.

"I don't want to ever go back there, though."

Collette hesitated for only a moment. "No. Of course not. Was it truly that disturbing?"

"Goodness, yes! Can you imagine Luke's reaction if he knew that not only had I gone into the gambling hall, but I actually placed a wager?"

Collette let out a musical laugh. "I would defend your honor! I would tell Luke that you were innocent, that I tricked you into going into the hall. Which is perfectly true and you should be very angry at me." Collette pouted, making Rose giggle.

"But you had nothing to do with my placing a wager," she said graciously.

"Not true!" Collette argued. "Why, I practically strong-armed you into placing that wager."

"I don't remember anything quite as violent as that."

Collette put the tip of her index finger into her bow mouth. "Now that I think back on it, you *were* entirely to blame. Why, as I remember it, it was your suggestion we go to that den of sin!"

Rose placed fists on hips. "I hope you plan to march right back into the church and confess that outrageous lie."

Collette suddenly became serious. "Truly, Rose. I hope you know that I am sorry about tricking you into going into the gambling hall. I thought it would be great fun. It never occurred to me that you would be so uncomfortable. I keep forgetting how different we are."

For some reason, Rose wanted to reassure Collette that she was just as adventuresome, that going to the gambling hall was a lark and placing a wager thrilling. But the truth of it was, Rose realized she was not like Collette. Going to the hall had bothered her a great deal and she would not pretend that it had not. "I wish I was more like you in some ways, Collette. You're a dear, dear friend." Collette looked away and Rose knew she was embarrassing her. "I didn't enjoy myself last night. I was a bundle of nerves all evening and almost fainted when we walked through that door and saw a gambling hall."

"I said I was sorry," Collette said, the impatience in her voice startling Rose.

"I know you are," she said softly.

Collette let out a little huff. "I have to go home now." Her tone still held a bit of a bite, but when she turned to Rose, she was beaming her sparkling smile. "Walk with me?"

"Of course." They walked side-by-side, saying little, and Rose again was besieged by the notion that she had somehow made Collette angry with her.

2

Midnight. Rose let out a sigh, hoping to empty her head of the thoughts that battered her and kept her awake. Her mattress seemed lumpy and uncomfortable, the blankets too hot, the air suffocating. But when she threw off the covers, she immediately became chilled. She tossed and turned with near-violence, yanking hair from her mouth with irritation, and finally lying flat on her back, her hands in two fists by her sides.

She stared at the canopy above her, dark gray in the moonlight, and thought about Luke, three doors down and sleeping like a baby, no doubt. After their heartfelt declarations of love, they had bewilderingly slipped back into normalcy. As if that warm embrace in Luke's study had never happened, as if she had dreamed Luke's sweet words. Though he was nice that morning at breakfast, he was not the amorous man he'd been in the study. "It's driving me insane," she said aloud in a harsh whisper. "And he doesn't seemed bothered a bit. Maybe I did imagine it."

Part of it was her fault, Rose readily admitted to herself. Guilt over her jaunt to the Supper Club had made her a rather silent dinner partner that evening. She hadn't wanted to say anything that would lead to a conversation about poker or the Taylors, which would inevitably force her to lie again. But in the days previous, they also had sat at the dinner table and in the parlor like distant relations passing a pleasant evening. Rose had toyed with the idea of calmly walking over to Luke as he sat engrossed in some law journal, and sitting in his lap. The mere thought heated her face and made her heart skitter ridiculously. He caught her staring at him and smiled, a distant, distracted smile that lasted perhaps two seconds before those eyes of his flickered down to read again.

Rose didn't notice that his eyes had stayed on one tiny spot on the page, that his grip on the journal tightened until the paper wrinkled, that he shifted in his chair with a little grimace. Her own eyes were staring at her hated needlepoint, taking in the imperfect stitches with indifference.

"He's made of stone. And for one magic day my fairy godmother sprinkled some dust on him and he became a different man," Rose whispered, her lips drawing down in a little pout. "And now my statue husband is sleeping like a rock while I'm here wishing . . ." What?

In one quick movement, Rose tore back the blankets and stepped out of bed. She took two hesitant steps before plunging ahead with determination toward her door, not bothering to put her robe over her white cotton nightdress. "If he's sleeping, I'll wake him up. Why should I suffer while he sleeps!"

She padded down the hall, her feet silent on the thick carpet, pausing only when she reached his door. No light showed beneath it and all was silent. Encouraged by her past visit, which had gone undetected, Rose quietly opened the door and slipped inside Luke's room. She narrowed her eyes. Just as she thought—he was fast asleep.

Brilliant moonlight gave everything in the room a silver glow, making the unclothed man on the bed look as if he were cast in sterling, a classical statue dipped in that precious metal and placed on a bed made to look like a man asleep. The window's shadow was sharply outlined on the carpet, a glowing rectangle rising halfway up the side of Luke's massive bed.

As before, Luke lay on his stomach without a stitch of clothing on. The pillow was on the floor, and only his feet were covered by the blanket. Rose stepped further into the room, her eyes riveted on her husband. With every step, her heart beat more painfully. What was she doing in here? What if Luke awoke— for she no longer intended to wake him. What possible explanation could she give to him to be skulking about his room in the middle of the night? As she stared at her husband, seeing him naked for only the second time, Rose knew what she would tell him. She knew what she would do.

She stepped closer and closer, almost willing him to open his eyes, and yet so afraid that he would. Once she reached the side of his bed, she took a deep, silent breath. His hair was tousled in sleep as it never was during the day, curling over his brow in a way that made Rose's heart wrench. Without thinking, she reached out her hand toward one errant lock, stopping herself just before she touched it, her hand shaking slightly. She began pulling away when her wrist was suddenly enveloped in an iron grip.

"Luke!" she shrieked. "Oh, goodness! You frightened me half to death."

Luke lay unmoving, except for those intense eyes of his. "I'm rather startled myself, Rose, to find you in my room in the middle of the night."

Rose tried to straighten, but Luke's grip on her wrist was unrelenting. "Yes. Well. I . . ." She was going to lie, make up some wild story: "I heard a noise in here and thought I would investigate." But with a short little breath, she knelt down beside his bed, her head just inches from his. With more courage than she thought she had, Rose drew the hand that still held her wrist toward her mouth and pressed her lips against his knuckle. He let go of her as if she'd touched his hand with a hot coal.

"Why are you here?" he whispered.

"I wanted to touch you," Rose said, and lifted her chin a notch. Luke closed his eyes and for an agonizing moment Rose thought he was about to banish her from his room.

"You may."

"But you can't touch me," she said.

His eyes snapped open. "That doesn't sound fair," he said, his voice low and his tone so serious Rose knew he had to be playing with her.

She bit her lip. "Luke. Please, I . . ."

"All right, Rose. I'll try." And he closed his eyes again as if he were planning to drift back to sleep.

Rose drew her brows together in a fierce frown. Her insides felt like a swarm of bees were buzzing about yet he could close his eyes and relax as if she waltzed into his bedroom every night asking to touch him.

"I hope I'm not keeping you awake," she said a bit testily.

Luke's eyes opened lazily. "Hmmm?"

Rose stood with a jerk, hands on hips, and walked to the other side of the bed so that she wouldn't have to climb over Luke to get onto the bed. She climbed aboard, marching over to him on her knees with the determination of a soldier readying for battle. She'd show him! Go to sleep, would he? She began twisting her ring in consternation as she looked down at his marvelous prone form just inches from her knees, which had become bared as she hiked up her gown to walk across the bed.

"I'm going to touch you now," she said, more to herself than to the still man in front of her. Why, it looked as if he'd already drifted off to sleep.

Rose laid a hand at the nape of his neck. Safe. She'd already touched him there many times. Her hand moved up and she watched her fingers become lost in his thick hair; only slices of silver showed where her fingers were. Feeling a bit braver, Rose moved her hands to his shoulders and smiled. Oh, this was wonderful, to touch Luke like this. His skin was warm velvet beneath her hands, and she felt something dark and thick swirling in her belly.

As if in a trance, she moved her hands down his well-muscled back, absorbing every animal curve, every powerful swell. His back dipped to his spine and she let her finger trail down that gentle valley until it reached the first swell of his buttocks. And there she stopped, her eyes darting to his face to see if his eyes were open. She moved her hand back up, then stroked him, up and down, reveling in the feel of his skin beneath her hands. Luke let out a long sigh and Rose knew he was not asleep. Good.

She began with her lips where she had been with

her hands, pressing a soft kiss against his nape. Following the path her hands had taken, she left a trail of lingering kisses down his back. Down down. Until her lips hovered over his muscled buttocks, round and firm, just inches from her mouth. She heard his breath catch in his throat, then brought her lips down to kiss him there, her hand resting lightly beside her mouth.

Rose watched as Luke's hand clenched at the sheets beneath him, the muscles in his arms bulging with the strain. For the first time, Rose experienced her woman's power. It was a wonderful, heady thing to realize that one's mere touch could drive a man to clench his fists in pleasure. She frowned. Certainly pleasure was why he was grabbing so convulsively at the sheets.

"Luke?"

After a few short gasps. "Yes. Rose."

He sounded quite normal, Rose thought, still frowning. "Was that quite . . . all right?"

He let out a strangled sound. "Quite."

"Then I suppose I'll continue."

"Oh, please do."

And she did. Feeling inordinately seductive and practiced, Rose grazed his thighs with her lips, darted her tongue out at the back of his knees, then made her way back up his glorious body very, very slowly.

"Luke?"

Luke was not sure he could manage speech. He swallowed. He thought of the Windmill Hill case. The fact that his brown shoes needed a good polishing. "Yes, Rose?"

"I've finished with the back. I thought I would proceed to the . . . front."

Oh, Jesus God. The front. He couldn't endure it. My God, he had been a hairsbreadth away from rolling over and throwing her down beneath him. It was only sheer will and the dawning knowledge that if he did not allow her this, it might never happen again that kept him from doing so. If she became frightened, he might lose forever the chance to love her.

He turned over slowly, watching with grim amusement as her eyes shot to the part of him that showed her just how successful her seduction had been. "Oh," she whispered.

"Yes, indeed." Luke propped himself up onto his elbows and gazed at his wonderful little seductress, thanking God for the bright moonlight that let him see her so well. She bit her lips and gave him a timid smile. Placing his hands beneath his head, Luke said with as much calm as he could, "You may proceed." He closed his eyes and waited a lifetime before he felt the first tentative touch of her lips on his jaw. He could only be thankful she was foregoing exploration by hand and was moving directly to those enticing lips, for he was quite certain he would not be able to endure on his front what he had on his back.

Rose kissed his neck, breathing in his male scent of outdoors and the tiniest hint of cigar smoke. She rested a light hand on his smooth and muscled chest as she kissed the hollow of his throat. Rose felt electric, as if every bit of her body could feel. Her nipples rubbed softly against the smooth cotton of her gown, such an exquisite feeling she wanted to moan aloud to let escape some of the wondrous sensation before she burst from it. Eyes closed, her hand skidded down his flat stomach, stopping momentarily at his navel, and moving lower . . . She jerked her hand back. Oh, she hadn't meant to touch him there. Not just yet. It seemed as if Luke stopped breathing at that whisper of a touch, and Rose smiled. She opened her eyes. There "it" was—in Rose's limited knowledge of body parts, the man-part had always just been "it" in her mind.

"Should I . . ."

In one smooth movement, Luke was kneeling on the bed in front of her, hands gripping her arms as he hauled her up so she kneeled before him. He dropped his hands. "Why don't we take off your gown. Would that be all right?"

Rose hesitated only a moment before untying the lacing at her throat and bringing the nightdress over her head. She wanted to be naked, she wanted Luke to touch her as she had touched him and that knowledge filled her heart to bursting. Luke let out a long ragged breath, his eyes sweeping over her. "You take my breath away," he said. "All this time you have been hiding this from me? It's probably better that I didn't know."

He leaned forward to kiss her, his chest brushing lightly against her erect nipples. Oh, it was better, so much better than anything Rose had ever imagined, this feeling of skin against skin. She pressed a little closer, experimenting with this new sensation. When she felt his arousal brush up against her thigh, her first instinct was to pull away, and a tiny spark of panic erupted in her belly, quickly doused by Luke's searing kiss. Letting out a moan that sounded more like pain than pleasure, Luke wrapped his arms about her and kissed her with near-violence. He ended the kiss abruptly, pulling back, out of breath.

"I'm sorry, sweetheart. I'll go more slowly."

Rose heard the fear in Luke's voice and she felt close to tears. "No, Luke. I want you to touch me. I want you to. I've wanted you to forever."

He looked in her eyes a long moment before dipping his head and kissing her, long and slow, his tongue making lazy circles with hers. It was crazy what that tongue could do to her entire body as it teased her lips, almost as if he were teasing all of her. His hands moved up and down her back, learning her the way she had learned him. His mouth was doing marvelous things to her ear, her jaw, her neck. Oh, he was good at this, she thought with wonder, letting out a pleasure sound. With a strangled groan, Luke dipped his head lower, teasing the swell of her breast with his tongue before finally, finally, taking her nipple into his mouth.

"What . . . Oh . . . Oh, Luke." She dropped her head back, all her thoughts centered on his mouth sucking first one nipple, then the other. She didn't care if this was quite proper, she only knew that she had never felt anything so lovely in her entire life. When Luke pulled away, she let out a little sound of protest, all thoughts of what was proper and dignified far gone, and pulled his head back to her breast. "That's quite nice," she managed to say between gasping breaths.

Luke let out a pleased growling sound before taking her hand and pressing it to himself. "Touch me, sweetheart. Please." As he continued to pleasure Rose with his mouth, she wrapped her hand around him, reveling in the impact that simple caress had on his powerful body. He stiffened, arching his back away from her, and let out a strangled sound before pulling her hand gently away.

"I'm so close, Rose. I can't let you. Not this time." He let out a chuckle. "Do you know how much I love you?"

Rose smiled, her white teeth flashing in the dark. Luke, one hand behind her neck, drew her to him for a long kiss that left Rose weak and giddy. "I want to love you now," he whispered against her lips.

"Isn't that what we've been doing?"

He laughed, a sound full of joy and happiness. "Yes, love. That's exactly what we've been doing." He kissed her again, drawing her down on the bed with him so that they lay side-by-side. He stroked one warm hand the length of her body as his mouth teased her breast again. With a hand that trembled slightly, he caressed the inside of one smooth thigh, giving Rose subtle instruction to open her legs for him. Rose, feeling decadent and wanton, did as he asked.

Luke lifted his head and gazed down at his wife. "I'm going to touch you, Rose." She answered with a kiss. At his first tentative caress, Rose closed her eyes and let herself feel. "Jesus, Rose. You're so . . . so . . . ." He began moving his hand between her legs and Rose gasped at the piercing pleasure his touch brought. She couldn't have imagined something could feel this good. From her breast to the very center of her, she was burning for his touch. Rose heard herself letting out frenzied little sounds, felt herself arch against him. Luke moved between her legs, his hand still pleasuring her, driving her to the brink of . . . something wonderful.

"I'm going to go inside you now, Rose." His voice sounded harsh in her ear.

"Yes, Luke. Now."

As he slid inside, Luke let out a choking sound and for a long moment he held there, not moving, his body taut, muscles bunched and quivering. And then he began to move, slowly thrusting, holding Rose close, kissing her neck, her breast, everything his mouth could reach. Rose moved beneath him, caught up in what was happening to her, letting herself flow with the river of feeling that was becoming more and more turbulent. And then she was there, a place she'd never imagined, spiraling down, all sensation, all pleasure. Oh, she thought, what a wonderful place to go.

Luke thrust one last time, his face buried in the nape of her neck, letting out a strangled sob. Rose moved her hands up and down his slick back, relishing the feeling of having been well loved. She slowly became aware that Luke's entire body was shaking and that the wetness she felt on her shoulder was not sweat, but tears.

"Luke?"

He let out another agonized sob and then he laughed. "Thank you, Rose. Thank you," he whispered raggedly.

Rose's heart overflowed. It was not possible to keep all the love she felt for this man in that little place beating so rapidly in her breast. They stayed together until they were both breathing normally, until those brief tears he'd shed had dried. Luke withdrew slowly, as if reluctant to move away even that much.

"When did this happen?" he whispered. "When did I begin to love you so much?"

Rose laid a hand on his cheek. "I've heard rumors that people in love are supposed to be happy."

He laughed, nuzzling her ear with his lips. "I *am*

happy, Rose. Happier than I've ever been. Happier than I ever thought I could be."

Rose lifted herself up on one elbow, no longer shy in front of him. "Then why do you sound so sad? Why did you cry?"

"Men don't cry," he teased.

"Luke Beaudette! Are you telling me you're not a man?" She shot a look between his legs as if to look for proof of his sex. He laughed, pulling her close, crushing her to him almost desperately.

"I love you so damn much."

"Don't swear," she said, kissing him softly. "I love you, too."

3

"You're late."

Rose looked up to see her mother, her mouth pulled down into a frown. Luke handed off his hat and coat then assisted his wife by removing her hat pin and hat as she tugged at her gloves. Unused to this duty, Luke pulled the hat off as he would have a man's, and mussed up her hair in the process. As Rose explained that the two had attended ten o'clock mass instead of the earlier service, he tried ineffectually to pat down the errant strands that came loose. Finally distracted by her husband's ministrations, Rose began laughing.

"What are you doing?" she asked, laughter in her voice.

He cocked an eyebrow. "I thought I was assisting you, madam."

"You seem to be quite good at mussing up my hair," Rose said jauntily, and then playfully made to ruin his hair, which he had carefully slicked back in a vain attempt to stop it from curling onto his forehead.

Rose's mother watched them, a frown deepening the lines around her mouth. "We were about to sit down for dinner," she said.

"We're in trouble now," Luke whispered into Rose's ear.

The older woman stiffened, and Luke quickly tried to make amends. "We're very sorry for being late, Mother," he said, kissing his mother-in-law's dry cheek. She seemed somewhat appeased, but gave them a disapproving look before turning and leading them to the dining room where the family had begun to gather for dinner.

"We'll be there momentarily," Luke called to the departing back of Aline Desrosier, her old-fashioned bustled skirt looking much like the stern of a departing ship. Rose made to follow her mother but was stopped by Luke's firm grip on her arm. Pulling her into a small parlor off the home's grand entryway, he swept her into his arms and gave his wife a long, passion-filled kiss.

"I've wanted to do that all morning," he whispered.

"Truly?" Rose asked, still breathless from the kiss.

"That . . . and more."

Rose flushed red and dipped her head. This burgeoning intimacy between her and Luke was still too new to treat lightly. They had made love twice more, laughing like children, losing themselves in each other. The last time had been just hours before. Rose had awoken to the wonderful feeling of a man beside her—or to be more precise, behind her. She'd been tucked into the powerful curve of his body, slowly becoming aware that Luke was awake, too. Very awake. He'd teased her nipples, brushed her shoulder with his warm mouth, pressed himself against her so that her entire body once again was on fire. He came into her that way, barely moving but for a hand that pleasured her and a slow, languid movement of his body as he pleasured himself. It had been astonishing to Rose, who had never imagined that a man and woman could make love in more than one way. Afterward, when she told him her surprise, his eyes had glowed as he told her there were many, many ways they would love each other. And he planned to try them all.

"Today?" she'd asked, anticipation clear in her voice.

Luke had thrown his head back and laughed. "We can only try," he'd said.

Church had been awful! Rose could not get images of her and Luke writhing naked together out of her head. She tried to pray, tried to listen to Father Beaulieu's sermon and get lost in thoughts of God. But with Luke standing beside her it had not been easy, especially when she had looked up at him through her lashes and he had given her a look that nearly burned the clothes from her back.

And now she would have to endure dinner with her family when she knew what Luke wanted to do, what she wanted to do. Just looking at him made her insides turn all hot and liquidy. Looking at Luke had always made her jittery and warm. But this new feeling was extraordinary. Surely, this was not normal. How could couples manage to go about their daily business feeling like this all day? Rose wondered. Perhaps she and Luke were unique. Then she recalled how Collette and John were together and she realized that she was not unique—simply fortunate. She felt sorry for those other couples, the ones who had been like Luke and she used to be, who never shared this wonderful . . . connection. It was a wondrous thing.

Rose smiled up at Luke and pretended to adjust his tie. Feeling wanton and wicked, she leaned against him, smiling when she realized he was hard for her. "I don't think my mother would approve of the 'and more' part," she said with a little pout.

He nipped her lips, letting out a low growl. "Who turned you into this little wanton?"

Rose gave him a look of pure innocence. "I believe, sir, that you did. This is entirely your fault."

"Mmmm." He nuzzled her neck above her high collar and she lifted her chin to accommodate him. "All the evidence has not yet been presented, madam. It may be you are somewhat responsible for your own behavior."

Rose let out a shaky breath. Oh, that mouth of his was doing amazing things to the tiny bit of flesh left exposed by her staid gown. "I concede that point, Your Honor."

"Oh, here"—Nicole stopped, a shocked look on her face—"you are."

In one motion, Luke maneuvered so that Rose stood in front of him facing Nicole, as her eyes moved from one to the other. It was impossible to see Nicole's expression, for the parlor was dark from drawn drapes and the entryway behind her was brighter, casting her in silhouette.

"We were . . . we were . . ." Rose stuttered.

"Kissing," Luke finished for her.

"Luke!" Rose exclaimed with embarrassment.

Having recovered sufficiently to leave the room, Luke guided Rose out of the parlor. "It's all right, sweetheart. We've been married seven months. It's allowed," he whispered with exaggerated drama.

Mortified, and not quite sure she should be, Rose looked at her sister to gauge her reaction and was relieved when she realized Nicole was trying not to laugh. "Oh, I wish I had let Mother come get you!" she said with a giggle. "Don't you know it is against house rules to kiss, show affection, or behave in any manner that could be deemed a pleasant activity?"

Rose laughed, but noted there was bitterness in Nicole's words.

With grave seriousness, Luke said, "Mrs. Baptiste, I'll have you know that I place kissing your sister in the category of duty, not pleasure."

Knowing he was joking, Rose nodded her head solemnly. "I can assure you, Nicole, it was entirely unpleasant."

Luke turned to Rose, a look of disbelief on his face. "Is that so?"

Rose glanced at her sister, who seemed to be enjoying the banter, before turning back to Luke. "I endured."

With that, heedless of Nicole standing there, Luke pulled Rose into his arms and gave her a searing kiss. It lasted only a few seconds, but it left Rose's knees weak. The couple could have lit the grand house with the electricity that shot between their eyes.

"From my objective viewpoint, you have clearly broken house rules," Nicole said dryly. Her face was red at having witnessed such naked passion between her sister and husband, but Nicole also was inordinately happy to see so much love between them. Obviously, the tiff they suffered had been resolved. Nicole had never seen the two of them quite so enamored, and part of her ached to see that happiness.

As she walked to the dining room, Luke and Rose following behind, she could hear their lovers' banter. They were so obviously in love, Nicole wondered what happened between them. Though she had been wrapped up in her own misery, she also had noted that Luke and Rose did not share a grand passion for one another. They had obviously enjoyed each other's company, could make each other laugh, but there had been something missing. Each had seemed sad somehow when looking at the other, a soft yearning that Nicole recognized and was saddened by. Now, though, all the sadness was gone.

They're in love, she thought. In love so deeply, they don't care who knows. It came upon her suddenly, a wave of envy that crashed through her, leaving her weak with it, that they could love each other so. Unbidden, Anthony's well-loved face invaded her thoughts, as it so often did. If she and Anthony had been free to love each other, that was how they would have been, the way Luke and Rose were now.

Nicole walked toward the dining room, her feet encased in lead, listening with growing bitterness to the couple behind her. She bit her lip, ashamed that she should feel anything but happiness for Rose, but she couldn't stop herself. She was walking toward a dining room filled with people she loathed. Her husband, with his thin little mustache and receding hairline, his paunch that so repelled her when he came to her at night. His hands, pale and thin and too feminine for the rest of him. And her mother, who never smiled, who never had a kind word to say, but who acted unaccountably hurt if she were not asked to accompany Nicole on an outing.

It is so unfair, her mind screamed. I hate them! I hate everyone! And then she heard Flora begin to cry, the high-pitched screech that meant she was truly distressed, and it took all her will not to scream and scream and never stop screaming. But when Nicole walked through the door, her face was passive, her step sure.

"You've coddled her," Louis said. "She hit her head on the table. Barely touched it, and listen to her. I told her to be careful, but she doesn't listen. I say let her cry."

Nicole pressed her jaw together until her teeth hurt. Kneeling down, she examined her little girl's head and spotted a red mark near her hairline. "Oh. That must have hurt, honey. Mommy will kiss it better." She did, but the little girl continued to cry.

"Let her cry." His voice went right through her, bossy, mean.

Nicole picked Flora up, ignoring Louis, and finally her cries turned into hiccuppy little things. "All better?"

Flora nodded, her expression so serious that Nicole had to smile and all those suffocating thoughts were swept from her mind. "Why don't we all sit down," she said.

"About time," her father muttered. They were the only words the man spoke all day.

"Mrs. Thibedeau died," Aline pronounced. It was how many Sunday dinners began, with a list of people who had died during the previous week or a recounting of wakes and funerals, most of which everyone in the room had attended. If no one had died, she came up with a list of people who were about to die, usually because of some bad habit or other self-inflicted malady. No one ever simply got sick, they became ill because of a specific reason, one usually related to the person's character.

Rose felt the familiar and unpleasant tightening in her stomach and looked across the table at Nicole to see if she thought the same thing. To her delight, Nicole crossed her eyes at her the way she'd done as a girl when the two were in agony over some boring dinner conversation.

"Did you go over to Collette and John's Friday evening?" Nicole asked when there was a lull in the obituaries.

Rose flushed. "Yes." Not a lie. She was there for a time.

"Whatever do you do over there?" Louis asked as he took a large gulp of red wine, clearly disapproving that Rose had friends outside the home whom she visited without Luke.

"We laugh." Rose could barely keep the animosity from her voice, especially now that she knew the lout was making Nicole so unhappy.

"They play cards, don't you, Rose?" Nicole said, her eyes beseeching Rose to try to be nice to her husband for her sake.

"Poker," Luke said, and Rose nearly choked on the water she was drinking. She shot him a look of disbelief that he would say such a thing in front of her mother. He got exactly the reaction he was looking for, apparently.

"Poker!"

"Yes, Mother. But only for fun. We don't gamble." And Rose cringed at the lie, picturing herself at the roulette wheel after she'd finally given in to Collette's cajoling. If her mother was shocked that she'd played poker, imagine how she'd feel if she knew her daughter had frequented an illegal gambling hall.

"Still. That doesn't seem right. You approve of this, Luke?"

"I've forbidden it, Mother. But she goes anyway."

Rose looked at Luke as if she would find great pleasure in killing him on the spot.

"Rose," her mother said, voice dripping with disappointment and disapproval. "You should obey your husband."

"Luke, you tell my mother the truth," she said, laughing at his play. "After all, you are the one who volunteered to teach me the finer points of the game."

It was Luke's turn to choke. "It's true, Mother. I was just having a little fun with Rose. She plays cards over the Taylors' with my blessings."

Her mother continued to frown. Now they were both the objects of her scorn, Rose thought. Her mother's disapproval would have paralyzed her in the past, but today, it was simply amusing. Still, guilt over lying to Luke about where she had been Friday night plagued her anew. She should tell him, she thought, and then almost immediately came to the conclusion she should not. Their newfound love was too wonderful to ruin with another spat. Luke would be very angry—and for good reason—if he discovered she had been at the Supper Club's secret gambling room. Though lying to Luke bothered her, the thought of his reaction if she told him the truth was much more bothersome.

"I don't like the idea of you playing cards with people I don't know," her mother persisted.

"They are very nice people," Rose said. Even as she said the words defending the Taylors, a part of her rebelled. The Taylors were not very nice, not in the way she knew her mother thought she would mean by such a description. They were exciting and fun and perhaps a bit dangerous, Rose thought, trying to tamp down the misgivings she'd had about her friends since Friday night.

"Do you like these people?" Louis asked Luke, and Rose tensed. She felt Luke's eyes on her, could almost see him weighing his words.

"I don't know them well enough to say," he said, finally. "But I trust Rose's judgment."

4

Luke walked into his office Monday morning, nodded to the two men sitting in front of his desk, and slapped a large leather folder down atop the polished surface. Still standing, he faced Arthur Ripley and Patrick Sullivan, the man who'd infiltrated the Supper Club. "Sorry I'm late, gentlemen. I've just come from police headquarters. Chief Farwell, needless to say, was not happy the raid was aborted. The man cannot understand that we would have lost months of this investigation had we gone ahead. The chief is champing at the bit to arrest Cardi and I wouldn't be surprised if he calls Max in on this thing."

"Do you really think he'd go above your head to the attorney general?" Arthur asked.

Luke shrugged. "I'd not be overly concerned about it even if he does. Max knows we're trying to put Cardi away for good. He's with us on this one." He brought out his watch. "I have a meeting with the mayor in one hour, gentlemen, so I want this briefing as concise and detailed as possible. Charles," Luke called to his assistant. "Takes notes on this, would you?"

Arthur shifted in his seat. "Why don't we hold off on taking notes for now, Luke," he said pointedly.

Luke gave his friend a searching look. "I'll call you when we're ready for you, Charles." Turning back to the two men, Luke sat down. Somehow he knew that whatever it was that Arthur and Patrick were about to tell him, he would be better off sitting. "You've something to tell me that you don't want in the official notations?"

The two men looked at each other with something like dread. Arthur began twiddling his thumbs and immediately stopped when Luke shot an irritated look at the restive movement. "This is damned awkward, Luke."

Luke, who had simply been curious, now felt fingers of fear at the back of his skull.

"Friday night, Sully was in the club. And . . ." Arthur took a deep breath, then apparently decided to spit out his information without any more dallying. "Luke, your wife was at the club."

Luke creased his brow and shook his head slightly. "Rose? At the Supper Club? You must have been mistaken, Mr. Sullivan."

Looking a bit sick, Sullivan said, "No, sir. It was your wife. I'm certain of it."

Luke looked from one man to the other and saw the same thing in each man's eyes—certainty and regret about what they were reporting. And pity. Luke's cheeks stained with color and his stomach clenched uncomfortably. "Give me the details," he bit out.

"Luke . . ."

"Give me the details," he repeated succinctly.

Sullivan straightened in his chair. "At approximately eight o'clock in the evening last Friday, your wife arrived with three other people. Two are unknown to us, a couple. We've since learned they are . . ." Sullivan began looking through his notes.

"Collette and John Taylor," Luke supplied, his lips tight.

"Yes. The third is a known small-time crook and big-time gambler, Thomas Kersey. He's in heavy with Cardi."

"How much?" Luke asked, trying to maintain control of his emotions. Thomas Kersey. It was a name he'd heard before from his own dear wife. The same man who'd gone swimming with her and the Taylors and the same man who'd played cards with them Friday nights. Quite a cozy little group they were becoming, Luke thought.

"About ten grand."

Arthur whistled and Luke raised his eyebrows.

"The Taylors and your wife ate dinner, then proceeded downstairs. Kersey was already down there."

Luke's mouth hung open in disbelief. "She went
into the gambling hall? Are you certain?"

"Yes, sir."

Luke shook his head once and gazed at his desktop.

"I knew it was your wife, sir, and I felt obligated
to follow them down."

"I understand. Go on."

Sullivan looked at Arthur uncertainly. There was
something fearsome about Luke at this moment.

"At first the two women and John Taylor simply
watched Kersey gamble. Watched him lose, that is.
Then they went over to the roulette wheel. From my
perspective, it appeared your wife was uncomfortable
and nervous. At first it did not seem as if she wanted
to join in, but she finally did, sir. Two or three spins
of the wheel. She won."

Luke leaned back into his chair, laced his hands
behind his head, and looked at the ceiling. "Are you
telling me that my wife played the roulette wheel?"

Sullivan swallowed. "Yes, sir."

He leaned forward suddenly, startling the other
men. "I'll be damned," he said.

An awful, thick silence permeated the room as the
two men waited to see how Luke was taking this bit
of news. Finally, he said, "Mr. Sullivan. What was my
wife's demeanor?"

"Excuse me, sir?"

He smiled a hard smile "How was she acting?
Happy? Frightened?"

Sullivan cleared his throat. "Uh, as I said before,
she seemed a bit nervous in the gambling hall."

"Just nervous."

Sullivan shot another look over to Arthur, clearly
hoping to get some assistance. "Tell him, Sully. Tell
him what you told me. He's her husband, for God's
sake."

"Well, sir, like I told Art here, if I didn't know that

one of the women was your wife, I would have thought they were two couples."

Luke's eyes, focused on the far corner of the room, held no emotion. "Did they . . . touch one another?"

"Jesus Christ," Sullivan muttered. "Kersey would put his hand on her back. Or she would put her hand on his arm. Like that. No kissing or anything I would call an embrace, if that's what you mean."

"But you thought it odd that a woman you knew to be married would be so friendly to another man?"

His voice heavy with resignation, Sullivan said, "Yes, sir."

The only sign that Luke heard him was a subtle tightening of his jaw. "Thank you, Mr. Sullivan. I realize that was not a pleasant thing to relate. Now, gentlemen, let's get down to business."

"Luke, if you want to take a few minutes . . ."

"I don't." He called his secretary into the room. "Mr. Sullivan. Any idea how Cardi learned about the raid?"

Sullivan discovered at the eleventh hour that Cardi had been tipped off that the police were planning a raid and had aborted the delivery of approximately two million dollars in opium. It became apparent, Sullivan said, that Cardi learned of the raid just hours before it was scheduled. "Which explains why the gambling joint was still running. He was in a panic to alter his plans for the opium. Unfortunately, I was upstairs in the restaurant when word came down that the raid was planned."

The three men mulled over that information. "Obviously, there's a leak," Sullivan said. "Probably in the police department," he added quickly, causing Luke's head to snap up at his tone.

"My wife was unaware of the raid, Mr. Sullivan."

"Oh, sir. I didn't mean to . . . that is to say . . ."

Luke held his hand up to stop the panicked disavowal.

"I'm sorry, sir."

Luke pressed the heels of his hands against his eyes.

"That's quite all right, Mr. Sullivan. You are only doing your job." He let out a heavy sigh. "Chief Farwell is not going to be pleased with your conclusions. He's not going to like our office pointing a finger at his department."

"But surely he cannot argue that someone tipped Cardi off," Arthur interjected. "And that it had to come from his department. He's stubborn but he's not stupid."

"Chief Farwell isn't interested in the drugs. He'd be happy shutting down the gambling den just to get the mayor off his back. Hell, maybe we are being too greedy."

Arthur shook his head. "You and I both know Cardi would be up and running within a week. We've got to get him with that opium."

"How long before you can pin down the leak?" Luke asked Sullivan.

"Hard to say. A week, maybe more."

Luke nodded. "Let's come up with our next move, gentlemen."

Luke spent the day in meetings, writing briefs, and assigning the Windmill Hill case to a displeased Arthur Ripley, who had decided that Byer was indeed up to the task. It was late afternoon before Luke had time to dwell on his wife's perfidy. Thoughts of her invaded his mind constantly throughout the day, accompanied by a slight feeling of nausea, but he resolutely pushed them away. But by five o'clock, with the spring sun casting the world in a pleasant golden glow, his thoughts turned dark. It could not be mere coincidence that she had come to him that weekend, suddenly "cured" of her unease of him. He walked over to the window, taking in the impossible green of new leaves, his heart so heavy he could not evoke the tiniest bit of joy in seeing the world outside his office look so beautiful.

His own words to Rose haunted him. *"Who turned you into this little wanton?"* She had told him that it was he. After nearly seven months of marriage, suddenly she had been drawn to him, wanted to make love to him. He closed his eyes. "You goddamn fool," he said aloud. "You pathetic fool."

All those changes in Rose had not been brought by him, but by another. His heart rebelled at the thought. It could not be true, it could not be. But his analytical mind drew the evidence together and produced an inevitable conclusion. Rose's beautiful body had been awakened by another. Was it guilt or lust that brought her to him, he wondered, that made her come to him in the middle of the night and touch him? Even as he tortured himself with such thoughts, his heart refused to believe it, a stubborn holdout with an innocent verdict when all else pointed toward her guilt.

Rose had lied to him; with a smile and a kiss, she had lied. Was he so blinded by his love that he could not see the woman for what she truly was? He knocked his head against the windowpane, the glass cool against his forehead, his hands pressed against the sill. When he first heard Sullivan's report, his first instinct was to immediately confront Rose, to force her to admit her lies. But time had inured Luke a bit, brought out the investigator in him. He wanted to see just how far Rose would go, how many lies she would tell before she finally caved in and told him the truth. The thought formed bile in his throat for he knew she would lie to him again.

"Damn you, Rose." Why couldn't it have been real? Jesus God, why couldn't I have been happy just this once? Luke heaved himself away from the window in self-disgust. He'd be damned if he'd let himself become weak over this. He reminded himself that he didn't want those softer feelings to rule him, to ruin him. He'd let himself become vulnerable. Hell, he'd welcomed love with the joy and guilessness of a child. He'd cried in her arms, thankful of her gift. He would be damned if he allowed it to happen again.

Satisfied with his resolve to harden his heart, Luke formed his plan as he made his way home that night. He would pretend, to the best of his ability, that all was well while inside he was filled with an anger he knew polluted his reason. Stopping outside his front door, he found himself unwilling to take those final steps, and a blinding rage swept over him at his weakness. Tightening his jaw, he resolved that she would never know how much he hurt.

5

Rose lay, to her vast dismay, in her own bed, staring up at her canopy. Just that day she had pondered the idea of turning her bedroom into a nursery, for certainly she would not be using it anymore. But here she was after a bewildering evening in which Luke went from the smiling man she loved to a brooding, remote stranger he'd never been. Luke had been distant and distracted but never cold and morose. It was almost as if he were *pretending* to be happy when he'd smiled at her that night.

He'd come home slightly later than usual, much to Rose's disappointment. All day she'd been looking forward to seeing him, missing him in a way she never had before. She hurried from her sitting room where she'd been pretending to read the *Ladies' Home Journal*—an utterly boring article about properly draping a window—when she'd heard the door close, marking Luke's arrival. When Luke saw her face, lit by a smile, he'd frowned, then quickly offered her a smile of his own. Except something even then had been wrong, Rose thought, tapping her index finger against her lips. When she went to kiss him, he'd turned his head just slightly, so that her lips pressed the corner of his mouth.

"Luke, we must practice more. I missed!" She'd gazed up at him with a teasing look of adoration, and he gave her another of those smiles that weren't really smiles.

Her heart plunging a bit and her gaze slightly troubled, she'd said, "Try again?"

And he'd dragged her into such a tight and desperate embrace, she'd almost been frightened by it. But Luke had laughed then, a rather unpleasant sound that Rose had tried to convince herself was a normal laugh. But it wasn't. It was self-mocking, as if Luke was disgusted with himself for kissing her that way. She'd asked if something were wrong and he'd said no.

Rose turned onto her side. Something *was* wrong. That evening, they walked like two strangers up the stairs and toward their bedrooms. Her heart thudding slowly in her breast, Rose watched as Luke stopped before her bedroom, clearly expecting her to enter it. He seemed to look everywhere but at her.

"I'm tired," he'd said, with a slight gesture toward her door. "Good night." And then he'd turned and walked to his room, entering without looking back, leaving Rose standing in the hall, hurt and bewildered.

Rose wrapped her blankets more tightly about her even though she was not cold. Perhaps, she thought, Luke wants another midnight visit? She bit her lips uncertainly. He certainly didn't seem to want to share his bed tonight. He didn't seem like he wanted to share anything with her. A sickening feeling of anxiety flooded her as she recalled their stilted dinner conversation.

"I've been thinking, Rose, about what your mother said about your playing cards over at the Taylors'. I hope you know I do not object to your evening out."

He sounded so serious, so much like a lawyer, Rose had simply said, "Thank you."

With a smile that seemed genuine, he'd asked, "Did you have a good time Friday night playing cards? I never did ask."

Rose's breath caught in her throat, guilt making her heart pound and her cheeks flush. "Yes. I always enjoy myself when I'm with the Taylors."

Now, lying in the dark, it seemed strange that Luke had mentioned the Taylors. *He knows,* she thought suddenly, her heart racing madly and a cold sweat breaking out, making her shiver. Just as quickly, she relaxed. Luke couldn't know, and certainly if he did, he would have confronted her with it. It was her own guilt that was making every gesture, every expression Luke made seem as if she were on trial. Perhaps Luke was exactly what he said he was: tired. Poor Luke. He probably thinks I expect another night of passion and would be disappointed to simply curl up with him and go to sleep, Rose thought happily.

As she had two nights earlier, Rose threw back the covers and marched to Luke's room. But this time, she simply knocked and walked in rather than skulking about like a person who didn't belong there. Not having heard a response to her knock, Rose assumed Luke was asleep—poor tired man!—and walked over to the bed. It was empty.

"What are you doing in here, Rose? I told you I was tired."

Rose threw a hand over her heart before turning to find Luke standing by the window, his form well-lit by the waning moon.

Rose walked to him and put her arms around his waist, ignoring the fact that he stiffened upon her touch. "I know you're tired, Luke. We don't have to. We can just sleep. Would that be all right?"

She thought she heard him curse beneath his breath. "Rose. I want you to return to your own room."

Rose felt herself ridiculously close to tears as she drew back to look at Luke. Why was he being so cold? "I . . . don't like sleeping alone anymore."

A short, low sound came from his throat, the sound a man makes when someone punches him in the gut. He turned toward her.

"You want to make love?" It was a question filled with anger and Rose was uncertain what to answer. She did want to make love, but the way he'd asked made her want to run from the room.

"I'm waiting."

Rose gave him a beseeching look. "Luke, what's wrong?"

He seemed to stare at something behind her. "Answer me," he demanded.

"I . . . yes, Luke, I do."

"Well then, we shall." He dragged her into his arms with near-violence and kissed her, a hard and demanding kiss. An angry kiss that almost instantly softened and teased her when she let out a small startled cry. Rose clutched him, already lost in the feeling of his mouth, his body. He pulled her nightdress off without a word, moving his hands and mouth over her in a way he never had, as if he were frantic to touch her flesh. Taking her hand, he pressed it against himself through his trousers, making her hand move over him in a way Rose found faintly disturbing. But then he knelt before her and drew her down, kissing her belly, her breasts, kneading her buttocks, and she became lost in the sensations, the urgency.

Luke laid her down, his hands stroking her, his mouth nipping and sucking until Rose writhed beneath his caresses. He was still fully dressed, and her hands moved restlessly at his shirt. He pushed her hands away and unbuttoned his pants. And then he was inside her, thrusting his hips against her as Rose wrapped her legs around him, wanting to share herself but feeling oddly separate from what he was doing. With a groan from Luke, it was over. He withdrew almost immediately, leaving Rose bewildered and unsatisfied in more than a physical way. She realized with confusion that Luke, but for his unbuttoned pants, was still fully dressed. He lay beside her, breathing heavily, one arm thrown over his eyes.

"Can we go to bed now?" Rose asked, her voice uncertain.

"Go to your room, Rose. Please."

Suddenly Rose felt dirty. What they had just done was not love, but raw mating. She sat up and searched for her gown, hugging it against her. She sat there, becoming aware of the cool wetness between her legs and a burning place on the small of her back caused, she realized, by the rough wool carpet. Luke had never seemed more distant, more unapproachable than he was at that moment. Even their awkward attempts at love when they'd first married had not left Rose feeling more lost. She thought of a million things to say to him, from angry retorts to pathetic pleas, but she remained silent. Finally, she stood and put her nightdress on, her hands shaking with emotion. He remained unmoving and silent as she walked toward the door.

The silence was too much. "I won't come to you again, Luke." She waited a moment for a response, and, hearing none, closed the door silently behind her.

6

Rose opened her eyes reluctantly the following morning, awakened by the rattling sounds of a servant pushing a carpet sweeper down the hall. The sun was out and Rose could hear birdsong through the window, but the cheerful sound only made her want to throw a pillow over her head. How dare the sun shine and the birds chirp when she was feeling so absolutely horrid? She heard the distant sound of the phone ringing and prayed it was not Collette calling, though she was certain it would be. She did not want to be happy today. She did not want to laugh and feel frivolous. She wanted to languish in misery.

Her maid poked her head into her room after a soft knock. "Mrs. Taylor on the telephone for you, Mrs. Beaudette."

Rose silenced a groan. "Tell Mrs. Taylor I will call back directly." After the maid departed, Rose felt her spirits rise despite her resolve to remain blue. Thirty minutes later, she was dressed and on the telephone with Collette, making plans to watch a bicycle race go through Springfield on its way to the Canadian border.

Thomas Kersey, whistling a jaunty tune, stepped up onto the curb at State and Main streets, an infectious grin on his face that Collette could not resist. She smiled, then giggled when Kersey swept up her gloved hand and planted a sloppy kiss, leaving behind a wet spot.

"Oh, Thomas, look what you've done," Collette said, eyeing the mark and wrinkling her nose.

Thomas shrugged, and slapped John's back in greeting. "How are you, old friend?"

John gave him a hard look. "You're in trouble, Thomas. I can't help you this time."

Thomas's eyes momentarily clouded. "Nothing I can't handle," he said with false bravado. "I've got a line on a horse racing tomorrow at Hamden Park. It's a sure bet. One win, John, that's all I need to get me out of this slump. Have you ever seen one of my slumps last so long? I've got a feeling about this horse. My bones are tingling."

John shot Thomas a look of disgust. "Where the hell are you getting money to bet with? If you've got any cash, I would highly recommend sending it Cardi's way. His patience is running thin."

Thomas waved a dismissive hand. "Cardi's all talk. You know that."

"Not this time."

Thomas just smiled.

Collette laid a hand on his arm. "Listen to John," she said, her blue eyes filled with concern.

"Hey, will you two stop it? How can a man have any fun with you two around? How about a little wager? I bet you a nickel the lead racer has blond hair."

Collette rolled her eyes. "You cheater. It said in the paper who was leading, including a rather nice description of the man. The blond-haired man," she said pointedly.

Thomas shrugged, then nodded his head indicating Rose's slim form walking toward them from across the street. He sighed dramatically. "Why is it every lovely woman is married?" he asked mournfully. Collette giggled, but John gave his friend a hard, assessing look.

"Over here!" Collette called. "My, don't you look sprightly today," she said when Rose reached the little group. Rose wore a pale blue skirt with a dark blue velvet sash that wrapped about her trim waist then dropped the length of the skirt. Her matching bolero jacket, worn over a plain white blouse, was accented with blue glass buttons of the same hue as the velvet. Rose closed her parasol, eyeing the sky which now held more clouds than sun.

"Have I missed anything?" she asked.

"Only me, making a complete fool of myself mooning after you," Thomas said, getting down on bended knee and grasping one hand. He looked up mischievously at Collette. "Shall I remove her glove so it is not soiled by my amorous lips?"

Rose pulled her hand away before he could do anything. "Oh, Thomas, really. While in public, you must learn to control your undying love for me."

Thomas got up and dusted off his knee. "I shall try . . . Ah, look, I would have lost that bet. The man is dark-haired." Suddenly, Thomas's good humor was gone as he looked at the lead bicyclist with pure malice. Rose gave him a curious look before turning toward the street and clapping heartily for the leader. It was several minutes before another racer flew by, his legs pumping an at amazing rate in an attempt to catch the leader.

The race had started the day before in Bridgeport, Connecticut, and would finish at the Canadian border in Maine, a schedule that allowed the racers only a few hours' sleep each evening of the four-day race, John informed the little group. He opened the newspaper that was tucked beneath his arm and turned to the page detailing the race.

" 'Whoever is leading at the end of a day, is allowed to depart in the morning before the other racers,' " John read. " 'If he is one minute ahead of the closest man in the evening, he is allowed a one-minute head start the next day.' Seems an awful lot to go through if you ask me."

"Is there a prize?" Rose asked.

John perused the article. "It doesn't say."

"I imagine they must get something for their effort," Thomas said moodily.

A dark-haired man whom Rose found faintly familiar stepped into their little group. "The five top finishers qualify for a national race," the man said. He had a slight Italian accent and was wearing white coveralls.

"Oh. You're my sister's milkman, aren't you? Mrs. Baptiste?"

Anthony nodded. "But no longer. My route has changed."

"Oh." Rose continued to look at him, searching her memory. Then she flushed. "You also work at the Supper Club. I saw you there Friday night but I couldn't place you without your overalls."

Anthony stiffened and shot a look to the others. "Yes. I assist the chef."

Not knowing what else to say, and feeling intensely uncomfortable beneath his unwavering gaze, Rose nodded. "You must be very busy, then." Though their brief conversation was obviously over, the man seemed almost reluctant to leave and continued to eye Thomas and her other friends warily. Just then, a group of bicyclists rode by, producing another cheer from the crowd. When Rose turned back, the milkman was gone. She said a quick thankful prayer that no one more important than a milkman had recognized her.

The novelty of watching the race soon wore thin and the crowd began to disperse. The four stood together for a while, clapping when a bicyclist rode by, but otherwise were silent. Rose tried to come up with something witty or clever to say, but each time she opened her mouth, she closed it again. It seems everyone is in a funk today, she thought. Even Thomas, who normally bubbled over with good humor, was disturbingly somber.

"I'm heading home," he announced finally, hooking his thumbs into his pants.

"Not to the track?"

Thomas gave John his characteristic shrug. "Don't feel as lucky as I thought," he said. But before the day was over, Thomas would feel lady luck tugging at him and he would lose another five hundred dollars that he didn't have a prayer of paying back.

7

Nicole sat at her kitchen table Wednesday morning as she had for the past four years, a cup of tea between her hands. Only four days since she had seen him, talked to him. Four days that stretched out before her, turning into forty days, then four hundred. Days of sitting at this table alone with a cup of tea between her hands, wishing . . . wishing . . .

Her heart flew up to her throat at the sound of a knock at the door. A familiar cadence: tap, tap-tap on the window. She turned her disbelieving eyes to the outline that showed through the curtain, then, still uncertain, she craned her neck and saw a shock of dark hair curling over a white collar.

Anthony.

Smoothing down her skirts and wishing she had time to check her hair—she just knew it was a mess—she walked as calmly, as slowly as she could to the door and opened it.

"Mr. D'Angelo."

"Mrs. Baptiste."

He had no milk in his hands, which were shoved deep into his pockets. "I'm come because of your sister," he said haltingly, still hovering outside the door.

"Come in," Nicole said, backing into the kitchen.

"I'm here only for a moment." He stood still, but his eyes filled with yearning as he looked beyond Nicole and into the cozy little kitchen.

"Then come in for just a moment," Nicole said,

sounding so calm, Anthony relaxed. He had feared that coming to see her would give them both false hope. When he'd left that Friday and said he would not return, he'd meant it. But he could not stand by and watch someone Nicole loved be hurt. Anthony followed her to the table, a familiar ache in his throat, and sat down in his chair.

"You know I work at the Supper Club assisting my uncle." At Nicole's nod, he continued. "I am ashamed to say that the Supper Club is not a good place. Bad things, evil things happen there. My uncle, he is simply the chef and pretends these things do not happen."

Nicole's eyes were wide. "What sort of things?"

"Gambling, and other things. Mostly illegal gambling." He would not tell her about the opium that was sometimes stored in the wine cellar, or his suspicions about Cardi and some rather convenient deaths. "I cannot convince my uncle to leave, as I plan to. He thinks of the restaurant as his, even though it is not. He will not hear an ill word about Mr. Cardi, the owner. He is a stubborn man."

Nicole shook her head in confusion. "Why are you telling me this?"

"Because I saw your sister there. And not only in the restaurant. I saw her go down to the gambling hall with two others. People who I know and do not trust."

"Rose? Are you certain?"

Anthony let out a heavy sigh. "I saw your sister yesterday watching the bicycle race. She was with those same people. Two men and a woman. She mentioned to me that she saw me at the Supper Club. I don't think she understands the danger of even mentioning that she was there. It is not a place for ladies. Even the restaurant is no such place for you or your sister, but to go into the gambling hall . . . It is not something I would want my sister to do. You understand?"

"Of course. Thank you, Anthony."

He looked down at his hands. "You know I do not want to see you hurt. It is why I came to tell you this.

I would die to know you were hurt." He looked up, then, his brown eyes unguarded and filled with such pain and love Nicole did not think she could bear it.

"I'll speak to my sister," Nicole said, choosing to ignore the deeper meaning of his words.

"Oh, Rose, how could you go into a gambling hall! And your husband the assistant attorney general right here in Springfield. What were you thinking?"

Rose sat in her parlor, squirming under her older sister's scorn and disappointment and cursing the inquisitive milkman who'd hurried and tattled on her at his first opportunity.

"I thought your milkman changed routes," she said, trying to deflect the conversation.

"He was so concerned, he made a special stop," Nicole said, pacing before Rose and gesturing angrily. "And I have to say I'm concerned as well, Rose. I *knew* that woman was no good. She's had too much influence on you, making you cut your hair and wear fancy clothes. Making you play poker and skulk about gambling halls!"

Rose crossed her arms stubbornly. She hated the way Nicole could act so straitlaced at times, throwing judgments about, and making Rose feel like she'd murdered someone rather than placed a bet on a roulette wheel. "Collette didn't make me do anything I did not want to do. You don't understand, Nicole."

Putting her hands on her hips, Nicole turned to her. "But I do, Rose. Of course I do. All our lives we've been constrained, made to believe we should apologize for any happy emotion. Don't you think most people would like to do as they pleased? But we don't. We know the rules and you've been breaking them. Don't you think everyone would like to throw away the conventions and rules that force us to conform to society's rigid expectations? But we don't!"

Rose thrust out her lower lip. "Perhaps more people should and then fewer people would go about their lives being so miserable." She didn't know why she was arguing with her sister, for she agreed with most of what Nicole was saying. She knew she'd gone too far; she'd felt awful about allowing Collette and John convince her it was innocent fun to play roulette, to go through that secret door. Still, Nicole couldn't know how exciting it had been, to take that step toward sin, to dance with it if only for a little while. Rose knew she would never be completely swept away into the world of sinners, and she truly regretted what she had done. But how wonderful was that feeling, when for just a little while, she forgot to be good.

"You're right. Of course, you're right, Nicole," she grumbled.

Nicole tilted her head and looked at her sister with a depth of understanding that made Rose feel even worse. When her big sister sat next to her on the sofa and put her arm around her, she wanted to cry. "It was fun, wasn't it?" Nicole said.

"Oh, Nicole, it was. It was awful. But I've never felt so alive. Isn't that horrible?"

"I suppose not. I believe I've fulfilled my obligation as the older sister and you may consider this lecture over."

Rose smiled. "I know my friendship with Collette is a bit . . . out of character. And I'm not blind to their faults. Luke loathes them, especially Collette's husband, John. Luke won't trust anyone who won't discuss his business. I have to admit, I've never seen the man actually working and he seems to spend an inordinate amount of time to do absolutely nothing." Rose sighed. "I've promised to visit them Friday, but I think after that I'll pull back a bit. Luke's angry with me and I suspect it has to do with my friendship with the Taylors."

"Luke doesn't know about your escapade, does he?"

"Goodness, no. And that has me feeling even more guilty. I lied to him about where I was Friday night."

Nicole took her hands in hers. "You've got to tell him, Rose."

Rose shook her head. She had avoided Luke all day Tuesday and this morning after Monday evening's disturbing incident in his room. The last thing she wanted to do was get him truly angry at her as she knew he would be if he discovered what she'd done. "I can't, Nicole. He'd never forgive me. Not only did I go to the Supper Club fully knowing he would disapprove, I lied to him about it."

"I suppose you know best," Nicole said hesitantly.

Rose didn't know best and long after Nicole departed, she wrestled with whether she should tell Luke or not. He'd been so distracted lately, she hated to drive another wedge between them. Rose decided Luke simply had been tired that night, and though she had not entirely forgiven him for being so callous toward her, she managed to muster some understanding. She resolved to get their marriage back on the rosy trail they walked briefly together.

8

Thomas Kersey was a dead man. He just didn't know it yet, thought John Taylor, a grim smile on his lips. Word had come down that Cardi's patience had reached its end. Though Cardi would not get his money from a dead man, he couldn't get it from the live one either. He would make an example of the freeloader in hopes of discouraging others from following suit.

When John had heard about the plan, he had, to his credit, tried to convince Cardi to let Kersey go. Certainly Cardi could afford a ten-thousand-dollar loss. But Cardi, his brown eyes as cold as mud in March, pointed out that he could not afford the damage to his reputation if he let Kersey walk away. John understood. He liked Thomas, but the man had gone too far, owed money to too many people. How could you respect such a man? As he sat in Cardi's opulent office, listening to plans to have his friend killed, excitement began to grow in his belly. It was perfect, he thought. Absolutely perfect.

"I wonder if you could do me a favor, Mr. Cardi," John had asked.

Cardi tilted his head, indicating that he should continue.

"I'd like the murder to happen here."

"In my club? No. Absolutely not."

John smiled. "What if I told you that by killing Kersey in your club you could get Beaudette off your back? Forever." That, as he knew it would, had piqued Cardi's curiosity. The man leaned forward, a gleam in his eye.

"Tell me."

And John had, laying out a plan so beautiful, he was nearly shaking from it. As John had watched that evil smile spread across Cardi's face, he could almost taste the sweetness of his revenge on his tongue. John left Cardi's office smiling and filled with elation. The only trepidation he felt was Cardi's stipulation. If the killing was to occur in the Supper Club, John would have to do the deed himself, for Cardi didn't want to take the chance one of his own men would be implicated. It was like making a deal with the devil, John knew. Cardi didn't trust him, had been angry that John even knew about the plan. He already knew he didn't want Cardi as an enemy, so it was crucial that all go as planned. Only one obstacle stood in his way of finally avenging his father's death: Rose Beaudette.

"You've got to get her there, Collette. I don't care how you do it, your little friend has got to be in the club Friday night." They were in bed, naked and satisfied from a wild midday romp.

Collette gave her husband a look of pure disbelief. "Maybe I can wear her down in a month, but there is no way Miss Goody-goody is going to walk through those doors Friday night. She was practically in tears Saturday when I saw her and I think she's getting suspicious of us. We're moving too fast. If we push her too far, we'll never get her. Why this Friday? Why can't we wait? We've waited this long." She crossed her arms over her gloriously plump breasts.

John gave his wife's breasts an appreciative glance before looking away. "I can't say."

"Something's going to happen. Something big." Collette's pretty face glowed with excitement. "Oh, tell me! Tell me, tell me. I swear I will not say a word to anyone." She pressed herself against him, knowing John could not resist her enticing body.

"It's better you don't know," John said, a stubborn set to his jaw.

Collette pulled away and pouted while John looked at her warily. "Don't make that face," he said, breaking into a grin. "You know I can't resist that face."

Collette tried to maintain her pout but found herself smiling instead. "I'll make it worth your while if you tell me," she cajoled, raking her well-honed nails over his chest.

"Aw, hell, I knew I couldn't keep this from you, darlin'." He kissed her. "We've got Beaudette and it's even better than before. There's going to be a murder at the Supper Club Friday night, and our little pigeon is going to commit it. Now, what could be more perfect than that?"

9

Rose could not believe she was again walking down those steep steps that led to the gambling hall. She was so tense, her entire body ached. Oh, how could she have let this happen? But as she watched John heave open the door, she knew she never had a choice. Thomas Kersey was in trouble and she was the only one who could talk some sense into him.

Collette had come to Rose Friday morning, desperate to see her, her eyes puffy and red from crying. Rose had ushered her through the door and brought her immediately into her small second-floor sitting room, giving them needed privacy. When Rose had Collette settled on a sofa, she took her shaking hand in hers. "What's wrong, Collette? Tell me."

Collette shook her head, truly distressed, for John had just told her moments before who Rose's "victim" would be. Poor, poor Thomas. So full of fun. So full of life. He'd be dead by this time tomorrow. The only consolation she had was knowing that John would have finally exacted the perfect revenge of his father's death. They could go on with their lives, leaving behind this little twittering fool looking at her now with such compassion. She wanted to rake her nails across her perfect face.

"It's Thomas," Collette had said, letting out a shaky sob. "He's in awful trouble. You know that he gambles. But apparently he's much more in debt than any of us imagined. The people he owes money to are getting angry. He won't listen to reason. John and I have tried to convince him he is being foolish, but it's like a sickness! He can't stop." Collette produced a handkerchief from her sleeve and buried her face in her hands. When she composed herself, she continued. "Tonight he plans to go back to the Supper Club. He insists he's going to win. He says he feels lucky." Saying that, Collette shuddered and fresh tears fell from her blue eyes.

"What can we do?" Rose asked.

Collette's expression had changed subtly. "John insists that we accompany Thomas to the club to make sure he doesn't get into any trouble. As soon as Thomas starts losing, we're to take him away. We can't stop him from going, short of tying him up, and John says that is not an option," she said, letting out a tear-clogged laugh and sniffing loudly.

"Well then, you and John should go. It sounds like a good plan," Rose said gently.

Collette had looked up at her with something like fear in her eyes. "You don't understand. When I said 'we,' I meant you, too."

Rose had clasped her stomach. "Oh, no, Collette.

You don't need me. I like Thomas, but he's really your friend. Not mine."

"You don't understand. Thomas won't listen to us, but John is convinced he'll listen to you. You see, Thomas likes you, Rose. Perhaps a bit more than he should like a married woman."

Rose jerked back. "That's not true. How can that be true? Thomas has a girl. He's mentioned her. And he's never given any indication he feels anything toward me."

"Perhaps not to you . . ."

"Are you saying Thomas has spoken to you about me?"

Collette shook her head. "Not to me. But he has spoken to John, who of course discouraged the feelings. Thomas hasn't said anything since, but John is certain the feelings are still there."

"Oh, goodness." Rose began fiddling with her wedding ring.

"So you see, you're Thomas's last hope."

"Oh, my. But I wouldn't want to do anything to encourage him."

Rose could almost hear Collette grit her teeth and she shrank away from the other woman's anger. "Rose! How can you be so selfish as to put your own petty little concerns before the life of a man in trouble? A man you profess is your friend."

"I wouldn't. I didn't think . . ."

"No. You didn't think of anything but yourself," Collette had said, standing angrily and turning toward the door. At Rose's frantic plea, Collette smiled. When she turned back, the smile was gone, replaced by a look of expectation.

"Can't I speak to him before he goes to the Supper Club?" Rose asked hopefully.

"That would have been the best plan, of course. But neither I nor John know where Thomas will be before this evening. I'm afraid we have no choice."

Rose looked hopelessly into her friend's eyes, which were glittering with anger. At that moment, she would

have done just about anything to erase that angry
look. She closed her eyes. "I'll do it," she said. Collette had smiled at her in triumph but Rose saw
only gratitude.

Now, standing at the entrance to the gambling hall,
she wished she had found another way to avoid coming here. As they were being seated for dinner earlier
in the evening, Thomas, his face already flushed from
drinking, had approached their table and hope had
surged through Rose that she could convince him not
to gamble and thus avoid going into the hall.

"Why, look who's here," Thomas said loudly, his
eyes resting warmly on Rose, making her feel unaccountably uneasy. Perhaps what Collette had told her
was true, she thought. He grabbed the single empty
chair, stumbling a bit, and made to sit down before
John's hand shot out and gripped his wrist.

"Go downstairs, Thomas. You're drunk."

Rose had given John a startled look. Why would he
send Thomas down to the very gambling hall that was
endangering him so?

Rose eyed John and Collette, who were looking at
Thomas with disturbing hostility and some other emotion Rose could not grasp. She only knew that she
must try to convince Thomas to stay for dinner.

"Perhaps you should eat something. It's all right,
isn't it, if Thomas joins us?" Rose said, not missing
the look of irritation of John's face.

"Of course it's all right," Collette purred. "Thomas,
please sit."

"Nah. I'll go downstairs and get a head start. Next
time you see me, I may be a rich man," he said, slur-
ring slightly. "I'll see you later, love." He grabbed
Rose's hand and kissed it. Rose pulled her hand away
immediately, not liking the possessive nature of that
caress, her eyes going about the room to see if anyone
saw the kiss. Even though everyone in the room was
a stranger, it still bothered her that they witnessed
such a caress. She'd never seen Thomas quite so tipsy
before and prayed it was the alcohol that was making

him act so strangely, and not his secret feelings for her.

Straightening, Thomas said, "Will you all be joining me after your meal?"

John smiled. "Certainly, Thomas. Try not to lose too much before we get there, hmmm?"

"Don't worry. I'm feeling lucky tonight," he said, again letting his eyes drift to Rose. She had the strangest feeling that Thomas was flirting with her. Not the silly way he had before, but with an earnestness she found disturbing.

"Thomas, why not skip the hall tonight? We could go to a play instead," Rose had said, angry with John for practically urging Thomas into the hall.

But he had waved her off with a jaunty flick of his hand, heading toward the gambling tables that Rose now searched in hopes of spotting him. As Rose looked about the hall for Thomas, so many emotions filled her she nearly felt faint. Collette and John seemed to have forgotten that they were here to save Thomas, and were in almost ridiculously high spirits given what their mission was that evening. Rose was confused and angry about the Taylors' behavior, sick about defying her priest, sister, and God by stepping foot into the hall, and concerned about Thomas.

The hall was even more crowded that evening than the previous Friday, and more women were in attendance. Again, Rose found herself scanning the crowd for a familiar face and praying she would not find one. She recognized some people from that last Friday—a little round man with cheeks so red it appeared they'd been painted on, the striking woman with hair so blonde it did not appear natural, the tall cadaverous man whose eyes drooped over dark black smudges, lending him a macabre air. It was noisy and smoky and exciting in an awful sort of way.

"A game of roulette, love?" a voice whispered in her ear.

"No more gambling for me," Rose said, stepping

back from Thomas. "Perhaps you should take a break yourself."

Thomas shrugged good-naturedly. "Losing tonight anyway," he said. He grabbed her hand and placed it in the crook of his arm. "Why don't we go somewhere more quiet?"

Rose looked about the cavernous room. "Unless we leave, I don't think we'll find anywhere quiet in this place," she said, hoping to put him off without hurting his feelings. Rose wasn't sure her unease was because of Thomas's actions or because of the seeds Collette had planted that afternoon. Would she have read anything into such a suggestion if Collette had not told her of Thomas's apparent tender feelings?

Thomas led her to a far corner of the room, hardly a private or quiet place, so Rose relaxed. With her back against the paneled wall, Rose looked beyond Thomas and took in the hall from this vantage point. "It's amazing how much money is in this room," she said. "I still can't believe people like to gamble. Why not just throw your money out the carriage window?"

"Now that's not very exciting," Thomas said, clearly mortified. "Losing can make a man sick. But winning . . . winning is magic, darling. Pure magic."

Rose wanted to point out that Thomas shouldn't call her "darling," but he'd always called her "darling." Thomas called every woman "darling." He was standing rather too close, his arm brushing hers, but it was not an entirely inappropriate touch, rather an inadvertent one. Rose was still looking at all the activity, when she realized that Thomas was no longer standing at what anyone would say was a proper distance from a married woman.

"Thomas, you're standing a bit close, wouldn't you say?" Rose squeaked out.

"I'd say not close enough," he said, his head just inches from hers.

Oh, this was too, too close, Rose thought. "Thomas. Please back away."

A frown marred his usually smiling face. "You and I both know you want me to kiss you."

Rose stiffened. "I want no such thing."

"I've been told otherwise," he said silkily.

"That's ridiculous and a lie."

"You're so sweet when you're pretending to be insulted." And then he moved his head quickly, so quickly Rose didn't know his intention until it was too late. She managed to jerk her head so that his lips hit her cheek instead of the intended target, but it was too late to avoid the kiss entirely. Bringing up her hands, she pushed him back, shocked and hurt that Thomas had betrayed their friendship in such a way. Without thinking, she slapped his face, and didn't even cringe at the resounding loud *clap* the impact made. Several people turned at the noise and Rose's face heated with embarrassment and anger.

Thomas rubbed his cheek bearing the red imprint of her hand. "I believe I was misinformed," he said with a little bow and a cocky grin. "You'd better have that hand checked."

Rose stared at his departing back, too angry to move. Had she somehow given him signals that she would have welcomed such a kiss? She thought back on the few times she and Thomas had been together, times filled with laughing and outrageous—and what she had thought was silly—flirtation. Not for one moment had Rose taken his overexaggerated declarations seriously. How could she have so misread the situation? When she realized she was blaming herself for Thomas's bad behavior, a new wave of anger washed over her—this one directed at herself.

Slowly, Rose became aware that several nearby gamblers and workers were staring at her with amusement. Mustering as much dignity as possible, Rose smoothed her skirts and stepped away from the wall. Oh, how she hated this place! As soon as she found Collette and John she was leaving. Maybe even sooner! As she walked the length of the hall, she kept her eyes darting about to ensure she'd avoid running into Thomas. He was nowhere in sight and she let out a sigh of relief. Maybe the man had left, too embarrassed by his bad behavior to remain.

Rose spent several minutes searching for Collette and John, getting more and more frustrated as time passed. The hall was so crowded, it was difficult to see past more than the most immediate crowd of gamblers. The couple could be anywhere, she thought in frustration. After conducting what she thought was a systematic search of the room, Rose decided to leave and explain to Collette and John tomorrow that she had failed to sway Thomas from his gambling ways and decided to leave. Just as she turned toward the door, Collette swooped down, her face filled with fear. John was several steps behind her.

"Meet me in the cloakroom in two minutes. I have to talk to you but I don't want John to know, so stay here while I go there," she whispered frantically into Rose's ear. And then she was gone, leaving Rose to stand awkwardly next to an agitated John. He kept jerking at his cuffs and vest. Rose wondered if the couple were in the middle of an argument.

"I'm afraid I failed with Thomas," Rose said.

John started. "What?" He seemed confused by her statement. "Oh. You mean the gambling. Of course. Well. That's okay. Gave it your best try."

Rose shot him a startled look. They had given her the task of stopping Thomas from gambling and she had failed miserably and John seemed to hardly care. "Your ear's bleeding," Rose said, nodding toward a speck of blood on his earlobe.

"What? Where?" He immediately took his handkerchief out and dabbed almost frantically at his ear, a strange look coming over his face when he saw the small red dot marring the cloth.

"It's all gone," Rose said with a little smile of reassurance. John appeared to be distracted, probably thinking about his tiff with Collette and how he could make it up, Rose decided. Her nerves, already frayed by the events of the evening, were unraveling even more as she waited the two minutes before joining Collette. Why be so secretive about everything? Why not just drag Rose away and cry on her shoulder if she had an argument with John?

"I'll be right back," Rose said, glad to get away from John who was obviously troubled. The entire time they'd stood together, he'd been shifting from one foot to another as if he was anxious to get away from her.

Rose excused herself to find Collette, nervous about traveling down the secret passageways alone. She felt conspicuous as she made her way toward the steep stairs and silly when she copied the special knock she'd seen John pound out the previous Friday. The door swung open, revealing the slitted-eye man, and Rose had to suppress a shudder. The restaurant had long since stopped serving, and only the sounds of kitchen staff could be heard above the noise of a handful of lingering diners. Rose peeked into the dining room, recognizing a few faces of gamblers who had been downstairs earlier in the evening, before heading to the small hallway that contained the cloakroom. She felt ridiculously relieved to finally arrive at the room, as if she'd just taken a dangerous trek and now found herself at her own front door.

The cloakroom was open and she walked in without a thought, expecting to see a tearful Collette. She turned and stopped, letting out a gasp. Thomas Kersey's bloodied body was lying on the floor.

10

Rose rushed to his side, sickened by what she saw. A puddle of blood had formed around Thomas on the wooden floor, an impossible amount. Rose knelt and then her heart lifted when he turned his head slightly toward her and let out a gurgling noise.

"Don't talk, Thomas. Lie still." She grasped his hand, and, turning her head toward the door, screamed for help. Thomas gripped her hand almost painfully, forcing Rose to turn back to him. The look in his eyes was one filled with horror and anguish, and something Rose could not read. The gurgling in his throat increased, a sickening, deathly sound.

"Please, Thomas. Don't try to talk." Blood came from his mouth then in a fiendish rush, falling over Rose's hand. She jerked her hand away and stared at it before turning back to Thomas, whose eyes were still open. It took a moment before Rose realized those brilliant blue eyes saw no more. Thomas Kersey was dead.

Letting out a sob, Rose looked over Thomas's body, finally seeing the hilt of a knife that thrust from his abdomen. It was wrong. It should not be there, she thought, sticking into her friend the same way a knife would be thrust into a side of beef. It was obscene. Rose only knew she had to remove it, had to give Thomas back some humanity. As she wrapped her bloodied hand around the smooth hilt, a scream came from the doorway. She turned to see Collette and several other horrified faces looking at her from the doorway.

"Murderer," Collette whispered. "Murderer! Murderer!" She screamed it over and over until John dragged her away from the door.

It was odd, that moment, for all Rose could think of was: How did John get up here so quickly? She stared blindly at the little crowd, finally taking in their stunned and shocked faces. With sudden clarity Rose realized her position. She was kneeling before a dead man, her hands and dress covered with his blood. She could see their accusing eyes sweeping over her, taking in the blood, the hand still wrapped around the hilt of the knife as if frozen in place. She jerked her hand away, suddenly realizing what it must look like to the horrified people.

"No. No. He was still alive when I found him." How false that sounded, even to her own ears. She heard someone say "Murderer" and Rose could do nothing but shake her head. *This could not be happening.* She stood and several in the ever growing crowd gasped. Her gown was soaked with Thomas's blood; it dripped from her hands, it glistened in the gaslight. All Rose could do was stand and wait for . . . something. Surely Collette and John would realize that she would never harm Thomas. Surely they would break through this muttering and angry crowd and come to her defense.

"Grab her!" A shout. "Don't let her get away!"

Rose thought that quite a silly thing to say, for she hadn't moved a step, and it would have been fairly impossible to escape through the surging throng outside the door. Two men squeezed through the door, their faces set, their eyes hard and accusing. Rose backed away, shaking her head.

"Don't touch me." Her voice sounded hysterical to her own ears, yet Rose felt oddly calm, as if she were a spectator, watching as these men approached a pitiful female covered with blood. Certainly that woman could not be her. Rose backed away until her heels bumped up against Thomas's body. The feeling of that solid, human, lifeless form was her undoing. She began screaming over and over, her eyes closed, her bloodied hands over her ears, "Get away, get away!"

When Rose finally stopped screaming, the silence was startling.

"Jesus Christ."

Rose opened her eyes at the rough-spoken expletive. A man stood before her, his sharp brown eyes taking in the scene with disturbing precision, and it almost seemed as if a smile lurked on his hard mouth. His dark, gray-streaked hair was swept back, revealing a broad forehead marred by the deep crevices of a man who has seen a difficult life.

"Everyone get out of here. Lou, get these people the hell away from here. Now!"

Rose stood as the crowd disappeared from view, ushered away by the slitted-eyed man, until she was left standing alone with the man and Thomas's body.

When everyone was gone, the man finally turned back to her.

"My name is Guido Cardi, and you, miss, are in deep trouble."

"I didn't do it," Rose whispered.

"I know," he said almost breezily. "That's not my concern. But I'm afraid convincing the police will be a bit more difficult than convincing me."

"Police?" Of course, the police would be called. There had been a murder. Rose shuddered. "You'll tell the police I am innocent."

Cardi let out a hard laugh. "You're on your own, sweetheart. As far as I'm concerned, this conversation never took place. And believe me when I tell you this, no one is going to believe you are innocent. No one."

With the certainty of someone who is innocently accused, Rose said, "I'm sure when I explain everything to the police, they'll understand."

Cardi let out another laugh. "You pathetic little girl," he said, shaking his head. His voice held contempt, not compassion. "You've no idea what's going to happen, do you?" He stared at her, that hard smile on his lips, as he swept his gaze over her blood-covered dress and hands. "The police have been called. Come on. We'll wait for them in my office." He glanced at her soiled clothes again. "Better yet, I'll put you in the chef's office. I don't want to get my office bloody."

Rose found she could barely walk, so weak and shaken was she. She stepped from the cloakroom, ignoring the few people who lingered and stared from the dining room. Her dress felt heavy and wet and Rose shuddered, knowing it was Thomas's blood weighing her down. The blood on Rose's hands was beginning to dry, stretching her skin and making it itch, making her want to scream.

"May I wash my hands?"

Cardi ignored her and continued leading her toward the kitchen. He led her to a tiny office off the large room where kitchen workers paused to stare at the disheveled woman being led through their domain.

"May I wash my hands?" Rose repeated, a slight note of hysteria in her voice.

"Best if you look just as you do until Chief Farwell gets here."

Chief Farwell. Oh, my God, Rose thought as the enormity of what was happening struck her. She knew Chief Farwell, had entertained him and his wife in their own home. Everyone would know. Everyone. It would be in the newspapers. Her mother! Oh, God, her mother would know. Luke. Luke would know she had lied to him. As she sat in a slat-backed wooden chair, all she could think of was how angry Luke would be to discover Rose had gone to the Supper Club and lied about it. She didn't think about the murder, for she had separated herself from that. She was innocent. At the most, she was a witness, and not a very good one at that.

Then she stiffened. Collette had sent her to the cloakroom! Collette had been there before her. Had she and Thomas had an argument? Had she panicked and then decided to blame the murder on Rose? While her heart tried to deny such a thing, her mind could think of no other explanation. She calmed down a bit, though she was sickened by what she was thinking, for now Rose believed she could prove her innocence.

The wait for Chief Farwell seemed interminable. When he finally arrived, Cardi headed him off, giving his rendition of events as an investigator took rigorous notes. Rose could overhear most of what Cardi said as he told police he knew very little. She pressed her lips together at the man's perfidy.

"I was told there was a murder in my cloakroom. When I arrived, I found a woman covered with blood standing by the body of a man."

"Do you know the identity of the man?"

"I do. Thomas Kersey. He frequented the restaurant."

"And the gambling hall?"

"I'm afraid I don't know what you are talking about, Chief."

The chief let out a grunt of disbelief, but did not argue with the man. "Let me see the woman now." Chief Farwell's great bulk moved through the door and his pale-blue eyes widened in surprise. He wore a suit without a tie and his thinning hair was slightly mussed, as if he'd been roused from his bed. "Good God, Mrs. Beaudette!"

Rose saw Cardi raise his eyebrows in shock, an expression that Rose thought looked practiced. "You know this woman?" he asked.

Chief Farwell clamped his mouth shut. Then he noticed her bloodied hands. "Jesus, man, let the woman wash her hands, for God's sakes."

"Thank you, Chief," Rose said. She wanted to hug this man with his familiar and friendly face until she saw something in his eyes other than disgust over Cardi's treatment of her. She saw doubt. Cardi led Rose to a large porcelain sink. With shaking hands, she poured soap powder into her palm and began to rub. Blood, dried and caked, stuck to her skin up to her forearm where it soaked into the sleeve of her gown. It ran with gruesome abundance down the drain, splattering and leaving little pink droplets on the white surface. Rose scrubbed until her hands were raw, scraping the blood from her fingernails in such a frenzy, several nails tore. She didn't care. She only wanted it off and wished she could immerse her entire body into the water that was nearly scalding.

"That's enough," Chief Farwell finally said, his voice gentle as he handed her a towel. He drew her away from the sink and led her back to the small office where he bade her to sit. "Why don't you tell me what happened this evening, Mrs. Beaudette?"

"Have you sent for my husband, Chief?"

He nodded. "One of the officers is looking for him; he was directed that Mr. Beaudette be taken to the police station. Now. Tell me what happened." The chief nodded to another officer to begin taking notes.

"I didn't kill him," Rose said, her eyes burning with unshed tears.

"No one is saying that you have." Yet. It was as clear as if he had spoken it.

Rose took a deep breath, fully aware of how important the next few moments were. "I came here with John and Collette Taylor. I didn't want to, but we wanted to protect Thomas," she began. "You see, Thomas has . . . had some awful gambling debts and we, that is, the Taylors thought I could convince Thomas not to gamble."

"You were in the gambling hall?"

Rose bit her lip and looked into her lap, deeply ashamed to admit something such as that to an officer of the law. "Yes. We all were. At one point, Collette came up to me and asked that I meet her in the cloakroom, that she needed to speak with me. I assumed that she and John had a fight and she needed a shoulder to cry on."

"Why did you assume that?"

Rose's brows creased in concentration. "Because she said something about not wanting John to know we were talking." She shook her head and shrugged. "It was rather secretive. She whispered in my ear to meet her, you see."

"And so you went to the cloakroom."

Rose, in halting sentences, relayed what happened, how Thomas was alive when she found him, how he tried to speak but could not, how she shouted for help and was discovered by Collette.

"That's all for now, Mrs. Beaudette. I'm going to have an officer accompany you to the police station."

Blood drained from Rose's face. "Am I being charged, Chief?"

Chief Farwell shot a look to the officer who was taking notes. Rose didn't like the smug expression she saw on the other officer's face. "No, Mrs. Beaudette. But we have to conduct several more interviews and may need to speak to you again. It's simply more convenient for us to have you at the police station. You understand."

"Certainly." But she did not. She wanted to go home. She wanted to draw a steaming hot bath and soak for hours then crawl into her bed and sleep for a week, a dreamless slumber where nightmarish images of Thomas's unseeing eyes and the hard accusing eyes of Collette were not present. Most of all, she wanted Luke to draw her into his arms and tell her everything was going to be all right. But the fear blooming in her stomach told her that nothing might ever be right again.

11

Luke stood outside the door where Rose was being held, looking at her through a tiny window set high in the door. She appeared to be about to fall asleep; her head dipped and bobbed, only to snap up as she realized she was about to succumb to exhaustion. Rose, who rarely had a hair out of place, looked disheveled and dirty, and terribly young. Her pale face was streaked with blood, her hair fell in tangles, her dress was stained. He watched in mute frustration as she fought to keep her eyes open. Just go to sleep, Luke wanted to shout. The officer in charge had been given orders not to let anyone speak to Rose until the chief arrived back from the murder scene. Though Luke could have knocked on the door to alert Rose of his arrival, he thought it would be too difficult for her to see him and not to touch him. For God knew he wanted to hold her.

The police had found Luke at his club just as he was about to leave for the evening. He'd had a miserable time, pretending he didn't care where Rose was, but found his will tested mightily. Twice he nearly left his club to pay the Taylors a visit to see if anyone were home. Rose had said she was playing cards at the Taylors' that evening and he forced himself to believe her, even though she'd fiddled with her ring in that restless gesture that told him she was skittish as hell.

When a young officer arrived and told him that the police were holding Rose at headquarters on suspicion of murder, he'd nearly laughed. Rose, who shooed flies out of the house rather than squash them, was being held for murder? It was too absurd to contemplate. He looked past the officer for one of his friends, fully believing someone was playing a prank on him. Officer Colvin, a young man who was obviously excited about having a role, no matter how small, in a murder investigation, assured Luke that it was true. Colvin was nearly giddy with the news, and when Luke finally realized the pup wasn't part of some joke, he nearly cut him in half with his words.

"Please try to hide your joy at imparting this news, Officer. I find the report that my wife is being held for murder rather unsettling. There had better be a damned good reason for it."

The officer instantly sobered. "Yes, sir."

Luke rode with the officer, plying him with questions, many of which the young officer regrettably could not answer. Colvin told him only that Rose had been found hovering over the body of a man at the Supper Club and was being held at police headquarters under suspicion of murder. The Supper Club. Luke had put aside a wave of anger, knowing that he would have to keep a clear head, knowing that what Rose needed was not a lecture, but comfort. He would get angry later, when all this ridiculousness was resolved.

Luke pulled out his pocket watch. It was nearly two in the morning. Where the hell was the chief? As if his thoughts conjured him up, Chief Farwell stepped into the hall. "Luke, I think we ought to talk."

"I want to see my wife." Luke looked at the chief and his belligerence faded. The chief looked damned tired, like a man who'd been through a battle. His usually florid face was pale and his eyes seemed to sag into the puffy bags beneath them. The chief looked at him with such sadness that Luke's heart dropped to his feet. "Why don't we talk first," the chief said firmly.

Luke nodded and felt his dread grow as the older man placed a fatherly hand on his shoulder and led him to his office. Three of the department's top officers were already there, all standing along one side of the small but elegantly appointed room. Chief Farwell nodded to a leather chair in front of his desk and Luke sat down, his hands gripping its padded arms painfully.

"I'm afraid I'm going to have to charge your wife with murder."

Luke felt as if the breath had been knocked out of his body. He might have had his differences with the chief, but he respected the man and knew he would not charge anyone with murder, particularly the wife of a prominent prosecutor, without some damned good evidence. He was wrong, of course, but that didn't make him feel any better.

"Who is the victim?" Luke said, keeping his voice remarkably even.

"Thomas Kersey." The chief saw Luke's reaction. "I see you know the man."

"He's a friend of a couple Rose is acquainted with." Luke wanted to vomit.

"I called you in here, Luke, as a friend. I wanted to warn you that this is going to get messy, that some things are going to come out about your wife that, well, are unpleasant. The investigation is still early, I'll admit that. But I hope you know I wouldn't make such a serious charge unless I was fairly certain that we have the right man. Or woman, that is."

Luke's gray eyes shot fire at the chief. "Your evidence is wrong."

The chief looked at him with pity and understanding, and in that moment Luke wanted to throttle his fat neck, even though part of him knew the chief was being kinder than he needed to be. "I know my wife, Michael."

The older man shook his head. "It's quite possible, Luke, that you don't know her at all."

Luke stood angrily, his expression so fierce, two of the officers in the room stepped forward as if to protect their chief. Luke shot them a scornful look. "I want to see my wife," he bit out. The chief nodded and one of the officers broke rank and gestured for Luke to follow him.

Rose had finally succumbed to sleep. She didn't even rouse at the sound of the door being opened or the quick footsteps of her husband. Luke knelt in front of her, taking in her blood-matted hair, her stained dress, and his stomach tightened. Her hands, folded properly in her lap, were clean, but the lace cuffs on her sleeves were dark red and stiff from dried blood. A tiny niggling of doubt filled him as he took in her appearance and he immediately thrust it away. He knew no details of the crime other than it had occurred in the cloakroom of the Supper Club and that Rose had been found with the body.

"Rose," he said, touching her hand. "Wake up, sweetheart."

Rose jerked awake. She let out a little gasp when she realized where she was and saw Luke kneeling before her. Her eyes immediately filled with tears.

"Oh, Luke," she said, thrusting herself into his arms. "I'm so sorry. Oh, God, I'm so sorry."

Luke held her to him, but went still at her words. He felt as if a part of him died in that moment as he held her shaking body to his.

Rose, who had not allowed herself to cry, let the tears flow, let herself mourn for her innocence, for the shame she was bringing to her family, for poor Thomas Kersey who hadn't ever hurt anyone except himself. Finally, her sobs turned to hiccuppy little gasps. Pulling away, she accepted the handkerchief Luke held out to her and blew her nose, not caring how unladylike the sound was.

"I think the police believe I did it, Luke. They think I killed Thomas."

"And you didn't."

Rose heard the slight question in his voice and was stunned. She stared at Luke in disbelief, gratified only when his cheeks flushed with shame.

"Of course I didn't," she whispered.

Luke pulled her to him. "I'm sorry, love. I know you didn't."

Rose shook her head. "No, you don't know. You don't."

He stepped back angrily, his eyes sweeping over her soiled dress. "Then what the hell are you so sorry about? Sweet Jesus, the first thing out of your mouth, Rose, was 'Luke, I'm sorry.' What the hell am I supposed to think when your dress is covered with the blood of another man and you say you're sorry?" He stopped, a hand behind his neck, massaging where a blazing headache was forming. "I came in here knowing you were innocent," he said more calmly. "What did you mean when you said you were sorry?"

Rose looked up at him, her eyes filled with hurt, her lips trembling as if she were fighting tears. "I lied to you. I was at the Supper Club. I was in the gambling hall and I knew you would disapprove. But I went anyway. That's what I was sorry about." Rose knew she was expecting a lot of Luke to believe she was innocent given what had happened. She wanted him to believe completely and totally in her innocence.

"When I was sitting there in the restaurant kitchen waiting for Chief Farwell to arrive, all I could think about was how angry you were going to be that I was in the Supper Club. I wasn't worried that anyone would think I killed Thomas because I didn't for a moment believe anyone would. I was more worried about your reaction when you discovered I was there at all."

Luke looked at Rose. Her eyes were clear and pleading with him to believe her. "Oh, Rose," he said, taking her hands and drawing her into his embrace.

"We're in big trouble here. You are going to be charged with murder and the police have an excellent case, according to the chief. How did you get yourself into such a mess?"

Rose could only shake her head against his shoulder, too weary to think about it or talk about it. "Can we go home now?"

Luke shook his head. "If the chief formally charges you, you have to remain in custody until the arraignment on Monday. After that, I'm quite certain Judge Mitchell will allow you to be released into my custody."

Rose looked up at Luke, her face stricken, fresh tears coursing down her face. "I can't go home until Monday?" She knew she sounded like a little girl, but she didn't care. She wanted Luke to pick her up and carry her all the way home.

"*If* Judge Mitchell determines you are no threat to society. You're being charged with murder, Rose. I don't think you understand the seriousness of it yet. I'm fairly certain you'll be released pending the trial. I do have some influence in the courts," he said, smiling ironically. "It's already Saturday, sweetheart, so you'll only have two days here. Think of it that way."

"Oh, Luke, a trial?" It was beyond comprehension. Rose was so tired, she swayed against him.

"It may not go that far. If I have anything to do with it, this case will be thrown out long before then. But there are no guarantees." Luke looked down at her and smiled gently. Poor little thing, she could barely keep her head up. He led her to a wooden bench and helped her lay down, then folded his suit jacket and placed it under her head. He laid his coat on top of her. "Try to get some sleep. I'll be back as soon as I can in the morning."

Rose was too tired to argue. She watched, her throat closing painfully, as Luke stepped to the door. He turned just as he was about to close it, saying, "Everything will be all right, Rose. Don't worry."

Rose smiled and closed her eyes, believing Luke with all her heart.

Chapter Five

1

"Bless me, Father, for I have sinned. It has been one week since my last confession." Rose sat in the cell where she had been brought hours before after being roused from her sleep by Chief Farwell. He had brought her into his office, solicitous and kind, and gently explained to her that she was being formally charged with Thomas Edward Kersey's murder. Numb and exhausted beyond belief, Rose simply had nodded her head when the chief asked her if she understood what such a charge meant. Then an officer had led her to a windowless cell with rough brick walls and a cold and dusty tile floor. The tiny room held a metal chamber pot and a cot with a single blanket.

She sat on the cot, her head bowed, as she prepared to confess her sins to Father Beaulieu. Luke had returned earlier that morning with a fresh dress, her rosary beads, and words of encouragement that rang hollow. He had assured her that his office was investigating the charges and predicted with false bravado that this entire messy incident would be cleared up within the week. Luke had arranged for Father Beaulieu to visit her to give her comfort, but Rose couldn't help but wonder if he believed her soul needed cleansing. She knew she should be grateful for the thoughtfulness that had brought the priest to her cell to hear her confession, but all Rose felt was resentment. Luke didn't believe she was innocent. Not in his heart and certainly not in his prosecutor's mind.

It was strange to confess her sins face-to-face. Rose felt oddly exposed, wishing for the dark confessional box and the screen that had given her at least the pretense of anonymity.

"I went back to the Supper Club when I knew I shouldn't have. And I only told my husband of my lie about going the first time yesterday, not immediately as you said I should." Rose bit the inside of her lip, trying to find other less serious sins she might confess to, but her mind was blank. She couldn't think beyond Friday night, beyond the moment her life had become a nightmare.

After a few moments of silence, Father Beaulieu, his faded brown eyes filled with compassion and sorrow, inquired if there was anything more Rose would like to confess to. The question caused anguish to surge through Rose, leaving her weak.

"Father," she whispered, "I'm innocent of the crime of which I am accused. If I had such a sin on my soul, I would confess it to you. You must know that. I felt heavily burdened by the lie I told my husband. And I confessed to God and to you that lie. Please believe me, Father. I have no other sin that I am aware of, else I would confess it."

Father Beaulieu gave Rose a searching look, and finally gave her a gentle smile. "I believe you, Rose."

Rose's eyes filled with tears for she knew that Father Beaulieu accepted her word without reserve. "Thank you, Father. You don't know how much it means for someone to finally believe me."

"Your husband?"

Rose shook her head. "Luke wants to believe in me, but he's an attorney, a prosecutor. He's trained to analyze evidence, to prove someone's guilt. I'm afraid the evidence against me is rather disturbing."

"When Luke came to me this morning he was beyond comforting. He's insane with worry about you. Don't lose faith in him, Rose."

"I don't want to. But it hurts to know he doubts me."

Father Beaulieu took Rose's hand and gave it a squeeze. "I know you are innocent and God knows.

And God is truly the only judge you have to worry about. Would you like to say a rosary with me?"

"Thank you, Father. I'd like that."

Priest and accused murderer bowed their heads and prayed, their fingers resting on their prayer beads, drawing comfort from each other and their faith. Police officers who saw them were oddly touched by the scene of the beautiful woman and the old priest whispering their prayers by the glow of a single light that dangled from the cell's ceiling. It was difficult to believe this gentle, soft-spoken woman, this lady, had thrust a knife into a man, not once, but three times.

"Impossible!" Luke shouted at Arthur Ripley, who had just come from a meeting with Chief Farwell. They were meeting in Luke's study, Luke pacing madly back and forth as Arthur sat and calmly relayed what information he had. An autopsy on the body conducted early that morning showed that Kersey had been stabbed three times. One of those thrusts had been so fierce, a rib had cracked. "Rose could not have driven a knife into a man hard enough to crack a rib. What else does the report say?"

Arthur took a deep breath before continuing. "The fatal blow, according to Dr. Petit, was one to the heart. But he probably would have died eventually of the stab that entered his lungs from the back. They were all deep wounds. His theory is that Kersey was stabbed twice in the back, then fell. The final and fatal blow, and the one that cracked the ribs, occurred while Kersey was on the ground, possibly unconscious. It's hard to prove, but he said that the angle of the wound, because it was horizontal instead of vertical like the back wounds, indicates that sort of blow."

Luke closed his eyes briefly. "Which makes it more likely that a woman could have delivered such a severe wound if she had put her entire weight into the motion. More likely, but certainly not proof that a woman could have done it." Luke stopped his pacing and sat down heavily across from Arthur. "I just can't picture it. I can't picture Rose being that filled with fury. Do you realize the amount of force needed to crack a man's ribs?" He shook his head.

Arthur only shrugged, fueling Luke's anger. "Don't you have an opinion on this, Art?"

Arthur gave his friend a long, solemn look. "You sound like a defense attorney, Luke. I'm a prosecutor. Chances are, I'm going to be the one in that courtroom trying to convict your wife. I can't have an opinion, understand?"

"Christ. You're right." Luke looked up at the ceiling blindly, his hands behind his head. "I'm going to represent her, of course."

"I figured you would. So I won't bother trying to dissuade you, although for the record I think you should hire someone like Rowse. You may not like the man but he's a damned good defense attorney. I suppose you plan to resign?"

"I plan to wire Max Monday morning." The two men were silent, each letting the impact of those words sink in. Luke, whose career path certainly would have ended in the attorney general's office in Boston, was not just another lawyer. His career was ruined, his reputation shattered. But Luke felt no bitterness, no anger directed toward Rose, just a feeling of hopelessness. All his goals, all his dreams were being swept away and there wasn't a goddamn thing he could do about it.

"The chief's got a helluva case, you know," Arthur said. "And I really shouldn't discuss it with you, but I suppose I'm not going to tell you something that you won't be able to find out on your own."

"Arthur, get out of here," Luke said without rancor. "We're in enemy camps now, friend."

A look of immense regret crossed Arthur's features. "Hell, Luke. It shouldn't be this way."

"But it is. Let me warn you of something, while you're here. You'd better prepare the best damn case you ever have. Because I plan to win."

Arthur gave his friend a half smile that held more

sadness than any other emotion. "Luke, I wouldn't count on it."

2

Luke stood outside the Taylors' brownstone and turned the doorbell. John Taylor, his face looking freshly shaved, his thinning hair wet and slicked back, opened the door. To Luke's surprise, he stepped back and immediately let him in.

"I'm sorry to disturb you so early in the morning, Mr. Taylor," Luke said, although he wasn't sorry at all. "I want to . . ."

"I know why you're here, Mr. Beaudette. I'm afraid I can't tell you anything more than what I've already told the police. I only saw your wife hovering over Tommy, her hand still on the knife. That's all."

Luke gave the man a tight smile. "I've actually come to speak with your wife."

"She's indisposed. As you can imagine, it's been a long and trying night. Collette is sleeping."

"That's understandable, Mr. Taylor, given the events. However, it is imperative that I speak to her as soon as possible to find out what happened."

"Why don't you ask your wife?" Collette said from the second-floor landing. She made her way down the stairs, glancing at her husband, a stubborn set to her jaw. She was dressed in a high-necked burgundy gown and her hair was pulled back into a simple knot at her nape. She looked, Luke noted with some unease he couldn't explain, decidedly sedate and respectable, like any number of women in their circle. John muttered a curse under his breath, obviously displeased that Collette was making an appearance.

"I'm here to talk with you, Mrs. Taylor," Luke said as he watched her descend the stairs.

"Collette, you don't have to talk to him. You should be resting, dear," John said, putting a solicitous hand on her arm. She patted him, a reassuring gesture that told her husband that she was perfectly well.

"I don't know much more than John," Collette said serenely, kindly. "Rose had disappeared from the gambling hall and I was looking for her. I suspected she and Thomas might be leaving together, so I went to the cloakroom hoping to head them off and say good night. That's where I found them." Collette reached out and grasped John's hand as if for support, her sky-blue eyes never wavering from Luke.

"Why would you think Rose and Thomas were leaving together?" Luke forced himself to ask.

Collette hesitated, seeming truly reluctant to answer.

"Tell him, Collette," John said.

Luke shot a glance at the man; he seemed to be enjoying this little scene.

Collette lifted her chin. "They were having an affair. I'm sorry, Mr. Beaudette. I did not approve of it, but there it is."

Luke blanched, then turned red. "You're lying."

"I'm afraid not. I know this is difficult for you, Mr. Beaudette. Rose didn't strike me as a woman who would . . . Needless to say, it did seem out of character for her. Perhaps that is why I found it so shocking. You see, Mr. Beaudette, the reason I became friends with Rose was because she seemed such a paragon. I had hoped that by befriending Rose, John and I would be welcomed into your circle of friends and business acquaintances. Unfortunately, Rose was seeking the same thing from me. She was bored with her own circle. She wanted to have fun, and I . . . Well, I'm afraid I was all too successful. I can't help but feel partially to blame for what happened, Mr. Beaudette, and I hope you can forgive me."

Luke's mouth went dry as he remembered Rose's complaints about their friends. Everything Collette was telling him rang true. Rose had changed seemingly overnight from the serene woman he married to a lively laughing girl she'd only hinted existed.

"It began the day we went swimming," Collette said softly, and Luke's entire body stiffened with the strain of remaining calm in the wake of the words that were killing him. "They were . . . carrying on. I told her afterward that I did not approve, but she did not listen. She alluded to the fact that . . ." Collette stopped, and looked at John. "Perhaps I shouldn't say this part," she said, all sweetness.

"Oh, I think it's important that he know, dear," John said.

"Rose alluded to the fact that . . . relations . . . between herself and you were not altogether warm." Collette blushed effectively. "She did feel guilty about the affair. And Thomas was terrified that they would be discovered. He was not altogether as enthused about the arrangement as Rose was, isn't that true, dear?"

"I did get that indication," John said.

With those words, Luke felt his world collapse around him. Hadn't he even suspected something? Certainly not an affair, but hadn't he been crazy with jealousy? And to know that Rose had discussed the marital bed with this . . . this . . . blonde creature was almost beyond bearing. It was that, more than anything, that made Collette's story believable. He remembered Charles coming back from the lake and reporting about the happy group enjoying an early-summer day. Rose had seemed so guileless, so innocent as she discussed the outing, Luke had felt guilty for even thinking there was something untoward about the excursion.

"In fact, Mr. Beaudette, as I told the police, they had fought earlier in the evening. Rose struck Thomas, slapped him. There are several witnesses who saw the incident. Apparently Thomas tried to break it off."

Liars! They had to be lying. They had to be! Rose, sweet Rose, would never . . . Oh, my God. At that moment, Luke's faith in his wife dissolved until all that was left were a few grains of hope that none of these sordid tales were true. Again he thought of that day she had called him at work with her oddly hesitant invitation to go swimming with her friends. Had she even then been contemplating an affair? He'd been filled with guilt at sending his assistant to spy on them, but now it appeared his suspicions, which had seemed illogical at the time, were well-founded.

"Thank you for your time," he said woodenly. "If I have any more questions . . ."

Collette gave him a dazzling smile. "Of course, feel free to stop by any time." And then, as if remembering she was destroying the man standing in front of her, her expression became mournful. "Please don't be too hard on her, Mr. Beaudette. Rose is my friend."

Luke whirled away, muttering something he hoped sounded like a good-bye. He climbed aboard his buggy and jerked the reins, sending the horse into a trot in the direction of Chief Farwell's home on Union Street. Before he spoke to Rose, he must talk to Chief Farwell. He could not trust himself to see Rose, not with Collette's words still ringing in his ears.

Beatrice Farwell opened the door of their modest Colonial, her gentle eyes immediately filling with sympathy upon seeing who their visitor was. It was a look Luke was beginning to hate. "Come in, Mr. Beaudette. Michael is out back in the garden."

The Farwells' tiny yard was almost completely taken up by an impressive garden that was just starting to send up green shoots. A rabbit hutch was built in one corner of this tiny farm in the middle of a city. Farwell was banging in a stake at the garden's far end when he saw Luke walking toward him along the perimeter of the patch.

"I thought you might be sleeping," Luke said, taking in the chief's dirty overalls and sweat-stained shirt.

"Couldn't sleep," the chief said, pounding at the stake twice more before tossing the sledgehammer to the side.

Now that he was here, Luke was unsure he wanted to know the truth. He glanced around the sunny garden rather than broach the subject they both knew he was there to discuss. To his horror, Luke felt his throat begin to close up and his eyes to burn, as Chief Farwell looked at him with fatherly compassion. He turned away and rested both hands on a split-rail fence that separated the chief's property from his neighbor's. He stared down at his hands, forcing himself to get hold of his emotions, but it was a difficult task, given that his world had shattered at his feet. He knew the chief would confirm what the Taylors told him, but he needed to hear it. Needed the words to be driven into his skull, needed the pain to drive away the terrible sorrow that nearly paralyzed him.

"I plan to defend Rose, Chief. In that capacity, I need to confirm certain aspects of the case with you." There, that sounded almost normal. Feeling in control once again, he turned to the chief, refusing to acknowledge the sympathy he saw in the older man's face. "I've interviewed the Taylors. Apparently Rose and the victim were involved in some sort of altercation not long before she was found with the body."

Chief Farwell let out a heavy breath. "Three employees reported they saw the victim and Rose kissing, then Rose slapped him. They claim the incident occurred in the ballroom."

"Ballroom?"

"That's what they're calling the gambling hall. Of course, by the time we went down there, there was no sign of a gambling joint. Cardi's a fast worker. That was the extent of the altercation. However, earlier in the evening, Thomas Kersey was seen kissing your wife's hand. It did not appear that she objected to that overture. That was witnessed by your man Patrick Sullivan." Chief Farwell had been speaking in a businesslike tone, trying to keep the conversation as impersonal as possible. But with the next, he softened his voice. "If you spoke with the Taylors, then you know that your wife and the victim were having an affair and that the victim wanted to break it off. We're going on the assumption that the breakup precipitated the altercation in the gambling hall and led, eventually, to the murder."

Luke could only nod. His prosecutor's mind would have built the same scenario, but his heart still cried out that something was wrong, that Rose was not the sort of woman who broke vows made before God. He knew his heart had no business in the courtroom, but he refused to hand the fate of his wife over to another attorney. Evidence! he shouted to himself. Look at the goddamn evidence. He could not let his emotions come between him and this case. His training as a prosecutor could help him guess at their strategy, but he must start thinking like a defense attorney. Whether Rose was guilty or not, he had to come up with a way to prove she was innocent.

"Have you spoken to any patrons other than the Taylors?" Luke asked.

"We've been unable to find any. Understandable, given that they were all engaged in an illegal activity."

Luke became aware of the day, the garden, the ordinariness of everything about him. It didn't seem possible that his wife, his Rose, was sitting in a cell at this very moment, accused of killing her lover. It was a glorious spring day, and the air was heavy with the scent of lilacs. Rose would have turned her face up to the sun and smiled, twirling her parasol ineffectually behind her. He was seized by the wrongness of it all.

"Pretty little spot, Chief."

The chief grunted and picked up his sledgehammer, knowing the unpleasant part of their conversation had ended.

"I'll see you in court on Monday, then," Luke said.

Chief Farwell, the sledgehammer slung over one shoulder, placed his free hand firmly on Luke's shoulder. "Good luck, son."

Luke could only nod, emotions he'd struggled with all day threatening once again. When he reached his buggy, he gripped the reins until they dug painfully into his hands, closing his eyes fiercely against the pain that nearly disabled him. He couldn't bear to see Rose now, for he was afraid of what he might say or do. By God, if she had been with another man, she was safer in jail than with him. His hands shook, the reins making little slapping sounds against the buggy.

Luke finally became aware of himself, that he was sitting still as a stone in the buggy, which was still parked in front of the chief's house, and that he was making a spectacle of himself. He unbraked the buggy, slapped the reins, and turned the vehicle toward home. He'd not visit Rose today. Maybe Sunday. Maybe by then he would be in better control of his emotions. Maybe by then he'd be able to look into her tearstained face and listen to her declarations of innocence without wanting to throttle her.

3

Rose awoke Monday morning to the sound of a drunk being noisily led into a cell down the hall from hers. The new prisoner's slurred protests and the guard's hearty laughter were unwelcome reminders of where she was. Her hip was numb from sleeping on her side on the hard cot and her neck was stiff from the lack of an adequate pillow. Rose turned and lay on her back, gazing at the water-stained ceiling, hopelessly wishing she could close her eyes and wake up beneath her silk canopy. Her bladder was full, but she dreaded taking care of her bodily functions in the openness of the cell. Though the officers were kind enough to give her warning when they approached, it was still awfully difficult to relax, knowing that someone could come around the corner at any moment and catch her in such a vulnerable position. Rose could only take heart that this would likely be her last day in the cell. Her hearing was today and everyone she spoke with told her she'd be home by noon. Though Rose was not sure she wanted to go home.

Throughout Saturday and Sunday, Rose's family had stayed with her, sitting in uncomfortable chairs outside her cell. Rose had been surprised and warmed by the fact that her mother, knitting in hand, sat outside her cell for hours at a time. She had been outraged to find her little girl incarcerated. How dared the police arrest Rose, she'd said again and again. She hadn't raised Rose to be a murderer and firmly believed some awful mistake had been done.

Nicole, her eyes red from crying, had been brave enough to ask Rose what had happened. And when Rose told her, Nicole had shaken her head, believing in her totally, but disappointed that Rose had been silly enough to go back to the Supper Club after her dire warnings. Her father had also come, as had Nicole's husband Louis. Even a few friends had stopped by, nearly as outraged as Aline to find one of their own sitting in a dirty cell. Rose was heartened by her family's unfailing faith in her, by their rage at the newspaper that wrote in such lurid detail—much of it false—about the murder. Rose refused to read the accounts that had her mother so livid, she'd threatened to sue the newspaper and Chief Farwell. She smiled and chatted as if she wasn't separated from her family by thick bars. And when they left for the day, heading home for supper, she'd waved cheerfully, only to clutch at the cold bars after they'd left and stare at the door that led out of the small cellblock. By Sunday night, it was clear that Luke was not coming and all the staring in the world would not produce him.

Rose rubbed her eyes and forced herself to sit up. The drunk, the only other prisoner, was snoring now. Other than listen to the snores, there was nothing for her to do except think about why Luke had stayed away. She could only think of one reason: He thought her guilty. Why else had he not returned?

She sat there for what seemed like hours, until she began to think, a bit hysterically, that the hearing wasn't this day after all. A young officer, who looked so nervous Rose nearly said "Boo," cautiously handed her through the bars a mug of coffee and a sack filled with sweet buns. She was so nervous, so downtrodden, she could barely force herself to sip the brew, made much stronger than she preferred. Finally, she set it and the unopened sack aside as she steeled herself against the tears that once again threatened. She sat on the narrow end of the cot facing the bars, her head leaning up against the cool brick, and waited.

Rose must have nodded off, for the next time she opened her eyes, Luke was there gazing at her impassively. "I've brought you another dress," he said, motioning to the gray silk he held draped over one arm.

"Thank you." Rose screamed at herself to demand to know why Luke hadn't visited, but she stopped herself. She knew. She saw it in his eyes, no matter that he tried to hide it. He didn't believe her.

Luke's gaze swept the cell, taking in the dirty chamber pot, the narrow cot, but his gray eyes now showed nothing. "I plan to represent you throughout the duration of this case. Today you'll be formally charged in court," he said, looking somewhere behind her. "Judge Mitchell will set bond and you will be released upon payment. I've little doubt that you'll be released, or that the bond will not be reasonable given your position in the community."

Rose bit the inside of her lip to stop her tears. How dare he stand there and talk to her as if she were merely a client? How dare he presume to represent her when he thought she was guilty?

He began to pace, hands behind his back. "Expect a hostile crowd outside the courtroom, given what was in the newspapers."

Rose lifted her chin. "I haven't read them."

"Just as well. It isn't . . . pleasant reading." Luke clenched his jaw and let out a shaky breath, the only indication that he felt anything at all. "I believe we should act as normally as possible, even in the face of the hostility. We should carry on as if nothing is wrong. As if we haven't a care." He stopped suddenly and turned away, swallowing as if he were trying not to be sick.

To Rose's disgust, she actually felt a moment of sympathy for him, the man who thought she'd committed murder. Anger replaced that short-lived, gentler feeling, but she remained silent. Nothing she said would change his mind about her. Let him think she was guilty, she thought wildly, let him suffer with it as she suffered sitting in this cell for two endless days, waiting for him to come and hold her and tell her everything would be all right.

"We should go on outings. Be seen together." He swallowed again, and Rose narrowed her eyes and shook her head.

"I'm going to live with my mother," she said, almost as surprised by her own words as Luke appeared to be.

"You are not," Luke said, turning to face her, every muscle in his body exuding anger.

Rose lifted her head a notch. "I will not live with a man who believes the vile lies he reads in the newspaper. Furthermore, I will not be represented by an attorney who believes I am guilty. Don't bother denying it, I can read it in your face."

"I wasn't about to deny it," he spat.

"Oh." It was a little gasp. Even though she suspected it, she'd expected Luke to at least deny he believed her guilty. "Well then, that truly leaves me no choice, does it?" Rose stood and turned away from him so that he would not see the hurt his words caused. "I'm going to live with my mother, Luke. You cannot stop me."

"As your attorney, I strongly advise you not to leave me. It would only make you appear guilty to the community, to the prospective jurors who will decide your fate. As distasteful as it is for both of us, for the sake of this case you must come home." Luke grasped the bars. "If you go to live with your mother, you might as well proclaim your guilt."

Rose's back stiffened. She couldn't help but recognize the truth in Luke's words. But how could she return to live with a man who thought she was capable of murder? She turned slowly toward him, trying to block out the anger and pain she saw clearly in his eyes. "Were you on the jury, Luke, what would your verdict be?"

"Knowing what I know now?"

All the frustration and anger, the pain and fear, the loneliness and despair welled up in Rose. "You know nothing! Nothing! Else you wouldn't be standing there looking as if you are the victim in this." She surged forward, throwing herself against the bars, the shock of the impact reverberating painfully up her arms. Luke backed away and Rose was gratified to see alarm in his face, though she wasn't certain whether it was for her or himself. "Get away from me," she said, her voice ragged. "Leave me alone."

"I won't!" he roared. He shoved the dress through the bars. "Get dressed. We have to be in court in half an hour." He turned his back and Rose realized she was expected to undress in her cell. Despite everything, she was bothered that Luke thought he needed to turn his back.

"Why are you doing this, Luke? Why are you defending me if you believe me guilty?" she asked softly. She watched as his back stiffened, then relaxed, almost sagging in defeat.

"I don't, Rose. Not entirely. God help me, I don't."

It was worse than Luke expected. The crowd in the courtroom was respectful and quiet as Judge Mitchell read the charge and Rose answered in a clear, steady voice. Her parents and sister sat behind her, lending their unfailing support. Charles Cutter, his assistant, stood beside him. Despite Luke's protestations, the man had resigned to continue working for Luke, leaving him humbled and exceedingly grateful. Outside, a near-mob had grown, curious people who were nearly giddy with joy that one of society's own had fallen to such a disgraceful level. The police were ineffectual,

Luke thought, apathetic toward the surging mass that waited for Rose to emerge.

It seemed almost all of Springfield waited outside the Elm Street courthouse, drawn by the drama of the case. It held all the elements that drove a crowd into a frenzy of curiosity. Reporters, some from as far away as Boston, hung about trying to get any tidbit they could from any source they could. And they reported the details, some true, some not, with the same relish. A high-bred woman, married to one of Springfield's preeminent citizens, arrested for murdering a man— possibly her lover: what could possibly be more scintillating? The crowd was nearly frothing at its collective mouth to get a glimpse of this notorious woman. When she appeared, the mob surged forward, shouting and calling out to her. Some threw rotten fruit at her, gleeful shouts erupting when one large, soft, and moldy tomato hit its mark. They spat, they screamed, they reached for her with outstretched arms and claw-like hands.

Luke wiped the rotten fruit from his face and huddled even closer over Rose, who seemed strangely unaffected by the savage crowd. Though police, with nightsticks flailing, tried to break a path through the mob to the awaiting closed carriage, the short walk seemed endless.

"Whore! Murderer!"

Rose cringed, the only reaction she gave that she was even aware of the mob.

"Hang 'er. Hang the whore!" Many in the crowd laughed and Luke drew her even closer, practically carrying her along.

Finally they reached the carriage, bruised and battered from the struggle. Luke heaved Rose inside as quickly as possible and yelled to the fearful driver, who hadn't needed any encouragement, to begin driving away. The crowd was so thick, it was several terrifying minutes before the carriage, the horses nervous and confused by the crowd, managed to break away.

Luke and Rose were silent in the carriage, which

smelled of the rotten tomato that still clung to their clothing. Rose's eyes looked impossibly big in her pale face, as if the full extent of the trouble she was in finally hit her.

"Why were they saying such horrid things? Why? They were all so . . . angry. I didn't even . . ." Rose buried her face in her hands and sobbed, the horror of the day finally overcoming her.

Luke watched her cry, struggling to remain impassive. He refused to let her tears sway him, refused to let emotions tell him which way to turn in this case. He needed to divorce his heart from his mind if he was going to successfully represent her. He damned his heart for its softness, for wrenching at the sight of those tears, for wanting to hold her against him.

"That should be the worst of it," Luke said, when her crying had abated. "They'll lose interest until the trial and I doubt we'll see a repeat of that strident behavior. The newspaper will run out of new stories to write. Things will calm down."

"My God, what *are* the newspapers saying about me?" Rose asked.

"Let's discuss the case later, shall we?"

"I want to know why . . . why they are saying those awful things. I don't even know those people." Rose let out a shaky little breath as she tried to control her tears.

"It's of little consequence as long as the stories now stop, which I imagine they will. Until the trial, the only story that should appear in the newspaper is mention of you attending various social events. Stories like that should somewhat diffuse the other."

Rose shook her head. "Oh, Luke, I can't go out. I can't."

"You can and you will."

"How can you be so cold?"

Luke looked at her, his eyes uncompromising. "I have a case to win. If you hide away in the house, people will think you guilty."

"I don't care!" Rose shouted.

"It is of no concern to me whether you care or not. The only concern I have is about winning this case."

"Is that all I have become to you, a case to win?"

Luke nearly flinched. "You know that is not true," he said, his voice low.

Rose turned away from him. "I don't know anything anymore."

4

Rose turned her head into her pillow, her own soft pillow in her own soft bed. Go away, world, she thought. But it rushed to her like a tidal wave, crashing around her, tossing her about and leaving her sick inside. For days, it felt like she had something stuck in her throat and no matter how many times she swallowed, it was still there. At odd times, the little lump would grow, until she was crying without knowing why. And then it would come to her, as she ate or got dressed or washed her face. I'm charged with murder. She'd giggle or cry, depending on the moment.

Rose had been home for two days and had rarely left her room. Perhaps if she stayed inside that little sanctuary, the world could never get to her. No one would ever shout "Murderer!" again, newspapers would not spout the horrific details of a crime for which she had already been convicted in the minds of many Springfield citizens. She'd been called a whore and a murderer, she'd been spat at and laughed at by members of the crowd who had gathered outside the courtroom Monday morning. Little Rose Desrosier, who had only wanted to do something as daring as climb trees, was now Springfield's most notorious character. She would not leave her house. Not ever again. She'd refused to see everyone, including Luke.

Those wretched tears that bloomed from that knot in her throat started again. "I hate everyone," she whispered. A polite knock on her door went firmly ignored.

"Rose, I'm coming in." Luke's muffled voice came through the door. "If I am going to represent you, we must talk."

"No! Why would you want to talk to a murderer anyway?" Rose shouted, feeling petulant and foul. She could almost hear the sigh she knew he was releasing. When she saw the door begin to open, she pulled the blankets over her head. "Go away!"

Luke didn't. He marched over to the bed and sat down so that his hip touched her legs. She moved away.

"Rose, I know how difficult this has been for you."

She snorted.

"But it's been hell for me, too."

"My heart weeps for you."

Luke frowned at her sarcastic reply. They needed to talk, Rose needed to know what the Taylors had been saying about her, and he needed to see her face when he told her. Since Rose's arraignment, he had become more and more torn, damning the evidence that pointed to her guilt and damning his heart for doubting that evidence. But he knew Rose like no one else did. He knew she was the sweetest creature God created. Her tiny bit of rebellion would not have extended to a full-fledged affair. He had prayed as he had never before that God give him the strength to believe in Rose. The doubt that came and went, growing large and horrific, only to be crushed by the single beat of his heart, was driving him insane. He needed to know, one way or the other, whether she was guilty or innocent—not only of murder but of adultery.

Luke dragged the blankets forcibly from Rose's hands until her angry face was revealed. "Hiding will not help you." She pressed her lips together as if forcing herself to not say what she wanted to. She looked so adorably young with her sleep-messy hair and her snapping brown eyes, Luke found himself smiling down at her. That only served to produce a deeper scowl.

"As your attorney, I recommend you begin cooper-

ating with my investigation," Luke said with mock
sternness.

"I don't know why you bother, you already know
what you need to know."

Luke ignored her. "There are many aspects of this
case that are puzzling." Rose began to open her
mouth but Luke held one finger to her lips. "Please
indulge me, Mrs. Beaudette."

She crossed her arms and looked away, pretending
disinterest.

Luke stood and began pacing. "There are many in-
consistencies. For example, you say Collette asked you
to meet her at the cloakroom, while she says she went
looking for you."

"She's lying," Rose spat.

"Please do not interrupt. Several witnesses saw
Thomas Kersey kiss you in the gambling hall and I
will assume that you will not dispute this." Rose remained silent and bile filled his throat. "Witnesses also
saw you strike Thomas in the face, and apparently not
long after, you were discovered with the body, your
hand still on the knife. The police have concluded that
you and Kersey were having an affair and he tried to
break it off, which precipitated the slap."

Rose could not help but react. Her eyes grew wide
in outrage. "That's not true! He did kiss me, but I
struck him because of that kiss. He had no right to
kiss me. I certainly never gave him any indication that
such a forwardness would be welcome. And he apologized to me."

"Then you were not having an affair with Kersey."

Rose looked at Luke with stunned disbelief, her
eyes immediately filling with those hated tears. "Of
course not. I'm married."

"Married women have been known to have affairs,"
Luke said, his tone even.

"How can you sit there and say such evil things?
How can you?" Rose looked at him, her eyes accusing
and hurt. "Do you love me?" she said suddenly, and

Luke jerked as if he'd been struck. He looked away from her. This was not going as he had planned.

"You know I do," he said quietly.

"Then how could you think such a thing of me? I'll never forgive you, Luke. Never. Believing that is worse than believing I murdered someone. I know that sounds horrible, but it's how I feel."

Luke massaged the back of his neck where the headache that began early Saturday morning had lingered and was now blooming. "I didn't say I believed it, Rose. I just wanted to let you know what others are saying. As your lawyer, I had to ask."

Rose brushed her tears away with the heels of her hands and sniffed loudly. "Who is saying such things?" she asked dully.

"The Taylors."

"Collette and John?" Rose shook her head in disbelief. How could they betray her like that, how could they lie? Why would they lie? "I don't understand," she said, choking back new tears. "Why would they say something like that? It doesn't make sense. They knew I would never. They knew . . ." Rose's hands began to shake. It could not be true. She could forgive them for believing she had killed Thomas, as outrageous as that was. After all, Collette had discovered her with Thomas and her hand on the knife. It had certainly been damning. But to lie about her and Thomas, to fabricate the story that they were having an affair and tell it to the police and her husband. It was more than her heart could take.

Rose looked at Luke, her eyes filled with profound grief. "I thought they were my friends."

"Apparently not."

"You're certain it was the Taylors who said such a thing?"

"They told me themselves. Collette even said she disapproved of it, but you ignored her."

Anger replaced the pain of their treachery. "She *what*? Why? Why would she lie? She is evil to say such things." Rose whipped off her covers and stood,

incensed and ready to confront Collette with her lies.
"How dare she?" The enormity of what the Taylors
had done finally settled on Rose. She started blankly
at her carpet, her mind a whirlwind, thinking back on
their so-called friendship. It was almost as if they'd
planned the entire thing. And that, perhaps, was the
most frightening thing of all. Rose sat down abruptly,
horrified by what she was thinking, that she had been
part of a well-planned and carefully executed plot to
frame her. They'd done one hell of a job.

"Oh, God, Luke. What are we going to do?"

"We're going to prove you didn't do it," he said,
standing.

Rose looked up at Luke. "Do you believe I'm
innocent?"

Luke hesitated only a hairsbreadth of a second, but
it was enough to break Rose's heart. Luke knew he'd
hesitated and cursed himself for his uncertainty. He
wanted to believe Rose was innocent as he had never
wanted anything before. But he couldn't help but
think that Rose had a far, far better reason to lie
about the events of Saturday night than the Taylors
did. Why frame Rose for a murder? What could possibly be their motive? Even as he asked himself those
questions, he became angry at himself for doubting
Rose.

"I don't want you in here," Rose whispered.

"Rose. You've got to understand. I'm no saint, and
only a saint could completely ignore the evidence."

"You're my husband."

"And you're my wife," he said angrily. "The same
wife who went to the Supper Club and lied to her
husband about it. The same wife who told her friend
that our marital relations were not satisfactory. The
same wife who was seen kissing another man. Jesus
Christ, Rose. I'm trying, God knows I'm trying, but I
refuse to be made a fool of."

It seemed impossible, but Rose's face grew even
more pale. "She had no right. No right to say that to
you. It was private."

"Yes," Luke spat. "Private. Between a husband and a wife."

Rose placed her fists against her forehead, unable to accept this newest betrayal. Collette had used everything against her, had framed her for murder, had made her husband doubt her. What a fool she was, what a silly, dim-witted little fool. How could she expect Luke to believe in her? As he listed all her sins, she wondered if she'd been expecting far too much from Luke. It was all too, too horrible. She'd never felt so alone, so miserable. And all because she'd been bored with her confining life. She'd let herself be drawn into a life of sin and she deserved whatever she got.

"I was unhappy. I don't even know how the conversation started. Collette was so blasé about the whole thing and I was . . ."

Luke waited for her to continue, but all Rose could do was shake her head, unable to speak past her clogged throat. How had she allowed this to happen? At that moment, the anger Rose felt toward the Taylors made a turn and shot directly into her. Everything was all her fault. She had become friends with Collette; she had let Thomas be too friendly with her, thinking it was all a game; she had discussed the most intimate aspects of her life with a near-stranger. Heat prickles of despair made her skin burn and she closed her eyes against it. Despite her self-loathing, she still wanted Luke to believe in her unconditionally. Was she asking too much of him? Perhaps. But she childishly wanted someone to believe her and she wanted that someone to be Luke. She was aware of him staring at her and Rose wondered what he was thinking. Was he thinking she was a murderess? An adulteress? She twisted her wedding ring mindlessly, letting it dig into her flesh, making it hurt so that she could feel something other than the suffocating pain in her heart. She'd make him believe in her, she decided with a particularly brutal twist of her ring.

"I'm innocent, Luke, and I'm going to prove it."

Luke sat down on the bed again and took her ringed hand, frowning at the mark she'd left on her finger. "Rose," he began, swallowing heavily. "I may not be able to convince a jury that Collette is the one who is lying. I want you to be aware of that possibility."

"But I'm telling the truth," Rose said, jerking her hand away.

"We need to build a case as strong as the prosecution."

Rose's shoulders slumped at his words. "I suppose people simply won't take my word for it."

"No, I'm afraid not. That's why you have to tell me everything you can possibly remember about that night. Everything you know about Thomas Kersey. Don't leave any detail out. Take some time to think about it and write everything down."

Rose nodded, feeling a tiny bit of hope surging.

Luke stood. "Your parents and sister have been calling and badgering me to let them see you. Do you think you're up to it? I've never seen your father as animated, or your mother as, well, motherly."

Suddenly, Rose wanted nothing more than to see her family. She needed to surround herself with people who believed in her. And for the first time in memory, she wanted her mother.

5

Nicole wiped a bit of raw egg from her mother's shoulder as they stood outside the Beaudettes' brownstone. The good citizens of Springfield had turned against them en masse, it seemed. When news of the murder hit the newspapers, the first reaction of their circle had been disbelief, which had almost immediately turned to scorn. In this case, the sins of the daughter were the sins of the entire family. Immediately following the first newspaper reports on Sunday, Nicole and Louis had been inundated with visitors who seemed sincere in their expressions of condolence and their conviction that Rose had been unjustly charged. Soon, though, and before Louis had an inkling of it, Nicole began to realize that the kind visitors were simply seeking gossip. It wasn't until Tuesday evening when Louis finally realized that his newfound popularity was founded on something vicious. In the evening edition of the *Springfield Union*, some of what they'd told their acquaintants appeared nearly word-for-word.

In a rage partly brought on by the bottle of wine he had consumed before dinner, Louis had turned his anger toward Nicole. It was somehow her fault that shame had descended upon the family. He'd called Rose all sorts of horrid names in a rather bizarre fit in which he expressed surprise that Nicole had not been implicated as well. Nicole had simply watched with detached curiosity as he ranted about the sins of Rose, turning so purple, she thought, and not without some hope, that he looked as if he might drop dead on the spot.

With that scene still firmly in her memory, she'd listened with unadulterated hatred as Louis fawned over her mother, agreeing whenever she expressed her disgust with the police and the entire legal system. How she hated that man! She'd almost been grateful when they'd been forced to stop their conversation by a loud bang on the outside of their carriage as they traveled to Mattoon Street. They'd drawn the curtains for privacy, but kept the windows open to allow air into the stuffy interior, and that was how the egg, thrown by one of Springfield's good citizens, made its way inside. The egg, regretfully, Nicole thought, splattered just above Louis's head, spraying them all with bits of shell and yolk. Louis had taken the brunt of it, and Nicole escaped with a tiny bit of egg white sprayed onto one cheek, but no one in the carriage had gone unscathed. The driver slapped the reins to speed up the team pulling the carriage, saving them from more damage. But outside, they continued to hear the bang of eggs striking the outside and the angry yells of the driver, as if someone were running alongside the carriage with missiles at the ready. No one within had the courage to stick his or her head out to investigate the commotion.

When they'd finally reached Mattoon Street and stopped in front of Rose's house, the smell of raw egg inside the carriage was nauseating.

"What awful people," Aline said as Nicole dabbed her shoulder. "I'd report it to the police, but I have no faith that anything would be done."

Nicole smiled at her mother, stunned by the woman's reaction to the events, and, if Nicole were honest, just the tiniest bit jealous. It was a curious thing to see her mother defend Rose so stalwartly when she had been one of Rose's most consistent critics. Rose was too loud, too flashy, too wild . . . and that was before her metamorphosis. Nicole couldn't help but think that her mother was secretly proud of Rose, for that was certainly how she was acting.

Nicole watched with worry as Rose tentatively entered the parlor where her family awaited her, as if uncertain about the reception she faced. She wore one of her old gowns, a dark gray silk that made her pale skin appear nearly colorless. Nicole, overwhelmed by the haunted look in her little sister's eyes, ran to her and embraced her with a mighty squeeze. "I'll scold you later," she whispered in Rose's ear.

Rose drew back with a little laughing sob. "I deserve a thorough scolding for putting you all through this," she said through her tears.

"Nonsense," Aline said, walking over to Rose, pressing her almost painfully against her. The embrace was short but moved Rose profoundly.

"Oh, Mother," Rose said, tears flowing freely. She threw herself into the older woman's arms. Aline seemed momentarily stunned to find her daughter weeping against her, but she slowly drew her arms around her youngest child and seemed to melt into her. Nicole watched, her eyes filling with tears, as her father joined them with his own awkward attempts at comfort.

"There, there," he said, his voice gruff. "That's enough tears for now."

"Yes. Certainly enough tears," Aline said, breaking away and sitting beside her husband. To Nicole's stunned disbelief, she saw that her mother's eyes were shining with unshed tears. Impossible! Again that unwanted stab of jealousy struck her as she watched the three of them recover from their display of emotion. Rose, she knew, gave her love in an unreserved way. But to have both parents practically blubbering over her was . . . startling. Nicole couldn't help but wonder if she would have garnered the same response.

To Nicole's utter disgust, Louis went up to where Rose had sat and patted her on the shoulder. "We've all been heartbroken over this," he said. Nicole smiled when Rose couldn't bring herself to do more than nod. Good girl.

"Have you seen the newspapers?" her mother demanded, now back in control.

"No. I don't want to see them."

"Good. All a bunch of lies." Rose's mother made her pronouncement with a sharp nod and her father muttered, "Lies," under his breath.

"Luke told us yesterday that he's resigned from the attorney general's office to represent you," Nicole said.

Rose looked startled. "I know he's representing me," she said hesitantly. "He didn't tell me he resigned, though."

"Of course he resigned," Louis blustered. "He can't represent a murderer . . . I mean, an accused murderer . . . and continue to work for the attorney general. He's a prosecutor, not a defender."

"No. I suppose not," Rose said, and Nicole's heart twisted as she watched as the full implication of Luke's resignation hit her.

"Papers said that his career's over," Louis continued, mindless of the warning look Nicole shot him.

"They even said he would have been the attorney general one day. Not now, though, that's for certain. Don't think the voters would elect a man whose wife was . . ."

"Louis! You're upsetting Rose. She obviously didn't know."

Rose clasped her hands in her lap. She hadn't known, though she should have. She hadn't thought about what it meant to have Luke represent her. She hadn't thought about anything but herself. Though she was angry with Luke for not believing in her innocence, she forced her mind to turn away from herself and to think how Luke was being affected. Luke loved his job as a prosecutor and she'd known he was thought highly of by the attorney general. She'd been so proud of him and had clipped every newspaper and law journal article that mentioned his name. And now, because of her, his career was in ruins. He'd be a laughingstock among his peers, a social pariah, an object of pity.

Luke chose that moment to enter the sitting room. He'd wanted to give Rose time to be with her family before joining them. The room was utterly silent when Luke entered, and he paused at the door as if uncertain whether to continue in.

"We were just telling Rose that you'd resigned your position," Louis said as a way of explaining the silence.

Luke's mouth tightened. "It's of no consequence," he said.

"No consequence?" Rose asked with a hysterical note to her voice. "How can you say that? You're ruined and it's all my fault."

"I think *ruined* is a bit of an exaggeration," Luke said as he walked into the room and took a seat opposite his wife.

"Luke can still practice law," Nicole said kindly.

"But who will want to be the client of a man whose wife is a murderer?"

"You're not a murderer, Rose," Nicole said firmly.

"I know I'm not but that's not what everyone will believe. Even if I'm found innocent, some people will believe I did it unless the real person confesses. No one will hire the husband of a murderer as a lawyer."

"Let me worry about my career, Rose. For now, we should only concern ourselves with the upcoming trial."

"But I've ruined everything," Rose said, her voice high-pitched and shaking. "Don't you see what I've done? Why is this happening to me?"

Rose's mother stood, crossed the room, and slapped Rose hard across the face. Everyone in the room froze, shocked expressions on their faces. Only Rose moved, her hand flying to her cheek. "Stop feeling sorry for yourself," Aline said angrily. "Your husband needs you to be strong now. I didn't raise you to be a weakling, I didn't raise—"

"That's enough," Rose's father said quietly. Amazingly, Aline clamped her mouth shut. "Rose is a good girl," he muttered.

Rose looked over to her father and gave him the tiniest of smiles. It was the first time in her memory that he'd ever stood up to his wife. Flustered, Aline returned to her chair, her cheeks burning red, as if she'd been the one slapped.

"Didn't mean to start all this," Louis said, scratching behind his ear. Nicole shot him a look of disgust but refrained from responding.

Rose, her cheek still hurting from her mother's slap, said, "I'm really very tired. I appreciate your stopping by, but . . . I just can't . . ." She seemed to deflate before their eyes. She wanted to curl up in her bed and disappear. Rose knew she shouldn't feel sorry for herself but she just couldn't help it. Be strong for Luke, her mother had said. She couldn't even be strong for herself.

Rose watched with detachment as Luke led her family out the door. What a miserable visit it had turned out to be. It had started so promisingly only to deteriorate into something ugly. With a twinge of regret, Rose realized that most family gatherings throughout her life had followed a similar pattern. Why did it always have to end this way, with bitterness and anger?

"Well, I'd say that went well," Luke said.

Rose groaned. "Can we leave the country? Go to China or maybe Antarctica?"

"We've got to face this," Luke said.

"I don't want to."

"Hell, Rose, neither do I."

Rose was startled by the weariness she heard in Luke's voice. "I'm sorry that you felt the need to resign." She couldn't help but think it was one more thing for Luke to be angry with her about. "After this is all over, maybe you could get your position back?" she asked hopefully.

Luke let out a bitter laugh. "I don't believe that will be possible."

Rose saw something in his eyes before he looked away that frightened her. Leaving his position was far more devastating than she'd thought. His life had been ruined by Thomas's murder as much as hers, she realized. Perhaps even more so.

"Luke, I'm so sorry. I never thought for one moment that something I did would hurt you so much."

"What did you think?" Luke said, letting out some of the anger he hadn't even known he'd been suppressing. "When you walked into that gambling hall, did it ever occur to you that your presence there was profoundly improper given your husband's profession?"

"Yes. I felt terrible."

"And yet you went back."

"But I explained all that. Thomas was in trouble."

"Thomas." He said the name like a curse. "If you'd thought more about your own family than of Thomas, we might not be in this position."

"I know that," she said, her hands drawing into two fists. "Every hour since this happened I've been torturing myself with those very thoughts. I shouldn't have allowed Collette and John to take me into that gambling hall. I should never have become Collette's friend at all. I know this is all my fault."

"On that point, at least, we agree," Luke said, no longer able to contain his anger. His hand massaged his neck as almost nauseating pain hit him. He hadn't slept well in days, he was tired and hurt and angry—more angry than he'd ever been in his life. He felt it rip through him, knew it was about to erupt, but he had neither the strength to stop it nor the inclination. He wanted to get angry, he wanted to tear something apart. He looked down at Rose, whose face was full of sadness and regret, and felt nothing but an anger that terrified him.

"How could you have allowed this to happen, Rose? You are not a stupid woman. It is one of the attributes I admired about you. That and your decency, your quiet manner. Your goddamn common sense." He let out a bitter laugh. "Where the hell is the woman I married?"

Rose surged to her feet. "You needn't curse," she said. "And I believe you should make up your mind about what sort of wife you want. For not a week ago, you were pleased that I was not the timid little mouse I had been. You were rather delighted with me on that occasion, as I recall." They both flushed at her obvious reference to their briefly shared passion.

"I did not believe even that woman capable of . . ." He stopped, sickened by what he was about to say. He looked away from Rose's stricken face, then irrationally turned his anger toward his wife. He strode over to her, his face an angry mask, his lips compressed so tightly they nearly disappeared. Taking her chin in his hand, he forced Rose to look at him.

"Did you secretly enjoy Kersey's attention? Did you wish it was him in your bed and not me that night? I did think it strange and rather out of character of you to come to me. 'I want to touch you,' " he mimicked cruelly. "Was it me you wanted to touch, Rose? Or Thomas?" He grasped her shoulder and gave her a little shake. "Tell me!"

Rose shook her head, tears streaming from her eyes, unable to believe the horrid accusations. She knew Luke had been driven by hurt, but that didn't ease the bite of his awful words—words that would never be forgotten by either one of them. This moment, with Luke looking at her as if he hated her, was the worst moment of her life. It transcended the horror of finding Thomas, the humiliation of being called a whore and a murderer, the pain of knowing the Taylors had betrayed her.

"How dare you, Luke," she said, with more sadness than anger. "I don't think I can ever forgive you for saying that."

"*You* cannot forgive *me*? You're the one who was seen kissing a man in a public place. A man who was not your husband. Do you know that we have a man investigating the Supper Club? That he told me in a meeting *last week* that he saw you there with another man? He felt it was his duty as a friend and a man of honor to tell me that my wife," he said with derision, "was walking about with another man. That if he hadn't known you were my wife, he would have thought the two of you were a couple. I stood there in the face of their pity and listened to him tell me my wife had been with another man. Do you know what it was like to hear a colleague say such things to me? Do you have any idea?"

"It wasn't like that." Rose thought back on that evening, her first in the gambling hall, and remembered how Thomas had led her about the hall. He had been animated and funny that night. And he had placed a hand on her elbow, and sometimes on the small of her back. Thomas was simply a naturally affectionate man who touched everyone as if they were a long-lost friend. He'd often have an arm draped about John's shoulder, and she remembered hugs given to Collette that lifted her off the ground. Rose had gotten used to his lively nature, but now she wondered what it would have looked like to a stranger. Obviously, it had appeared improper.

"Then tell me, dear wife, what it was like. Tell me how many times he kissed you that were not witnessed. Tell me how many times you let him touch you. Tell me why friends of yours would accuse you of having an affair with Kersey if you were not. Tell me you weren't *fucking* another man."

"Stop it, Luke! Stop it, stop it!" She turned away, unable to look any longer into his ice-cold gray eyes, to hear the awful venom in his voice. Rose took a step away only to stumble on her skirt, and she fell hard to her knees. She was unhurt, but it was simply more than she could bear at that moment and she buried her head in her hands and cried, loud wracking sobs that ripped at her heart.

Luke took a step toward her and stopped, telling himself he was unmoved by the display. Of course the woman would cry. She ought to cry, long and hard, for what she had done to him and to their marriage. Even as he tried to strengthen his resolve, his damned heart was acting the traitor, and he already regretted his harsh words. Still, he could not bring himself to go to her. The anger still swirled about his veins, polluting his thoughts.

"Get up, Rose. Your mother is correct. You must be strong. There are worse things, much worse things you must face than my doubt."

"I hate you," Rose whispered.

"You don't mean that," he said coolly.

"I've never meant anything more."

6

Rose sat in her rocking chair, the same one in which she had pictured herself holding a baby, and stared at her rain-splattered window. She'd been there for more than an hour watching the rain drip down in rivulets and trying to come up with reasons she should want to live. Had it only been a week ago that she had never felt happier? She'd been in love, Luke had loved her. She'd had the greatest of friends. She'd been pretty and young and carefree. One night of bad judgment and her life was ruined. She hadn't spoken to Luke in two days, partly because she'd felt so horrid about saying so vehemently that she hated him. She didn't; she loved him so much it hurt even though, she reminded herself, he was being so awfully mean. For two days she refused to think about the case, refused to leave her room. She prayed Luke wouldn't make good on his threat to force her out of the house. Just the thought of stepping out of this sanctuary caused her heart to pound frantically in her breast. Tonight she and Luke had planned to attend a concert at the town hall and she knew he would try to keep that appointment.

I'll refuse, she thought, pressing her head back against the rocker until it hurt. He can't make me go. She began twisting her ring as she acknowledged a terrible truth. She would go, she would smile and keep her back straight and wish she was dead every moment. Rose knew, as much as she loathed admitting it, that Luke was right when he'd said it was important that they act as normally as possible. The only reason she had been allowed to hole up in her room for so long was that it would have seemed odd for her to immediately go about town. It had nearly been a week; mentions of the murder in the newspapers had ceased, as had the vandalism. It was time.

Rose's heart pounded as she heard footsteps outside her door, knowing it was Luke. He knocked, then entered without waiting for a reply. He was already dressed for the concert and looked magnificent in his black evening clothes. His stubborn dark blond waves were tamed, his lean cheeks shaven. Rose felt a piercing longing in her heart at the sight of him, despite the unwelcoming expression on his handsome face.

"Why aren't you dressed?"

Rose felt her spirits, already low, slip down even more at Luke's cold tone.

"I'm not going," she said, wondering even as she

said it why she was provoking him when he was already clearly angry.

"You are. Be ready in twenty minutes or I will come back up and drag you down as you are." After this frigid speech, he turned to leave, stopping as he reached the door. "And wear one of your old gowns, please." He closed the door firmly behind him.

"I'm not going!" Rose shouted, not meaning a single syllable. "Oh, God," she whispered. "I can't do this. I cannot face those people." Breathing as if she'd just run up a flight of stairs, Rose stood and pressed the buzzer to call her maid. Moments later, she arrived.

"Mildred, I need to dress for the symphony. Please get me my brown . . ." She stopped, feeling a surge of rebellion. "Get me my rose gown." It was the same one that Luke had looked at with alarm, the same gown she'd worn to the Supper Club that first evening. Wearing it would be sure to anger Luke, and for some reason, that produced a smile on Rose's lips.

Mildred pulled on Rose's corset laces until she was gasping for breath, then slipped the beautiful gown over her head and proceeded to attack the multitude of buttons up the back. It seemed to take forever, but Rose didn't mind. She planned to walk down wearing a light hooded cloak that she hoped covered enough of the gown so Luke wouldn't notice what she was wearing. After the gown was secured, Mildred quickly put her hair up in a simple but elegant style, pulling down a few curling tendrils to frame her face. Rose looked in the mirror worriedly. She looked awful, she thought. Her face was unusually pale and dark smudges marred the skin beneath eyes that were wide and fearful. Rose took a deep, calming breath and forced her expression into something more bland.

"You look lovely, madam," Mildred said as she put another pin in her hair. The woman, not much younger than Rose's mother, gave her a timid smile.

Rose forced herself to smile at the maid. "Thank

you, Mildred." She donned her cloak and made her way downstairs where Luke waited impatiently.

"We're going to be late," he said, snapping his watch closed and jamming it into his vest.

"Perfect," Rose said lightly. "We're always late, so it will appear quite normal."

The rain had turned to a light mist, leaving the air heavy and humid. As she stepped toward the carriage, Rose looked up and down their quiet street, fearful that someone would be about. The street was deserted and Rose relaxed as she climbed aboard the carriage, placing a gloved hand in Luke's. She ignored the quiet strength of his hand, which released hers, it seemed, as soon as she was safely aboard. Luke sat across from her, his face in the shadows, his expression unreadable. Rose looked resolutely out the window, refusing to look at Luke even when he spoke to her.

"We need to appear, as much as possible, to be a happily married couple."

Rose stiffened. "You mean," she said, her eyes never straying from the window, "we need to appear as we always have, indeed as most couples of our set appear. Bored and disinterested in one another. If we appear too happy, if we smile too much or pretend adoration, our friends will certainly be suspicious."

"Be quiet," Luke bit out.

"I'm just trying to fully understand what is expected of me."

"You're antagonizing me."

"Only if you allow yourself to become antagonized," Rose shot back. They rode the rest of the way in uncomfortable silence.

The carriage slowed, then stopped. Luke leaned forward and touched Rose's sleeve. "Rose. I cannot stress enough the importance of this evening. People will be looking at us, wondering about us. They cannot know that we . . ."

Rose turned to Luke as he hesitated and immediately wished she had not. For Luke's eyes were filled with pain and a longing that wrenched her heart.

"They cannot know that we dislike one another," Rose finished for him in a ragged whisper.

Luke looked away, as if her words surprised him. When he turned back, though, Rose thought she must have imagined the pain she saw, for his eyes were as hard as slate. "Precisely, my dear."

He stepped down from the carriage and immediately turned to assist Rose. She hesitated a moment and Luke's lips compressed in ill-concealed anger. "You'll have to do a better job of acting than that, Luke, if people are to believe us," Rose said as she accepted Luke's hand.

Luke had been correct, they were late. Most of the concertgoers were already seated, and those few who remained in the hall's lobby were unknown to them. They walked up the thickly carpeted marble stairway to the town hall's balcony, where Springfield's elite sat in small clusters that imitated the private boxes of finer concert halls. As they moved toward their "box," Rose was immensely relieved to find that the house-lights had already been turned down as the crowd awaited the entry of the conductor. The two dimmed gaslights behind them gave the Beaudettes enough light to safely find their seats, but little more. As Luke helped Rose remove her cloak, she suddenly remembered what she was wearing, already regretting that impulsive move. He slipped the cloak from her shoulders, the satin lining sliding smoothly and soundlessly over her gown. Rose immediately stepped forward and sat down, her nerves so raw she felt like screaming.

As soon as she sat, her hands unknowingly gripping the railing, the murmuring began. At first, Rose was aware that others sitting on the same level had noted their late arrival. The rustling of skirts as women adjusted themselves subtly to view who the latecomers were was deafening to Rose's ears. And then those patrons in the orchestra seats inevitably noticed something or someone was creating a stir in the balcony. Rose watched in horror as nearly every head, like a wave in a placid sea, turned toward her. She could hear the whispering, though the words were lost to her, until someone below had the nerve to shout "Murderer!" Someone laughed, a woman's nervous giggle.

Rose's face, held stiff, burned, her eyes stared straight ahead as she tried to focus on the small orchestra that sat silently on the stage. She removed her gloved hands from the railing and clenched them tightly in her lap. I will not cry, I will not cry, I will not cry.

Then she felt Luke's hand, strong and warm, grasp one of hers. She couldn't look at him, could only hold onto his hand as if to let go would send her plummeting into the crowd below. Luke did not turn to her, just held her hand in his on his thigh. Thankfully, the conductor walked on, his steps slowing as he waited for the applause that always came upon his appearance. The faces turned away from the balcony and the applause began.

The orchestra had been playing for several minutes before Rose let herself relax even a bit. She could still sense some patrons gawking at her. As she looked across the great hall, she saw women's heads bent toward one another as they whispered and she knew several sets of opera glasses were pointed her way. The urge to run was nearly overpowering.

"Luke," she whispered. "I can't . . . Can we go now?"

"No," he said without turning toward her.

She bit back a sob, then, as if realizing people were watching, forced herself to smile. "Please, Luke. I'm not strong enough for this."

He turned to her then, gazing at her with intensity and an emotion she could not read. "You have to be," he said in a low voice. And that's when he noticed her dress. Rose thought he'd be furious, but instead he smiled, a genuine smile that reached his eyes.

"You little scamp," he said, letting out a small laugh. Rose didn't think that admiring look was for the benefit of the crowd, but couldn't be sure.

She bit her lips and looked appropriately guilty. She leaned toward him, unaware that by doing so, the tiny bit of cleavage she displayed while upright became more apparent. "You made me quite angry with your holier-than-thou pronouncement: 'Wear one of your old gowns,'" she said saucily, aware that his eyes had dipped to her breasts. When he looked up, she saw something in his eyes she hadn't seen in weeks—raw desire. His hand, which still held hers, loosened its hold and he began to stroke her exposed wrist with his thumb, sending delicious sensations through her. Rose was quite sure Luke would not want anyone to see what he was clearly saying with his eyes at that moment. As if realizing it himself, he turned away and shifted in his seat, looking almost angry.

"Luke, you mustn't appear angry with me, remember?" Rose whispered harshly, shaking the hand he still held. She reminded herself just as harshly that she was still angry with Luke for not believing in her and forcing her out this evening. One look of desire from Luke and she was ready to forgive him, ready to throw herself in his arms, she thought with disgust. Luke's expression immediately became bland and bored.

"Perfect," she said, and withdrew her hand.

Rose would have enjoyed the concert if she hadn't been plagued with the fear of facing the crowd during intermission. She could not hope that Luke would allow her to remain in their seats. All too soon, the orchestra was taking its bows and the conductor was marching offstage. The houselights went up and Rose could feel the crowd's perusal grow. Her entire body tingled with mortification and her face felt seared by their interest.

Luke looked at her, his eyes drawn against his will to the creamy flesh exposed above Rose's neckline. Damned little rebel refused to listen to him, he thought, not without some grudging admiration. Rose's skin was flushed from her breasts to her cheeks as she faced the crowd. He was not immune to his wife's suffering, and he certainly did not enjoy her humiliation, but he refused to regret his decision to take her out into public. Someone in this crowd might sit on a jury that would decide her fate. Perhaps they would remember this brave lady attending the concert and would think it impossible for a guilty woman to dare show her face.

Or they would think her unconscionable and without remorse for the horrid deed she'd done.

Luke knew it was a gamble forcing Rose out in public and it was imperative that she not act like a fallen women. Thus far, Rose had been perfect, appearing embarrassed by the stir her presence had created, but keeping her chin up, her gaze steady. Luke stood and held out a hand, which Rose took without hesitation. He smiled down at her.

"You're doing well, Rose."

"Do we have to go down?" She looked up at him, her eyes so filled with fear, he almost gave in and allowed her to remain in their seats.

"Yes. And smile."

That demand immediately produced a frown and Luke nearly allowed himself to laugh again. It would not do to seem overly happy, he thought. They needed to display the perfect combination of restraint and ease—not an easy feat when their nerves were coiled dangerously tight. The balcony had nearly emptied out and he began maneuvering her toward the door, his hand firmly on the small of her back. Just as they reached the door, Rose whirled around and tried to push past Luke. He caught her arm, holding it firmly against his side.

"I can't, Luke. Please don't make me," she said over her shoulder.

"You can, Rose. Don't fail me in this." Luke knew he was pushing her, but he could see no other way. Rose tried to pull away to head back toward their seats, but Luke stopped her, his grip on her arm tightening. He was aware of murmurs from other patrons who still mingled on the balcony, as if some in the crowd were hovering about to see what this notorious couple would do next.

Rose turned around slowly. She held her head high, her eyes straight, but her mouth trembled slightly. "I won't forgive you for making me do this."

"I know."

He took her cold, limp hand and placed it in the crook of his arm. With his free hand, he pushed open the door and led his wife to face the vultures that awaited them.

It could have been worse, Rose thought as she huddled in her rocking chair later that night. Springfield's elite had simply snubbed her but in a way that left open a door in the case this matter was all a horrible mistake. Luke had assured her that, barring her circle gathering around her in a protective cloak, it was the next best thing. No one demanded that she leave. No one dared say a thing about the horrible crime for which she had been accused. They simply ignored it and her, leaving Rose faintly thankful.

A few friends, Mrs. Agatha Trumbell among them, came up to them to lend her support. That she hadn't looked at Rose during this grand gesture was obvious to Rose and she realized a message was clearly being sent. Luke was considered the victim in this scenario, the poor, beleaguered, and wonderfully loyal husband who was standing by his errant wife no matter her great sins. She'd be angry, she truly would, if she hadn't also, begrudgingly, begun to realize just how profoundly Luke was affected by this all. She certainly would not forgive him for not believing in her, but after this evening, after seeing the strain on his face, she allowed herself the tiniest bit of sympathy for Luke.

Despite the sometimes hostile looks from people Rose hadn't even known, Luke had stood by her, clasping her hand firmly in the crook of his arm, pressing gently if someone approached them. The only person Luke seemed to openly dislike was a man who introduced himself as Martin Rowse, whom Luke later identified as one of the best criminal defense attorneys in Massachusetts. Despite Luke's obvious animosity, Rose liked the man, possibly because he was the only person all evening to directly speak to her.

"Very brave of you, Mrs. Beaudette," Rowse said without a speck of censure. "And good show, Beaudette. Risky business, this, but it appears you gambled well. The crowd is shifting a bit in your direction. Keep her looking woebegone and you'll get your acquittal despite the evidence." Though to Rose's ears it had sounded like praise, his words angered Luke.

"This isn't a show, Rowse," Luke bit out, and Rose gave him a curious look. Hadn't Luke himself said how important it was to go out into public simply to show that all was normal? It seemed rather duplicitous to become angry with Mr. Rowse because he pointed out something Luke had freely admitted to doing. She confronted him on that later.

"It wasn't what he said, it was the manner in which he said it. Getting praise from Rowse is like getting praise from the devil himself. I suppose I should be flattered that Rowse would have tried a similar tactic. Rowse is a good criminal defense attorney. I simply cannot stop thinking like a prosecutor."

Rose gazed at her husband's profile and had the odd urge to grasp his hand the way he had held hers in the town hall. She hadn't, though. She'd simply sat next to him, watching as he flexed his hands again and again, as if he were in some sort of pain.

Rose pulled her shawl closer against her thin nightdress and told herself she didn't care if Luke had been uncomfortable. She tried to remain angry with him for forcing her into that crowd, but her intellect told her that he had been right. Why did he always have to be so darned right all the time? Why couldn't the infallible, perfect Luke Beaudette ever make a mistake?

As she had done.

Then a happy thought hit her. Luke was wrong about her. Very wrong. When he realized his error, as she was certain he would, Rose planned to relish his discomfort. She'd get some salt and rub and rub. With that oddly pleasant thought, Rose uncurled herself from the rocker and walked drowsily to her bed, so exhausted that sleep came blessedly soon.

7

The morning after the concert, Luke sat in his study going over every bit of information he had on Rose's case. On one sheet of paper, he had written a list of witnesses, those for the prosecution and those for the defense. His own list was woefully and depressingly short, a simple and ineffectual list of people who knew Rose and would testify to her good and docile nature. He hoped his trip to Holyoke to talk to Kersey's mother could produce some helpful information.

Luke glanced up to check the time. It was nine o'clock and Rose had yet to emerge from her room. He'd be heading out momentarily and hadn't wanted to leave without seeing her first, though he'd no idea what he would say to her. He couldn't get her haunted eyes out of his mind, or the feeling that he was failing her in her greatest time of need.

"Rose is innocent," he said aloud. He cursed harshly. Why couldn't he simply have faith in her? Why put her and him through this hell because of this damned nagging doubt? How could he say he loved Rose and then believe she could have committed the most heinous of crimes? Was he a fool, a contemptible cad for still having doubts? He glanced at the stack of papers that contained what he believed to be the prosecution's case. How could he completely ignore the evidence, the witnesses, the police investigation that all pointed to Rose as the culprit? That was what Rose expected of him, he knew. It was what he wanted from himself. Lord knew he did not want to doubt Rose. But he did. Damn him to hell, he did.

He remembered telling Rose he didn't believe her

to be guilty, *not entirely*. Even with her pain-filled eyes begging him to believe in her, he couldn't. Not entirely.

As the clock chimed the quarter hour, Luke stood. He could not wait any longer for Rose to make an appearance. It was an hour's trolley ride to Holyoke and he wanted to be back home in time for dinner.

The ride to Holyoke was pleasant, the open-air cars letting in the sweet early summer air. The trolley was not crowded, so Luke was able to sit the entire trip, entertained by a group of young men and women who sang songs along the way, thoroughly enjoying the ride, the glorious day, their youth. Luke, glancing back at the laughing young people, felt uncommonly old. He realized with a start that he always had. He'd never sat in the back of a trolley simply for the enjoyment of the ride and sung songs until his throat hurt. The most fun he'd had was . . . His mind went blank. He'd always been so damned serious, even as a child. Luke realized with a jolt that he'd never felt as free-spirited as he guessed the young men sitting behind him did.

And then he thought about Rose. Serious, solemn, sedate Rose, who wasn't truly any of those things. He could picture Rose among those young people. He could almost hear her laughing. But when he tried to place himself there, all he saw was someone who was impatient for the ride to end so that he could . . . do something important. No wonder Rose had slipped so easily into the world the Taylors built for her. All she'd wanted to do was have a bit of fun. He hadn't understood Rose's behavior—the new dresses, the swimming, the card-playing, the secret thrill of eating at the Supper Club. But now he did. He'd forgotten what it felt like to open up the window, take a deep breath, and wish and wish. But Rose hadn't forgotten.

Luke shook his head, irritated with himself. No, Rose had impetuously decided to do whatever she wanted to do and look what it had led to. Suddenly, the laughter, the singing became bothersome noise and he couldn't wait to get off this damn car and get about the business of building his defense.

Anne Kersey lived in a tiny house along a dirt road that bordered the Connecticut River. Its whitewash had long since peeled off, leaving the shingles gray and marred with white specks of old paint. The shutters fared better, their black paint peeling but hanging on in enough abundance so that they still appeared black. The house, nearly entirely surrounded by oak trees, seemed deserted upon first glance. A screen door, the copper mesh turned green and pulled away from the frame, hung crookedly open. It was only an orange-and-white cat waiting patiently on the stoop that suggested to Luke that someone lived inside. The cat rubbed up against Luke as he knocked, obviously hoping that his appearance would gain it access to the inside of the house. The screen door, hanging precariously from a single hinge, rested lightly against Luke's left shoulder.

When the door opened, the cat shot inside, momentarily distracting the woman who stood there. Seeing Luke, she immediately looked wary, her faded blue eyes taking in his well-cut suit. Luke swept his hat off his head and introduced himself.

"Mrs. Kersey? I am Luke Beaudette. I've come to talk to you about your son."

"Ah you another police offisah?" she asked, her New England accent pronounced. "Don't lookit," she observed, her round and wrinkled face holding a slightly hostile expression.

"No, ma'am. I am an attorney for the woman accused of killing your son."

The woman stepped back and led Luke into a remarkably pretty and neat little parlor. The furnishings were slightly shabby, but meticulously clean. Even the fireplace looked to have been scrubbed, for not a single ash marred its brick surface.

"Would you like some tea?"

Luke declined and nodded to Mrs. Kersey for her

to sit. She wore a jet black gown that had not a single bit of ornamentation upon it. The stiff material rustled loudly in the little room, as did the creak of the sofa as she set her rather round body down with a grateful groan. "Rheumatism," the woman explained, wincing as she adjusted herself. "Now. Go on with your questions, Mistah Beaudette."

Luke smiled at her straightforward manner. "I'm not certain how much you know of this case, Mrs. Kersey."

"I've read the papers. I know the woman accused of killing my boy has the same last name as yourself."

"She is my wife," Luke said evenly.

"Is she guilty?"

"My wife did not murder your son, Mrs. Kersey. I'm here hoping you will have information that will lead me to the true killer."

Mrs. Kersey stared at Luke for a long moment. "Police are pretty definite they got the right killah. But I didn't believe a word of it, and I told the police that too. Yes, I did. See, Tommy had himself a pretty little girlfriend up in Agawam, Feeding Hills way. Farm girl, she is. I didn't see Tommy but once a month and he always brought her along, especially since the trolleys went electric."

Luke sat forward. "Your son had a girl?"

Mrs. Kersey nodded. "They weren't engaged, though Tommy hinted that someday they'd get themselves married up. Tommy liked the fast life, he did. It was a curse, that's so. And his little girl, Lenore Potter is her name, she's as wholesome as they come. But Tommy'd go up to the city and see things he wished for. Fancy houses, fancy clothes. I think the thought of living in Feeding Hills was suffocatin' him. He would have settled down eventually, though." Suddenly, Mrs. Kersey's eyes filled with tears that fell thickly down her wrinkled face. Luke, who had admired the woman's spunk, was taken by surprise by this sudden show of emotion. As quickly as the tears began, they stopped, with Mrs. Kersey waving a dismissive hand at Luke's offer of a handkerchief.

"Got my own," she said, opening the drawer of a little table. She patted her cheeks dry and daintily wiped her nose. "It's not right to outlive your children," she said. "It's not right." She was silent for a few moments as she continued to blot her eyes. "To get back to what we were saying, Mr. Beaudette. That's why I didn't believe what the police said. Tommy never mentioned any gal named Rose."

"Given that Rose was married, do you think he would have mentioned her?"

Mrs. Kersey gave him a shrewd look. "Well, now, that's a question. Tommy never visited without his Lenore. But I'll tell you this, Mr. Beaudette, that boy loved Lenore, despite those fancy dreams of his. He loved that girl with all his heart. He never let her be part of that other side of him. He was always a gentleman with her. Oh, he was such a fun-loving boy. Such a good boy." The tears began again.

"I'm so sorry for your loss, Mrs. Kersey," Luke said, touched by her tears. He had cast Thomas Kersey as a villain. He'd had some small trouble with the law, petty stuff, like skipping out of a restaurant without paying the bill. He wasn't the saint Mrs. Kersey believed her son to be, but he wasn't the scoundrel Luke had thought him to be, either. But just because Thomas Kersey had a loving mother and girlfriend hidden out in Feeding Hills did not mean he hadn't been making a play for Rose, Luke forced himself to think.

Mrs. Kersey could tell him nothing more. After getting directions to the farm where Lenore Potter lived with her family, he thanked her for her time. He left the old woman at her door holding her friendly cat, and felt overwhelmingly sad to think about such a nice woman living there all alone without even those monthly visits from her son to look forward to.

Lenore Potter was nowhere near as good at hiding her grief as Mrs. Kersey had been. Her brown eyes were red-rimmed, and her pretty face was pale, with circles so dark marring her skin, it almost appeared as if she'd been struck. She sat on the porch, a bowl of potatoes on her lap, which she skinned with expertise as they talked. As she finished each potato, she dropped it with a plunk into a bucket of water.

"If you're here to say awful things about Thomas, you may leave now," Lenore said, in a surprisingly strong voice. "I'll not hear another word castigating his character. The police were here, but I sent them off."

This was no meek farm girl, Luke thought, his respect for the girl growing. "I apologize in advance if any of my questions offend you, Miss Potter," he said kindly. "I simply want to discover the truth about what happened Friday night. My wife's life is at stake."

Lenore nodded, and Luke knew he had struck a romantic chord in Miss Potter's heart. "I understand, Mr. Beaudette. But the police said just awful things about . . ." Her throat closed up and she quickly placed the bowl of potatoes on the porch. "I keep thinking I can't have any more tears left and then . . ." She wept, burying her face into a handkerchief, as Luke watched feeling decidedly uncomfortable in the face of such grief. "I'm sorry," the girl said, shaking her head, her face still covered with her handkerchief.

When she seemed to recover sufficiently, Luke asked her his first question. "Did you know the Taylors?"

Lenore nodded her head. "I didn't approve of the fast company Thomas kept when he was in the city. I met the Taylors a year ago in Boston, but didn't like them. I didn't fit in with them. Thomas knew it and kept that part of his life separate from me."

Luke sighed in disappointment, fearing this trip would produce nothing but more glowing praise of Thomas—the type of testimony the prosecution would use to evoke sympathy for the victim, but which was worthless to him.

"Were you aware of Mr. Kersey's gambling debts?"

Lenore looked down at her hands folded in her lap. "I was," she said softly. "Thomas knew I didn't approve, but he was so proud. He wanted to buy me things. Things I didn't even want, really." She began crying again, this time quietly, tears slipping silently down her cheeks. "The last time I saw him, a week before . . ." She swallowed. "He seemed worried. He said John Casey was getting on him about some money. He told me . . ."

"John *Casey*?"

Lenore looked up, startled. "Oh. I mean John Taylor. I keep forgetting he changed his name. Thomas told me John *Taylor* warned him about his debts. I think he owed quite a bit. He . . ." She stopped, looking miserable.

"Go on," Luke said, trying to hide his excitement at what she was saying.

"Thomas asked me for money. And I gave it to him." She flushed with shame. "He told me he would use it and be able to pay his debt. I never would have given it to him, but he seemed . . ." She looked up at Luke, tears flooding her eyes. "He seemed frightened, Mr. Beaudette. Truly frightened."

Luke spent the fifty-minute ride home in a state of pure exhilaration. Lenore's revelations did not prove a thing, but they gave Luke another track to take. Thomas Kersey had felt threatened by someone over his gambling debts. But by far the most interesting revelation was that the Taylors were using an alias. Now, why would an upstanding citizen use a false name? Feeling more alive than he had in weeks, Luke vowed to find out.

8

Anthony D'Angelo stood hidden in a shadowed alley between two houses across the street outside the

Beaudettes' pretty brownstone for an hour before he gathered enough courage to knock on the front door. Nicole had been at the house yesterday for he'd seen the Baptiste carriage, which was why he did not approach Luke Beaudette then. Though he'd come to Mattoon Street early, he wanted to be sure Nicole was not visiting her sister. He could not bear to see her again and not touch her. He thought at first he would die from not seeing her, but the passing days eased his pain just enough for him to realize that he would live despite the emptiness inside.

Just the thought of seeing Rose made his gut twist, for to him the sisters looked so much alike, though most people would not think so. Rose, like her name, was as beautiful as a flower. Next to Rose, some would think Nicole plain, but to Anthony, she was the very definition of what was beauty. Nicole was smaller in almost every way, except that the features in her face were startlingly vivid—her mouth slightly too wide, her eyes too large, her brows too sharp. Only her well-shaped nose seemed to fit properly. The only feature the sisters shared was their brown eyes and those thick and curling black lashes that framed them. Looking into Rose's eyes was almost like looking into Nicole's, except his beloved's eyes held a fathomless sorrow where Rose's had only been filled with delight. Perhaps now, the sisters would be even more alike, he thought.

He couldn't help but worry that he was putting his body in far more danger than his heart by talking to Luke Beaudette. No doubt if word got out that he'd been seen talking with Beaudette, his own life would be in danger. Anthony was no coward, but he was not fool enough to ignore the real peril he faced. He told no one of his plans, not even his uncle. So if Cardi came to his uncle demanding to know where Anthony was, his uncle would not have to lie. Anthony planned to help Rose as much as he could, and then he planned to disappear. He found he could not bear to live in the same city as Nicole anyway, not if he wanted to have a hope of a normal life. He wanted a wife and children, and though he wanted Nicole to be part of that life, he knew it was impossible. Anthony told himself he would get over this love that left him wretched and so lonely he ached.

He walked across the street, trying to look casual as he attempted to determine whether he was being watched, and stepped up to the Beaudettes' front door with its pretty etched-glass windows. He heard quick footsteps from within the house and for some reason his stomach clenched. The door opened. *Oh, sweet Jesus.*

"I didn't . . . I wouldn't have . . ." Anthony stuttered as he looked into his beloved's face.

Nicole stepped forward so that one foot was outside, the other still resting on the home's marble entry hall. "Anthony," she breathed. "What are you doing here?"

It was madness that drove him to do what he did next, that and the fact that she had so clearly been on his mind. He'd planned to leave Massachusetts forever without ever seeing her again. He didn't want to see her again. But here she was, her soft lips slightly parted, her eyes looking at him with concern and love. He pulled her outside with one hand behind her head, fingers buried in the wonderful softness of her hair, and did what he swore he'd never do anywhere but in his dreams. He kissed her. Long and hard, possessing her with his mouth, searing the taste of her onto his tongue, the feel of her onto his heart. That kiss seemed to last forever. Anthony stopped only when he heard her let out a moan that held passion and painful yearning.

When the kiss was ended, he looked down at her stunned face, panting slightly as he tried to get back the breath that she had stolen from him. "I'm sorry, *cuore mio.* I never meant to do that. I don't know . . ."

Nicole placed one finger on his lips, quieting him. She stared at his lips for a long moment, then smiled. "Thank you," she said softly. Then, as if they hadn't shared anything more than pleasantries about the weather, she backed into the hall and ushered him in.

"You're here to see Luke?"

Anthony could barely speak. "Yes," he croaked out. Oh, God, why had he kissed her, why hadn't he lived on his dreams? Now he knew that reality was better than his dreams and leaving her wouldn't simply break his heart, it would kill it.

"He's in his study. I'll tell him you're here," she said sedately.

Luke Beaudette lifted his head as Anthony entered and nodded to a leather chair placed before his desk. Luke's eyes swept over him, taking in Anthony's ill-cut suit and his extreme discomfort with one assessing look. "Mr. D'Angelo, please have a seat." Luke was taller than Anthony and was his physical opposite. Where Anthony was dark, with chocolate brown eyes and wavy brown-black hair, Luke was light, with gray eyes and dark blond hair. But both men exuded power and confidence, despite the disparity in their stations. "How can I help you?"

"I think I can help you. And your wife."

Luke's gaze sharpened. "Go on."

"I work with my uncle in the Supper Club's kitchen. I am assistant chef," he said with defiant pride. "I know of your wife through her sister, Mrs. Baptiste. I delivered milk to her," he said, hoping Luke could not see his skin flush. "I saw your wife at the Supper Club two weeks ago on a Friday night and I was concerned. The people she was with, I didn't think she knew who they were, so I told Mrs. Baptiste about my concern."

"Nicole knew Rose had gone to the club?"

Anthony nodded, but waved his hand as if that were of little consequence. "I saw Mrs. Beaudette again last Friday, the night of the murder. She was with the same people. These people, Mr. Beaudette, they are not the sort of people I would want my wife to be with."

"Why do you say that?"

Anthony suspected that so far he hadn't told Luke

anything he didn't already know, but he continued. "As I say, I work in the kitchen but I see a lot. One of the men your wife was with, the balding one, he met with Mr. Cardi last week. He was with him a long time. Mr. Cardi is a good businessman, he runs a good restaurant, but he is not a kind man."

"He's a criminal," Luke said.

"Yes, there is that," Anthony said in an almost dismissive way. "But he is a man with a strict code, a man no one would want to cross. The dead man owed Mr. Cardi a great deal of money."

"Ten thousand dollars."

"Yes. And now he is dead."

"Are you saying that Cardi murdered him?"

Anthony breathed in deeply, knowing that he was putting his own life in danger by saying such things to Luke. "I am saying only that the man owed Mr. Cardi money and now he is dead. I am saying only that the man your wife was with Friday night met with Mr. Cardi last week." Anthony stopped, uncertain whether he should say more, only certain that if he did, he would have to leave Springfield immediately and never return.

"What I am telling you, Mr. Beaudette, I will never testify to. I am telling you only to help prove Mrs. Beaudette is innocent. She did not kill that man in the cloakroom," he said with such utter certainty, Luke's scalp tingled.

"Are you telling me you know who killed Kersey?" he snapped.

"I did not see the murder, no. The night of the murder I came into the washroom and saw the bald man washing his hands and face."

"Taylor?"

"If that is his name, then yes. The basin he had been using had little pink and red specks all over it. I know what blood looks like, Mr. Beaudette, and it was blood in that basin. At the time, I thought perhaps the man had cut himself, but after the murder . . ."

"Jesus Christ," Luke whispered. "You have to testify."

Anthony shook his head, his brown eyes filled with regret. "I am sorry, Mr. Beaudette, but I cannot. Perhaps I am a coward, but I do not want to die and not at the hands of a man such as Cardi. It would not be an honorable death."

"And not testifying is honorable?" Luke spat, angry that his best witness was not cooperating. "I'll subpoena you."

Anthony looked at him and sadly shook his head. "I am sorry, Mr. Beaudette, but you will not be able to find me."

"My wife's life is at stake here, Mr. D'Angelo."

Anthony flushed. "I understand that. It is why I came here. Even now I am putting my life in danger simply by talking with you."

Luke let out a curse. "You make me sick," he said with a snarl.

Anthony looked away, deeply ashamed. The man was right, but he'd be damned if he'd walked into that courtroom like a lamb to the slaughter. He'd told Luke what he knew, he'd done more than he should have. "I am not proud of what I am doing," he said, finally. "I am sorry."

"Don't you realize that your information is worthless to me unless you agree to testify?"

Anthony stood. "Again, I am sorry. I am leaving Springfield today, Mr. Beaudette. I wish you luck."

"You bastard!" Luke shouted, slamming his fist onto his desk. "My wife may go to prison without your testimony. How can you live with yourself?"

His words rang in Anthony's ears. He hadn't imagined this. He'd thought Luke would thank him for the information and let him go on his way. Anthony stopped at the door, realizing that Nicole would find out that he was a coward and she would likely grow to hate him. And that, more than anything, helped him to make his decision.

"Mr. Beaudette," he said, turning fully toward

Luke, "I find it very hard to live even now." He walked out the door, ignoring Luke's curses, ignoring Nicole who hovered in the entryway, obviously drawn there by the shouting. Let her hate me, he thought, let her hate me more than she hates her life. In his heart, he believed he was doing the best thing. He didn't stop to consider that he would be stealing from Nicole one of the few good things she had in her life: her love of him.

For the second time in as many days, Luke, a man who prided himself on controlling his emotions, wanted to destroy everything in sight. He'd never felt so helpless in his life. Luke knew the case the prosecutors were building was a damned good one, and without witnesses like D'Angelo it would be difficult at best to convince a jury of his wife's innocence. His eyes fell on a crystal paperweight that had once graced his desk in his office. It had been a gift from the attorney general after Luke won a high-profile case two years ago. He grasped the crystal globe in his right hand and squeezed until his arm was shaking. With impotent rage, he flung it toward the marble fireplace where it shattered with an unexpectedly loud explosion. A gasp from the door brought his head whipping around to see Nicole standing there, one hand still on the doorknob, her eyes wide and frightened.

"What happened?"

Luke turned to look at the hundreds of glass bits scattered upon the rich red carpet, already regretting that the piece was destroyed. Turning back to Nicole, he let out a short laugh. "I lost my temper," he said unnecessarily.

"I can see that," Nicole said, stepping into the room, having assessed that the storm had abated. "What I meant was, what happened to make you so angry?"

"It seems your milkman is a material witness in a murder investigation and he is refusing to cooperate.

He's more concerned about protecting his own skin than saving Rose's life."

"That doesn't sound like . . .." Nicole stopped, realizing that it would seem rather odd for her to know her milkman's character enough to make such a statement. ". . . a very nice thing to do," she said quickly.

Luke gave her a sharp look and Nicole's guilty mind was positive he could see through her to her heart. "No. Not nice at all."

Nicole wanted to hear no more about what had happened in this room, afraid her heart would cause her to defend the man Luke was so obviously furious with. She made an excuse to escape. "I'll send a maid in to clean up the mess." At Luke's curt nod, Nicole hurriedly left the room. After bidding the maid to sweep the glass, she headed to the tiny garden behind her sister's home. She wanted to be alone to think about Anthony, to savor that kiss, to wonder why he refused to help Rose.

The garden was enclosed by a high wall at the far end and wrought-iron fences on each side, dividing the area from the neighbors' plot. Rosebushes, sprouting new leaves, would soon be entangled in the fence, their stems heavy with flowers. It was still too early for many flowers to be blooming, but a lilac bush filled the air with a sweet smell that filled Nicole with longing. Oh, Anthony, Anthony, why did you kiss me? She placed a finger against her lips, trying to preserve the feel of his mouth against hers. Perhaps if she thought about that kiss every day for the rest of her life, she would never forget how wonderful it felt to be kissed by a man she loved. And who loved her. She had thanked him for giving her such a memory, for the aching longing she felt in her heart was much better than the emptiness it replaced.

Nicole strolled to the lilac bush and pressed a bundle of the tiny purple flowers to her nose, breathing deeply. She didn't want to hear anything more about what Anthony had told Luke, she decided. She didn't want to know if what he had done was awful or good.

The only memories of Anthony she wanted were of him in her kitchen sipping the tea he hated, his laughing eyes, his tender words. And that one wonderful kiss.

9

Luke held the piece of paper containing Rose's fine penmanship in his hand. She'd handed it to him with all the aplomb of a seasoned attorney presenting evidence to be submitted to the court. Then she'd walked away from his desk without a word and sat, back painfully straight, upon a chair angled in front of the fireplace. He could only see her profile, but he thought he detected tension in her lovely face, as if everything were riding on his opinion of the words she'd written.

He hadn't yet told Rose about Anthony D'Angelo's visit. First, he wanted to see if what Rose wrote confirmed D'Angelo's claims, and second, he was afraid the knowledge that his best witness was now gone would send her over the edge that she seemed to be teetering on. She was clearly annoyed with him for doubting her, despite what Luke thought had been just cause. Now that he'd spoken to Anthony, Luke's guilt over doubting her gnawed at him.

His lips quirked slightly as he began to read: "I, Rose Beaudette, to be called 'The Innocent One' for the purposes of this document, hearby submit to Luke Beaudette, to be called 'The Doubter' for the purposes of this document, the events leading up to The Innocent One's false arrest." The sentence's pseudo-legalese had him shaking his head in mirth. Rose must have looked up and seen his smile for she stiffened even more and pressed her lips tightly together as if to prevent her from shouting at him. Luke's smile faded, however, as he continued to read. For the information his wife had painstakingly transcribed had not been written in a single report he had read about the case—and he had read them all.

"It seemed extremely important that the Taylors take me to the Supper Club on both occasions," she had written. "The first time, I was brought there unwittingly for I had no idea that such an establishment existed. We left abruptly with no explanation. Having given it great thought, I had concluded that the aborted raid precipitated this departure and is consistent with my overall theory that the Taylors were somehow trying to frame me. On the second occasion, the Taylors devised a rather convoluted story (which to my shame I believed) that Thomas Kersey's gambling debts had reached a point where he was in some sort of danger. I was pressed upon by the Taylors to stop Thomas from gambling. However, the Taylors expressed a curious lack of concern about Thomas's gambling once we were actually in the gambling hall."

The three-page document continued, offering Rose's detailed recollections, including some startling revelations that had Luke snapping his head up. "You saw blood on Taylor's face? Why the hell didn't you tell the police that?"

"I only remembered just now. As I was writing, trying to remember all that had happened, little details like that came back to me."

Luke let out a weary sigh. "Rose, that little detail was immensely important the night of the murder, but I'm afraid that unless someone else saw blood on John Taylor's face it means nothing." He silently damned Anthony D'Angelo. His testimony, along with his wife's, would have been enough to instill into the jurors' minds the reasonable doubt he needed to establish.

"Because it will simply be my word against his," Rose said dejectedly.

"Exactly. Had you mentioned the blood that night, perhaps the police could have found that handkerchief on his person and that would have given credibility to your story. Now it simply sounds like the desperate attempt of a desperate woman. I'm sorry, Rose." He debated whether to tell Rose immediately about Anthony D'Angelo's information, but it seemed even more cruel now. It was damned frustrating to know that Cardi evoked such fear in his employees that it was highly unlikely that any of them would come forward, never mind testify against the man. Though he was still angry with D'Angelo, Luke recognized that the man had displayed some courage to speak with him and had probably put his life in danger. But dammit, it took only slightly more courage to testify.

"*Everything* is my word against theirs," Rose said, pounding a fist into her thigh so hard she winced.

"Not everything. If Taylor killed Kersey then someone knows something. Unfortunately, I've a feeling that the people who know are the same people trying to cover for Taylor. Or are too afraid to testify. They've done one hell of a job, Rose."

Rose's face brightened. "You believe me."

Luke didn't answer but brought his head down again to continue reading, ignoring Rose's little huff of impatience. His gut clenched as he reached the part of the story concerning Rose's kiss with Kersey.

"Thomas had been acting strangely all evening. His lighthearted and completely innocent flirtations had subtly changed. I was rather disconcerted by his attention, but because I knew he had been drinking, I decided it was the drink and not any change in feeling that was causing him to act strangely. He led me to the far end of the gambling hall and kissed me. I slapped his face, shocked and angry that he would do such a thing. Thomas appeared embarrassed. And then he apologized and said (I believe this next is extremely important) that he had been misinformed. Misinformed! I assume now that he meant someone had told Thomas that I would welcome his advances."

Luke put the page down. The Taylors had set Rose up. It was as if he'd been suffocating under the heavy weight of a wet wool blanket for days and someone had whipped it off. Rose was innocent. Of everything. He'd known yesterday after D'Angelo had left that Rose was innocent of the murder, but part of him still wondered whether Rose and Thomas had been more than friends. The only question remaining was why. Why would anyone target Rose for such an elaborate scheme?

Rose watched warily as Luke stood up and began pacing. He hadn't finished reading her report, but seemed to have come to some sort of conclusion. He paced back and forth, his hands thrust into the pockets of his trousers, and Rose realized then why his pockets were always tearing away. He paced until Rose thought she'd scream if he didn't say something soon. Finally, she could not stand another moment. She was getting dizzy just watching him.

"Well?"

"Hmmm." That was all. Just a maddening little *Hmmm,* and he continued pacing.

"Luke."

He held up one hand, silencing her, and Rose angrily crossed her arms and slumped, quite unladylike, into her chair. He stopped suddenly, a broad smile on his face.

"I'll be damned," he said to himself.

Rose instantly straightened. "What?"

He looked at her and tilted his head. Then he slapped his forehead so hard Rose flinched. "It wasn't you. It was never you."

Rose looked at her husband with narrowed eyes. "Of course not. I'm glad you finally realized it."

"No, no. Not about the murder. I know you're innocent."

Rose looked at him with shock, and then Luke walked over and knelt before her, took her head between his hands, and gave her a loud smacking kiss on her lips. "I'm the one they wanted. I'm the one they were setting up."

Rose looked at her husband as if he'd lost his mind. "What are you talking about? You weren't even there."

Luke stood, holding his index finger in the air as if he were addressing the court. "Ah," he said. "But *you* were there. Both nights. You were there the very night my office planned a raid. And you were there the night of the murder, and were carefully manipulated to become the prime suspect."

"Luke, I still don't understand what this had to do with . . ." Rose stopped, her mouth forming a little O.

"Exactly! It would be rather embarrassing for the wife of an assistant attorney general to be found gambling in the very same illegal gambling establishment that his own office was investigating. Arrested, technically, by his own men. Can you imagine the newspaper reports? The outcry?"

Rose was getting excited. "But the raid was called off. John somehow found out about the raid and made sure I was at the club. And when it was called off, we left. I remember he seemed almost angry and now I know why. That's why it was so important that I be at the club the next week, so they could set me up for murder!"

Luke smiled down at his wife as if pleased with her. "Cardi met with John Taylor a few days before the murder. I suspect that's when the two planned the entire thing. I don't know if Cardi's been involved from the beginning—I doubt he would have allowed a raid simply to embarrass me—but I'm damned sure he helped set you up for murder."

"Oh, Luke!" Rose said, hopping up from her chair. "Now it will all be over. You can tell Chief Farwell what we know and they'll drop the charges and . . ." She stopped when she saw Luke's face. "What wrong?"

"Sit down, Rose," he said in a tone that frightened her.

"I don't want to sit," she said stubbornly. She let him lead her to the sofa anyway and sat when he pressed her down. Luke sat next to her and massaged the back of his neck.

"We can't prove any of it," he said softly.

"But . . ." All the happiness she'd felt fled in an instant. "We can't prove any of it? How do you know John met with Mr. Cardi?"

Luke pushed his hair back with an impatient hand. "That's just it. Most of my information comes from a man who's disappeared. Rose, sweetheart, he saw John in the washroom. He saw blood in the basin, but unless I find someone who will testify to that, I can't use it to defend you."

"Who saw him? What are you talking about?" Rose asked through a tightening throat.

"Anthony D'Angelo. He worked in the kitchen. He saw Taylor in the washroom and apparently he left a bit of blood behind after he washed his hands."

"Nicole's milkman."

Luke nodded. "He's afraid his life would be in danger if he testified and he's probably right. I couldn't convince him to stand up in court and say what he told me. I wanted to kill him myself when he refused."

Rose looked at Luke, her graceful brows creasing over troubled brown eyes. "When did Mr. D'Angelo tell you this?"

Luke looked decidedly uncomfortable and his eyes shifted away. "Yesterday."

"Yesterday! You've known I was innocent since yesterday and didn't say a word to me?"

Luke squirmed like a little boy caught putting a tack on the teacher's chair. "I never truly believed you murdered Kersey."

"Don't lie to me, Luke Beaudette."

Luke drew himself up as if facing a skeptical jury. "Despite the overwhelming evidence that pointed to your guilt, I did not—at least not in my more self-possessed moments—believe you were capable of murder."

"How gratifying to know I instilled such confidence in you," Rose said bitterly.

"I'm sure, my dear, that you do not want me to again list your misdeeds that ultimately pointed toward your guilt."

Rose flushed and looked mildly put out. Lifting her head a notch, she said, "That is not necessary." She raised one finger. "However, in my own defense I would like to say that had our roles been reversed, I would have believed in you."

"Even if I had lied to you?"

Rose looked to the floor, opened her mouth, and snapped it shut. "Even so," she said finally, but her words lacked a certain conviction and Luke gave Rose a smug look. Seeing that look, Rose again went on the attack. "But that does not explain why you waited a full day before telling me you believed me to be innocent."

Luke stood and crossed over to his collection of banks and idly touched one of the iron toys. "I knew you to be innocent of murder, that is true. There were other issues, however, that were unresolved."

"Other issues?"

Luke turned explosively. "That goddamned kiss! I drove myself mad thinking about it—even when D'Angelo came forward I couldn't get that kiss out of my mind. You've no idea how the thought of another man's lips upon yours . . ." He stopped, taking a short hard breath. "You've no idea."

"I've explained how it came about."

"In light of everything else," he said angrily, "it was the one thing I could not come to grips with."

Rose lifted her head, her eyes angry and hurt. "And now?"

Luke lost all his bluster. "It was all part of the game. I see that now. The Taylors set you both up, told Kersey you wanted him, hoping that when he acted on it you'd create a scene that everyone would remember. They thought about everything. They even gave you a motive for murder. And, by the way, I have some information that 'Taylor' isn't even truly their real name. Apparently, it's Casey, but I've yet to prove it."

"How could I have been so stupid," Rose said, overwhelmed by all she had heard. And then realizing she was still angry with Luke for doubting her, she added, "And how could you have believed it of me? Really, Luke. I'd barely worked up the courage to kiss you; how could you think I'd been having an illicit affair with a stranger?"

"Because I'm a goddamn idiot," Luke shouted. "And because you," he said, pointing an accusing finger at Rose, "allowed yourself to be manipulated."

Rose jammed her fists onto her hips. "Anyone could have fallen for their lies. I didn't *allow* anything."

Looking maddeningly smug, Luke pointed out, "I never trusted Taylor. I knew something wasn't quite right."

Rose narrowed her eyes. "Oh, yes, but you were so concerned that I continue to enjoy their company, you defended them in front of my mother."

Luke appeared momentarily nonplussed. "That was simply for your benefit. I was never truly comfortable with the Taylors. And I was damned uncomfortable about Kersey."

"You never even met Thomas," Rose said. "And stop swearing."

"I had been informed about him," Luke said through tight lips.

"Oh, yes, I forgot about your spies," she said dramatically.

That was enough! Luke strode over to Rose and watched with a certain amount of satisfaction as fear replaced the bravado in her expressive eyes. "Believe me, dearest, the last thing my men expected to find when they were investigating the Supper Club was my wife gallivanting about with another man." What began in a low menacing tone ended in a near shout.

"Gallivanting!"

They stood face to face, their eyes shooting sparks, their mouths set and angry, and all Luke could think of was how he wanted to kiss that mouth until it was soft and pliant against his. Rose must have seen the subtle change in what he'd thought was quite a threatening look, for suddenly she looked more confused than angry.

"Rose," Luke said thickly. "Why are we still arguing about this?" He watched as her gaze touched his mouth then moved back to his eyes.

"Because you're so stubborn." The spell was broken.

"*I'm* stubborn! Why, you . . ." A knock at the study door interrupted what would have been a fine catalogue of Rose's own stubbornness.

"Yes," Luke called, giving Rose a final glare.

A maid ushered Arthur Ripley into the study. He looked tired and disheveled, as if he'd been up all night. "I thought you should know, Luke. John Taylor's dead and his wife has disappeared."

Arthur looked pointedly at Rose, and Luke said, "She can stay. Tell me what you know, Art."

"Not much. Only that Taylor's body was discovered early this morning by a worker down by the river." He gave Rose an uneasy look. "His throat had been cut and a rock tied to his legs. Apparently the rock wasn't heavy enough and the current dragged him. His body was found stuck in some debris."

"Oh, my God," Rose said, turning pale. She ought to hate John Taylor, but she still hadn't come to terms with his betrayal. Part of her refused to believe that her friends were never her friends at all, though she knew she was being foolish.

"The wife has disappeared. Chief thinks maybe her rock worked better. They've been dragging the river for her body since dawn."

"I'm filing a motion tomorrow that the charges against my wife be dismissed," Luke said.

Arthur gave him a startled look. "On what grounds? If anything, Taylor's death is damaging to Rose. A key witness being found dead is rather prejudicial."

Luke's eyes turned to ice. "Are you saying the police suspect my wife?"

"No. They don't suspect Rose, but . . ."

"But what?" Luke bit out.

Arthur sighed in resignation. "But I wouldn't be surprised if Chief Farwell pays you a visit and asks about your whereabouts Wednesday night."

"You are joking."

"I'm afraid not, friend."

To Rose's amazement, Luke began laughing. "Oh, this is grand. Next you'll be arresting Rose's mother."

Arthur wasn't smiling. "They do plan to interview her father."

"What?" Rose shouted. "My father is the gentlest man I know."

"It's just routine, Rose."

"It's a witch-hunt is what it is." Rose turned to Luke. "Tell him what we know. Tell him about John."

"We've no proof," Luke said.

"What proof do they have that you murdered John? Or that my father did? This is absurd." Rose threw her hands up in disgust and frustration.

"Sweetheart, calm down. From the police's perspective, I would be a likely suspect. Once they interview me and the servants, they will realize that they have the wrong man. Then perhaps they will be more receptive to our theory."

Rose curled her delicate hands into fists. "It's not a theory. It's the truth! And I think it's about time we started telling someone about it."

Arthur, obviously uncomfortable to be caught in the middle of a domestic spat, began edging toward the door. "I just stopped by as a friend to give you fair warning, Luke."

"Arthur, before you go, I'd like to give you some friendly advice. If I were you, I'd turn your investigation Cardi's way."

Arthur gave Luke an assessing look. "It's been done. Perhaps not to my satisfaction, but we've turned up nothing thus far."

"Dig deeper. Thank you for stopping, Arthur," Luke said.

Rose kept her back resolutely to Arthur and refused to say good-bye. When he was gone, she turned to Luke. "If you won't tell Chief Farwell the truth, then I will."

"I would not recommend that, Rose," he said uncompromisingly.

"Why?"

"We have no proof," he said succinctly. "No evidence, nothing. We don't even have a witness. I've done all that I can by pointing Arthur toward Cardi."

Rose chewed on her lip, knowing that Luke was right but refusing to acknowledge the logic of his words. "Well then, let's find a witness. If we could only find Collette. She must be frightened out of her evil little mind about now. If we could find her and convince her to testify, perhaps then the police would listen to us."

"She'd only be hurting herself if she were to testify that her husband killed Kersey. She'd be setting herself up for a charge of conspiracy."

"But certainly that is better than being killed. If Cardi killed Taylor—and we both know he did—then he probably would have no compunction killing Collette. After all, she's the only other person who could point her finger at him. And she knows it." Rose rushed over to Luke, stopping herself just as she was about to clutch his arm. "Oh, Luke, we've got to find Collette before Cardi does."

Luke looked down at his wife's determined and hopeful face. "She may already be dead. I haven't the resources or the time to search for a woman who is likely dead. I can't spare Charles. He's off trying to find out who the Taylors were and whether their real name is Casey. I'm running out of time. The trial is at the end of this month."

"So soon." Rose seemed lost in thought. "Without the Taylors, what sort of case does the prosecution have?"

"It's not as good, I'll give you that. But they still have their statements and several other witness who saw you at the Supper Club."

Rose hung her head and Luke fought the urge to comfort her. But it wasn't defeat that brought Rose's head down, it was deep thought, he realized. "If we find Collette . . . if we convince her to testify, we'll win. That's the only way."

10

Collette Taylor, born Collette LaFrenier, married John Chasen when she was just eighteen. She'd loved him to distraction, turning her back on her family so she could spend the rest of her life with a man who frightened her sometimes and loved her always. A man who was now dead. Her grief was inconsolable, her fear uncontainable. What can I do, she thought wildly. Where can I go?

Collette was a prisoner in Massasoit House, one of Springfield's oldest and most distinguished hotels. She had nowhere to go, no hope of escaping the city unnoticed by the police or Cardi's men, and so she stayed in her room, made immobile by fear and grief. John, dear, dear John, had suspected he might be in danger when he saw two well-dressed hulking men at the door Wednesday evening. They were Cardi's men. Quickly, he had shoved a thick handful of bills at Collette and pushed her out the back door, not even taking the time for a brief kiss. Collette, terrified, had followed his instructions to the letter and gone directly to the hotel where she was to wait for him.

But he never came. And so she never left, knowing in her heart that something horrible had happened to him. It wasn't until Friday that she learned by reading the *Springfield Union,* which she obtained from the bellboy, that a body police identified as John Taylor's had been found in the Connecticut River. When she'd read the story, all Collette could think of was that they would put the wrong name on the tombstone. It bothered her so much, just that thought nearly drove her from her sanctuary. She'd actually made it to the hallway before she stopped herself and fled back into the room.

"Oh, John, what am I going to do?" she whispered for the hundredth time. She sat on the hotel bed wearing only her combination, saving her dress for when she knew she would be forced to leave, for she only had enough money to live in the hotel for slightly more than two weeks. Perhaps by then, everyone would have forgotten about her, she thought. Collette let out a bitter laugh. No one would forget the key witness to a murder and the widow of a man who also was murdered. She wondered idly if the police would come to suspect her for both murders and realized with a start that could be a real possibility.

"Oh, John, do you see what you've done?" She balled her little fists and struck the pillow she clutched against her stomach. All this for his father, a man who hadn't made an honest living his entire life. For all the man's faults, John had loved his father deeply, had worshipped him in a way that Collette could not understand. She'd never said it aloud, but she'd often thought that John's anger toward Luke Beaudette was misplaced. His father, after all, had been guilty of the crime for which he'd been convicted. But for the first time, thanks to Beaudette's vigorous prosecution, John's father would be doing hard time. The thought of spending ten years in prison, rather than the few weeks he had in the past, was too much for the older man to face, so he had killed himself in his cell using his shirt as a noose. John's rage toward Beaudette was unfathomable, and his plan for revenge, brilliant. Death, he'd decided, was too kind for the prosecutor. He'd wanted him ruined, he'd wanted him to suffer for years.

Collette had been proud of John—until he got in with Cardi. Then she'd been mostly frightened for him, and now it seemed her fear had been justified. Cardi had turned John into a murderer, into a man who had justified killing a man he'd thought of as a friend simply to advance the ultimate goal of revenge. Collette had been sick about the entire plan, but grateful that everything would finally be over. John would be happy again.

But now John was dead. Dead. Tears filled her already swollen eyes. Whatever was she going to do without him?

Chapter Six

1

"Bless me, Father, for I have sinned. It has been three weeks since my last confession."

Rose had never gone so long without seeking absolution, but the thought of exposing herself to public scorn had been too, too much. With Luke by her side, she'd forced herself to go out, but she could not gather the courage to go out alone. The trial was set to begin next week, and Rose feared that if it did not go her way, this would be her last opportunity to kneel in this old familiar church. That thought gave her the courage she needed.

"How have you been, Mrs. Beaudette?" Father Beaulieu asked, ignoring the thin pretense of not knowing who the confessor was.

Rose smiled, then grew somber. "Not well. The trial will likely begin Tuesday or Wednesday and Luke is terribly discouraged."

"Does he believe in your innocence?"

"Yes." She said the word softly, unable to hide the sadness in her voice. "Luke is a good man, Father. But I believe he is very, very angry with me. He thinks I am foolish and I know he blames my foolishness for this entire ordeal. I think, perhaps, he is correct." Luke had been more than cool toward Rose and it seemed the closer he got to the trial, the more frigid he became. It had gotten so he could barely stay in the same room with her. When Father Beaulieu did not dispute that she had been foolish, her entire body heated with shame.

"Have you any sins?"

"My greatest sin, Father, has been my failure to tell Luke I have forgiven him for doubting me. I have forgiven him, but . . ." Rose bit her lip. "I am angry that he is angry with me."

"You must have faith that God's love will heal you both. You must be patient with your husband, even if he is not patient with you."

"Yes, Father." Inside, Rose couldn't help but think that it was not fair to ask her to forgive Luke when he clearly had not forgiven her. Why else would he draw further and further away? After listing a few smaller sins, reminiscent of her former life as a godly woman, Rose stepped from the confessional after receiving her penance and walked to the bank of holy candles flickering softly in the dimness of the church. Dropping in a few coins, Rose lit a candle and prayed for Luke, prayed that he would forgive her, that he would love her again. She stared at the candle for a long moment before dropping in a few more coins and lighting another. Kneeling again, she said a prayer for Collette.

"Dear Lord, please watch over Collette and forgive her." As Rose kneeled, she realized she meant the prayer. Perhaps I am the silliest woman alive, but I cannot think Collette is completely evil. Or that she was never truly my friend. Rose knew Collette had betrayed her in a way that most would find unforgivable, but she couldn't help but miss her. That their friendship was mostly a lie only made the pain of losing her worse. Her fate rested in the perfidious hands of a woman who might be dead and was certainly missing. And yet Rose could not hate her. She had, in fact, forgiven her. Silly, silly woman, she thought, if I don't learn to harden my heart, it will be ripped to shreds by the time I'm thirty.

The trial would certainly begin this week after a jury was selected and Luke was terrified. The prosecution's case was strong—it was more than strong. He knew if he'd been sitting across the aisle in the prosecutor's chair, he'd be celebrating a victory already. He was going to fail and Rose was going to prison for the rest of her life. Luke had barely slept, had been unable to eat well for days. Every time he looked at Rose he wanted to scream, to tell her the truth: I cannot do this. I am going to fail you. She looked so damned hopeful, those eyes of hers so trusting, gazing at him like he was some sort of Supreme Court justice. An innocent woman, the woman he loved, was going to be taken away from him forever and there was nothing he could do about it.

He'd sat for hours in the new office he'd rented near the courthouse, trying to come up with something—anything—that he thought would insert enough reasonable doubt into the minds of the twelve men who would judge Rose to make them acquit her. The only thing going for Rose was that she was a woman and quite lovely. It would be difficult for any man to believe such a woman could produce enough passion to murder a man as brutally as Kersey had been murdered. Charles had been unable to substantiate the fact that Taylor's name had truly been Casey, Collette Taylor was still missing, and his only other witness, Anthony D'Angelo, had also disappeared. It was as if the world were conspiring against Rose to get at him.

The only good thing to happen was that the police were satisfied that neither he nor Rose's father had anything to do with John Taylor's death or Collette's disappearance. Though sometimes he wished he *had* been responsible for their demise. Luke had convinced himself that the Taylors would not have gone to elaborate lengths to frame Rose. Unless he was the target of such calculated enmity. Unfortunately, he could not fathom why he would be the target of people who were strangers to him. Either the Taylors were hired by someone else, or they had reasons he was unaware of for wishing him ill.

The list of people who would like to extract revenge against him was long. After all, he was a prosecutor, a man who had sent numerous people to prison. He'd gone over his entire history case by case, hoping to find a Casey among those he had helped put into prison, but he'd found nothing. As he reviewed each case, he remembered the defendant, wracking his brain to recall some incident—something that would cause someone to exact revenge. Before him was a list of ten cases, ten defendants who had some reason to want revenge. He didn't have time to investigate one, never mind ten. Charles had sent letters to wardens concerning each case to determine if anyone had escaped, but nothing had come of it. His motion to delay the trial had been refused, leaving Luke with little hope of putting together a defense that he felt was adequate.

He was going to lose.

"Goddammit!" he shouted, pounding a fist painfully against his desk.

Charles's head immediately popped past the doorway. "Something wrong, sir?"

"Yes, there's something wrong. I've got an assistant who can't accomplish the single assignment I gave him."

Charles turned pale, then flushed pink at Luke's harsh words. Luke rubbed the back of his neck and shook his head, angry with himself for losing control. "Sorry, Charles. Out of line entirely. I'm tired and worried sick about this trial. Nothing has gone our way."

Luke leaned forward, propping his elbows on his desk, and rubbed his eyes with the heels of his hands before resting his head in his hands. "You just get back?" Luke had sent Charles to New York in an attempt to find D'Angelo. His uncle did not know where his nephew had gone, but had volunteered that the man had several relatives living in New York and Providence.

"I found Mr. D'Angelo's mother and father, but they said they hadn't heard from their son. I . . ."

"Go on."

"I didn't believe them, but I couldn't force myself

into their home. Besides, they could barely speak English and looked scared to death. But I may have something for you. About Casey."

Luke dropped his hands and brought his head up. "If you've got something we can use, Charles, I'll take that bar exam for you and nominate you for a federal judgeship."

The younger man grinned. "It might not be what we are looking for. I couldn't find anything on a Casey anywhere. But . . . and I believe you will remember this . . . I did find something on a John Chasen, Sr."

"That's one of my cases," Luke said, and began shuffling through the stack of files on his desk. "Here is it. John Chasen, Sr., armed robbery, burglary, and simple assault. He was sentenced to ten years. Did he escape?"

"He's dead, sir. He committed suicide last year. His only known relative is a John Chasen, Jr."

Luke tried to still the excitement in his heart. Could Kersey's girlfriend have been wrong about the name? He repeated the names silently and decided she could have been mistaken, especially if she'd only met him once or twice. He remembered Chasen only because it had been one of his first cases, one that he had vigorously prosecuted. He remembered Chasen shouting at him, threatening to kill him. At the time, he'd been disturbed by the outburst—enough to recall the case and pull it as a possible connection to current events.

Charles continued, "I received this letter from the warden on the case. Only three wardens have responded to my inquiries, by the way. The warden included a transcript of the suicide note Chasen left behind. In it Chasen basically says he cannot serve out the ten years. He does not name you specifically in the note, but complains about the sentencing."

Charles handed the transcript of the note to Luke, who read it silently. He stood and began pacing rather ineffectually in the confining office. His heart was pounding almost painfully as his excitement over this discovery grew. A small smile appeared on his face and slowly spread into a full-fledged grin. Now he knew why Chasen had targeted Rose. It was as if a black veil had been lifted from his eyes. Walking around the desk, Luke grasped Charles's hand and gave it a hearty shake.

"Well done, sir. I'll have that nomination for you as soon as you pass the bar."

Charles flushed with pleasure. "Beg your pardon, sir, but you also promised to take the exam for me," he joked.

Making a fist, Luke swiped the air in a victorious gesture. "We've got a case now! We've got a goddamn case!" That alone would not be enough to set Rose free, Luke knew, but it would insert some doubt into the minds of the jurors that perhaps John Taylor, also known as John Chasen, had framed Rose for a murder to gain revenge on himself. It was the kind of intrigue that jurors found compelling, that they were unable to disregard during deliberations.

As the day wore on, though, Luke's elation wore thin and doubts returned. By the time the sun was low in the sky, he had once again convinced himself he needed more of everything, particularly more time. At least now he had some defense to lay before the court. Kersey's girlfriend would testify of his devotion and his gambling debts, and Luke would make sure the jurors believed that perhaps it was those debts and not some failed love affair that led to his death. The prison warden could testify about John Chasen, Sr., and the suicide note that could have given the now-dead son a reason to exact revenge.

Luke needed more. He needed Anthony D'Angelo and he needed Collette Chasen, but both were as far out of reach as the stars.

2

Rose looked up from her book to the clock. Luke was late again, and it was Saturday. She wondered if all these hours he worked boded well or ill for the case. He had spoken hardly a word to her about it in two weeks and one look into his weary eyes told her not to broach the subject. Each night when he came home he looked defeated, hopeless, angry. It is all my fault, Rose thought. He is driving himself to death to free me. No wonder he could barely look at her when they were forced to be in a room together.

The front door opened and Rose tensed as she listened to his footsteps grow near. He appeared in the doorway looking as tired as he probably felt. His face was pale and drawn from lack of sleep, his hair mussed from hands that had been run through it all day. But still, even with the deep circles under his tired eyes, Rose thought he looked impossibly handsome. She wanted to go to him and pull him to her, to kiss away the weariness. But he could hardly look at her, it seemed, and she knew he could not bear even to be in the same room, so deep was his anger.

"You look tired," she said, hoping to draw him into the room. She laid down her book.

"I *am* tired," Luke said. He remained standing in the doorway as if uncertain whether to enter. "I've had some good news about the case. Some good. Not enough, not nearly enough." He said the last to himself, but Rose heard him, heard the note of defeat.

She chose to dwell on the positive. "Good news?" she asked, forcing her voice to be light.

Luke looked to the floor, his eyes seeming to search for something as he let out a ragged breath. "Not good enough," he bit out, and Rose blinked rapidly at his harsh tone. Unaware of the effect he was having on Rose, Luke continued.

"Your friend John Taylor's real name was John Chasen. His father, a man I successfully prosecuted five years ago, committed suicide in prison. Chasen was trying to get revenge on me through you." Luke looked up to see that hopeful, hero-worshipping look on Rose's face. "So, you see, my dear, none of this was your fault at all. I was the target. I was the reason this all happened. You were just a silly little pawn, a perfect dupe for Chasen's evil plans. And let's not forget Cardi. He wanted me out of his way, too. So when you're sitting in your cold cell at night you can comfort yourself with the fact that your husband caused all this and then couldn't prove a goddamn thing to set you free."

Rose, her eyes wide with shock, shook her head. "Luke, stop saying such things."

Luke strode into the room and ignored Rose's plea. "I won't stop! I've been silent too long, allowing you to believe your husband is going to save you from life's injustices. Well, it's not going to happen, Rose. Because I'm going to fail. Because the case against you is nearly airtight, because every witness I need has disappeared."

"Please stop, Luke." Rose stood and put her hands on his arms but he shook her off angrily.

"Don't you understand, Rose? You are going to prison. *I am going to lose.*"

Rose had never seen Luke—solid, serious, confident Luke—like this, and she felt afraid for the first time, truly afraid that things would not turn out all right, that just because she was innocent did not mean she would be found innocent by the jury.

Luke saw the truth finally drawing in Rose's eyes. He'd known for some time that he was fighting a losing battle, that without Collette Taylor or Anthony D'Angelo the chances for acquittal were remote. But Rose, with her trusting looks and her tentative smiles, was driving him mad. He was glad she finally knew the truth. Glad she now knew that he could not save her.

"I didn't realize," she said softly.

"Now you do," he bit out, being purposefully cruel. It would be more cruel to let her believe he would win, to stare stunned at the jury as the final verdict was read. She should be prepared. He watched as she lifted a trembling hand to tuck a curl behind one ear as her other hand groped behind her to find the chair she'd vacated. Rose sat down heavily, her hands clasped together in her lap, and let out a shaky breath.

"If we lose, we can appeal."

Luke flung his arms wide. "Wonderful strategy! If we lose, which I am going to do, we'll appeal. Good idea."

Rose frowned at his scathing sarcasm.

"Meanwhile, you can rot in prison. Perhaps you don't know what prison is like, Rose. I do. I've seen them. I've seen the rats and smelled the feces. I've heard the screams and the cries. I've seen what they can do to a woman, I . . ." Luke stopped and turned away, unable to look at Rose a moment longer.

"I'm tired," he said, finally. "I'm going to my room. Good night." He walked through the door without looking back.

"Good night." He did not hear her, those softly spoken words filled with sadness and yearning.

Luke insisted they carry on as they had for the past several weeks: as if their lives weren't falling apart. Sunday morning they attended eight o'clock mass, Rose sitting in the pew so stiff-backed that not even the small bow attached to the back of her dress touched the pew. Though the parishioners stared, some with open hostility, the scathing remarks whispered just loud enough for Rose to hear had ended weeks ago thanks in part to one of Father Beaulieu's sermons. "Do not judge lest ye be judged," he'd boomed out at the congregation. Few people there had not known to whom the sermon was directed.

As always, Rose looked straight ahead, appearing to be captivated by the activity of the altar boys, repeating her responses by rote. But Rose felt nothing. Part of her knew that this day, perhaps the last Sunday she would be free, should be filled with prayers in which she beseeched the Lord's help. She did not have the energy to do more than sit with her back straight, to kneel and stand when it was required, and to say words that suddenly had no meaning to her. She didn't even realize she had begun to cry as she knelt, waiting for communion to end, until she felt Luke's hand on hers.

Rose turned to him but he was looking forward, his jaw clenching and unclenching and his hand uncommonly gentle upon hers. With her free hand, she wiped away her tears, hoping no one would notice her crying. For every tear she wiped away, another formed, until her face was almost ridiculously wet. Rose would have laughed had she not been so aware that everything she did was carefully scrutinized. The more she tried not to laugh, the more she wanted to, until she realized she was no longer crying but trying with all her being not to laugh. I'm insane, she thought, biting her lip painfully as her body began to shake. Luke turned to her, giving her a look of alarm as he realized he was looking not at a wife who was crying, but one who was laughing.

"Rose, get control," he whispered.

Rose nodded vigorously, then let out a little noise as air escaped her compressed lips in a most unladylike fashion.

"Rose!" Luke whispered, this time with a bit of mirth in his voice. "There is nothing funny about this." He sounded angry but Rose could tell he was simply trying to get control of his own self. Rose squeezed her eyes closed and said her first heartfelt prayer of the day. Please, God, forgive me but I cannot stop . . .

And her entire body began to shake as tears—this time of mirth—escaped her eyes. Next to her, Luke lost control, letting out a rather unpleasant noise as he tried to control his laughter. Rose looked up to find Father Beaulieu raise an inquiring eyebrow at her just as he was handing a parishioner the Body of Christ. Rose immediately sobered, but Luke clutched his middle as if he were in pain.

"Luke, stop laughing," Rose whispered, leaning toward his ear. "Father Beaulieu's looking this way."

Luke covered his eyes as if deep in prayer as his

body shook convulsively. "I . . . can't . . . stop," Luke managed to whisper. And Rose, who'd barely had control of her emotions, dropped her head to her folded hands and lost the battle as well.

"What in God's name happened to the two of you in church this morning? The entire congregation knew you were laughing. In the Lord's house! The day before the trial begins. *Mon dieu!*"

Looking and feeling appropriately chagrined, Rose apologized to her mother as the family sat for dinner. "Our emotions are so raw, we couldn't stop," she said. "I hate to think what it must have looked like."

"It looked like the two of you do not have a care in the world, that's what it looked like," Aline said with a sniff. "And Lord knows you do."

"I think that laughter did a world of good," Luke said, coming to Rose's defense. "I know I feel much better."

"You might have chosen another place to have your fit," Aline shot back with a frown that left deep crevices along either side of her mouth. "By the way, Rose, your Aunt Flora wrote to me and wanted me to pass on her prayers to you and Luke. She said she is not up to traveling from Pittsburgh for the trial. You may read the letter after dinner. Perhaps you could find time to write to her?"

Rose smiled at her mother's broad hint. She wrote to her Aunt Flora monthly, long detailed letters that took more than an hour to write. But she hadn't written a word since her arrest, even though she was long overdue. She did not want Aunt Flora to worry about her.

"Yes, Mother, I will."

"See that you do."

Rose bit her tongue. Why did her mother have to always be so abrasive? That woman who'd embraced her had made only a brief appearance and her old mother was back in full force, as disagreeable and complaining as always.

"Mrs. LeClaire's wake is Monday. I don't suppose you'll be able to go."

Rose easily detected the reproach in her mother's voice but refused to take the bait. This could be her last Sunday dinner with her family and she refused to argue. "With the trial about to start, I don't think the LeClaires will miss me. Please pass on my condolences, Mother."

She sniffed. "Life doesn't stop just because of this trial."

"Mother, I'll let the LeClaires know Rose regrets being unable to attend the wake," Nicole said gently. "Lord knows poor Mr. LeClaire will have enough to worry about without having someone as notorious as Rose walk through his front door."

If Rose's mother knew she was being gently chastised by her oldest daughter, she gave no indication. "Rose hasn't attended a single wake in a month. People are beginning to talk."

"I'm sure they'd be talking more if I did go," Rose said, feeling anger heat her face.

"Forget I mentioned the wake."

"I will!" Again, she felt that hand on her arm, there, she supposed, this time as a warning, not to give comfort. She shook Luke off, irritated that he would try to calm her. But when she turned to him, expecting to see censure in his eyes, she saw only kindness. And that, illogically, irritated her even more. As much as she'd wanted to laugh in church, she wanted to get angry now. Good and angry at . . . at . . . everyone. Luke, her mother, Collette, Nicole. The world.

"Rose, Mother is just worried about what people think, that's all," Louis said.

"Why doesn't everyone just leave me alone! I don't care what people think. I'm sick to death about worrying what people think. Let them think I'm a murderess. Let them think I don't give a whit about Mrs. LeClaire. And do you know something? I don't. She was a mean old lady and poor Mr. LeClaire should dance on her grave and say good riddance." Rose stood, red-faced and already regretting her childish outburst. She'd gone too far. Her entire family was looking at her with shock at her behavior. Except Luke. He started to laugh, damn the man. This time, because he did not have to worry about disturbing a mass, he laughed loudly, big body-shaking guffaws. And then Rose was chuckling, too, her anger swept away by her laughing husband.

"They've both gone mad," Louis said, and that only produced more laughter.

Nicole lost control then, her hand coming up to her mouth as if she were mortified that she, too, was giggling. Even their father had a smile on his lips. Only Louis and Aline remained frowning.

Having shared such laughter, Rose found herself bewildered and hurt that Luke, once they were alone, reverted back to the unapproachable man he'd been since her arrest. They drove home in silence after Rose unsuccessfully tried to draw Luke into conversation. She needed him, but she refused to let him see how much. Night after night, she squeezed a pillow against her breast and fought the desire to go to him. She'd said she would not that night all those weeks ago, and she *would not*.

Luke didn't even seem to notice. He didn't seem to give it a thought. It was as if they'd never made love with such abandon all those weeks ago. Did I dream that weekend? Rose studied Luke's hard profile as he looked out the window of the hired hack, a conveyance they'd starting using since her arrest. The trial would likely begin Tuesday. She could be in prison for the rest of her life by Friday. Didn't he realize that? Didn't he understand that they needed to fit a lifetime of making love into a single week? He must. But apparently even that thought failed to move him, Rose thought grumpily.

He must come to me. He must. I need you, Luke, she pleaded silently. I need you so much.

But when they arrived home, he politely opened the door for her, stepping back so that he might enter first. As she handed her hat and gloves to a maid, Luke turned to her and her heart hammered in her breast.

"Tomorrow will be a long day. You ought to get a good night's rest."

Rose stared at him, willing him to see what was in her heart. "Are you going to bed?"

"I have work to do," he said, not meeting her eyes. "Opening statement. It needs work." With that, he hurried to his study, leaving Rose frowning at his back.

3

By the time the first day of the trial had ended, Rose felt as if she'd been beaten by the mob of people who waited outside the courtroom. Though the small courtroom held many supporters, including her parents, there were just as many detractors in the crowd and she could feel every pair of their accusing eyes boring into her back. She sat stiff and straight in her chair as she listened to the whispers behind her back discussing everything from the murder to her choice of dress. Rose wore a conservative dark brown silk dress with jet beading, large bell sleeves, and a tiny waist that required her corset to be cinched uncomfortably tight. Her maid had clucked her tongue and warned Rose that she would be uncomfortable sitting in that dress for hours at a time, but Rose had ignored her. Now, according to the whispers she heard, the dress was entirely too modern, too stylish for an innocent woman to wear.

The testimony for the prosecution was long and tedious and terribly damning. It was awful to listen to Arthur Ripley say such terrible things about her during his opening statement, to know that he likely believed every word he uttered. Luke had told her to try not to show too much emotion during the testimony, for it could be misinterpreted by the jury. A flush of anger or embarrassment could easily be seen as a flush of guilt. Rose tried but it was not easy. Behind her, she could hear her mother's gasps of angry outrage and Nicole's quietly spoken entreaties for her mother to be quiet. It broke Rose's heart that her family had to listen to such lies and then face their friends with as much grace as they could muster. Although Luke had been angry, Rose was relieved when his parents, still in Europe, wired to say they could not make it back in time for the trial.

The prosecution examined witness after witness who said they saw Rose with Thomas Kersey at the Supper Club on more than one occasion. When one man, a club employee, mentioned the kiss, the members of the jury looked at her with what Rose knew was scorn. She tried to ignore the testimony, but her face flushed despite her best efforts. Though Luke did his best to reduce the damage done, the testimony was damning . . . and all true. Rose knew none of the witnesses had lied, and yet she wanted to stand up and scream, "It wasn't like that. Thomas was my friend!" By the end of the second day, Rose would have voted to convict herself.

The only bright moment of the trial came when Luke cross-examined the doctor who performed the autopsy on poor Thomas's body. Luke honed in on the broken ribs.

"What kinds of breaks were they, Doctor? Hairline fractures? Minor fissures or cracks?"

"No, sir. The fourth and fifth ribs were broken clear through."

Luke raised his eyebrows as if surprised to hear such a thing. "Broken clear through! I imagine it would take a considerable amount of force to crack a rib in that manner."

The witness shot a look to Arthur Ripley. "A considerable amount," he agreed.

"In your experience, Doctor, would you say that such a force could be produced by a woman?"

"It's possible."

"*Really*. A woman of small stature could with a single blow crack two ribs?"

"In my opinion, yes."

Rose's heart plummeted—until Luke asked the court to indulge him in a little experiment. He then produced a board upon which two human ribs had been attached and asked the doctor, a rather frail man, to attempt to break them with his fist. Luke presented him with a pair of leather gloves to protect his hands. The doctor, looking a bit panicked, asked the judge if the demonstration was necessary.

"I'll allow it." Judge Mitchell seemed to be enjoying the doctor's discomfiture.

It took the doctor three attempts, but he finally broke both the ribs clean through, shaking his hand after the successful blow was delivered.

"Thank you, Doctor."

"But it's not the same at all," the doctor said hurriedly.

"Thank you, Doctor. I'm finished with you."

Arthur stood up. "I have another question for the good doctor," he said.

The judge nodded.

"Doctor, you theorized that the final blow was delivered when the victim was already down, is that correct?"

Having regained his composure, the doctor calmly answered, "Yes, that is my testimony."

"And, given that, it is possible that a woman, falling down with her entire weight behind the blow, could have broken those ribs, isn't it?"

"It certainly is," the doctor said pompously.

Arthur had won a small point, but Rose noticed the men on the jury looked thoughtful. She reached over and gave Luke's hand a small squeeze.

As grand as that victory was, it wasn't enough, not nearly enough to convince the jury that she was innocent, Rose knew. The prosecution had painted her as an adulteress and a murderer and had done a fine job. Luke would begin his defense on Thursday, stretching out his meager witness list as long as Judge Mitchell's patience would allow. Charles was still looking for Anthony, but it was becoming painfully clear that Luke's defense was woefully weak.

Wednesday night, Rose and Luke sat at the dining room table staring at their still-full plates. Rose knew without being told that things were not going well. With great purpose, she sawed at a piece of roast beef but simply couldn't bring herself to eat the morsel. She laid down her fork and knife.

"I'm frightened," Rose whispered. "I don't want to go to prison." Her voice sounded very small, even to her own ears.

"I know," Luke said raggedly. "I'll do everything in my power to keep you free."

Rose laid a hand on Luke's arm and he turned toward her. "If we lose, I don't want you to feel responsible. You've tried your best. All we can do is pray for a miracle."

Luke let out a short laugh. "I have been. I've prayed so much, I'm sure God is mightily sick of hearing about you."

"It's all we have left," Rose said. "Let's pray together, Luke. Let's pray for that miracle."

At that moment, their miracle was almost dying from fright.

Collette, bored and restless, had taken to going for strolls after dark. The first time had been so frightening, it had hardly been worth it to venture out. But each day that passed that she went undiscovered, Collette became more confident that perhaps no one was searching for her after all. She still took the time to disguise herself by covering her signature blonde hair and wearing a veil, but she strolled freely about downtown as soon as the sun went down.

At least when she was outside breathing the heavy night air she could be free of the thoughts that plagued her. Collette missed John terribly, and, to her great shame, found she also missed Thomas. Thomas, whom John had murdered, whom she had helped set up for that murder. Great waves of guilt crashed over her when she caught herself smiling at some happy memory that included Thomas. It seemed so many memories included the man that made her laugh so. At times, she actually found herself getting angry with John, then chastised herself for her disloyalty. Perhaps her greatest feelings of guilt came from knowing that Rose Beaudette, one of the few truly good women she'd had met, would likely be convicted of killing Thomas. She tried not to feel that stomach-curling guilt, she tried to tell herself that Rose was nothing but an irritating goody-goody and the world was better off without her forcing her charms on the unsuspecting blackguards of the world. But her arguments never rang true. She'd even had moments, sitting in her hotel room, when she'd come close to turning herself in. Reason, thank goodness, always returned quickly. She might not feel completely good about Rose being falsely accused of murder, but she certainly wasn't stupid enough to implicate herself. Only a ninny would turn herself in.

On those long nighttime walks, Collette could forget everything. She could look in darkened shop windows and dream of the day when she felt safe enough to walk about in daylight, when no one was looking for her or picking out a rock weighty enough to keep her body on the bottom of the Connecticut River. Once Rose Beaudette was safely in prison, she would be free. If that thought gave her a twinge of guilt—or perhaps more than a twinge—so be it. She, Collette, had not killed Thomas. She comforted herself with that thought when images of the devil waiting for her at the entrance to the bowels of hell caused her to wake up screaming in the night. If Rose Beaudette had not been so gullible, she would not be facing a murder charge. Rose's stupidity had more to do with her predicament than Collette's maneuverings did. Collette told herself these things over and over until she thought she'd go crazy from it all. Until darkness came and she could escape her room and her thoughts.

Collette rode up the hotel's elevator to the top floor of the four-story hotel with a sleepy operator at the controls, who brought the car to a halt so that Collette had to step up to reach her floor. She suspected the young man did so simply so she would have to raise her skirts, which she did with a huff. As she stepped into the hall, she immediately noticed two men outside her door—and they immediately noticed her.

"Down! Oh, God, hurry, hurry. Down, down," Collette screamed at the startled elevator operator as she jumped into the car, skirts lifted high above her knees. "Down, you dimwit!" Collette whacked him on his head, denting his little cap. Spurred into action, the boy pulled the lever that shut the cage and started the elevator with a jerk.

"Oh, God, can't it go faster than this?"

"Ma'am," the boy croaked, "is someone after you?"

Collette was silent, twisting her hands together as she watched the dial that displayed the elevator's slow progress. "We're here. Stop it!" The boy immediately brought the elevator to a jerking halt and opened the door, even though they were still a foot above floor level. Collette leaped and fell to her knees, her skirts billowing out around her. Her foot got caught on one petticoat as she tried to get up, sending her sprawling again. With a screech, she lifted her skirts high, hauled herself up, and ran for the door, heedless of the gaping stares of the few patrons in the lobby. The doorman, seeing her hurrying his way, calmly opened the door and stepped back. He didn't have time to complete his bow before Collette, blonde hair and skirts flying, disappeared.

4

Luke was awakened from a deep and much-needed sleep by an insistent tapping on his arm. He opened his eyes to see their housekeeper, Mrs. Jones, her nightcap askew atop her head, looming over him. She immediately withdrew from the room without saying a word and, clutching her wrapper about her rotund body, waited for him in the dimly lit hall. "There's a woman downstairs in the kitchen. Claims she's Collette Taylor."

Luke grasped the older woman's pudgy arms. "What did you say?"

Mrs. Jones's eyes grew wide. "I've never seen her, but the voice sounds right. She says she's Collette Taylor and that she needs to talk to you. Ain't that the one everyone's been looking for?"

"Yes. Go on to bed, Mrs. Jones. I'm sorry for the disturbance," Luke said absently as he turned to go.

Luke made his way down the hall, hesitating only a moment in front of Rose's room as he contemplated awakening her. Then, fearful Collette would lose courage and disappear, he hurried on. Why would Collette come here of all places? Certainly this was the last place on earth she would run to. But despite the incongruity of such a thing, when Luke walked into the kitchen, Collette Taylor, looking disheveled and very frightened, turned to him.

"Mrs. Taylor."

Collette swallowed. "Cardi's men are after me. I . . . didn't know where else to go."

Luke gave this woman who had set his wife up for murder, who had allowed her to be falsely accused, a hard, condemning look. "Certainly you cannot feel safer with me than with Cardi's men."

"Oh." Suddenly, Collette looked unsure of herself. "Yes. I can understand that," she said finally. "You must be quite angry with me."

"Angry doesn't begin to describe what I feel toward you."

She swallowed again, her blue eyes wide and uncertain. "But I'm here . . ." She stopped and squeezed her eyes shut. "I'm here to turn myself in." Her voice dropped to a whisper. "I thought if I did, you could help me."

"You want me to help you."

"Well, yes. I thought that . . . because I imagine things are not going well with the trial . . . and I thought I could help."

Luke crossed to a chair and sat down, nodding to Collette that she should join him at the table. "I believe your testimony—your truthful testimony—would help Rose, yes," he said cautiously. He was very much aware that he had sitting in that chair, her lying blue eyes wide with fear, the means to free Rose. A noise from outside filtered into the kitchen and Collette nearly jumped from the chair, her eyes immediately filling with fear-induced tears.

"Cardi's going to kill me," she said, her eyes darting toward the door.

"If he finds you, I'm sure that is his plan," Luke said without emotion. Collette looked quite ill, he thought.

"I'll speak up for Rose, but I don't want to go to prison. I want you to talk to someone, to protect me."

"I have no power to make deals, Mrs. Taylor. As you may know, I no longer work for the attorney general's office." A thought occurred to Luke then, a wonderful liberating thought. Collette would not only help him free Rose, but could also help him put Cardi away for good. *If* he was still in the attorney general's office. Max had not been happy when he'd resigned. Although he clearly regretted accepting Luke's resignation, he agreed that Luke could not remain as a prosecutor with a wife accused of murder. But now he could clear Rose's name in a way that would leave no doubt as to her innocence. A verdict in her favor would have left such doubt. Despite a verdict of innocence, people still would have wondered if she had indeed killed Thomas Kersey. With Collette's testimony, Rose would be free, Cardi would be convicted. Luke had to stop himself from rubbing his hands together in happiness.

"Mrs. Taylor, I can make no promises about

whether the state charges you with a crime in connection to the murder in exchange for your testimony. But I will try."

Collette, her face pale and despondent, nodded, sealing her fate. A gasp at the door brought her head snapping up.

"Rose!" Collette stood up and backed toward the kitchen door. Luke immediately shot out of his chair and placed a restraining hand on her arm.

Rose couldn't help herself. She smiled. Collette and Luke gave her a cautious look, as if unsure what that smile could possibly mean. Indeed, Rose was not certain why her mouth had curved upward. It was, she decided an unconscious reaction to seeing a friend before realizing that Collette was no friend at all. Immediately, she sobered.

"Why are you here?"

Luke answered for her. "Collette is going to testify on your behalf. She's going to tell the truth, Rose."

Rose looked from Luke to Collette, taking in the other woman's disheveled appearance and her haunted blue eyes. Rose wanted to be glad Collette had fallen so low, but all she could feel was pity.

"I'm sorry about your husband," Rose said, and watched dispassionately when tears filled Collette's eyes. Why was she being so polite to the woman who had framed her for murder? She should be scratching her eyes out, not spouting inanities. Somehow, Rose could not muster up the hatred she knew she should feel.

"He killed Thomas," Collette said, biting her lip.

"I know."

"It wasn't my idea. None of it. It was all John. He wanted to get back at Luke for killing his father. It was eating him up inside. It ate away any goodness he had. I just did what he said."

Luke made a face, as if Collette's attempt to exonerate herself sickened him.

"It does not excuse his behavior," Rose said. "Or yours."

Collette hung her head, her blonde curls falling limply over her face. "I know. That's why I'm here."

"You're here," Luke said, his voice hard, "because you are afraid Cardi will kill you, no other reason. Please do not act as if you are here out of the goodness of your evil little heart. My wife has heard and suffered enough from your lies."

"I'd been thinking about turning myself in," Collette said petulantly.

Luke let out a snort.

"It's true! Do you think that I have no conscience whatsoever? I never felt right about what we were doing to Rose. After Thomas . . . I was tortured daily by thoughts of what Rose was going through."

"Bully for you," Luke said scathingly.

"I'm sure she did feel badly, Luke," Rose said, causing Collette and Luke to give her a look of disbelief for her defense of an indefensible act. Realizing what she was doing, Rose stiffened her spine and explained. "What Collette did was reprehensible, but what she is doing now is admirable."

Looking exasperated, Luke said, "But she's only doing it to save her own skin!"

"Are you, Collette?"

Collette looked from Luke's angry face to Rose's trusting one, her expression slowly turning hard and cynical. "Your husband is right. If Cardi's men hadn't shown up at my door, I never would have come here. Never. But I figured I was better off in prison than dead. Honey, that's the truth and I'm sorry. I did feel bad about what we'd done, but that's as far as it goes."

Rose lifted her head up a notch, ignoring the pain Collette's words brought, but knowing she was telling the truth. "I see. In any case, I thank you for coming forward and finally telling the truth."

Collette looked away, unable to meet Rose's gaze. But before she could turn, Rose thought she'd seen something in Collette's eyes that helped her to harden her heart: utter contempt.

5

Rose, Luke thought, looked lovely sitting in the walnut witness stand; her navy blue dress, trimmed with black lace, was somber yet attractive. He had been forcing himself to think of Rose as simply a client, rationalizing that if he distanced himself from her emotionally, his representation of her would be more thorough and capable. It hadn't worked. Instead, he'd spent hours set aside for much-needed sleep thinking of her, remembering how she looked naked, remembering how she tasted. Like everything else in this case thus far, it was a strategy that hadn't worked.

Rose gave her name and swore in a clear voice to tell the truth, but she looked frightened, Luke thought with a slight inward grimace. Rose should not look frightened. She should look confident. Innocent. Knowing that every expression, every gesture he made toward Rose would be taken in by the intensely curious jurors, Luke walked up to the witness stand and gave his wife a smile. Rose instantly relaxed and smiled, very, very slightly, back at him. Perfect, Luke thought with relief. He patted her hand and stepped away.

"Rose, did you kill Thomas Kersey?"

Though they had rehearsed the question hundreds of times, Rose still flushed when Luke asked it now. He showed no outward reaction to that flush which could be interpreted as guilt, but inside his stomach clenched painfully.

"No."

"But you were found hovering over the body, the knife in your hand."

They had gone over this, time and time again. Rose seemed to have settled down after that first difficult question. "Thomas was still alive when I arrived at the cloakroom, but he was mortally wounded. He was bleeding from his mouth and appeared to want to say something, then he died. The knife . . . it looked so horrid . . . I didn't think, I just wanted it out of him."

Luke gave Rose a smile that only she would see. *Good girl,* that smile said.

"Were you having an affair with Mr. Kersey?" That question, coming from the woman's husband, produced a murmur and a few snorts from the spectators.

"No."

"But you were seen kissing him. Several people have testified to that fact."

"The kiss was unexpected and unsolicited. It is why I slapped him. He apologized."

Having disposed of those two major points, Luke shifted to other questions, hoping to ask everything that the prosecution would. But by asking first, he was able to better control how Rose answered. He asked her why she was in the Supper Club, even though it had a rather notorious reputation. He asked why she returned, whether she gambled, whether she'd won. He laid everything out before the jury, letting them see that Rose had perhaps been foolish, but she was not a murderer. Finally, he asked about the Taylors in preparation for Collette's appearance on the stand.

"They were . . . I thought they were my friends," Rose said, unable to keep the hurt from her voice.

"You trusted them."

"Yes, I did."

"The night of the murder, was either of the Taylors acting strangely?"

"They seemed quieter than usual. And although they got me to the gambling hall on the pretense of helping Thomas to not gamble, once we were there, they seemed not to care whether he did or not."

"Where were you just prior to discovering Thomas?"

Rose took a deep breath. "I was in the gambling hall. Collette told me to meet her in the cloakroom, but she wanted me to wait so that John wouldn't know we were talking."

"How was John acting?"

"He seemed nervous. Especially when I pointed out that he had blood on his ear."

Several members of the audience gasped and Luke could barely suppress a smile.

"And then you went to the cloakroom?"

"Yes. And that's when I discovered Thomas."

"And who discovered you?"

"Collette and John Taylor."

Luke smiled. After that first damning flush, Rose had been perfect. But it wasn't over. Arthur Ripley would now get his chance to cross-examine Rose. Though the two had gone over every question he thought the prosecution would ask, Luke's stomach twisted nervously at the thought of Rose being so vulnerable. He'd seen Arthur work a witness numerous times. He was a damned good attorney.

As Arthur approached Rose, she stiffened slightly, as if preparing for an onslaught. Arthur smiled. "Hello, Mrs. Beaudette." Rose simply nodded a greeting, her eyes darting to Luke. He made a fist and gave it a little shake. *Be brave, darling. It's almost over.*

"Mrs. Beaudette, I have here, as entered, statements signed by Collette and John Taylor describing a rather torrid love affair between yourself and Thomas Kersey. You've just testified that you and Mr. Kersey did not have an affair. Were the Taylors lying?"

"Yes, they were."

"For what possible reason?" Arthur asked, looking at the jurors with an expression of pure puzzlement. Many of the jurors smiled at Arthur, a shared joke between men.

Luke stood, irritated with Arthur even as he knew the man was simply doing his job. "Objection, Your Honor. The witness cannot be asked to testify about the motives of a third party." Luke wanted to wait for Collette to take the stand before introducing the matter of the Taylors' plot.

"Sustained," Judge Mitchell boomed.

Arthur smiled and shrugged, eliciting more grins from the jurors. Luke gritted his teeth.

Arthur made a great show of searching the police reports before asking Rose, "Mrs. Beaudette, I can't seem to find mention of any blood on Mr. Taylor in these police reports, which were written based on information you gave police the night of the murder and in subsequent interviews."

"Oh, well, that's because I had forgotten about it."

Arthur clearly looked surprised. "You had just been accused of murder and you forgot to mention that someone you saw that night had blood on them?"

"I . . . At the time I thought it was John's own blood." Rose shot another look at Luke.

Arthur gave Rose a kind smile. "And it could have been Mr. Taylor's blood. Am I right?"

"Yes. It could have been." Rose looked heartbroken and Luke wanted to rush up and reassure her that all would be fine. Once Collette Taylor testified, everything would tie together in the minds of the jurors.

Arthur then drilled Rose about her relationship with Thomas Kersey, asking questions in such a way that no matter what Rose answered, her face flushed and she appeared to be lying. Rose, Luke thought miserably, was a horrible witness. If someone had asked her if she'd shot Lincoln, he feared she would flush with the appearance of guilt. By the end of the cross-examination, Luke could do little to salvage the truth from the lies. The circumstantial evidence against Rose was so damning and so believable that the truth appeared to be a weak and ridiculous defense of a guilty woman. Thank God, Luke thought, for Collette, for without her testimony, the case would surely be lost. If he hadn't loathed the woman so, he would have kissed her feet in thanks.

But even Collette's testimony was not a guarantee of success, Luke knew. The woman had lied to police and Luke was quite sure that Arthur would attempt to capitalize on that fact. The only saving grace was that Collette's testimony would implicate herself in a crime. Surely the jurors would note that and realize she was telling the truth.

"I call Collette Chasen, aka Collette Taylor," Luke

said with near relish. All heads turned to the back of the courtroom as the sergeant escorted Collette through the door. The murmuring grew so loud Judge Mitchell pounded on his gavel and demanded quiet. Collette, head held high, looked positively beautiful in her black widow's weeds, which accented her trim little waist and made her blonde hair appear luminous. Arthur shot a look of admiration to Luke, which went ignored. For the first time since this hell had begun, Luke felt in control.

Luke questioned Collette carefully, starting with her friendship with Rose. He quickly established that Collette, at the request of her husband, had worked to frame Rose. Now the testimony given by Kersey's girlfriend and the testimony from the prison warden about John Chasen, Sr.'s suicide began to make sense. He watched with satisfaction as the men in the jury box leaned forward, as they wrinkled their foreheads in thought, then nodded when the realization of what they were hearing began to gel.

"Mrs. Chasen, the testimony you have given is quite damning. Why on earth would you implicate yourself and your late husband in such a scheme, knowing that criminal charges will likely be brought against you?"

"Because I'd rather go to prison than be dead like poor John," Collette said, dabbing her eyes with a handkerchief. She had been crying, much to Luke's secret delight, throughout much of her testimony.

"Are you saying John was murdered because of his role in Thomas Kersey's death?" Luke asked, as if surprised to hear such a revelation.

"That's exactly what I'm saying. And I'm next. I'm the only other person who knows what really happened. I'm the only one that knows John killed Thomas so that Guido Cardi could teach a lesson."

"Those are very serious charges," Luke said solemnly. Finally, for the record, he asked: "Did Rose Beaudette kill Thomas Kersey?"

"No," she said, shaking her head and pressing the

cloth to her delicately pink nose. "My own John did it."

Luke let out a sigh. "Thank you, Mrs. Chasen. That's all I have for now."

Arthur was furiously writing and looked up when he realized Luke had finished. He stood.

"Would you say you are a liar, Mrs. . . . Let me see, Chasen, is it?"

Collette stiffened indignantly. "No, I wouldn't!"

Arthur scratched his head. "Wouldn't you say introducing yourself as Collette Taylor when your real name is Chasen is a lie?"

"I suppose," she said, glowering at him.

Arthur gave her a tight smile. "Were you Rose Beaudette's friend?"

Collette looked started by the question and unsure what to answer. "I . . . Well, no."

"No?" Arthur shuffled through his notes. "And yet you went to dinner together, played cards, attended a bicycle race, and went swimming with her. Are those not activities one engages in with a friend?"

"I was only pretending to be her friend."

"I see," Arthur said, nodding in understanding. "Then you lied to her. Consistently. Over a period of several weeks. Lied again and again."

"Yes," she said through compressed lips.

"You seem to lie quite a bit," Arthur observed lightly, and several members of the jury chuckled. "And this—" Arthur picked up the statement signed by her and John and placed it in front of her. "This is also a lie."

"Yes."

"Do you ever tell the truth, Mrs. Taylor? Oh, forgive me—Mrs. Chasen?"

More chuckles.

"I'm telling the truth now," she said, lifting her head.

"Ooh. You're telling the truth *now*. How nice for us all," Arthur said grandly.

Luke stood angrily. "Your Honor, I would request

a sidebar." Judge Mitchell nodded and Luke stalked over to the bench as Arthur casually stepped up next to him.

"What the devil are you doing, Art? You know damned well Rose is innocent and this woman is telling the truth."

Arthur shot Luke a look of irritation. "I'm doing my job, Luke. You know that. And I've got to be honest with you, I don't know what the truth is in this case. I only know what the testimony tells me."

"Gentlemen, this is not proper discussion for a sidebar. Is there a point of law you wish to discuss, Mr. Beaudette?"

Luke snapped his head up. He'd half forgotten about Judge Mitchell. He clenched his jaw. "No, Your Honor. My apologies."

Luke knew he'd made a mistake when he saw the worried expression on Rose's face. Now, more than ever, he needed to remain confident. He'd let his love for Rose interfere with his better judgment. By letting the jury see his concern, he was letting them know he was not as confident about his witness as he should be. *Idiot,* he thought, a bit of panic building in his breast.

"I apologize for the interruption," Arthur said to Collette, neatly capitalizing on Luke's display. Damn the man.

"You say that now you are telling the truth. But what if you are not? What if you are the best of friends with Mrs. Beaudette and are lying to protect her?"

"That's not true."

"How can we know?" Arthur asked, bewilderment and skepticism in his voice. "You expect us to believe that the true guilty party is the one person who cannot defend himself. A dead man. Quite convenient."

"It's the truth," Collette said, her elegant brows snapping together.

"We cannot ask John Chasen, can we?"

Collette's eyes filled with tears. "No. We cannot."

"Because the man you claim killed Thomas Kersey

is dead. And the woman who you claim was never your friend, whom you said you discovered in the cloakroom, her hand still about the knife—something that was witnessed by several people other than yourself, I might add—is innocent?" His tone said he clearly did not believe her.

"Yes."

"Are you lying, Mrs. Chasen?" Arthur asked, driving home the point that the woman was, indeed, a liar.

"No."

"That is all I have," Arthur said, stepping toward his table with confidence.

Luke stood. "Mrs. Chasen. Where have you been the past month?"

"At the Massasoit House."

"And why were you there? Surely you knew the police wanted to question you about the death of your husband."

"I was hiding from Guido Cardi."

Luke gave Collette an encouraging smile. "And why were you hiding?"

"Because I'm the only other person who knows he had John kill Thomas Kersey because Thomas owed him money."

Luke prayed he had undone some of the damage Arthur's questioning had wrought. He'd known Arthur would attack Collette's credibility, but he had miscalculated how well-executed that attack would be.

Collette was given permission to step down, which she did with obvious relief.

Luke felt sick as he wondered whether Collette's testimony did any good at all. Rose looked pale and worried and his heart wrenched as he saw her twist her ring around her finger over and over. She turned to him, her brown eyes wide. "I thought Arthur was our friend," she said, and looked to be on the verge of tears.

Luke had no answer for his wife and no other witnesses. He felt paralyzed with the knowledge that despite Collette's testimony, Rose could still be found guilty. He had failed. Miserably. The attorney general's protégé, the up-and-coming star, had failed. He knew it in his gut. His head suddenly shot up as he realized Judge Mitchell was talking to him.

"Because of the late hour, do you have any objection if we recess for the day, Mr. Beaudette?"

Luke beamed a smile at the judge. "No objection," he said, and he secretly wondered if somehow Judge Mitchell knew just how desperate he was.

6

"That didn't go well, did it?" Rose asked, as if afraid the question might anger Luke. They'd been home fifteen minutes, each trying to come up with someone—anyone—who could help Rose's case.

"No, it didn't."

Rose walked up to Luke and stopped his pacing with a gentle hand on his chest. He stiffened but did not walk away and Rose took heart. "Luke, look at me."

Luke shook his head. "Rose."

"Look me in the eye," she persisted. When he finally did, looking impatient and slightly belligerent, she smiled. "You are not going to lose."

He began shaking his head but Rose gave the sleeve at his upper arm a little tug. "You, Luke Beaudette, are not going to lose."

Luke let out a sigh of defeat. "How can you have such faith in me?"

Rose looked into his eyes, then focused on the collar he had partially removed, her eyes filling with tears. "Because I love you."

"I wish love was enough to convince the jury."

"It's enough to convince me. And that's all that matters." Rose gave Luke's sleeve another tug, seeing that he continued to resist her.

The look he gave her was filled with regret, sorrow, and an abiding love. "I'm going to lose, Rose."

"Tonight, I don't care. I don't want to think about it. I just want . . . everything to go away."

Luke crushed her to him, holding her in an almost desperate way, burying his face against her neck. He let out a low sound and pulled her impossibly closer. "I don't want to lose you," he whispered harshly against her ear.

"You won't."

They drew apart and gazed at each other. Silently, Luke took her hand and led her out of the room and up the stairs to his bedroom. He didn't speak until they were both naked and standing facing one another, his hands lightly caressing her cheeks. "I tried to convince myself that I didn't want this. That I could focus better on the case if you didn't share my bed. I was wrong. Do you forgive me?"

Rose leaned forward and placed a soft kiss on his mouth. "Yes."

Luke drew her down with him onto his bed. For the longest while, he just held her and Rose thought that perhaps he'd fallen asleep. She didn't care, truly; it was nice enough simply to lay there in his arms. But slowly, she became aware of a light caress, a soft kiss upon her hair, and a warmth filled her that made her smile in anticipation.

Sweetly, he kissed her, his mouth brushing her lips, cheek, neck, breast. His hands moved lightly over her and she felt languid and wonderfully alive. She let out a happy sigh and turned her mouth to his so that she might taste him. With a groan, what had been sweet caresses turned torrid, their hands moving over each other, touching, squeezing, trying to get a lifetime of love into a single night.

When he entered her, she welcomed him by raising her hips and letting out a sigh of wonder that it should feel so good. They moved together, silent, intense, feeling each other in a way that transcended any other moment they had shared. Rose reveled in the feel of him, his every thrust giving her pleasure, sending her toward that place where everything was gone but

Luke. She arched against him, losing herself, disappearing, taking him with her. Gone, gone.

Slowly they came back, aware of their breathing, of their still-joined bodies slick with sweat, of their pounding hearts. Slowly, the world returned: the crickets and night birds, a carriage driving by, a distant barking dog. It was all still there.

They spent that night together sharing themselves with no one. For the first time in their married life, they did not go down to supper. Instead, after making love for an hour, they went to Forest Park and strolled along the flower-lined paths, holding hands as the night enveloped them. Their love was not the giddy and brief thing they had shared before, but a deeper, quieter love that filled their hearts far, far more. Every look, every touch filled them up and helped block out the nightmare that awaited them both. For if they touched and made love as if it might be their last time, it was only because both knew their time together might be cut horribly short.

The worst moment was when Luke and Rose came upon a couple bent over their newborn baby. The baby lay nestled in a froth of white lace that nearly made it impossible to see what lay amidst the fabric. It hit Rose then with a pain that was stunning: I might never share a moment like this with Luke. I might never have a child.

Rose had looked at Luke with such raw torment, he had clutched her to him, immediately discerning what had caused the pain. The couple, oblivious to the drama being played out behind them, only made matters worse when they lifted their little bundle out of the well-sprung carriage and held it aloft. Their pure happiness at holding their child was like pouring salt into a gaping wound. Rose turned abruptly and nearly ran from the happy scene, a sob tearing from her throat. She stopped under a large maple tree several yards from the path and the bench that held the little family.

"I couldn't bear it a moment longer," she said, burying her nose into a handkerchief. "It's not fair. It's not fair," she railed. It was the first time Rose had displayed anger about her predicament and Luke was oddly glad to see her release some of the pain she'd kept well hidden. "Why won't anyone believe me? Why?" She spun around and punched Luke hard in the chest.

"Even you!" she sobbed. "You believed I did it. If it took so long to convince my own husband, how can I expect twelve strangers to believe in me?" Rose blew her nose nosily, oblivious to the odd stares other strollers were casting her way. "I'm doomed," she cried, looking so pathetic Luke didn't know whether to laugh or join in her tears.

"Oh, this is the worst. The absolute worst!" Rose blew her nose again, hiccuped, then let out a laugh.

"Feel better?" Luke asked.

Rose gave what could have passed for a smile if her eyes hadn't looked so damned sad and shook her head, her gaze drifting to the family. "I don't think I'll ever feel better."

Luke wanted to hold her against him and make it all go away. But he couldn't. He could only use his brain and his experience as a lawyer to convince the jury that Rose was innocent. Other than that, he was as helpless as the baby that had brought about Rose's tears.

When they returned home, long after dark, they made love with a fierceness that left them sated but melancholy. As Rose lay abed nestled in the crook of Luke's arm, her head resting on a muscular shoulder, she couldn't help but think of the time wasted that could never be regained. She breathed in his scent, willing herself to remember it always.

How could she possibly live without him? How could she endure it? How could he?

7

"Have you any more witnesses, Mr. Beaudette?" the judge said the next morning.

Luke stood, feeling as if he were facing a death squad. No. There were no more witnesses. Rose could go to prison for the rest of her life. She would be ripped from everything she knew and thrust into hell for something she did not do. And Luke would not be able to stop it. He could only give his best try during final arguments and pray the men on the jury believed him. Or would they simply pity him, the cuckolded husband who was too blind to see the truth?

"Your Honor," Luke said, swallowing the bile that threatened to rise, "the defense . . ."

"Has one more witness."

All heads turned to the back of the courtroom, where a handsome, dark-haired man stood, his eyes not on Luke or Rose or even the judge, but on Nicole Baptiste, who looked at him and smiled.

Nicole's heart filled to nearly bursting. He'd come back. She drank in the sight of him, his dark brown hair, those wonderful love-filled eyes, framed by dark and ridiculously thick lashes. Oh, Anthony, Anthony. You've come back.

She was aware, horribly aware, of Louis standing next to her. "Who the hell's that guinea?" he asked, and Nicole stiffened.

"Our milkman, Louis. He also works at the Supper Club."

Louis gave a grunt, acknowledging Nicole's answer. She couldn't help but compare Louis to Anthony. Louis wore a fine suit, but one that was beginning to be too small about his growing stomach. The buttons had begun to pull slightly. The flesh around his neck was loose and folded over his stiff collar, his rather full mouth wet from a tongue that was constantly darting out and wetting them, leaving them split and chapped nearly year-round. Looking at them made Nicole's stomach heave, so she looked away. Right into Anthony's eyes as he swore to tell the truth.

Nicole smiled, hoping that smile said everything she longed to say. I'm proud of you, Anthony. I love you. Thank you, my love.

"Mr. D'Angelo," Luke's booming voice said, breaking into her reverie. "On May twenty-fifth, where were you employed?"

"I worked for Brown's Dairy and also for the Supper Club in the kitchen as a chef's assistant. My uncle is the chef there."

"On the night of May twenty-fifth, were you working?"

"Yes, sir."

Nicole loved his voice, his accent, his quiet yet firm way of speaking. People would believe this man. His eyes did not waver. He did not flush or fidget when asked questions.

"Do you recall where you were shortly before the body of Thomas Kersey was discovered?"

"Yes, sir. I was in the washroom."

"And was anyone else in the room?"

"A man. He was washing his hands. There was blood in the basin."

"Did you recognize this man?"

"I knew him only from seeing him frequently at the club. I had also seen him at a bicycle race with his wife and Mrs. Beaudette. Mrs. Beaudette had accompanied this man to the club the Friday before the murder."

Luke showed a photograph of John Taylor to Anthony.

"Yes, sir, it is the man."

Luke smiled. "Let the record show that the witness has identified John Taylor as the man he saw in the washroom."

Nicole looked at the members of the jury panel, who were listening intently to Anthony's testimony. She knew that Anthony, more than any other witness, would help free her sister.

*   *   *

The crowd murmured, but this time those voices did not bother Rose for she knew there had been a shift in the case. She felt it in the way the jurors looked at her with a strange intensity that held none of their earlier scorn. When Luke sat down, hardly able to contain the smile on his face, Rose grasped his hand. And that smile he'd been containing burst through with a radiance that had Rose wanting to whoop and shout.

"It's not over yet, love," Luke cautioned. But Rose could tell from his tone that the tide had turned.

Arthur asked only a few questions of Anthony, his brow furrowed in thought as he walked back to his seat. His assistant appeared angry but Arthur ignored the man and glanced over to Luke, who turned, sensing his perusal. When Luke turned back, he leaned toward Rose. "Darling, we've won."

Indeed, Arthur's closing argument was lackluster. Though he could not withdraw the state's case, it was clear to Luke that Arthur now had doubts about the charges brought against Rose. In contrast, Luke's words were emotional and had many women spectators dabbing at their eyes before he was finished.

"Gentlemen, I'm sure you are aware that the defendant is my wife and you think I am either a fool or a very lucky man. I'll tell you now that you are looking at the luckiest man alive." With that he turned to give Rose a wink and a smile, and Rose blushed prettily, looking not guilty, but very much in love.

"I'd like to tell you a story, gentlemen. It is a story about a husband who doubted his wife but decided to defend her despite the doubt that gnawed at his guts and made him sick inside. It is a story of a strong woman who never stopped loving her husband even when he was a complete and utter ass."

Many men on the jury chuckled. The ever-severe Judge Mitchell frowned.

"I realized long ago that Rose was innocent," Luke said, as if he were talking to a group of close friends.

He went on to outline the major points of the defense, managing not to sound like a professor giving a lecture.

"She has forgiven me for doubting her, by the way. But proving it to strangers was another matter. I think I've done that. My wife made mistakes. She befriended a woman she should not have. She went to the Supper Club and she gambled. She trusted." Luke walked over to the jurors and put his hands on the walnut railing that separated the twelve men from the rest of the courtroom. "Trust. She trusted that people who behaved as friends were indeed her friends. They weren't. She trusted that society would stand by her." He scanned the crowd and watched as many faces flushed with shame. "It did not. She trusted that the police would believe her when she told them the truth. They didn't. Finally, she trusts you, gentlemen. Rose believed, even when it seemed the evidence was stacked against her, that you would make the right decision. She trusts you." Luke swallowed, suddenly overcome by the importance of this moment. "Please don't betray that trust."

The silence was an almost tangible thing as Luke walked back to his seat and grasped Rose's hand. Rose turned and gave her family a small smile.

It was in the hands of those twelve men who had looked at Rose with scorn, interest, and sorrow. Their faces were now passive as Judge Mitchell gave them instructions and dismissed them to begin deliberations.

"Now, we wait," Luke said, his face tense and unreadable.

"But you said we'd won," Rose said.

"I shouldn't have. Arthur still has doubts about the facts, else he would have withdrawn the state's case. If he still has doubts, so do the jurors."

"Oh." Rose looked so crushed, Luke was hard pressed not to tell her what she wanted to hear—that the jurors were certain to come back with an innocent verdict. He was quite sure they would, but he'd been wrong before.

An hour later, they were still waiting. Charles brought them a lunch of ham sandwiches, which Rose forced down past a growing lump in her throat. What was taking so long? Were they deadlocked? Did one or more jurors think she was guilty despite Collette's and Anthony's testimony? She just knew it was that balding man with the bushy eyebrows and constant frown who believed her guilty, Rose thought. The old coot glowered at her throughout the trial. Or perhaps it was that studious-looking young man. The one whose suits were too tight and whose cuffs were frayed. Did that mean he detested the wealthy?

"This is maddening!" Rose muttered, putting down her half-eaten sandwich.

"It hasn't even been two hours, Rose. Not even enough time to review the evidence and take a few votes. Remember, if even one man thinks you're guilty, the rest have to convince him he is wrong. That can take quite a while. I've seen juries deliberate for days."

"Days?" Rose looked sick.

"It is rare, but it does happen."

"But it's so obvious I'm innocent."

Luke chuckled at his wife's naiveté. "Apparently not."

Two hours later, word came down that a verdict had been reached. Though it had been what Rose was waiting for, she became physically ill. Clutching her stomach, her face an ungodly shade of pale green, she said, "I think I'm going to be sick."

"Wait until after the verdict, sweetheart," Luke said, nonplussed. Rose narrowed her eyes at Luke, who seemed decidedly energetic now that the verdict had arrived. She could barely keep up with the man as he headed for the courtroom, which was already filling with spectators.

"Good luck," Nicole mouthed, crossing her fingers. Her mother patted the underside of her own chin: Chin up! Rose gave her a brave smile and lifted her chin. If the verdict was guilty, she would remain composed. She would keep her back ramrod-straight, she would betray nothing to the curious crowd murmuring behind her. She would keep her chin up.

The jurors filed in, eyes pointedly away from Rose, and her heart plummeted. They all looked so serious! Certainly if they had just decided that a woman had been falsely accused of murder and they'd just voted to free her, the men would look a bit more chipper. Rose closed her eyes briefly. It's going to be guilty, she thought, bracing herself against the words. Guilty, guilty, guilty. She said the word over and over so that she would become accustomed to hearing it, so that when that word was read, she would be prepared.

"You have reached a verdict?" Judge Mitchell asked.

"We have, Your Honor." Guilty, guilty, guilty.

The sergeant walked over and retrieved a slip of paper and handed it to Judge Mitchell, who read it without emotion. Guilty, guilty, guilty.

He handed it back to the sergeant, who presented it to the foreman.

"We, the jury, find the defendant Rose Anna Beaudette . . ." Guilty, guilty, guilty.

". . . not guilty of the charge of murder."

The courtroom erupted. Judge Mitchell pounded his gavel, his brows snapping together. Rose, her eyes wide, whirled around to Luke. "What did he say? What did he say?"

Luke didn't have to answer. The smile on his face told Rose everything she needed to know.

"Innocent, sweetheart. They found you innocent."

Rose, all thoughts of maintaining her composure gone, flung herself into Luke's arms and kissed him long and hard. So happy were they, they were unaware that the courtroom had become silent. When they finally broke apart, the silence turned to laughter and clapping.

Suddenly Nicole was there hugging her, followed by her mother who also pulled her close. Those who had stuck by Rose from the beginning surrounded her, smiling and laughing. Arthur congratulated Luke, holding out his hand as if unsure of his reception. Luke grasped it, his eyes telling his friend he understood.

"I wouldn't be surprised if Max takes you back, Luke," Arthur said above the din.

Luke shook his head. "Now that I have such a fine reputation as a defense attorney? Not on your life." Both men laughed. "Just do me a favor. Try to cut a deal for Collette Chasen, will you? And get that bastard Cardi."

Arthur grinned. "The warrants have already been written. Considering what Mrs. Chasen's testimony will do for our case against him, I'm sure Max would be willing to work something out."

Luke shook Arthur's hand again. "If you'll excuse me, I think I'd like some time alone with my wife."

Rose was surrounded by family, friends, and reporters eager to file yet another story about this notorious woman. Suddenly, she felt a familiar iron grip on her upper arm and was slowly dragged away from the well-wishers. Happily waving an apology, she laughed delightedly when Luke pulled her into a room off the court and swept her into his arms. She found herself in a book-lined office with high molded ceilings and rich furnishings, which she took in with a blur before her vision was completely filled with Luke's handsome face.

He kissed her as if they'd been separated for weeks. She sagged against him weakly as he turned her body to liquid and still his mouth ravaged hers. "Oh, Luke," she sighed, lifting her chin to give him access to her neck.

"Excuse me," Judge Mitchell said, his face red with embarrassment.

Rose made to jerk away from Luke, but he held her fast. "I'm sorry, Judge Mitchell, I thought this office was empty."

"Obviously."

Luke looked at Judge Mitchell, then at Rose's mortified face, as if deciding what to do. Rose's eyes widened with surprise as she realized his decision. He lowered his head for another kiss, ignoring Rose's weak protests and an odd strangled sound that came from the direction of the judge. He kissed her until Rose forgot to protest. And when the door clicked shut, she could not be sure, but it sounded as if the habitually cantankerous Judge Mitchell was laughing.

Epilogue

"Bless me, Father, for I have sinned. It has been one week since my last confession."

Rose bit her lip, knowing that for the first time in weeks, she truly had an honest-to-goodness sin to report. Now when she entered the confessional, her soul nearly pure, she was glad of it.

"Father, I lied to my husband."

Father Beaulieu straightened. Many Saturdays had passed since Rose Beaudette had done much more than list inane sins that most of Springfield's good citizens would not have even bothered to report. Was Rose headed down the path of sin again? Surely she learned her lesson the first time.

"Lying to your husband is quite serious, Mrs. Beaudette."

Rose lowered her head, but smiled. "Yes, Father."

"You don't sound repentant, my dear. You must tell your husband the truth immediately," the priest said sternly.

"Oh, I intend to. Soon."

"God cannot truly forgive you until you do."

"But I wanted to wait until I finished. You see, Father, I'm knitting booties and I told Luke they are for my sister's new baby boy."

"And?"

Rose smiled again. "I'm afraid that was a lie. The booties are for our baby. Do you think God would mind very much if I finish knitting them before I tell Luke the truth?"

"Only a very little," Father Beaulieu said, beaming

a smile at the screen. "I'm sure He would forgive such a small sin."

Rose accepted her penance of three Hail Marys and two Our Fathers and headed to the pews to pray. Behind her, confessors came and went and still she kneeled, breathing in the candle wax and incense as she prayed. And knitted a little pair of booties.